DAGGER
IN THE
HEART

A Historical Novel

Ahuva Ho

To

Harel, Claire, Ofer, Joyce, Noemi, Tamara, Oren, Noa, Deena

In Gratitude to

Joyce Tamanaha-Ho
Howard Mirowitz

TABLE OF CONTENTS

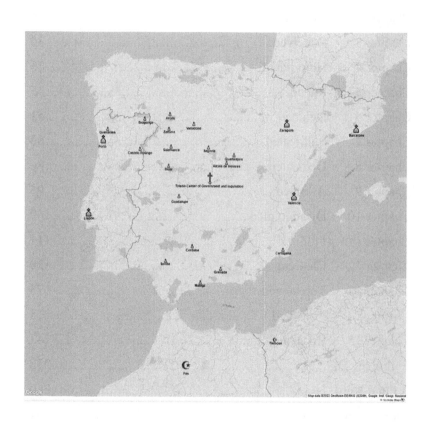

FOREWORD

In accordance with his own annotations and messages, this story is based on the life and work of Alfonso de Zamora, a famous Crypto-Jew in 15th–16th-century Spain. The historical background is based on facts recorded by Alfonso de Zamora and through additional research. The adventures of the Jewish and Ottoman pirates of the Mediterranean Sea are also factual, though the participation of the two Zamoran brothers is fictitious. The murder of the Archbishop of Toledo Francisco Jiménez de Cisneros, Primate of Spain, by the Moorish prince Adalberto Muntaquez, is fictitious as well, although based on the historical rumor of his poisoning.

Jewish life in Spain can be traced to as early as the first century of the Common Era when they were brought by the Romans as slaves. Forced conversions and persecutions began in early 7th century by the Catholic Church, and then concurrently by the Moors. The last auto-da-fé in Spain took place in 1826, and the Inquisition was finally abolished only in 1834. The number of Jews living in Spain up to the royal Expulsion edict of 1492 is estimated to have been between 250,000 and 350,000. One-third of them were forcibly baptized.

CHAPTER 1

Shielded

Happy are those who dwell in Your house, they forever praise You.
Psalms 84:5

The Campanton Yeshivah was situated on top of a hill overlooking the Duero River. Only three students remained at this late hour to study in "havruta". Tonight, their study was so intense that they forgot the time.

"Hey, comrades, it's time to go home," Jacob, the taller among the three, said to Eliezer and Samuel. "We're the last students in school and our parents must be worried. You know how dangerous it is outside at this time of night."

They looked at each other for courage and nodded. They closed their books, laid them neatly in the desk drawers, grabbed their coats and rushed outside. The thumping of the boots coming from the main gate of the *Juderia,* could be clearly heard. If they were caught at this late hour, the beatings would be merciless. The *matones* of the newly arrived Bishop Diego Deza roamed the streets of the Jewish quarter looking for any excuse to show who was in charge. And if they were in a good mood, they would drag Jews to their headquarters or to the Church dungeons for interrogations. The Jews of the *Juderia* knew well the outcome of such encounters: broken ribs, bloody limbs, and often, demands for ransom. And yet, defiantly, they kept their yellow bands, the compulsory sign of ignominy, that identification marker of the prostitutes, deep in their pockets.

Jacob, Eliezer and Samuel continued to rush home. Even though it was late spring, the evening was chilly. The faint streetlamps and the lights flickering from the windows threw wavering shadows onto the alleys.

The uneven cobbled pavement hurt the runners' feet. They reached Plaza Mayor and turned sharply left, groping the walls. Each of them thought as their hearts pounded with the exertion: 'Don't let the priests and the police, who sat outside drinking wine and munching on roasted pork, notice us for they can stop us for no reason.' The young boys ran down the alley, careful not to slide, then turned left again. Samuel's home was the closest, on Cobblers Street. His mother was already at the slightly- open door.

Without a word he went in, and his friends continued on, accelerating their pace. A few doors up the street they saw Eliezer's mother at the window. She disappeared and a few seconds later the door opened and swallowed the young student. Jacob's house was next door. He unlocked the door and slipped in, as quiet as a mouse. His mother Sarah, a lamp in hand, motioned him toward the kitchen. The aroma from the steaming bean soup reminded him how hungry he was. On the table a bowl and a spoon were already set for him.

"Wash your hands, son," his mother said with a hint of anxiety in her voice as she poured some of the soup into the bowl. From the oven she brought a warm roll. Jacob took off his cloak and hung it on the peg in the vestibule. He went to the corner of the room where soap, water and towels were permanently stationed. He murmured the blessing as he washed his hands and sat down to eat.

Sarah sat opposite him and watched her son rapidly slurping up the contents of the bowl. "What were you studying today that kept you so late?"

"The laws of public fasting during drought years. Do you know, *madre*, that even pregnant women had to fast?"

"It doesn't seem right, does it?" His mother looked straight into his bright green eyes anticipating a learned *drash*. 'My precious first born,' she thought, 'he will grow to be as smart and as studious as his father and grandfather.' She smiled. Her darling son will be destined for greatness.

"Well, it depends," Jacob spoke in between mouthfuls. "You see, there are three sets of days of fasting in case the drought continues, and no rain has fallen. The first two sets are made up of three fast days each, while the third set lasts for seven days because

2

of the severity of the situation. Some say the pregnant women fast on the first set of three fast days, but only from sunset to sunrise. In this way, if more fast days are declared, they are exempt. Others say only on the last fast days, because no one knows when will the last days be. However, and you will like this, dear *madre*, one *beraita* teaches that they do not fast at all, neither in the first nor in the last days of the fast. But to reconcile the dispute, the Rabbis agreed that pregnant women are obligated to fast only on the second set of the three fast days." Jacob ended gleefully, expecting his mother's approval.

"This is clever," Sarah said. "In this way there is a greater chance of not fasting at all."

"Exactly. Our Rabbis cared about the well-being of their women, hoping that there would be no need to declare a second set of fasting." He went on sopping up the soup that was left with a crust of bread. "Anyway," he continued happily, "this law was valid only in the land of Israel, and many centuries ago."

"Oh, that's good. I could always trust the Rabbis to come to the right decision."

Jacob's father, Hayim, entered from his study. Tall and handsome, his black hair covered part of his forehead and his bright hazel eyes lit up with relief when he saw his son. Jacob rose from the table out of respect and ran to embrace his father. Hayim stroked Jacob's head, intoning: "Well, little rabbi, did you have a good day in school?" Jacob looked so much like his beautiful wife, that he smiled joyfully.

"Yes, *padre*," he replied as his face became somber.

"What is the matter? Did something happen? Did you forget your lesson or were you reprimanded by Rabbi Avraham Sabba?" Sarah turned to watch her son respond.

Jacob did not hasten to answer. He looked worried and contemplative. After a pause that seemed to be eternal, he said:

"Rabbi Avraham Sabba convened all the students and warned us of dangerous times ahead. The new Bishop Deza has already rounded up some Jews for interrogation. His alliance with the Grand Inquisitor Torquemada is well known. The establishment of the Inquisition's Holy Office in our land nine years ago portends more troubles, and the Rabbi does not know how long our school will survive. He cannot foresee whether the disasters will come slowly or swiftly." Jacob breathed heavily.

3

Hayim and Sarah sank into their chairs. "What does the Rabbi suggest we do?" whispered Hayim.

"He told us to minimize our contact with the Christian population and to go on with our schooling. Knowledge and faith in our God, blessed be He, are our shield. We must survive as Jews no matter what." Jacob's face lit up with resolve and pride. He was the best student in the *Ways of the Talmud*, the beloved Rabbi Canpanton's system of study, analyzing the sacred texts by understanding every aspect: their intent, their language, their interpretations; by delving into past commentaries and offering innovative perceptions; and, most of all, by developing independent learning through acute questions. He had already mastered the *massoretic* chanting of the Torah *parashiot*, and he had astounded his family and community with his facility with Hebrew as he read the Torah at his *Bar-Mitzvah*, just two months earlier. His sermon that morning on the *tzara'at*, a variety of skin diseases, and the ways the Priests treated them, combined with his own new approaches to these afflictions, had dazzled the audience. He was determined to become a rabbi, following in the footsteps of the masters: Rabbi Isaac Canpanton, Rabbi Isaac de Leon, Rabbi Isaac Aboab and Rabbi Avraham Shem Tov, the giant minds who had graduated from his *Yeshivah*. Now, as a young Jewish adult, he had to exhibit maturity for the sake of his parents and his two younger brothers.

"Yes," nodded the father, taking his wife's hand, "your duty right now is to ensure an honorable future by doing well in school." After a short pause he continued: "You will also start coming to my shop to learn shoemaking. With these two skills you will secure a respectable living. As you know, our esteemed Rabbis of the Talmud, of blessed memory, were skilled artisans."

"Yes, *padre*, I will be honored to learn from you." Jacob was pleased, anticipating the opportunity to spend quality time with his beloved father. Looking eagerly at him, Jacob enthusiastically continued, "When do I start?"

"Tomorrow afternoon will be a good time. Come home at the end of school. Don't stay later to study with your *havruta*. Hard days are ahead of us, and we should not raise any pretext for Deza's men to harm us. Always hurry home with a friend or two. We have to be ready for any trouble."

Jacob did not know what his father meant by being ready, but he knew he counted on him to know the right thing to do. After all, he was the *gabbai* of the community, the one who oversaw the smooth running of the synagogue, as well as the care of the poor and the needy. He could tell that his father was worried about those taken for interrogation. Would the Jews need to pay ransom to free them? Any Church cleric could trump up charges against anyone in the community in order to collect a ransom or to confiscate property. That was happening more and more often since the country-wide pogroms of 1391.

"Jacob," Sarah rose, and hugging her son she said, "I'll prepare your hot water to wash up, then you go to bed. A busy day is ahead of you, so get some sleep. Don't make noise. Your brothers are already asleep." She spoke in short sentences to her children for she had learned having raised three, that young children's memories could not internalize long sentences.

At the age of thirty, Sarah was still attractive. Her beauty was mirrored in her sons' faces. They will grow to be tall men, like their father, she mused. She was as in love with her husband as on the day they were married fifteen years earlier. She was so young then, shy yet skilled in the running of a home with three generations living in the same compound. Her father, a physician, was of the Melendez family, who boasted a long line of men educated in science and religion. Whereas her first born showed keen interest in the rabbinate, her second son, Isaac, favored science like his grandfather. The marriage between the Gabbai family and hers was expected and blessed by their community.

The two families fostered close ties as the new generation grew up as siblings. Among the children of Jacob's aunt Devorah, Sarah's sister, was Isabel, who was a couple of years younger than Jacob. Their relationship blossomed with time into a true friendship.

Meanwhile, Bishop Diego de Deza's days of terror continued to escalate in the late 1480s and the Jews prayed for his demise or replacement to no avail. Rabbi Sabba called the community leaders for a meeting at his house to discuss their options. As the sound of voices filled the air, the Rabbi called for silence:

"Let us send a delegation to the newly-elected Pope Innocent VIII, for Deza is his protégé. He appointed him as the Cardinal of Zamora. Perhaps the Pope will show mercy to our people."

Despite expressions of doubt, at the end of the meeting they all agreed with the Rabbi's advice. Fernando de Granda was an eloquent businessman, who on his frequent trips to Rome befriended Rabbi Solomon Tzarfati, the leader of the Jewish community there. "As you know, I have business in Rome. I am willing to go and present our concerns to the Pope. My friend Rabbi Tzarfati is the Pope's personal physician. He will surely facilitate an audience to speak on our behalf."

"Very well," agreed the Rabbi. "Will anyone else join Fernando?" He looked around for a volunteer or two. His eyes fell on Pedro López, a trader in home furnishings. "Pedro, would you be able to spare three weeks of your busy life?"

All eyes focused on Pedro. He mumbled a few words but then spoke up: "I will go with Fernando, Rabbi. My Latin is not as good as Pedro's but together we shall represent our community with honor."

"So that's settled. I shall write a letter to the Pope, and you prepare to leave in two days' time."

As planned, Rabbi Tzarfati arranged an audience with the Pope, who asked them to return the next day for his response.

Sitting high on his bejeweled chair, the Pope declared the next day: "Bishop Deza is a learned man of great prospects. I trust that his handling of the Jewish situation is just and compassionate. He is admired by the Bishops and the Inquisition as a most devoted one to our Holy Faith. However, since other complaints of his behavior have reached me, I have written a letter in which I request him to extenuate his zeal." The Pope felt completely justified in his prudent response.

"This is the best I can do. I have no power to exert pressure on the Pope who otherwise is benevolent to our community," Rabbi Tzarfati said outside, with disappointment in his eyes.

López and de Granda did not expect this mild response to their desperate situation. Back in Zamora, Rabbi Sabba heard their report and agreed with their assessment of the situation: "I fear that Deza might retaliate against us for daring him."

The Rabbi was right. Deza's zeal only intensified. The celebration of *Shavuot* lacked its usual enthusiasm as fewer people came to dance with the Torah. On the following *Shabbat*, the Rabbi looked out to see several empty seats in his *sinagoga*. He spoke from the *Bimah* and said:

"Your troubled mood is justified. We are in a grave situation. Since that letter from the Pope to Bishop Deza, our taxes have increased, and with them our level of poverty. Zamora, a wealthy Jewish presence for centuries, has been experiencing a marked decline. Some prominent traders have moved their businesses and homes to Algiers and Morocco, while the business of others has been curtailed as a result of new regulations. Because of this, social and trade relationships with our Christian neighbors have significantly suffered."

A few weeks later, as the toll of the new laws weighed heavier and heavier upon the community, another meeting was convened, this time at the home of Doctor Melendez. After welcoming the attendees, the Doctor who was well-informed by his many highly placed Christian patients, said: "The only gate to the *Juderia* is now under police control, which forces Jews to avoid staying out of the city for long periods. Those caught after hours will be subject to heavy fines. Please do not give the police the satisfaction of further impoverishing us."

Luís Álvarez was concerned about the safety of the school children: "Children under 18 should walk to and from school with chaperones," he advised. Voices of agreement were heard.

Rabbi Sabba, the last to speak, said: "Family and religious celebrations must be toned down and done in private. Only on our special Holy Days shall we hold communal gatherings at the *Yeshivah* and at the three remaining synagogues. Soon the dwindling number of our community will only support the survival of a single synagogue."

Hayim Gabbai watched the diminution of the community as the 1480s gave way to the year 1490. It was then that a messenger from Málaga arrived and spoke at another private meeting: "My honorable brothers, dozens of our people in Málaga have been taken captive and our coffers are emptied. We are desperate. We beg you for help while there is still time to prevent the languishing prisoners from being put to death. I have traveled from one town to another, but the response has been modest."

Hayim reminded his brethren of their obligation: "Whoever saves one Jew, it is as if he saved the whole world. We are responsible for each other."

And indeed, the Jews of Zamora rallied to redeem the Jewish captives in Málaga. This episode hastened the exodus of more people, lured by letters from their relatives, to move to Tlemcen, Algeria, where the local governor encouraged Jews to settle. The stories of peaceful living and prosperity there attracted Hayim, but he could not leave his community. The Jews of Zamora depended on his leadership. He and the rabbis called for the deepening of their faith by sincere prayers and charitable giving. Perhaps a miracle would come, they all hoped.

As his father suggested, Jacob focused his energy on his studies. His insights on the disputes of the Talmudic Rabbis and his deep understanding of the Medieval grammarians and commentators, elicited much admiration from his teachers and classmates. He especially loved Ibn Gabirol's *piyyutim*, those moving and lyrical liturgical poems he learned by heart. They were chanted in synagogue rituals on the Sabbath and on festivals. His place in the Rabbinic school was secure.

Abner Melendez, Sarah's father, came over with disturbing news: "Rumors have spread that the Catholic Kings are preparing a very important declaration concerning the Jews. Soon after the fall of Granada to the Christians in January of 1492, it was reported that the Grand Inquisitor, the most vicious and zealot Tomás de Torquemada, increased the frequency of his visits to the royal court. Knowing his close relationship with wicked Deza, we may brace ourselves for further escalation of our situation."

The rumors were true. Soon, Bishop Deza began to appear in the Jewish quarter more frequently, riding in his official carriage, dressed in his ostentatious regalia, flanked by his private police holding batons, and by several junior priests, who marched behind him with religious icons and symbols held in their upraised hands. Notices were glued to doors and walls in the *Juderia* with the new rules:

"Tomorrow, Saturday, 8 of February in the year of our Lord 1492, all Jews are ordered to come out of their homes and synagogues when the herald blows his trumpet, and to wait on both sides of the main streets in complete silence. Whoever breaks the silence will be severely punished, regardless of age or gender. The yellow badge must be clearly seen on the right arm. All heads will bow in reverence and capitulation."

The time was not stated and therefore the Jews rushed to their house of prayer early morning to supplicate for mercy and miracles from God almighty. As they were saying the Shema, they heard the trumpet making its round in the empty streets. They hurried outside holding on to their wives, children and aged parents. It was the 15th of Shevat, the festival of the trees, when the first white and pink blooms adorned the fruit trees of the *Juderia*. The rebirth of nature, its smiling colors and fragrance, seemed to laugh at the anxious thousands of Jews. With hands on their children's mouths, they waited motionless with anticipation. Only the sounds of the procession pierced the silence.

From his high seat, Deza appraised the Jews' properties with his roving eyes. If a single movement or a sound emanated from the terrorized audience, that person would be dragged to death under the horses' feet and the carriage wheels. Everyone knew that there was no place for defiance.

A new notice was plastered in the *Juderia* three months later: "Early Wednesday, May 1, in the year 1492 of our Lord Jesus, when you hear the herald's trumpet echo throughout the *Juderia*, all Jews will line up in the *Plaza Mayor*, in front of the Cathedral, for an important announcement."

Again, the time was not stated but the Jews assembled there at the break of dawn. On edge, Jacob and his family were pushed to stand in straight lines alongside their entire community. They stood motionless in the cool of the day for a long time, afraid to move lest they catch the eye of one of the *matones* or the *policia* who surrounded the crowd armed with swords and spears.

Eventually, Bishop Deza emerged from the Cathedral donned with regal vestments and shining jewelry. He mounted a platform and read from a parchment in his rattled high-pitched voice: "By the edict of the blessed Queen Isabella and King Ferdinand, all Jews must leave Spain by the first of August of this year. Jews who decide to join the Holy Faith will be excluded and will fare well. No silver or gold or jewelry will be allowed to leave our sacred land ..." Jacob rapidly calculated that the date of expulsion would fall on the ninth day of the Jewish month of Av, the date on which all Jews had mourned for centuries over the destruction of their first and second Temples in Jerusalem. Jacob, his mind strangely clarified by the shock of the news, realized instantly that this was no coincidence.

Former Jews, true Marranos, were no doubt behind this terrible schedule.

They were dismissed as the Bishop and his entourage were smiling triumphantly. Deza's words reverberated in Jacob's ears.

All the people around him were stunned and numb. "How could we, who have been living here for centuries, since before the Visigoths, who disappeared from history, even before the Spanish were Spanish, be thrown from our homes and the land we love?" said one.

Another answered him: "This edict cannot last! The Kings will come to their senses and rescind this abomination. Didn't France expel its Jews five times between 1182 and 1394? We propel the Spanish economy! Their greed will readmit us by the new king!"

A third spectator joined the discussion: "On the other hand, England expelled its Jews in 1290, never to return. What will happen in Spain? There is no certainty for Jews in exile!"

That same night Rabbi Sabba, Hayim Gabbai and several heads of the community met at the Gabbais' home. As a Jewish adult, Jacob was permitted to attend. Rabbi Sabba was the first to speak.

"We cannot wait for the possibility that the Kings will change their minds. We must take painful steps to survive. I suggest that schools will continue to operate until the 13th of *Sivan*, a week after *Shavuot*. In the meantime, every family should organize its affairs: prepare the sale of the house, pay off debts, collect debts, procure horse-drawn carriages, pack the most important items for a long journey, prepare food and water, and send letters to family and friends in North Africa for accommodation. We shall travel to Portugal with the aim to end up in Algiers or Tunisia to see if the edict is rescinded. If not, we shall either find refuge there or continue to farther locations. The land of Israel is waiting for us."

"But not every one of us has relatives outside of Spain," called out José Medina.

"How do we know Christians will repay their debts to us?" asked the butcher Martín Padilla.

"That's right!" interjected Mose Carnoy. "How can we prepare for a long trip without sufficient financial means?"

"What shall we do with our communal properties, the synagogues, the schools and the *miqvaot*, the ritual baths?" asked Fernando de Granda.

Here, the men fell into silence. Personal properties were one thing, but the centers of Jewish culture and identity were ultimately the responsibility of the entire community. They all looked at Rabbi Avraham Sabba.

"We have no choice but to abandon the buildings. However, we shall divide the books and the Torah scrolls among us. I hope you shall rebuild our communities wherever you settle. Do not let the Jews of Zamora and their centuries-old rich culture cease. Our sages are known throughout the diaspora."

Salomón, Hayim's younger brother, was the first to volunteer to carry at least one Torah scroll and other holy books. Others followed suit. The discussion continued, with one after another voicing further questions and concerns.

"We have less than three months to settle our affairs. Let us be vigilant. Give your debtors two weeks to respond. If they refuse to honor their debts, we shall send petitions to the Kings to mediate."

Before the meeting came to a close, Rabbi Sabba raised his voice and said in Hebrew words everyone in attendance knew by heart: *Hazaq, Hazaq, VeNithazaq,* "Be strong, be strong, and let us strengthen each other. May God be with us."

The Jews' doubts as to the honoring of their debts turned out to be prophetic. Petitions to the Crown fell on deaf ears. Locally, reciprocal credit agreements were brokered by *corregidores* between Jews and Christians. However, Christian debts were allowed to extend and were ultimately not enforced. By August 1, the deadline of the Expulsion, some impoverished Jews converted to Christianity. Their debtors were ordered to pay back their outstanding loans and due debts.

As in most of the households in the *Juderia*, the Gabbais, with their extended families, attempted to sell their homes and property, but few were the buyers. Some decent Christians paid off their debt, while others bartered for goods. The Gabbais could not sell their home. They decided to leave it behind. Perhaps it was a good omen that they shall return with God's help and the recission of the royal edict. They estimated that their savings would be sufficient to make the journey to, at least, North Africa.

Seeing his wife's ashen face, Hayim tried to allay her fears: "I do believe the edict would be reconsidered and abolished. Is not the eminent Avraham Senior, the Queen's personal and trusted adviser, working hard on our behalf? How could she turn her back to him, the one who guided her like a loving father since her youth to the alliance with King Ferdinand and the throne over the united Castile and Aragon?"

But Senior's pleas and arguments against the Expulsion made no impression on Queen Isabella and King Ferdinand. However, Torquemada's enormous cross and the thundering words of Archbishop Cisneros did. Avraham Senior was baptized on June 15, 1492, in Guadalupe, along with his son-in-law Rabbi Meir Melamed and other members of the Senior family. Yet, several members of the family, among them his daughter Reina, left Spain. His friend and business partner, Don Isaac Abravanel, also pleaded with the Crown, but without success. He took his family, his fortune, and his library with him to exile.

As Zamora was situated a short distance away from the Portuguese border, the city became a transit center for thousands of Jewish deportees. The crowded conditions that resulted posed a health hazard for the entire population, and therefore many homeless Jews were forbidden entry.

Within the walls of Zamora's *Juderia*, preparations to go to exile went into high gear as June arrived. The most important items to pack were the holy books and ritual items Sarah cherished: The *mezuzuot*, the Sabbath candlesticks with boxes of candles, the *havdalah* set, prayer shawls and phylacteries. Sarah carefully stashed these precious items among the clothes. Water and food were packed in containers. Any household goods that were not needed for the coming journey were put on sale to raise funds. Much had to be left behind for as the deadline drew near, fewer and fewer Christians came to buy.

"What are we going to do with the heavy holy books?" Sarah asked her husband whose face and body showed increased stress that bore down on him each day.

"We will have to place them in water-proof metal boxes, together with other books and items, and bury them under the basement floor. Who knows? Perhaps we shall live to see the reversal of the royal decree and rescue these precious items when we return home." Basements were flooded from time to time from the Duero River that flowed a short distance away.

Sarah wondered whether her husband might be losing his grip on the reality of their situation. "We have to face what our lives will be, Hayim. Once we leave Spain, there is no real chance of our ever returning. Have you completed packing your parents' belongings?"

12

"Yes. I am afraid that most of their property will have to be left behind. I am worried that the ordeal of the expulsion will be too traumatic for them. They are our responsibility." A tear escaped from Hayim's eye and rolled slowly down his cheek. "My brother Nahum vowed to protect them as long as he lived."

"Me, too, I am so very worried about my parents' physical and mental strength, about their ability to withstand the coming catastrophe. I don't know if I will ever see them again." Sarah began to cry.

Jacob and his brothers helped to choose their most precious things and stacked them in the few trunks allowed for each family by the governments of both Spain and Portugal. Jacob especially cherished Isabel's brooch she had entrusted him to keep. This he kept in his inside pocket. "We are cousins," she had told him a few weeks earlier: "We do not know what the future holds for us. Remember me with this brooch wherever you go. Let us pray for God to shine His face upon us." They covered their eyes and prayed. "Our God and God of our ancestors: Lead us in Your path that we do not stumble and stray. We vow to forever love and trust in You and live by Your words of our Torah. May our people stay united and strong. Amen." They turned and fell into each other's arms in a long embrace.

Shortly after Shavuot, the night before their departure, the Jews of Zamora met one final time in the Yeshivah to hear their Rabbi's last directives.

"Many of you asked me for guidance as to where we should go as a community," Rabbi Sabba began. "I suggest that we cross the border into Portugal at Bragança and find our way to Guimarães, a short distance from Porto, from where we would be able to aboard a ship that will take us through Gibraltar to Fes. We should avoid Lisbon, where fierce anti-Jewish sentiment shows its evil face. The faster we get off the soil of Portugal, the better. Remember, our faith is our strength. Trust in the God of Israel. *Hazaq, Hazaq, VeNithazaq.*"

"What about crossing at Castelo Rodrigo where the local tax collector, Diego de Aguila, has shown compassion to our plight by either reducing the crossing tax for Jews or waiving it altogether?" asked Hayim. "Lisbon is a safer and larger port with a wide range of boats." Businessmen muttered sounds of agreement.

"My concern is the long and treacherous journey along the Spanish border," Rabbi Sabba replied. "The way I recommend will take us through a Portuguese terrain with less population, although it is mountainous. In Guimarães and Porto we shall find people of our faith who will help and guide us." He looked around him. "Who among you are planning to join me?" The majority raised their hands, including Hayim. The unity of the community was essential for the success of their plan to find a haven outside of the Iberian Peninsula.

The Rabbi was reassured by the response: "We have seen enough persecution in this cursed land, and it is time to leave here, where we are hated and unwelcome. The North African kings offer us a haven and freedom. Portugal is not our panacea. The Inquisition will reach there, too, and then what will we do? Please remember," he continued, "our journey will be long and strenuous for both young and old. May God be with us." As he spoke, he felt strongly confirmed by the vision he had seen in a dream several nights earlier, and so he added: "This Expulsion was a divine omen that the exile was coming to an end, and that it was time to return to the land of Israel. After all, in the Jewish calendar, it was the year 5252, *we shall multiply* in gematria.

As though responding to an unseen signal, everyone present began to cry, adults and children, hugging relatives and neighbors. David, Salomón's son, hugged his cousin Jacob and urged him: "Do not waste your talents among people who hate us. You will be a great Rabbi in Morocco or Algiers, or perhaps even in the land of Israel. There are famous schools there where we both can excel and become leaders of our people." As he continued to speak, Jacob began to picture in his mind the beauty of Zion where he wished one day to settle. He imagined the land dotted with the forests on the mountains of Benjamin and Ephraim, and the tributaries of the flowing water that feeds the Jordan River or the Mediterranean Sea; the juicy fruits of every variety, and the wheat and barley fields, the olives and dates trees that spread from the Negev to the Galilee, the Sharon and the Valleys.

He woke from his momentary reverie when he heard David's words, "May HaShem, blessed be He, help us all." David turned and joined his family on their way out the door. He could not hear Jacob's words, "May it be so." Jacob wiped his tears with his sleeve and joined his own family. Early next morning, they transferred their belongings onto the sides and the roof of a large carriage harnessed to two horses and set off with prayers and trepidation. The grandparents' cargo had been loaded as well. Their health was of great concern to the Gabbai family.

The Melendez clan, along with other wealthy and professional families, decided to set out for the small hamlet of Bejar, deep in the mountains in the province of Salamanca, to find a hiding place from the Inquisition there. Bejar was an isolated village controlled by the House of Zuñiga, a known protector of Jews. They said that the village was founded by Jews who escaped the Visigoths, following the pogroms and the forced baptism of 612–620. Bejar, in Hebrew "in the mountain," became a place of refuge for Jews in the next few centuries. Others said that the first escapees reached the mountains on the week of *Parashat Behar*.

The cavalcade of defeated people moved slowly out of Zamora. Some revised the Psalmic verse: "By the River of Duero, there we sat and wept." With a heavy heart, they were leaving home to an unknown and perilous destiny.

CHAPTER 2

Defeated

Go into exile from your home to another place before their very eyes. Ezekiel 12:3

Portugal was the main destination of the Jews of Zamora. It was Rabbi Isaac Aboab of Toledo who obtained King John II's permission of passage for the Spanish Jews in return for a capitation tax. The conditions limited the asylum to only eight months, with the understanding that the King would provide them with suitable ships at moderate rates.

On their way out of the city of Zamora toward the Portuguese border, they crossed the ancient Roman bridge over the Duero River. As they drove away from the city, the procession of carriages filled with fleeing Jews from Zamora and other nearby towns, grew in number and length. They progressed slowly in silence. Sensing the gravity of the moment, the children kept their eyes fixed on the road.

Farther on, the line of carriages came to a halt as it frequently did. Jacob suddenly felt a dark sense of foreboding flood his mind. Could Bishop Deza's men be waiting just before they reached the border, pulling Jews from their wagons and ransacking their belongings? He recalled the Israelites' exodus from Egypt and the pursuing Egyptian army on chariots, so like their wagons. He kept praying for a miracle as he looked at the eastern shores of the Duero.

"*Padre*, why are we stopping now? We are almost at the border, right?" Jacob asked.

"I do not know, son," his father answered. "But I'm sure we will start moving again in a short while. The line has been stopping and starting like this ever since we left Zamora."

"Do you think we can trust the King of Portugal to provide the ships that will take us to North Africa?"

"We have no choice, Jacob. We have very little influence on such matters now. We must trust in *HaShem* to provide the ships." Meanwhile, Bishop Deza and his cortége, together with the officials of the city of Zamora and the Christian populace, remained in town, seizing property abandoned by the Jews. Public buildings were painted with large 'X's for demolition. Blocks of stones, torn-down from Jewish synagogues, were reused by the Church to build new churches following the order of the Catholic Kings to turn all synagogues into churches. Several of these stones showed Jewish symbols and Hebrew inscriptions. Jewish stores had been divided among Christian artisans by the city council. The official aim was to erase all evidence of Judaism in the city and in Spain. That was the Inquisition's official *raison d'etre* from its inception.

Eventually the line of refugees began to move again, and Rabbi Avraham Sabba and his family, joined by most of his flock, headed to Bragança. It was unusually hot and humid for late July. They had to stop several times to water and feed the horses and themselves. The terrain was a steady incline which curtailed the speed of the horses even though they traveled along the valleys. The many tributaries of the Duero and the Sabor Rivers that flowed through Portugal provided an abundance of water. As the sun set in the west, the Rabbi motioned to the trailing carriages to stop at the roadside for the night.

Families gathered to have dinner and chat. Being a physician, Haim's younger brother, Salomón, checked on the well-being of his family: "How is everyone?"

His parents murmured words of hope. "We shall soon be on our way to Algiers," his mother said. "And all this episode will be behind us," his father continued his wife's thought.

"Thank God we are all bearing well," interjected Sarah. "I am more worried about my parents on their way to Bejar."

"How are you doing?" Salomón asked Luís Álvarez, the wealthy businessman, who joined the conversation. Luís smiled confidently: "So far the travel is going smoothly. We must have patience and resolve in our plans. I trust that money will open doors and hasten our exit out of Portugal."

Pedro López joined in. He was a close friend and a trade partner of Álvarez. Pedro was less optimistic than Luís. "I have no doubt that money will get us room on the ship. My concern is the Church in Portugal. Their power is immense, and they will pile hurdles in our path. I will not be surprised if soon they will collude with the Spanish Church for our souls. What do you think, Hayim?"

Hayim looked around and saw his sons. He agreed with Pedro's suspicions, but he did not want to alarm the boys. "It is only the first day of our exit. Let's deal with each situation as it comes. As long as we are united and strong, we shall overcome any hurdle. Trust in *HaShem*, my friends."

Sarah called her sons to go to bed. "A long day is waiting ahead of us, and we are not on vacation!"

They all got up and went to their temporary sleeping arrangements.

Early next morning, after the morning prayers, the Gabbai family prepared themselves to continue the journey. Hayim kept his purse deep in his light coat. He knew that the crossing tax was between 2 and 3 *reales*. After several hours in the hot sun, they reached the Spanish border. The official at the gate could not hide his hatred, but he had orders to collect the tax and move them on. His eyes fell on the very attractive Sarah, who sat in the back with her head covered. It was a tense moment. Hayim conjured up another beautiful Sarah, Abraham's wife, who was taken to the harem of Pharaoh in Egypt. His lips moved slightly in prayer: "God of Abraham, save us from the lust of this uncircumcised." He did not realize Jacob could hear his prayer, until Jacob whispered "Amen."

"Twenty-one *reales*," the official's voice shook Hayim from his momentary reverie. Hayim hastened to produce his purse, counted *reales* and handed them to the tax collector, murmuring "Thank you, sir. May God bless you with an abundance of goodness." The official looked at him with contempt. He then looked back at the endless line of deportees and yelled at them to hurry up and move on.

"This is just the beginning, my dears," Hayim said, turning his head back to his family. "Brace yourselves for a long and arduous journey." He turned to his parents and asked. "How are you doing, my revered *padre* and *madre*? God, blessed be He, is trying us as He tried our righteous Fathers." He changed from Ladino to Hebrew, and with closed eyes he prayed: *Shema Yisrael Adonai*

Eloheinu Adonai Ehad! The rest of the family, even seven–year–old Barukh, covered their eyes with their hands and repeated the statement of faith.

When they reached Bragança they were directed to the municipal citadel. At the gate, under a canopy, the *recaudador de impuestos* sat at a table laden with water jugs and an assortment of food. He was heavy set and red-faced and sweated profusely. A junior official checked the Gabbais' Spanish passes. He circled the carriage, while eying its occupants who were holding their breath in fear and anticipation and inspected their luggage. Hayim's lips began to move softly in prayer.

"Are you cursing me, dirty Jew?" yelled the young man.

"On the contrary, your Excellency," responded Hayim at once, "I was praying for your good health and prosperity. May God be my witness."

"What God? Repeat after me: May Jesus our Holy Savior be my witness." He looked at Hayim with hatred.

"Yes, he, too. And his mother. Don't we all adore our mothers?" Hayim retorted with a straight face.

The young Portuguese did not know how to react. He was not certain if he was supposed to respond to this Jew or humiliate him further. He decided to resolve his dilemma by harshly asserting his authority: "Fifty-six *cruzados*, filthy Jew. *Rápido!*"

Hayim counted the money and handed it to the young brute. Like the rest of the Jews, they had converted Spanish *maravedis* into Portuguese *cruzados* before crossing into Portugal. The going rate was one *cruzado* for 365 *maravedis*, or about 11 *reales*.

In the few remaining hours to sundown, they slowly continued in their journey through the harsh terrain. As the sun was setting, they stopped for the night at a flat clearing. The families in the convoy exchanged information and experiences. Yoseph HaLevi, a skilled tile setter, was furious: "Did you hear that bastard *recaudador*? I almost hit him for offending my wife! Thank God for Estelle. She reminded me that we needed his good grace to reach our destination in peace."

"What did he do to her that upset you so?" asked Lorenço Tasarte who loved to listen to gossip.

"This asshole grabbed her leg and pulled up her dress. But no one messes with my Estelle. Oh, no! She dug her nails into his hand so hard that it bled. He howled from pain and jumped backward as though bitten by a scorpion. I was ready to smack his filthy face when Estelle held me back. Anyway, the asshole was so shocked that he let us go at once."

The group laughed. Sarah lauded Estelle's response: "I salute your wife, Yoseph! Tell her that!"

Shem Tov Arditi, a junior teacher at the *Yeshivah*, wondered about the road ahead. "Today a wheel came off the carriage and it took me an hour to reinstall it. It seems that the road is not going to improve and further breakage is expected."

Salomón, the forever optimist, responded: "Thank God it was the carriage and not your bones!" The friends laughed. "Don't worry, Shem Tov, we are here to help each other."

"Look, *amigos*," Saúl Ambron followed suit, "we have been lucky so far, thank God. No one has been robbed or killed or fell sick. This journey will eventually end, and we will be on the ships out of this cursed land in no time."

They raised their voices in agreement "May it be so," "God willing," "Amen."

The young cousins were happy to see each other. As the dinner wares were being washed at a Duero canal, the men recited grace. A short while later they congregated to say the evening prayers facing east toward Jerusalem.

With the first rays of the new day, they proceeded to Guimarães in northern Portugal. They knew they were approaching the town by the change in scenery: The hills on both sides of the valley shimmered with the variegated greens of fields of vegetables and orchards of fruit trees and olive groves. The circling terraces were bordered with small and large stones, an enjoyable sight to behold. The refugees could not afford to stop and marvel at the breath-taking view, for with the signs of habitation there came the local hooligans cursing and pelting stones. Some braved to come near to rob the caravan, but the Jewish men stood firm and thwarted the raids with batons and stones.

It was an arduous two-week journey to reach Guimarães. The local Jews welcomed them with water and refreshments and opened their homes to them, but many remained to spend the night out in the open. Rabbi Avraham Sabba and his family were invited with great honor to the local Rabbi's home. Rabbi Nissim Perez had been Rabbi Sabba's classmate at the Campanton Yeshivah.

Throughout the night the two friends assessed the fate of the Spanish and Portuguese Jews.

"My dear friend Avraham," began Rabbi Perez, "I have no doubt that the catastrophe of the Spanish Jews will sooner or later jump the border. The King's cosiness with the Spanish kings portends only gloom for the future."

"You are right, Nissim. We must awaken our people to leave this land, and the sooner, the better. What are your plans?"

Rabbi Perez took a deep breath. "I have already alerted my congregants and encouraged them to think seriously about getting out. In a year or two I will pack up my life and head for Zafed or Jerusalem. Life's permutations are converging on the coming catastrophe, and everyone will be affected. Our people are on the precipice of one of the most disastrous historical events ever; perhaps even since the destruction of the Second Temple."

"I agree. But we should not lose hope. Our people depend on our strength, resolve, and spiritual guidance. I am worried that King John's promise to avail us of ship transportation will turn out to be nothing but empty words."

After a few days of rest and filling up with fresh food and water, the caravan continued its journey southwest along the side of the main road leading to Porto. That city was a center of shipyards with a burgeoning economy. From Porto the Portuguese fleet sailed in search of new territorial discoveries, putting Portugal on the map as a great European power. Rabbi Sabba led his community to the Porto *Juderia*, hoping to find a short respite from weeks of stressful and weary travel.

The local Jews welcomed the Zamorans with food, water and temporary shelter in small inns. Rabbi Sabba addressed his congregants in the local synagogue: "No one knows how long organizing the voyage will take so we had better resign ourselves to a temporary settlement for some time. We shall maintain a quasi-normal daily life to reinforce the stability and morale of our families. The children will be schooled by the adults, and the older children will teach and monitor the young. The women will take care of the daily chores. I, together with Hayim Gabbai, will concentrate on securing affordable sailing."

However, ship captains refused to transfer Jewish refugees to north Africa. To go to the African coast in order to import slaves and natural resources to Portugal was much more profitable. The King's promise was dismissed with contempt. "Go to Lisbon, you will find there captains who will agree to take you," they said and turned their back.

Rabbi Sabba and Hayim did not give up. For three months they approached every captain in the port and haggled on a passage that everyone could afford. Seeing the urgency in the Jews' situation, the few captains, who deigned to engage in a conversation with them, raised their prices to exorbitant levels. Negotiations failed from the start, and the two leaders returned to their inns discouraged and deeply worried. A prompt exit did not appear promising. In the next meeting convened by the Rabbi, the anxiety of some of the wealthier families surfaced.

"It is taking too long to find a ship, and the longer we negotiate, the higher the price gets. We are desperate. My family has decided to negotiate on our own and pay any price," said Luís Álvarez.

The next morning Luís and his close friends went down to the port and found a captain who was willing to take them to Fes for a hefty price. The terms were signed, and the sailing date was set for two weeks from then. At that time, a fleet of 25 ships was being organized to leave with 250 Jews among other groups of passengers. It was late autumn, and the departing families bade goodbye to their friends and former neighbors, relieved to be at last away from the harassing priests. They looked forward to living in relative freedom in tolerant Muslim lands. The remaining Jews stood on the quay as the ships glided slowly out of the port until they disappeared in the horizon. On the dock, friends and relatives kept waving their hands to the smiling passengers. No one on the quay was smiling.

During the winter months no ship left the port. The High Holy Days came and went, and the Jews debated about how they might be able to leave Portugal, considering their dwindling savings. The local Jews could not—and some would not—support their Spanish brothers. Rabbi Sabba and Hayim pled with the authorities to extend their eight-month residence permit. The extended permit was granted for a considerable fee. Throughout this period, the Rabbi and his community continued to engage the children in Torah studies. Rabbi Sabba dedicated much of his time to the community's needs, and in the evening, he would write bible commentaries, Kabbalistic and philosophical essays.

He brought most of his library with him and his study became the cultural and religious center of the Zamorans. Personal disputes came before him, for no Jew would take his case to the Portuguese civil courts. As Jacob wrote many years later: "For whoever goes to the Gentiles' court debases HaShem, may He be blessed, and honors the name of idol worship. God forbid if we choose them as our judges and say that we follow the Gentiles' courts! Thus, we acknowledge their laws to be better than our laws, and their courts better than our courts."

Jacob would study with the Rabbi, and the two challenged each other in the scholarly methodologies of the late master teacher, Rabbi Isaac Campanton. The Rabbi's sons would join in occasionally, and the *havruta* became strongly bound in the joy of learning.

It was still chilly that May of 1494, when some ships returned to Porto. They were severely damaged, with large gaps in their sides and ruptured masts. Typically, the arrival of ships was a day of celebration in the local tradition. The people of Porto, who rushed to welcome the ships, were aghast at their ravage. People wailed and clasped their hands in sorrow. The few Jews who happened to be there, could identify some familiar faces. They ran to their quarters with the sad news and called on Rabbi Sabba. Jewish refugees rushed to see if any of their friends or loved ones, whom they had not seen for months, might be aboard. To their utter surprise, 97 formerly wealthy Zamorans descended, their clothes torn, some with no shoes on. They held their children close, but their heads were bent in shame. They appeared to be infected with typhoid or scurvy. They were emaciated and jaundiced, eyes bulging with oozing yellow mucus. When they reached Rabbi Sabba they fell and cried out:

"May *HaShem* forgive us. Our suffering has been unbearable and for the sake of our children we succumbed to the Cross." They touched the Rabbi's coat, but he moved away. One of them, Pedro López, clutching his son, looked desperately around for someone to hear their story. But the Jews stepped back to avoid the infected in body and soul. Miriam Lopez, a relative, was highly worried as she stood a few steps away. She called out:

"Pedro, pray, what happened? Where is everyone else? Are they among the living? Please tell us."

Pedro turned to her with relief. At least someone cared. When he replied, his voice was shaky and breaking off:

"On the second week of our voyage our ship was stormed by pirates who took away our food and water and anything they desired. Our wives were raped, and several children were thrown overboard. Whoever tried to save his family was stabbed to death. When they were gone, the ship sailed on with only 27 of us surviving. The captain cheated us by heading to Palma de Majorca instead of Fes. But the storm forced the nine ships in our fleet to find shelter in Cartagena." He paused for a deep breath.

By now some Zamorans dared to come closer. Pedro continued, encouraged by the growing audience: "In Cartagena the Bishop came aboard and promised us food and water if we abandoned our faith and accept the holy water. We asked for three days to decide. We prayed to God with all our hearts. We reminded Him of the merits of our righteous Forefathers. We looked at our wives and children, and there was no one to save us." Someone from among the Jews came with a jar of water, bread and cheese. As he thanked him, he shared the food with his son, and both devoured it. He drank the water, spilling over his tattered clothes.

After a short pause, Pedro continued: "Having no choice, we decided to accept the bishop's offer, as our faith commands us to survive. This fate will not last. The Kings will come to their senses. No, we have not abandoned our God." He swallowed his saliva and went on: "Dozens of us were baptized and promised a free voyage back to Porto. We remained in Cartagena for a month to be disciplined by the local clergy. We were given crosses to bear," he murmured, showing his cross under his clothes, "but we spit on them in private. Three families could not face another ordeal on the high seas and remained there. They took an oath before us to never abandon our traditions. The Church promised to settle them in the old *Juderia*, now emptied of its population."

He looked at the people watching him and said: "Please do not condemn us. We all went through diabolic tortures." Pedro began crying again, recalling that event. He wiped his face with his filthy torn sleeve. He choked by his tears and collapsed on the ground, sobbing uncontrollably with the pain of being shunned by his once loving community.

"Please go on, go on," egged on Miriam.

He took a deep breath and continued his story. "On the way back from Cartagena, the storm almost broke our ship. People died. I lost my beloved wife, Rebeca, and two of my children

Gabriel and Hannah. Now I am left with my only surviving son, Rafael."

Pedro began to cry again, uncontrollably. Raphael hugged his father with his little hands and put his head on his father's chest. Pedro stroked his son's head, pulling him closer.

"What happened to the rest of our people?" Miriam persisted. Were her family and friends, the Álvarezes and the Padillas, among the survivors who reached safe land?

Pedro struggled to control himself and finally answered Miriam. "Because of the storm, all the ships stopped again to find shelter in Málaga. Along with the nine of our ships that anchored there, eight others arrived with 54 more surviving Jews. Their fate was like ours. I learned that your entire family perished. May *HaShem* avenge their deaths!" He lifted his face and looked at his audience, seeking sympathy and forgiveness. "We could not withstand the unbearable tribulations. Haven't we suffered enough? God, have mercy on our souls!" His breathing was quick and short. He was choking on his own sobs and tears.

Someone handed him some more water. Another called out: "Go on, Pedro, we understand you. May God avenge their blood." Pedro continued with some gained strength: "The 17 ships left Málaga with 112 baptized Jews. The stormy sea and a frenzied epidemic took 15 more lives." He bent his head in shame and weariness. The Jews were crying, raising their heads and hands to heaven in prayer. "What a catastrophe! What a calamity! What human can bear such suffering? How long, God!"

Fernando de Granda cried out: "What happened to the rest of the eight ships that left Porto with our brothers and sisters? Please tell us."

Pedro turned his face to him and replied with a sad voice: "We do not know. We only hope they reached Fes."

A procession of priests, holding their huge crosses and icons high in the air, drew near the dock and rounded up the baptized Jews. Cardinal da Costa lived for such occasions. He stood on a dais of crates and declared:

"Quiet! Listen up! No New Christians are permitted to maintain contact with their former community. All of you must come to Church every Sunday, and everyone will be observed and monitored for heresy. Any infraction will be met with severe consequences from our holy Tribunals." He paused and looked at the miserable lot with satisfaction. "After two months of further indoctrination in our holy faith, you will be allowed to return to your former towns in Spain. All privileges and rights of true Christians will be bestowed upon you, and all your properties will be returned to you. Now, form a line and follow us. You will be settled in a separate location away from the *Juderia*."

With this, the new converts stood up with much difficulty, and dragging their feet, followed the pompous and ceremonial procession.

The Jewish population stood numb, thinking about the horrors these poor people experienced and worrying about the rest of the voyagers whose fate no one knew.

This episode left a deep mark on some Jews who were determined to leave Portugal by way of Lisbon, where, they believed, more opportunities were available to find safer ships to North Africa. And thus, twenty-two families packed their belongings and back they went on the wagon trail. Blessed by the Rabbi, they bid farewell to their teary-eyed brethren. Other families followed, and the number of Zamoran Jews in Porto decreased to a few hundred.

The Hantavirus plague that originated in England at the end of the 15th century, was a pulmonary disease that spread in Castille and then in Portugal by the exiles, which left many either as carriers or scarred for years to come. Hayim Gabbai's elderly father was infected and had died a few months before. His mother's health was holding on by a hair's breadth. The children were not affected. Hayim and Jacob, now with the help of Isaac, were keeping the family afloat with their shoe-making business.

King John II, who had permitted Jews to overstay their initial welcome, resisted the introduction of the Inquisition, fearing the potential drain on the Portuguese economy with the exile of the Jews. Yet, he promulgated cruel edicts that nevertheless persecuted both refugee and domestic Jews in his goal to convert as many as he could without the intervention of the Church. But *O principe perfeito*, as he was known, died in October 1495 as the pressure to give way to the Inquisition was mounting. With no heir of his own, after his son died in a horse-riding accident four years earlier, his cousin, Don Manuel I, ascended the throne.

King Manuel I took note of his predecessor's failure to solve the "Jewish question." He began by revoking King John's edicts and restoring the Portuguese Jews to their former positions. Imprisoned Jews were released hoping to convince them to abandon their faith by his mercy. His advisor, with whom he consulted on everything from naval voyages to personal matters, was astronomer and astrologer Rabbi Avraham Zacuto, who had previously taught at the Salamanca University until his exile from Spain. But this was the calm before the storm. Not a year had passed since his ascension to the Portuguese throne when King Manuel began ardently pursuing the hand of Donna Isabella, the zealot daughter of the Catholic Kings of Spain. She agreed to the marriage on the condition that all Jews be either deported or forcibly baptized.

The new edict did not tarry. Two days before Passover the decree was posted on the houses of the *Juderia*: "In the name of our blessed King Manuel I, may our Lord Jesus protect him, all Jews still remaining in Portugal, are either to leave in ten days or enter the holy congregation of Christ. All children under the age of fourteen will be seized forthwith to be immediately handed over to Christians for instruction in the new faith."

The panic among the Jews was heart-rending. Parents hid away their children, even among sympathetic Christians, but they could not escape the diligent search by the authorities. On the first night of Passover gendarmes broke into Jewish houses and plucked the remaining children as they were seated around the tables. The parents rose in their attempt to shield their young, but the gendarmes moved fast toward the main cathedral in the *Plaça Principal*. They ran after the hunters shouting, pleading to let their children go. The priests were gathered at the entrance of the cathedral to receive their prey, and as they were receiving each child, they rushed them to the baptismal font. The helpless parents were stopped at the entrance. "In the name of God and decency, let our children go! These babies need their parents! Please, for Heaven's sake, return our children!" They called out the names of their children: "Benjamín, Moise, David, remember who you are! Remember us! Don't let them take your soul! Trust in the God of Israel! *Shema Yisrael!*"

Among the helpless parents were Rabbi Avraham Sabba and his wife Leah. They could not save their two younger children. They could only call out to them to keep their faith. That same night the Rabbi gathered his books, a few bare necessities, and his three older children. The next morning the Sabba family headed to

Lisbon. To those who saw them off he said: "Get out, now! Save your children! May HaShem save us all."

The news spread like wildfire throughout the community of the Zamoran exiles. The Rabbi's last words were still echoing in their ears when the King's officials reappeared in the streets and one by one the rest of the young children were caught and taken away. The heart of Hayim's mother could not bear the anguish any longer, and she passed away in her sleep.

Hayim and Sarah Gabbai saw their young son Barukh dragged from his hiding place in the courtyard well to the cathedral. They rushed after him but were stopped at the gate where hundreds of Jews huddled, crying out to their children to resist the water, to curse their abductors, or even to commit suicide. Hayim and Sarah pulled their hair and called on God to see and avenge. At the entrance to the church, priests stood holding crosses addressing the multitude of distraught parents:

"Accept our Lord and Savior! Come closer, kiss the cross. Our Lord Jesus is compassionate and wants you to enjoy his blessings. Come to the font and you will be reunited with your children. If you reject our generosity and love, your children will be given to faithful Christians around the country, and you will never find them." Very few parents stepped forward and were immediately pushed to the font. Others pretended to capitulate. They entered the sanctuary, grabbed their children and with the words "Here, *Adonai*, our pascal sacrifice to You, may *HaShem* be blessed," they slaughtered their children then killed themselves. The majority stood helpless, some for hours, some for days. The Gabbais hugged their two older children, Jacob and Isaac, their feet glued to the street, unable and unwilling to move. Hayim was the first to move. "Nothing can be done tonight, my dear family. Perhaps something good might happen tomorrow." They went to their rented home sobbing and praying for the strength to go on living.

Devastated, the Gabbais joined a group of Jewish leaders who tried to change the King's edict, but the reaction was even gloomier.

The new December proclamation constituted worsening conditions. Salomón, Hayim's brother, did not wait for a miracle. He asked Hayim to join him, but Hayim and Sarah would not leave without Barukh. Salomón and his family left for Lisbon without delay. They boarded the last ship before all exits were closed to the

Jews and reached Fes safely. Being a doctor helped him in finding a place on the ship, on the condition that he took care of the sick captain.

Like Salomón, resilience and quick action were the only way for resourceful Jews of means to escape in time and circumvent the royal decrees.

CHAPTER 3

Deceived

They plot craftily against Your people ... They say: "Let us wipe them out as a nation; Israel's name will be mentioned no more."
Psalms 83:4–5

It was not planned out of love for the Jews. It was simply an economic necessity when the new King of Portugal, Manuel I, released those who had been imprisoned by the late King John II. "Let us give them a false sense of security so that by the time we drop the blow upon their heads, they will feel obligated to obey," he announced to his inner circle of advisors. He held tight his ever-present golden staff to either dramatize his plan or to prove his superiority.

The King's calculation was not too far from the truth. Soon a delegation of the Portuguese Jewish merchants met with the King to express their gratitude, bearing gifts from the New World and India. His brown beard was neatly trimmed, his dazzling crown sat firmly over his pale face. Manuel praised their contribution to the growing Portuguese economy and influence in faraway territories.

"My reign will usher new ventures around the world to increase our economy and our holy faith. Your duty will be to accomplish my enlightened vision to surpass all other empires. And together we shall smite the Ottomans and their allies and reach new lands with resources to put us on the map of global maritime power," His Highness promised, pleased with his own newly-elevated status. He still could not believe his good fortune, for he did not expect to succeed his first cousin who had died suddenly at the age of 40 without a legitimate heir. He stirred slightly in his throne, ironing his filigreed brown coat with his right hand and touching his golden necklace, heavy with precious stones, with his left. He sat erect to stabilize the weight of the necklace and the newly acquired crown from falling.

Delighted, the Jews bowed and looked up to their new King with beaming faces. "Your visions are our visions. Our beloved country shall lead the world under your courageous and divine leadership," said Carmo Hazan, the leader of the delegation. His comrades uttered words of consent, raising their hands as though holding glasses of wine. The king smiled benevolently.

"May we raise another subject, Your Majesty," dared Hazan as he bowed his head.

"You may. What is the subject?"

Hazan raised his head in deference. "Your cousin, the late King John II, promised our brothers, the refugees from Spain, to avail them with proper ships to leave our shores. Ships are scarce and many refuse or take advantage of our destitute brothers. Would Your Majesty extend the promises of the late king so that these poor families can leave as was decreed? May God keep and watch over our gracious King!" Hazan bowed his head again.

"I shall see to it that your people from Spain shall have the proper transportation." His face turned grim, and then he added: "Their stay should not be extended any longer." With these words *the Fortunate King,* as he was called, dismissed them with his raised bejeweled hand.

The mood on the streets among the Portuguese and the exiled Spanish Jews overflowed with joy. Even the weather was optimistic as spells of warm days erupted in the Fall of 1496. However, a royal proclamation, pasted on the doors of the Spanish and Portuguese Jews in December of that year caught everyone by utter surprise:

"By the decree of His Majesty Manuel I, and the blessings of God and His holy Church, I hereby order all Jews in the land of Portugal, to either convert to our holy faith, or be expelled outright. Children of the said nations are ordered to remain in order to enjoy the blessings of our Lady Mary and her son our Lord and Savior, Jesus Christ. All Jews who refuse to see the light of Christianity are ordered to arrive in Lisbon no later than March 31, 1497. Ships will be ready to take them off the Iberian Peninsula for a moderate fee. God save the King!"

Slowly rumors began to circulate that Manuel was begging for the hand in marriage of Isabella of Aragon, the daughter of Queen

Isabella and King Ferdinand and heiress to the Spanish throne. The King was passionate about uniting Spain and Portugal under his crown, of course. He reasoned that Isabella and Ferdinand would not reign for long. Their only son John was said to have spent his days and nights in bed with his lovely young wife, Margaret of Austria (both 18), their widowed daughter Isabella was in deep mourning, and their daughter Joanna, married to Philip of the Holy Roman Empire, brother of Margaret, was mentally unstable, sealed off from the palace.

This alliance worried the Jews, for Isabella's zealous hatred of the Jews was well known. The princess had blamed them for the accidental death of her beloved first husband, Afonso V of Portugal, in July 1491. Christ, she believed, was displeased with Portugal for accepting the Spanish Jews into its territory that her parents had banished. Manuel was persistent. It took a year to convince the melancholy princess to agree to the marriage under one condition: that by the time the wedding took place, no Jews would be in the land. The wedding was set for September 1497 under strict fog.

The Jews were alarmed when the weekly audiences of their business counselors and representatives with the King was abruptly curtailed without explanation and they were barred from any further contact with the royal court. Carmo Hazan convened several heads of the leading families to his estate outside of Lisbon. Lights from the gate to the front door lined the two rows of flower beds beyond which the manicured lawn lay in the shadow. The usual lights around the house remained extinguished. Each nobleman arrived in his carriage after dark and was immediately ushered into Hazan's study. When all the guests gathered and took their seats, the host faced them with a somber countenance:

"My friends, the latest dissimulation of our King is a grave concern for all of us. We were there when he praised our contribution to our beloved country. We trusted him and a glorious future was promised. What could have changed his attitude toward us, I beg of you? What is the message he has been sending us?" All eyes focused on this distinguished man, tall in stature with penetrating blue eyes. He kept silent and watched his friends for some answers.

The silence was broken when Emilio Levy suggested: "I wonder if the new policy is associated in any way with the ongoing envoys sent to the Spanish royal court? We know the King wishes to be married to secure an heir to the throne and to unite the two kingdoms."

"Whom does he have in mind? The Catholic Kings have two available daughters," interjected Hazan impatiently.

"Not two, but one. It is said that the eldest, Isabella, vowed to never remarry."

"That's good because she is the most devout and a Jew-hater like her mother," mused Hazan. Another silent pause enveloped the men.

Inacio Cardoso got up and paced about the room, pausing behind the sofa to ponder aloud, "Something is going on for certain. But what?" Clasping his hands, he sank into deep thought and regained focus: "I would not be surprised if the King's words of praise were meant to lull us into a false sense of security. I don't trust him." He shook his head and walked slowly to the next chair and leaned on it, back in his mentation. Cardoso was known for his gentleness and clear thought. They all turned to him in reverence.

Castello Diés was a practical man. "You may be right, but what should we do? Should we begin liquidating our businesses and move somewhere else? Are we in danger of losing our rights?"

"Not rights, but perhaps our lives," prophesied Cardoso. He looked around with fear in his eyes. "I see cloudy days ahead, days of utter destruction."

"You may be right again," responded Diés, "but what do you suggest we do? We are all intelligent people with considerable assets. We have families and many dependents to support."

"Liquidate! Liquidate and leave!" Cardoso was emphatic. They all turned their faces to him, shaken. "Anywhere else we shall be appreciated and welcomed. If we start right now, by the end of March our assets and lives will be saved." His determinative voice, unmatched to his mild manners, raised everyone's attention.

"I agree with you," said Diés. "But how would we move our assets safely? We all know the difficulties of finding proper ships. We have also heard of the robbery aboard ships and the abuse by the captains." Hazan, the wealthiest among them, raised his voice. "I shall prepare my two ships to take as many of us as they can manage." He paused to think further. "I suggest to arrange two voyages. The first will be in three weeks from today. The elderly, women and children will be smuggled first. The second ship will leave two weeks later, not to alert the authorities. If there are extra spaces, invite your friends and neighbors. Let all know to get ready. We shall have to be discreet and fast before the authorities realize our children and wives are gone. Do we all agree?"

They agreed unanimously. Cardoso's wisdom and Hazan's generosity electrified them with a call to action. The fate of their Spanish brethren was still fresh in everyone's mind. They rose to their feet murmuring "May God help us," thanked their host and left hurriedly. These men had worked hard to reach their social and economic status. Some of them descended from noble families of centuries old. But they were realistic, for powers much stronger than their own were at work to ruin them.

Each head of household sold his estate without exhibiting urgency to the interested buyers. Their plan ran like clockwork and by the end of February 1497 they all arrived safely in Thessaloniki, at the northeast corner of the Aegean Sea, within the Ottoman Empire. By the nick of time their lives were saved, but their hearts ached for those left behind.

CHAPTER 4

Humiliated

Keep my soul and deliver me; let me not be ashamed, for I have taken refuge in You...Redeem Israel, O God, from all his troubles.
Psalms 25: 20, 22.

No one suspected that King Manuel's latest order to leave Portugal in ten days was a deceptive tactic designed to gather all the Jews to a single location. With the exit date approaching, Hayim Gabbai's family, Spanish refugees from Zamora, and now refugees in Porto, prepared for the voyage. He took with them their remaining few precious possessions, and within a week they arrived in Lisbon looking for a ship. However, no ships awaited them, only twenty thousand stranded Jews, desperate and frightened. At the dock, policemen on horseback and Church officials appeared and chained their hands and feet, and herded them like cattle to the *Estáos*, a large walled military camp with gates on three sides and a few windows on the fourth wall. In the large front yard, a few trees offered some shade. After some time, the police officers approached them and removed the chains. The Chief of Police stood on a raised platform and announced:

"We have gathered you here until His Majesty King Manuel decides your fate. In the meantime, we have provided you with comfortable accommodation. Enjoy His Majesty's hospitality and generosity. The gates will always remain locked and except for three hours a day you will remain indoors. We will not tolerate any uprising."

Each of the twenty barracks was designed to host five hundred soldiers. The number of mattresses and thin blankets in the barracks were not adequate for the twenty thousand detainees. Two or three, and sometimes even more people, huddled on one bed. Children clung to their parents, refusing to let go of their clothes. Not knowing how long they would be detained, the inmates distributed their food in tiny portions twice a day. Water was limited. The price of basic food set by street vendors, who sat at the gates from early morning until sunset, increased as the number of days of incarceration lengthened.

On the third day, dressed in his long colorful robe, embroidered red cape and fancy pointed hat, the heavy-set cardinal, Jorge de Costa, appeared with a large entourage. Dressed in less ostentatious clothes, the other priests held crosses as they passed through the north gate and sang hymns. There was no need to silence the frightened Jews. From his high seat, the cardinal looked contemptuously at the crowd and began his first sermon out of many to follow in the coming days.

"You, the murderers of our Lord, the son of the Holy Mother, have taken advantage of our grace, and our compassion, and have taken over our blessed land even though we have saved your lives from the Spanish Inquisition. But what have we received in return? You enriched yourselves on the backs of our good Christian citizens without an iota of gratitude. As tax collectors, you further impoverished the indentured farmers and took over the sea commerce. You are incapable of living among noble people like the Portuguese. You are leeches, blood-suckers of the innocent."

He picked up his big cross, kissed it and said loudly: "This cross will heal you of your diabolical blood. Come and kiss it! Come and save yourselves! Kneel before Lord Jesus! He will surely cleanse you from your filthy body and soul."

No one moved. Fear paralyzed them. The cardinal looked at the people as they tightly held on to their children and resumed: "Even your God has called you a stiff-necked people. He wants you to follow his only son. So do the right thing and join the holy flock."

Realizing that no one was stepping forward, his face flushed, and his voice thundered with anger: "I will give you two weeks to decide. If you do not voluntarily step into baptism, you will be dragged by force. It is your choice."

He motioned to his assistant who stood to his right to help him get off the stage. He hurried out of the *Estao*, with his entourage trailing behind.

The pressure to convert to Christianity began the next morning. The *Estao* guards demanded strict obedience as they walked among the Jews with a stick in their right hand and a cross in their left. "Convert to Christianity!" they shouted, "Damn people! You do not love life? Kneel before Him, cursed people!" As the Jews turned away in terror, one guard grabbed a girl and ordered her to kiss the cross. She burst into sobs. Her parents shouted, "Leave her alone! Leave her alone!" A group of Jews surrounded the guard who recoiled from their threatening faces and let her go.

The intimidation continued in various ways. Every morning the Jews were ordered to gather in the front yard to hear a sermon by a senior cleric. No matter what rank he was, the content was the same: The sermon began with seductive rewards of full citizenship: the right to live, work and trade among Christians; the possibility of admission to universities and ascension to public, royal and ecclesiastical positions. He would then enumerate the harsh punishments of forced conversion, separation from children, deportation to isolated islands, imprisonment, torture and death for those who refused to obey.

The cleric would end the sermon on the virtues of Christianity and the shortcomings of Judaism. "Your God has forsaken you. You are disrespectful and useless. Where is your wealth that will save you? You have shed the blood of this land with greed and malice. Come to our Lord Jesus and be saved. They will feed you abundantly, and your property and your children will be returned to you." And so, he continued as he sat under the shed and the Jews crowded against the cold winds. Despite the low mood and hopelessness, no one rushed to him to be saved.

Small groups huddled for warmth under the few trees in the yard. While people exchanged news about Jews who had managed to leave Portugal, Sarah, Chaim's wife, found herself talking to a Portuguese woman named Emilia Ferreira and her husband. "Perhaps you happened to see our rabbi, Avraham Sabba, and his family?" Sarah asked, "They left for Lisbon many months before the king's decree was issued. Without our leader we are like sheep in the desert without a shepherd."

The woman was happy to recount what had happened to the Rabbi. She was living on the outskirts of Lisbon when the rabbi and his family traveled on their way to the capital. "We invited them to stay with us. One trunk contained his books. We informed him of the new law banning the transfer of any Hebrew books within Portugal. The immediate unmitigated punishment was death. The authorities searched all the belongings of every Jew coming to the city. Because of that, he buried his books under an olive tree in our area. In Lisbon he and other community leaders were arrested by the authorities, who were under pressure to convert them to Christianity. Despite everything, he managed to escape six months later. To the best of our knowledge, he and his family found a ship to Fez, Morocco. We hope they arrived safely."

The two women breathed a sigh of relief. "With the help of HaShem," Sarah prayed, "perhaps we will be able to meet our dear and beloved Rabbi."

Haim, Sarah's husband, approached two women carrying the bread and cheese they had just purchased from the street vendors at the gate. One of them, Emilia, Sarah's new friend, introduced him to her husband, Claudio.

"We used to be among the richest families in Portugal with ships carrying goods to and from the New World." Claudio said, "We believed in the Portuguese kings who would protect our rights as contributors to the country's economy. Several times we were invited to the royal court for rewards and appreciation."

"Yes," replied Haim, "like you, we lived in Spain in a dream world. We believed the kings needed us. Their closest advisers were our people. Their loyal tax collectors were Jews. The best scientists, philosophers and poets were Jews. Jewish blood flowed in the veins of many of the leading aristocratic families, and even among the royal family and the church. We thought it would last forever. We forgot Zion!"

"It's too late now," Emilia said in despair. "We are like sardines in a net without water and hope. They brought us here to convert us from our religion and nothing more."

"I think you are right," Claudio said. "We are lost."

Everyone was silent, pondering their past lives. Haim was the first to return to the present. He sighed and said: "How did you, Portuguese citizens, get into this situation of being imprisoned? We thought only the Spanish refugees were the king's target."

"We thought so, too," Claudio replied. "It is evident that those Spanish Jews who fled the riots of a century ago in Spain and settled in Portugal like us, were never considered equal citizens."

One afternoon, the Ferrara couple approached the Gabbays with frustrated faces. To Sarah's question, Claudio replied in a whisper: "Yesterday I offered a bribe to one of the guards to allow us to escape after sunset, but he took the money and did not show up as agreed. I am afraid other guards will do the same. We are definitely doomed."

Sarah found no comforting words to offer.

Some people had little money left for food and water. The detainees organized the distribution of food among the needy. Despite this, several cases of dysentery began to appear that worried the rest of the people greatly. The doctors among them isolated the patients to the corner of one hut and increased their dose of solid food and water.

When the two weeks the cardinal set for them had passed, the deacon-cardinal entered the northern gate with a unit of policemen and took his place on the dais at the entrance to the prisoners' camp. He unrolled a scroll and exclaimed aloud: "Your stubbornness has reached the ears of our blessed King. You have chosen to defy the King and our Lord God, and therefore, His Majesty King Manuel had no choice but to issue a new order: children from the age of fourteen to twenty will be taken from their parents and baptized." He signaled to the policemen, and they hurried into the crowd and pulled out those who looked the right age. In trying to protect their children, some dared to harm the police, but the resistance was useless.

Haim and Sarah Gabbay's middle son, Isaac, matched the age group. As he was dragged, kicking and fighting, he was heard shouting, "Hear, O Israel, the Lord is our God, the Lord is One!" Other children joined him in the declaration of faith. The sound of their voices pierced the air in the plaza outside the gate. The gate closed with a loud thud.

Sarah, Chaim and their eldest son Jacob watched in horror. They recalled the abduction of their youngest son, Baruch, eight months ago in Porto. The heavy load of wailing parents at the gate took them out of the temporary stupor that enveloped them and pushed them toward the gate as well. The children were dragged by the raiding policemen while a Portuguese crowd remained standing outside the gate mocking the mournful Jews.

And so, the defeated parents were left standing in front of the north gate, hugging each other and sobbing.

Shortly after, while the Gabbay family headed for the barracks, Sarah fainted and fell to the floor. She felt the blood pool in a puddle as the soul left her dying foetus. Women rushed to her aid, carried her aside and as privately as possible, coped with her loss. Haim and Jacob stood helpless, clenching their fists and swearing, tears streaming down their cheeks: "God, take this baby's soul in love and mercy. See our suffering! You have tried us and yet we will continue to cling to you."

The next day, officials returned with a new order: "All the Jews left in the *Estao* will be forcibly baptized in five days."

To their astonishment, the officials discovered that eight Jews had fled during the night. The guards were severely reprimanded and fired. New and more vicious guards were brought in immediately. Four days passed and officials declared: "The resistance will not be tolerated. Whoever remains stubborn will be tortured and will never see his children again." The Jews were given another day to reconsider the offer, but they remained steadfast in their spiritual tenacity.

The next day, early Sunday morning, hundreds of priests and their assistants raided the *Estao*. One by one, men, women, and the elderly were dragged by their hair and arms to the cathedral. Thousands of spectators jeered: "Look at these chosen people! Where is your God when you need Him? He abandoned you as you abandoned our Savior when you killed Him. Murderers! No holy water will purify you, filthy Jews! The blood of our Savior is upon you, God forsaken people!" The crowd threw stones at them and whipped them as they danced in demonic fervor.

Despite the new baptismal basins prepared for this event, the lines of resistant Jews stretched a long way. Sarah was still bleeding and weak. After the baptism, Haim and Jacob supported her for no one was allowed to sit.

In a daze, Jacob wondered how this could have happened to them, the most righteous and God-fearing Jews. As he clenched his hands and gritted his teeth, Jacob put his hand in his pocket and held his cousin's brooch for some comfort that did not come. His tears flowed down his cheeks as he recalled their last embrace. His thoughts wandered to the last act the Jews of Zamora before leaving for exile, which was to visit the graves of their ancestors. Some even carried the tombstones of the departed. He recalled Rabbi Sabba bitterly weeping over the grave of his brother, Rabbi

Shaul, a renowned Kabbalist, who had been executed by the city courts on a trumped-up charge of blasphemy seven years earlier.

They sensed the diabolic symbolism of the baptism, and the physical and emotional betrayal of their existence. Those in line moved slowly, whispering softly to each other: "We have no power to change the decree, but we have the power to remain Jews. We must survive!" Some shouted: "This is the War of *HaShem!*" Cursed be Amalek!" "We shall see the downfall of our enemy!" "This is just water!" "God will show us His arm of redemption!"

But the arm of God was yet to come. Now, here in Lisbon Cathedral, His family, along with thousands of Jews, stood wet from the "holy water," their heads bowed in shame and anger. Each was given a new name upon baptism. Haim was called Juan, Sarah—Leonor, Jacob—-Alfonso, and Isaac—-Enrique. The Gabbay family, cursing the church and the cross, vowed, like most forcibly converted, to observe their faith secretly.

The priests strutted around, their chests bloated with satisfaction, diverted their attention to create neat and fast lines to the fonts of baptism. The Jews continued to protest by dragging their feet, reluctantly touching the cross that was pushed into their hands. Some spat on it, others threw it on the ground.

When the last of the Jews was baptized, the cardinal appeared again dressed in his colorful garb. He ascended the dais and sat down on the high, lavishly decorated chair as his deacon called for silence. The cardinal opened and said:

"You, lost sheep, have now seen the light of our Messiah, the Lord Jesus, and the power of our holy faith. From now on you are considered "new Christians," with all the rights of our Holy Congregation. When you complete your indoctrination, your young children will be released to you, and you will be able to return to your land. It is strictly forbidden to use your previous names, speak Hebrew or keep your holy books, especially the Talmud. If such books are found in your possession, they and their owners will put to the stake without any exception. Now, follow the instructions of the good priests in utter silence." The deacon helped him down from the dais and the entourage followed him holding crosses and symbols.

Juan, Leonora, Alfonso and Henrique were transported to a local monastery for a month of indoctrination in the new faith. When this was achieved, church officials deemed the converts ready to be released into Christian society. Each family was given a certificate of rehabilitation and permits to return to their homeland. Young Barukh, abducted in Porto, now named Miguel, was reunited with his family.

During that period, King Manuel and Princess Isabella, who initiated all the anti-Jewish decrees, finally married. But their happiness was short-lived. A month after her marriage, in October 1497, her only surviving brother, the Spanish regent, John, Prince of Asturias, died. Within a year of her marriage, Princess Isabella died shortly after giving birth to Regent Miguel de Pas. Miguel survived for 22 months and died. King Manuel I was left not only without a wife and heir, but his ambition to unite the two Catholic kingdoms faded with the heat waves of the Portuguese summer.

King Manuel I, ironically called "the Fortunate One," a devout Catholic, continued in his attempt to unite Spain and Portugal. He hoped to fulfill his goal by marrying Maria of Aragon, Isabella's sister. Her condition for this unification was the introduction of the Inquisition into Portugal. The approval of Manuel's request was given twenty years later by Pope Paul III after the royal couple was no longer among the living.

God's ways are not always mysterious.

CHAPTER 5

Raped

Even when I walk through the valley of the shadow of death, I shall fear no evil, for You are with me. Your rod and staff comfort me.
Psalms 23:4

The Gabby family found their way back to Zamora in early 1498. The Church restored their home and store to them, and their debtors were compelled by law to pay back their debts. Many other Conversos were already back in their homes, like Fernando de Granda, whose store in the *Juderia* was restored to him. Granda's many influential friends in town ensured his full rights and privileges as a respectable merchant. Others trickled back throughout that year. They met each other at the market or in the alleys of their old *Juderia*, avoiding eye contact out of shame and embarrassment. What could they say to each other when they were still carrying the marks of their wretched- ness?

The Spanish Inquisition was reigning unchallenged with the full support of the Crown. The Inquisitorial machine reached every corner of society without mercy, stifling any independent thought or scientific research and publication. The slightest suspicion of heresy, be it from clergy or royals, did not escape the long and evil hand of the Tribunals. Since the pogroms of 1391, many prominent Conversos had joined Catholic seminaries to reach high positions, hoping to find safety in the Church. Yet, several of them were caught or accused of secretly practicing Judaism, or even Judaizing.

Such was the state of the Zamoran Conversos. The majority continued to observe their former faith in private; first as individuals, then in groups, especially during major Holy Days. On winter Friday nights, Church spies would roam the streets of the *Juderia* to see if no smoke came from their chimneys. Since no Jewish books, and especially the Talmud, were allowed in Spain, agents would raid homes, then arrest their occupants for Judaizing. In most cases, the Tribunals would result in the confiscation of home, business, and execution. Books were burned in huge public bonfires as the locals drunkenly danced.

Some cases could take years for resolution during which the miserable Conversos suffered abominable torture and humiliation. The condemned would be donned with the infamous *Sanbenito*, the penitential garment decorated with dragons and devils, crosses and flames to indicate where their soul would go.

But the cruelty of the Inquisition did not deter Conversos from being careful in their covert life. Hayim-Juan had buried holy books under his basement floor, now back in his possession to read and study. The basement was turned into a mini synagogue with a raised platform facing east where the Torah would be placed. The platform faced a low window that could easily be boarded for privacy. When standing in front of the makeshift holy ark, the voice of the reader would carry forth. Behind the platform, a set of steps led to an opening in the back wall in case of an emergency exit. In the two sidewalls Juan built three arched niches for lamps. The entrance to the basement from the ground floor was through a secret door in the floor covered by a crate over a rug. High and winding stairs led to the basement.

The *mezuzah* that had adorned the right doorpost had been brutally uprooted by a Church official. Juan, like others, smoothed that spot into a concave, to pass the hand over it in reverence. On the lintel, to ward off suspicions, they engraved the sign of the cross emanating from a shape that suggested an inverted *menorah*. They named it "the Jewish Cross."

The Conversos watched as their once vibrant *Juderia* was vanishing before their eyes. Parents would tell their children, "Here was my school, *Torat Emet*" and "Here was my synagogue, *Rodef Tzedeq*," "Here was Don Eliahu HaCohen's Kosher store, may his soul be bound in the bond of everlasting life! Don't ever forget this. Pass it on to your children!" The parents would shed tears as their children would do the same, tears rolling down their cheeks in thunderous silence.

Sarah-Leonor and Hayim-Juan conducted several furtive talks with their three children to set the kind of life under the new conditions: "We shall continue to lead our former life but with utmost caution not to raise any suspicion of the scrutinizing authorities. Remember our vow in Lisbon. Water does not wash off our sacred faith. We shall continue to be true to our God, tradition and people."

Leonor continued to pass on the Jewish traditions and customs to her three sons, be it through liturgy, proverbs, or Ladino literature. She strictly followed the marital relationship laws, dipping in the Duero River or in private *miqvaot*. Sabbath candles were lit behind an inner door and a Sabbath tablecloth covered the dinner table. A maid was hired during the week only. A small statue of the Madonna stood on a small table at the entrance, but when no outsider was at home, they would turn the statue to face the wall. A large cross was nailed above the statue. Juan and Leonor turned their house to reflect a devout Christian residence, if only for the outsider's inspection.

Life as Christians took on the character of a split personality with the major difference that each personality was very much aware of the other. Going about everyday activities outside the relative security of home, engendered an extra sense of caution from former co-religionists or even neighbors. One never knew whom to trust. Once devout Jews could be now detractors for a variety of reasons, the main one was self-preservation. Conversos communicated by signs, whether words, phrases, body language, or insinuations. There was a constant effort to ascertain the other's mode of life: Did he choose to live as a Jew underground, or did he resort to live as a Catholic? Conversos groped in the dark to reveal the other's true mind-set and practice.

Despite the natural degree of suspicion and fear, Zamoran Conversos knew each other and with time, they careened into groups that resumed their Jewish life. They developed customs and routines. The kosher slaughtering was designated to a former butcher who moved his enterprise outside of the city to a remote and secluded estate. Those with private vineyards made kosher wine, others made wine at home, even from cocoa beans. Often, the Church laid snares at their feet when they ordered them to eat pork or other non-kosher foods in public. However, no pork was brought indoors. *Yom Kippur* and the ninth of Av were observed on pre- consented dates and not according to the Hebrew calendar, for the Inquisition inspected Conversos on those days. Even

Passover was moved by a day or two and celebrated simply, by eating vegetables and *matzot* baked by the wives. Years later, when Hebrew Bibles were unavailable, the story of Passover and other festivals like Purim, were read from Latin or Spanish translations. Understandably, *Succot* and *Purim* had to be relinquished.

Forced to keep their stores open on the Sabbath, the owners used a variety of means to evade sales. Juan and Alfonso organized games and took orders without writing them down. Alfonso later alluded to lighting candles every day to cover for the Sabbath and *Hanukah*. These and other customs had to be either adapted to the new circumstances or invented. A typical example for the latter was the dedication of a son to the priesthood for an extra level of protection. That priest would establish his own church to provide the needs of the community. And indeed, from the first generation of Conversos in the Iberian Peninsula, this custom continued for centuries even in the Americas.

Every former Jew was obligated to follow the Christian customs of Sunday Mass and Communion, fasting on certain days, donating money and gifts to the Church, participating in holy processions and so on. On their required confessions, they talked about any subject but Judaism. Conversos could be easily detected as those who hesitated at the entrance to the Church, who murmured a curse or an apology to God upon entering the sanctuary. There, they avoided eye contact, for shame and embarrassment weighed heavily on their collective conscience. Now they were called *Anussim*, "forced, raped."

Soon after their return to Zamora, a bride was found for Jacob-Alfonso from among the Conversos who returned with them from Portugal. This act of marital arrangement became the responsibility of the mothers or grandmothers. It was 16–year-old Guiomar Carbajal whom Alfonso knew as a little girl playing in the neighborhood. Alfonso was just shy of 24. The two families met at the Carbajal home to discuss the conditions for the marriage. Alejandro Carbajal was a heavy-set man, a skilled tailor for men, unlike his wife Bianca who was petite and slim. His family owned a textile factory in the outskirts of the city to where sheep owners brought their wool. Occasionally a trader in fabrics would come by with his merchandise carrying mostly exotic material set apart for top officials and clergy. Mateo Carbajal, Alejandro's brother, specialized in fabrics for women. His wife, Estelle, supervised the design and the tailoring aspects of the business.

At the dinner table, Guiomar put down her fork and asked her parents: "Dear madre and padre, I see you are pleased with the future prospect to unite our family with the Gabbais. Like our Matriarch Rebeca, I, too, have the right to accept or decline this matrimony. To help me decide, what can you tell me about him?"

Her parents stopped eating. Alejandro looked at his wife. Bianca smiled, eager to oblige: "Oh, my dear daughter, he was the future scholar of the *Yeshivah*. His career as the next great Rabbi of Zamora was sadly curtailed by the evil forces." She lowered her head and became contemplative for a minute. "But he kept on studying in Portugal with our beloved Rabbi Sabba." She continued as she raised her head in pride. "Like his father, Alfonso is dependable, honest, and hardworking."

Alejandro, the businessman, joined in the conversation: "He is a skilled cobbler with a growing clientele. I heard people praise his dexterity and good nature. He will no doubt expand to build a factory with many employees. You will see!" He looked at his wife congenially. Bianca nodded to her husband and returned to her plate.

"Then I shall be looking forward to meeting him face to face. When do we expect to meet him and his parents?"

"A week from today, my dear. Your new dress will be ready by then, so promised your Aunt Estelle." This settled, they went on with dinner.

The Carbajals welcomed Alfonso's family with smiles and hugs. Both families served the Jewish community for centuries and earned much honor and appreciation. They were also brothers in secrecy.

The guests were invited into the living room where the maid immediately appeared with trays of cakes and tea. When they were all seated on the plush sofas covered with opulent multi-coloured fabric, Guiomar entered dressed in a modest new dress. She wore no head cover. The men rose to their feet. She smiled but her gaze remained on Alfonso's face a few seconds longer. She saw a young man exuding wisdom and great confidence. 'He would be a fine provider who would take the obligations of marriage seriously,' she thought to herself. She smiled and sat next to her mother facing the guests.

Bianca beamed with pride as she introduced her young daughter to Juan and Leonor: "Guiomar has been studying our tradition well and is knowledgeable of our rules of deportment. Not only does she excel in her dress-making skills, but she is well trained as a home maker. She will be an excellent wife to your accomplished son." All this time Guiomar sat poised with head held high and looked inquisitively at the young man sitting between his parents. 'Quite handsome man,' she thought, 'I like how he gazes at me. Not insolent or bashful, but rather secure in himself. I like it!' She smiled at him approvingly. 'How beautiful this little girl has become,' he thought. 'I like how she looks at me as an equal. She will be an asset as a wife.' He returned her smile.

"We are pleased to join our families in matrimony," said Alejandro, looking lovingly at his daughter. "It has become uncomfortable for Guiomar to appear in public under the lustful gaze of the local men, especially the repugnant priests and the city administrators."

"Even on Sundays in church they have no shame to get close to her, even only to rub their fat bellies against her body," added Bianca, her face reddened in revulsion.

Alfonso focused his face on Guiomar's reaction. He saw her shiver, her lovely face contorted as she remembered those humiliations. Leonor noticed that too. "How awful, my child," she said. Guiomar smiled at her in agreement and said: "Let me pour the tea for you, our honored guests." When she finished, she offered cakes to all present. Bianca said: "Guiomar insisted on baking the cakes. She is such a blessing." Mother and daughter smiled at one another.

They were registered at the city registrar and were wed by a priest with Jewish ancestry. With time, this priest became the official cleric of the Zamoran Conversos. But before the Christian wedding took place, the two families met in Alfonso's basement for a Jewish matrimony. The two fathers officiated and two witnesses from among the secret group signed the *Ketubah*, the marriage contract. Juan read it aloud and then handed it to Bianca for safekeeping as customary. The attendees laughed in happiness. Leonor lifted the kiddush cover and called out: "Here is the bread and wine."

Juan raised the two loaves, said the blessing, cut pieces and dipped them in salt. Then he distributed them to every person in the room. He continued to bless the wine in his goblet as each one held his own cup of wine. Together they said the blessing and drank and congratulated the newlyweds: "*Mazal tov!* May God bless you with children," "May God bless you with good fortune," "May God bless you with good health," and so on they went. The small group sat around the table, now laden with festive food. The party went on for another hour. Someone said, "It is time to leave one by one to avoid suspicion. Be quiet and greet the policemen without stopping to chat." The guests dispersed. Alfonso and Guiomar went upstairs to Alfonso's room for the customary privacy.

Guiomar's personal effects had been already put away in the closet and drawers. Their night gowns were hanging neatly, and their house shoes placed at the foot of the new bed. They stood looking at each other, embarrassed. Then they laughed. Guiomar was first to speak: "Turn around. I shall change into my nightgown and go under the covers. Then I shall close my eyes and you'll change clothes. Agreed?"

"Good idea." Alfonso could not find anything else to say. He was relieved that his new wife, ten years younger, could be so mature.

He put on his nightgown and slid under the blanket. He had never been with a woman. He was afraid he would be clumsy or even offensive. He lay there motionless and speechless. He felt Guiomar's hand searching for his hand and squeezed it gratefully as he turned to face her. She moved his hand to touch her body, first her breasts, then on down, slowly and gently. He kissed her, first tenderly then passionately. She responded in kind, wishing to please him. She let him take control and followed his lead in silence. She knew she married the right man and she loved him.

Alfonso wished to move out of his parents' home, which provided little privacy. It was also too close to the local cathedral and the police station. He needed to start his own business of shoemaking anyway and to think of a future family. "We must find a small and isolated village," Alfonso explained to his young bride. "Arcos de la Polvorosa is a good choice. It is only about 43 miles north of Zamora by the Esla River. I shall open a leather store for I have learned well from my father. Fishermen, travelers and farmers need shoes, belts and saddles."

"This is a splendid idea. You have a good reputation as a master of leather goods. We will do well. My only reservation is the distance from our families."

"It is not too far, dear wife. They will be welcome anytime they wish to visit. The isolated house will allow me to study in peace and safety. As long as we participate in the local church routine, we shall not be bothered."

Alfonso de Zamora was not a prophet.

CHAPTER 6

Deluded

My mind is confused, I shudder in panic. My wishes were turned into terror. Isaiah 21:4

Three months after the wedding, Alfonso and Guiomar moved to their refurbished rustic little house. They both adopted the name "de Zamora," to avoid Christian surnames. One night, Alfonso packed his holy books and moved them to the basement, which he designated for study and ritual purposes. Both wore crosses and visited the local small church every Sunday, silently cursing as they entered.

Alfonso's name as a skilled laborer spread among the locals and his business flourished. At night he would copy books and further his studies. As a result of studying Maimonides' *Guide of the Perplexed,* he began delving into Jewish and Aristotelian philosophy, as well as astronomy. For this purpose, he began to study Greek. Maimonides' *Guide* in Hebrew, which his father had rescued from the *Yeshivah,* opened his mind to the sciences, thus sharpening his cognition of Ralbag's and Ibn Ezra's philosophies. But alas, he had to show up in his shop on the Sabbath, dallying not to conduct business and apologizing for the incompletion of work. There, he would recreate synagogue services in his mind, whispering and mouthing the prayers, and softly chanting the *piyyutim.*

Alfonso and Guiomar enjoyed their peaceful life in Arcos. And indeed, as long as they appeared faithful to the Church, no one harassed them. On the contrary, Alfonso's dexterity, honesty and good manners were widely appreciated by the local populace.

It was one Saturday morning when two young Friars from the local Franciscan monastery entered his store. Their brown habit was hooded with a white cincture tied by three knots on the right. On their left a rosary dangled. Carrying identical bags, they were both tall with kind faces rounded by short beards. If not for the difference in hair color, they could pass as twins. One's hair was dark, the other, reddish. As they entered, they pushed back their hoods. 'They cannot be over twenty or so,' Alfonso thought, wandering what they wanted. "Welcome to my store, sirs. How can I help you?"

The dark-haired friar was the first to speak. "Our sandals need new soles." He opened his bag and took out a worn-out pair of brown sandals. The other did the same.

"I have not seen you before. Do you reside in St. Francis de Assisi?" "Yes," they answered in unison. They looked at each other laughing.

Alfonso smiled back. "Will Tuesday be convenient to pick them up?" He returned to his business-like manner. He thought, 'be careful how you handle these two youngsters. They have come to test you.'

"Yes," they answered again in unison eliciting more chuckles. The red-haired friar said: "How rude of us, I am Antonio Herrera, and my friend here is Luís Gonzalo. We have heard about your skills and propriety and have decided to bring our business to you."

"Glad to be of service. I hope to be worthy of your trust." Alfonso extended his hand to the two who enthusiastically shook it.

Luís picked up the book on the seat and perused through it. It was the Septuagint with Spanish translation. "Why are you reading the Septuagint?" wondered Luís.

"If I want to study astronomy and the sciences, it is important to read Greek. At the same time, I improve my understanding of the holy Bible," Alfonso responded, hoping he did not say anything incriminating.

Antonio was excited: "Would you like us to teach you Greek and you will teach us Hebrew? I assume you know Hebrew, don't you? This is a fair exchange, don't you think?"

Antonio came closer and lowered his voice: "Do not fear, my friend. We read unauthorized books such as Erasmus' *Antibarbarorum*. We like his emphasis on the spiritual interpretation of Scriptures and the study of Greek and Latin.

So here we are, ready to promote Greek to our new friend." He smiled conspiratorially.

"Would it be agreeable if we meet here every Saturday morning to study, you Greek and we Hebrew?"

Before they left, they hugged Alfonso. He stood there unsure if this pact was sensible or even beneficial. Were they plotting to monitor his behavior? Were they here to lay traps? Or were they truly sincere in their hope to exchange knowledge and views?

The two friars found themselves every Saturday morning spending more time in Alfonso's store, teaching and learning, and discussing biblical and philosophical topics. They were impressed by Alfonso's strive to learn Greek and the sciences and encouraged him to take on Latin as well. "It is a worthwhile investment in a future of free thought," they said. But alas, their spirit constituted the minority of clergy, for the Church, and especially the uneducated Inquisitors, declared war against the new ideas blowing from the Netherlands, Germany, and Italy.

One day he came home to find Guiomar elated with excitement. Alfonso noted her happy mood and asked: "My beloved, you have good news to tell me?"

At first, she blushed, then she held his hands in hers and looking at his bright green eyes she blurted: "I am with child, Alfonso! We are going to have a baby!" Her eyes shone with glee as she waited for his reaction.

Alfonso took her in his arms and kissed her passionately. "Praised be God! I am so happy, my love! From now on you will not do any strenuous work. We will get a maid for you."

"Oh, no! I am young and strong! I don't need help around the house. Perhaps after the birth."

"We can afford a part-time maid to come for one or two days during the week. You deserve to be pampered. I will look for a maid in the village."

In mid-1499, Gabriel was born bearing the name of Pedro López's son who had perished on the ship going to Fes. Pedro and one son survived the tribulations at sea, forced to receive baptism and returned broken in body and spirit to Portugal. Pedro did not survive for long and soon he took his own life after killing his son by strangulation during the time of their indoctrination. This episode only strengthened the resolve of Juan and his sons to cling to their faith. No Christian name was added. "Gabriel is a perfect name for our first-born," was Alfonso's explanation to his wife, "for it means 'God will prevail.' As our tradition teaches, the angel Gabriel is God's messenger on earth to save Israel from fire, the fire of the stakes. The soul of Pedro López's son will live through our son."

Right after baptism, baby Gabriel was cleansed of the "holy waters." He was then secretly circumcised. In case someone noticed, the parents would answer that the baby developed a deadly infection, which necessitated the procedure. They could rely on Doctor Rodrigo Calderón, a Crypto-Jew himself, who served his community with utter confidence.

Alfonso appreciated Guiomar. Not only was she a devoted wife, but she was also a devoted mother to baby Gabriel. Her mother had taught her the Jewish customs and rituals well. They lit candles every day to mask those lit for the Sabbath. She was careful ridding the house from unleavened bread before Passover. No pork entered their house. To keep her marital purity, she would immerse herself seven times in the Esla at night, accompanied by her husband. On cold nights, she would go to a private *miqveh* in one of the homes of wealthy Crypto-Jews, who built them in their basement or cut into the rock in their backyards away from onlookers. To dispel sudden raids on the Sabbath in winter, they prepared the fires in the kitchen oven and in the hearth just before sundown. Life was complicated but manageable. At times, in order to survive, they had to compromise.

Diego was born in late 1500, and Francisco two years later. Guiomar's mother would occasionally come down to help with the three babies and the house chores. Their modest home and lifestyle did not attract Church spies or nosy neighbors. After all, they believed, God wanted them to live. Their hope for the rescission of the Expulsion edict faded away as the years passed. The opposite was more likely as the power of the Inquisition and its cruelty reached unfathomable dimensions. If suspected, no one could escape its poisonous clutch.

Soon after Francisco Jiménez de Cisneros was introduced to Queen Isabella in 1492, he became her confessor and closest advisor. When the Archbishop of Toledo died in 1495, Isabella forced Cisneros to accept the most powerful position in Spain after hers. By then he served in various royal positions, notably the bishop in charge of converting the Moors of Granada. He was known as an ascetic and a non-compromiser who promulgated strict edicts not only against non-Christians, but against Catholic orders as well. During these years of exerting power and influence, he amassed considerable fortunes. As a graduate of the *Studium Generale* (so universities were known since they first opened in 1293) in Alcalá de Henares, he wished to expand the small institution by building several new faculties, each in its own house. It was in 1499 that he was granted his wish from Pope Alexander VI in concert with the change in name to Universitas Complutensis (Complutum was the Latin name of Alcalá de Henares).

Despite his zealotry, he was influenced by the new thoughts of the Renaissance and its emphasis on the Classics, Hebrew, Aramaic, Greek and Latin. As a result of this trend, he planned a new cathedra for the "Oriental Languages". The new trend was already being studied in the older Salamanca University where New Christians taught. In Alcalá, Cisneros envisioned a more modern University to compete with that in Salamanca. Five new schools were in operation in the 1509–1510 school year. Each school operated as an individual village, with administration, dormitories, library, police, and even punishment rooms for students who broke the rules. Cisneros's grand vision was to produce the first Polyglot Bible in Hebrew, Latin, Greek and Aramaic. Only one volume would feature the New Testament.

It was 1504 and Cisneros was looking for former Jewish scholars to fill the teaching positions. The new Chair of Oriental Languages required that teachers be knowledgeable in the four Classics. There was a large group from which to choose, but he needed to find them. He sent messengers to churches around Castile where Conversos were registered and monitored. Antonio Herrera and Luis Gonzalo, the Franciscan Friars in Arcos, endorsed Alfonso de Arcos/Zamora with enthusiasm.

The letter from Cisneros's secretary to Luís Gonzalo arrived quickly. "In two weeks' time I will arrive at your monastery to interview Alfonso de Arcos. Expect me for lunch after which I will see your recommended man." The two monks rushed to the shoemaker's workshop where nearly out of breath, they slumped on the chairs. 'It is not Saturday, so they did not come to learn or philosophize,' Alfonso thought, with some trepidation, to which he said: "My esteemed friends, you seem to have some news to share. Please speak up. But before that, let me offer you a glass of water."

From a corner in the room, he picked up a jar of water, poured some into two glasses and handed them to the red-faced clerics. When their spirits were revived, Gonzalo spoke as he held the letter up for Alfonso to see.

"We have great news for you, Alfonso! We had recommended you for a very prestigious academic position in Alcalá de Henares. Here is the official response by Jorge Baracaldo, the secretary of the most eminent Archbishop of Toledo, Francisco de Cisneros. He wishes to meet with you in our humble monastery. Such an honor, Alfonso! We are honored to have known you!"

They looked at the astonished shoemaker, who was speechless at their recommendation and trust. as was their impression. But Alfonso was rather worried to be thrown into the lion's den of the top cleric in the land, the Inquisitor General. Alfonso had heard of the slaughter of the Moors in Granada and their forced conversions thus nullifying the agreement of tolerance the surrendering forces had signed with Cisneros himself. He had to compose himself and think fast for a response. After all, the two Friars meant well and truthfully respected him.

"Who am I to find a seat among the academia of high learning? I am only a provincial shoemaker. I am afraid I am not worthy of your trust in my scholarly abilities. You are too kind, my friends."

"No, no, no, Alfonso!" said Herrera, "You are too humble. You have opened our minds to new approaches of learning the Holy Scriptures, to philosophy and the sciences. You ought to share your great knowledge with our young minds in the renewed University of Alcalá. Here, read the Secretary's letter."

Alfonso read the short letter and returned it to Friar Herrera. "Well," the latter said, "you have no choice but to rejoice."

They beamed with satisfaction. "It is all set, then. We shall see you in one week from today after lunch." One week had already passed since the letter was written.

Alfonso was still troubled when he arrived home. Guiomar sensed that something unusual had happened to her husband. She stopped setting the dinner table and looked at him, worried. Has anyone delivered him to the Inquisition?

"What has happened, Alfonso? Are we in trouble?"

He picked up five-year-old Gabriel, stroked his brunette hair and sat down with a heavy sigh. He told Guiomar of the unexpected news and then added:

"I have no choice but to meet this important man. I will dissuade him from choosing me as a university teacher. This is not what I desire for our family. Alcalá de Henares is a big and unknown town to me, and who knows if we would be able to keep a low profile there?"

"And it is too far from our families. It will be unwise to leave them. How will our children grow up away from their grandparents and religious, albeit secret, environment? We have lived in the county of Zamora for generations!"

"Yes, I agree. What's more, living within a Catholic institute will threaten our hidden life and will be dangerous for us. No, I will do my best to stay in the quiet environment of Arcos."

Dinner was ready and Alfonso watched over Gabriel, who was seated in his chair feeding himself. Guiomar picked up four-year-old Diego and put him in his chair and began feeding him. Two-year-old Francisco was asleep in his crib. After their nightly washup, Guiomar sang Ladino lullaby songs to her children. The one they loved most was: *Durme, durme, ijiko de madre; Durme, durme sin ansia y dolor; Sienti joya palavrikas de tu padre, las palavras de Shema Yisrael; Durme, durme, ijiko de madre, con hermosura de Shema Yisrael.*

The day came and Alfonso walked to the monastery to meet with Secretary Baracaldo. At the gate he was met by Friars Herrera and Gonzalo who looked more excited than him. "We are taking you to the Abbot's office. Secretary Baracaldo will see you there." They patted his back in encouragement as they led him through the maze of the gray building. At last, they stopped in front of a large and solid wooden door. To their knock, a voice from the inside called them to enter. Herrera whispered, "Don't forget to stand in obedience with your head down. Talk only when you are addressed."

"Thank you," Alfonso whispered back.

They opened the door and gently pushed Alfonso in. They remained standing in the corridor.

Alfonso was afraid something in his mannerism would reveal his thoughts of revulsion. 'God of Avraham, stay by me,' he was thinking again and again like a mantra. The room was large, with cabinets along one wall, paintings of a Christian nature hung on the walls, a small round table with jars of water and wine, and an imposing desk under a huge cross, where Jorge Baracaldo was seated. He was dressed in rich garments, as befitting Cisneros's chaplain and secretary, his embroidered collar reaching his rounded bearded chin. Several jeweled rings adorned his fat hands. He looked well fed and content.

"Come closer, Alfonso de Arcos." He waited until Alfonso stepped forward. "Now," Baracaldo resumed, "I understand that you are a Hebrew scholar and a philosopher. We need people like you to teach and copy books we need for the new University library. We are going to establish a new Chair for Oriental languages. What are your credentials? Are you skilled in Hebrew, Aramaic, Greek and Latin? Speak up!" Despite his effort to show respect to the potential candidate, Baracaldo barely hid his displeasure of his task. Many in the Church hierarchy and the academia loathed the Conversos whom they suspected as untrustworthy. But Cisneros's goal forced him to seek those Conversos.

"No, sir. My knowledge is in Hebrew and Aramaic. I have started studying Greek on my own, but I am far from mastering it. I do not know any Latin, sir."

Alfonso was encouraged, for he would not be the right candidate, and that meant staying in small-town Arcos.

Baracaldo looked at him sternly. He did not like this tall and handsome man. He could not despise him for his looks, for Alfonso did not fit the stereotyped image of a Jew, so he mused. Alfonso's face exuded knowledge and wisdom that came from generations of scholars. He would be an excellent teacher, but he was not perfect for the position. Baracaldo thought long and hard for the right response. All that time Alfonso kept standing motionless with his head lowered. In the end the Secretary said:

"We have heard of your quick and remarkable mind. My decision is thus: You will move to Salamanca where you will be tutored in Greek and Latin for the next two years. In the new academic year of 1506, you will join the faculty as a teacher and scribe. This decision is final. You have two months to organize your move. In the meantime, an appropriate lodging will be arranged in the teachers' zone for you and your family." He looked at Alfonso as his face darkened with worry and fear. "You should not worry.

Your first two years will be provided financially by our beloved and generous Cardinal Cisneros," Baracaldo added. 'These bloody Jews think only about money,' he thought. Alfonso was thinking, 'look how this pontifical guest is enjoying his power over my destiny.'

"But sir, I have a family with three little children. Our families have been dwelling in Zamora for generations. How can I ..."

Baracaldo cut him short as he raised his bejeweled hand: "You have no right to argue. My decision is final. Go now!"

Alfonso moved as though he was covered by swarming vermin. He trudged backward until he reached the door. Outside, the two monks smiled radiantly with pride of their "protégé's" good fortune. Alfonso smiled at them and murmured: "I have to rush back to work. I appreciate your friendship." They accompanied him to the gate and bid him goodbye. "Do not worry. We shall continue our study sessions with you until you leave."

'Sure,' Alfonso thought, 'may it be my only worry.'

Alfonso was too overanxious to resume his work or go home. He found himself wondering among the tall trees that grew along the river. How will he tell his wife of the order? Yes, he always wanted to be a Rabbi, but not to the hated Catholics. The shadows grew longer and soon darkness fell. 'Guiomar will be worried,' he said to himself as he hurried toward the village.

His dinner was kept in the oven when he entered the house. The children were each in his bed. Guiomar stopped pacing the kitchen when Alfonso opened the front door. She rushed to see him. "Did the interview take so long? What did he want from you? Were you able to turn down his offer?" She took off his coat and hung it on the hook. "I am hungry," was all he could utter. At this moment he missed his mother's kitchen and her warm embrace when he would come home from school, late from over-studying. Life was secure at his parents' home in those days. His only concern then was to do well in school. But now, 'how deep we have fallen!' He washed his hands, said the blessing, and sat at the kitchen table. He blessed the bread and began eating. Guiomar sat opposite him staring at her deflated husband.

His body was full, but his soul was empty. At last, he raised his head and began relating the day's events. "I am sorry, my dear wife, but I cannot change my fate. We will have to move to Salamanca in July to start my classes. On August 18th the school year opens. A house will be prepared for us, and a small grant and tuition fee will be covered by Archbishop Cisneros, may *HaShem*, blessed be He, strike him."

Guiomar was stunned: "You know how I feel about leaving this area. I cannot leave my parents and grandparents and the rest of my family in Zamora and uproot us to a big city where we will be under constant surveillance by the Church. We will be living, if I might use this phrase at all, in the lion's den. How safe will it be to continue our children's secret Jewish learning? How safe will it be to keep our furtive Jewish tradition?"

"I had time to think about it while walking in the woods. We will do our best to continue our secret life. We will find a way. There are probably hundreds of other people like us there. Come with me. Without you and the children I shall be lost. You are the rock I lean on; you are the reason for surviving this life of slavery in this evil country." Alfonso burst into tears. He got up and reached to her with his hands and held on to her like a drowning man. "God of our fathers is a shield to all who trust in Him," Alfonso quoted from Psalms. He went back to his seat and covered his head with his hands.

Somber, Guiomar cleared the table. "Hot water is ready for your wash." She left the kitchen. Alfonso said Grace after dinner and dispirited, went to wash up.

Throughout May, Alfonso worked long hours to save for the dreaded move. Anticipating a small stipend, he had a family to support for two years until he would hopefully be paid a respectable salary. While Guiomar no longer expressed her objection, her demeanor changed. Now uptight and moody, she sometimes burst out crying to which Alfonso would hug her tightly and try to console her with words of love. They were both helpless, knowing they were not masters of their own fate. Alfonso organized the horse carriage, crates and food supply. His precious books were packed at the bottom of their belongings together with his ritual possessions. Guiomar attended to the children and the house belongings. The candlesticks and candles she received from her mother were wrapped with the clothes deep in a crate.

A few days before their departure in mid-July, they stopped in Zamora to bid farewell to their families. Alfonso was surprised not to see his brother Isaac/Henrique. Juan took Alfonso aside and apologized for not revealing Isaac's whereabouts. "Your brother left Spain through Gibraltar and reached Fes safely. His abduction by the priests in Portugal left him with a trauma he could not overcome. He was not willing to raise his children in this damn land, and that is why he never married. It was too dangerous to send you a letter with a messenger."

"How could he leave without saying goodbye? Did he really believe I was going to betray him? He knows me, the brother he always looked up to!" He choked on his grief. "Please inform me of the news whenever you receive a letter from him." After a few seconds he resumed: "I am happy for him. He is a master of his own now. He had the courage to do what we all wanted and should have done. May *HaShem*, blessed be He, watch over him." This hope strengthened his wounded spirits.

He turned to his father and asked: "What does Barukh plan to do? He was very close to Isaac."

Juan lowered his voice and said: "He is leaving us soon to join his brother. The less people know, the better."

"Didn't the Bishop inquire about Isaac's disappearance when he did not show up at Mass?"

"We told him he found a job in Málaga. When Barukh leaves, we shall say that he missed his brother."

Father and son returned to the family room strengthened by each other in the hope for a better life for Alfonso's siblings.

Both sets of parents and Guiomar's grandparents clung to the children and showered them with gifts. "Now, be good and keep up your studies your parents teach you. We shall miss you very much, but we shall do our best to visit you." Each grandparent put his hands over the children's heads and blessed them. "May *HaShem*, blessed be He, keep you and watch over you"; "By the merits of our righteous forefathers, may *HaShem*, blessed be He, shine His face upon you, little ones." And so on they blessed their children and grandchildren, tears rolling down their cheeks. In these turbulent times no one could foretell if they would ever meet again.

In that meeting Alfonso was informed of his aunt Devorah Melendez's events since she and her family left Zamora in 1492, eight years prior. Leonor recounted: "Their initial move to Bejar was encouraging. The local Duke Zuñega welcomed the Conversos. Because of its remoteness from major towns, situated deep in the mountains, they could rebuild their businesses and practice their tradition in peace. The locals were instructed to support their efforts to integrate for it was beneficial for the entire population, especially for the Duchy."

"How is Isabel doing?" Alfonso was eager to hear news of his beloved cousin.

"She married one of the local Conversos who had found shelter there ten years earlier. Since he was originally from Guadalajara, he decided to join his family who had remained there. It was too late for Isabel to protest."

Alfonso was just about to ask another question when his mother responded quickly with a smile: "Yes, her devotion to Judaism is as strong as ever."

Alfonso put his hand in his pocket and squeezed the brooch Isabel had given him at their last meeting. Their last embrace seemed to be eons ago, in different times, on a remote planet.

CHAPTER 7

Suffocated

Desolation, devastation, and destruction! Spirits sink, knees buckle, all loins tremble, all faces turned ashen. Nahum 2:11.

They left early morning in order to reach Salamanca before sunset. Most of the approximately 50 miles ascended amidst hills and fields. From afar, the city walls of Salamanca on the hill looked immense and suffocating, shaded in a menacing gloomy gray. Guiomar shuddered. "Here we go into the lion's den of oppression," she muttered. Alfonso's face turned ashen with anticipation. "God, help us," he implored quietly, as though the Inquisition could already hear every word. He stretched his hand to his wife and held it tight. He searched for encouragement which did not come.

Huffing, the horses reached the main gate, engraved with religious symbols, and stopped to take a deep breath. The guard asked for a permit to enter for he could see this family was coming to settle. He looked suspiciously at them. No Catholic in Salamanca, or in Spain, approved of the Conversos. But the law obliged that New Christians be tolerated. Alfonso handed the guard the letter he had received from Secretary Baracaldo with the seal of His Eminent Archbishop Cisneros stamped at the bottom. The guard immediately bowed his head down in reverence and returned the letter to Alfonso with a shaken hand.

"Welcome to Salamanca. We have been expecting you. I am ordered to accompany you to the University cathedral." He turned to his young assistant and said: "Take my place until I return." He groped one horse's reins and pulled. They climbed the narrow pebbly streets passing homes and churches; small squares and stores led to the grand *Plaza Mayor*. On its four sides, the artisans' workshops and the market buzzed with people: selling, bartering, shouting, and arguing. The cathedral soared over the plaza with its tall walls, turrets and bells competing with the noise below.

This time Guiomar clung to Alfonso as she whispered: "It looks like the devil has sucked the life out of this place."

The smaller plaza in front of the Cathedral's main door hummed with activity as priests and nuns in their brown, black or gray garb were coming and going, or conversing with each other in small groups. Such intense level of activity was foreign to the Zamorans, and in a way, frightening. 'The Church is undoubtedly the center of power and strength. It may not be so easy to live as Jews in secret in this wasp's nest,' Alfonso and Guiomar thought.

The guard left them in the plaza and rushed toward the imposing entrance, and soon he was swallowed by the darkness inside. He stood for a few seconds to get accustomed to the soft lights that came from the many lamps around the main hall. He turned right to the seat of the local bishop and the Church administrators. He was shown to the office of Baracaldo, a large room with all the comforts of the day. He was not there, but his assistant came forth to take over the case of the Zamorans. With him was a young priest in a different habit. The assistant ordered the guard to bring in the newcomers. Bowing repeatedly as he was stepping back, the guard left the cathedral in a hurry.

"Please, sir, follow me," he told Alfonso, "I will take you to the honorable Father Franco who will take care of you."

Guiomar held on to her husband's hand, troubled by the multitude of clerics around her. "Do not worry, my love," Alfonso could read her fears, "you will be safe." The guard sensed Guiomar's anguish and looked around. He saw a young man waiting for work and called him. "Stay here until I return and make sure no one harasses this lady. You will be paid." That was comforting. She murmured words of thanks.

Alfonso's meeting with Father Franco was short. "Your house is ready for you. Deacon Conejo will take you there." The deacon gave the guard a coin and dismissed him. Alfonso bowed and thanked the Father who was already halfway out. The Deacon was a young man, wearing a cassock too big for his slim and medium-height body. His sandals seemed to be the same as he wore as a teenager. He asked Alfonso to follow him and walked briskly without waiting to see if Alfonso was keeping step. The guard was already standing by Alfonso's carriage. Alfonso gave the young man a coin and sent him away. He then held the reins and followed the young priest. All this time the children were looking wide-eyed at the commotion around them. They had never seen so many people in one place and so many robed men and women, for in Arcos they remained indoors most of their lives.

A road led through rows of homes that reminded him of the Zamora *Juderia*. He could recognize the smoothing of the doorposts where the *mezuzahs* used to be and the exaggerated number of awkward crosses on the sides and top of the doorways. As he walked to his new location, he thought about how many of his people still lived under the same conditions as his people have been in Arcos and in Zamora, each one hiding his own story and fears.

"So many churches in this neighborhood!" Chattered white-faced Guiomar.

"So, you can imagine how many synagogues used to be here," answered her husband with suppressed rage.

Alfonso was startled out of his reverie when the deacon stopped and said: "Here is your new home. Let me give you a hand." He helped Guiomar descend the carriage while she embraced baby Francisco in her arms. Diego and Gabriel jumped off and coyly stood close to their mother taking in the exterior architecture of the house, which resembled very much that of their grandparents'. There were two elevated windows with closed shutters left of the wide entrance door. The second floor had two windows and a wide balcony with artistic balustrades decorated overhead.

Conejo went in first and the rest followed. The house was dark. Conejo lit a lamp and opened the windows' shutters. With a sparingly furnished living room, the interior looked abandoned by the former owners who probably fled the country when they still could. There was a bedroom on the right and a bathing area. The kitchen was in the back facing the yard. Guiomar examined every corner of the kitchen and found it somewhat adequate. The second floor had two bedrooms and a sitting room, again minimally furnished. With the few extra belongings they brought, the house will be habitable. A canopied balcony surrounded the cluster of homes around a shared tiled backyard. A well with a narrow shaft in the middle of the yard was covered for safety. A few children were noisily playing. Alfonso and Guiomar suppressed their delight when they saw the basement.

Conejo and Alfonso transferred the cargo into the living room while Guiomar and the children carried the light objects. In two weeks' time Alfonso would begin his classes at the University. By then, he hoped, the house will be comfortably organized to Guiomar's satisfaction. They would need a maid for a few days a week to fetch water and help with house chores.

Before he left, Conejo said: "Welcome to our city. Our university is highly prestigious, and I wish you success in your new venture. I would be happy to lend a hand when you need spiritual guidance." His words did not sink in. 'Just another priest,' thought Alfonso. He gave Conejo a coin and all thanked him for his kindness.

For the next few days, Guiomar was busy settling down. A week later two women came by to welcome her to the compound carrying refreshments. Coincidentally, their husbands, too, were recruited by Archbishop Cisneros to teach and to prepare for a once-in-a- lifetime endeavor. They could not be specific. One of the women appeared to come from a noble family. Her name was María Nuñez Coronel. She had delicate features and her outfit lacked extravagance. She seemed to wish to repulse undesirable attention. 'Is it modesty or surreptitious strength? Or something else? It is too early to determine,' thought Guiomar. The other was Esmeralda de Alcalá. She was also dressed modestly but her body language conveyed friendship and a need to connect.

"To which church do you belong?" Asked María nonchalantly as they were munching on the baked goods.

Sheepishly Guiomar answered: "No one. We have not had the opportunity yet to attend church." 'Why is she asking me this question?' Guiomar pondered. But before she could form a possibility, Esmeralda added:

"Just wondering, because our families attend Mass at the church of Deacon Conejo down the street. He is very good with the children."

Guiomar began to form an idea of the reason behind María's question and Esmeralda's volunteered information. She remembered Conejo's parting words. She thought she understood why she was directed to that church. Conversos insinuated in order to scout the others' true religious tendencies. She realized now that

Secretary Baracaldo was recruiting former Jews with credentials to fill the university's teaching positions, as well as to attract the bright students of Converso families to the declining institute of learning. Many Jewish teachers and scientists had left the University in 1942, like the rabbi and astronomer Avraham Zacuto.

They continued to conduct small talk to know each other better: How old are the children? Where do you come from? What is the reason for your move to Salamanca? Guiomar was impressed by her guests' education and demeanor and suggested that they all meet for lunch on Sunday in two weeks' time to meet the spouses. After morning Mass, of course.

Alfonso was pleased to hear of Guiomar's social event which might signal acceptance of their move. Like his wife, Alfonso figured out as much concerning the scouting efforts of *señoras* Coronel and Alcalá. He was looking forward to meeting the two professors. He did not know then how close the three would be working just a few years from now. In the meantime, he acquired school material for his Latin and Greek classes.

That night, as they were alone in their bedroom, Alfonso said: "I wonder if this Professor Nuñez Coronel is related to the late infamous Avraham Senior who sold his soul to save his fortune. Many of his family members were noted rabbis and Jewish scholars."

"Imagine the irony if he were a crypto-Jew like us," whispered Guiomar. "The wives were very cautious in their choice of words."

"I would not be surprised. One cannot trust his Converso neighbor on the first meeting. We should play the part of devout Catholics until we are completely certain of their affiliation."

"Yes, I agree," said Guiomar, half asleep.

The two weeks passed quickly. Guiomar and Alfonso established a routine that kept them busy: Alfonso with his university demands and Guiomar with house chores. The basement turned into a *heder*, a Hebrew school for little children, where they were taught to read and write, Jewish traditions and songs, and basic sciences. The children knew not to talk to anyone about their activities in the basement.

The guests showed up as planned. Guiomar and her part-time maid worked for two days to prepare the lunch. The house was meticulously cleaned and in order. While the Zamoras were dressed in their finest as befitting the Christian Sabbath, the guests' apparel exuded wealth and comfort. 'Well,' thought Guiomar, 'these ladies make a public statement on Sundays! It is expected. But not me!' As they entered, the Zamoras welcomed them and showed them inside. The table was set for six people. The guests' children, as was the custom, remained with their nannies. However, Diego and Gabriel had been fed and now were playing quietly in their room. Baby Francisco was asleep in his crib.

"Please come in. Lunch will be served shortly," said Alfonso as he shook hands with the men. Each introduced himself and for the first time Alfonso and Guiomar faced the two couples. In a way, Alfonso felt inferior to these professors, but he immediately thought of his own education and value in Jewish literacy. As they were seated, Guiomar excused herself and soon came back with the *Koftes de Prassa* (leek patties) followed by the *Bulemas de Berendjena* (pastry with eggplant filling). She chose these two dishes, for they were typical to the Jews of Spain. It was now her way to plant codes for a response. A pitcher of wine mixed with water was stationed at the center of the table. Alfonso stood up to pour the beverage into the guests' cups.

"Well, we are happy to meet you at last. We thank your wives for their friendliness to my wife. It is hard to move to a new place with three little children," began Alfonso.

When Guiomar at last sat down next to her husband, she noticed the sudden silence as the guests looked at the vegetable dishes. They then looked at her with acknowledgment and Guiomar returned with a smile. She was proud of her tradition and was not going to apologize or defend her position. It was who she was.

"Indeed," Pablo Coronel responded, "we remember when we moved from Segovia two years ago with two children. But fortunately, the university was very helpful with providing the accommodation. However, we preferred to purchase a larger house, but this possibility was not afforded to us. In fact, not to any of the new teacher recruits."

The hint was received. Segovia was the hometown of Avraham Senior's family. Their family palace as well as several manufacturing plants there were well known among many Conversos. So, Pablo was willing to open up! What about Alfonso de Alcalá? Alfonso de Zamora turned to him.

"And you, sir," opened Alfonso, "did you also move with children?"

Alcalá swallowed his mouthful and answered flustered: "Not exactly. We do have three children, but I was born in Alcalá. I met my wife here in Salamanca during my study at the university. However, we understand your situation very well." Esmeralda smiled as she remembered their youth. Alcalá continued: "I, too, was recruited by Archbishop Cisneros."

"What was the purpose of that recruitment?" asked Alfonso.

"The archbishop has pioneered a ground-breaking venture based on the ancient Greek Hexapla by Origen of the third century. He has named it the Polyglot Bible and its aim is to revive the languishing study of the Sacred Scriptures, as the Cardinal officially stated."

"What is the Polyglot Bible?" Alfonso did not want to show his ignorance of the Hexapla.

"It will contain six volumes of which the first four will center on the Hebrew Bible. Each page will contain the Hebrew text, and parallel columns of the Latin Vulgate and the Greek Septuagint with an interlinear Latin. For the Torah there will be Aramaic Onqelos and its Latin translation. The fifth volume will contain the New Testament, and the sixth—-Hebrew grammar and dictionaries."

Pablo interjected when Alcalá took a breath: "We are still in the organizational stage. The Cardinal began collecting manuscripts a few years ago. He has organized a committee in which we are members headed by Diego López de Zuñiga. I know we are expecting one more scholar who specializes in the Hebrew and Aramaic, but who is also skilled in Latin and Greek. We do not know who he is yet." Pablo stopped and looked at Alfonso: "Are you the one? Why have you moved to Salamanca?"

"I'm afraid I don't think so. I was hired to teach Hebrew and Aramaic since ..." He stopped before blurting out 'many Jewish scholars left Spain.' He did not know how far he could go with his boldness. "... some seats have been vacant. I was ordered to study Latin and Greek to be able to teach in two years' time." With this, Pablo and Alcalá understood that Alfonso was a *Yeshivah* student, where these two languages were not taught. They also sensed his reluctance to uproot himself from his previous life, and even acerbity toward Baracaldo and Cisneros. They shared the feeling but by now they have accepted their inferior and repressed situation. It was especially hard for María who had known luxury and freedom only the nobility enjoyed.

"We are both teachers of the Classics and if you need help, don't hesitate to ask," Pablo said.

Alfonso thanked both teachers. They continued to talk about the children and their education in the local church. Guiomar proudly said she home-schooled the eldest two. "The children are too young to leave home," she reasoned, "they still need their mother." The faces of the lady guests projected either envy or admiration, Guiomar did not know which.

As the main dishes were being consumed, Guiomar got up and brought the *Biscocho*, the round and braided cookies, typical to Spanish Jews. The eyes of Esmeralda and María opened wide. They had not enjoyed them for at least fourteen years, but now they could without compunction. They appreciated them not only because of their deliciousness and the happy memories, but more so because they knew the complicated and lengthy process of making them. Guiomar truly respected them and was not afraid to send them the obvious message of defiance and pride. If only they had her courage! The lunch experience was a success for all participants involved.

Now everyone knew where the others stood in terms of their religious affiliation. Perhaps it was not yet the time to be fully trusting, though, but the preliminary steps had been made.

The time was passing fast. On Sunday they all went to Deacon Conejo's church where they met many more Conversos. From time to time, they would have lunch with their newly found friends, the Coronels and the Alcalás. The two professors helped Alfonso with Latin and Greek, and he taught them Hebrew Grammar and new methodologies to read Hebrew Scriptures. They showed fundamental knowledge of Jewish culture and traditions but kept a low profile.

In the summer months the *Juderia* was emptied from its residents as families left to visit relatives. In Zamora, Guiomar felt at home surrounded by her and Alfonso's families. It was a happy time for her even more so since she found out she was pregnant. Alfonso was busy either going over his classes and furthering his surreptitious Jewish studies or helping in his father's shoemaking business. For Alfonso it was too painful to see the new church built where his *Yeshivah* once stood; many of the synagogues' building blocks, still embellished with Jewish symbols, were reused and thus stood desecrated in the walls of new churches.

Back in Salamanca in early August, Guiomar felt extremely lonely and cheated. The more she stayed there, the more resentful she became. Most of her childhood friends had married Zamoran Conversos and remained in Zamora. Salamanca was too big with too many churches.

Soon, her attention shifted to her new baby girl they named Princesa. However, Guiomar's exuberance was short-lived. In the winter of 1505, a devastating typhus outbreak spread from Barcelona in the north to the Mediterranean coast in the south. The poor, the old and the very young were the first to be blighted. The rich and the Church leaders in Salamanca fled the city causing unrest and misery. Many died. Alfonso and his family stayed indoors but little Princesa succumbed to the disease despite the heroic efforts of Doctor Carlos Heredia to save her. They buried her in the old Jewish cemetery outside the city walls, now a Christian burial ground. Guiomar could not be consoled. She plunged into depression and resentment. She saw the death of her baby as a dark omen for having moved to Salamanca. They put stones on Princesa's grave and slowly returned home. She knew she would never overcome the loss of her little princess. Alfonso would sneak to the grave site to say prayers whenever he could.

Alfonso achieved a high standard of mastery of the Latin, while his proficiency in Greek trailed behind. As he studied Jerome's Vulgate, he noticed the many errors in translation that accumulated throughout the centuries due to multiple copyists, or more so, due to the intended Christianization of Scriptures. On the other hand, he knew of the changes in translation made by Jewish translators of the Septuagint centuries earlier in order to avoid certain pitfalls with the Ptolemaic King for he had studied that in the Talmud. In a secret notebook he began to keep at home, he noted all these errors. One day he would come to need them when he became a teacher.

Alfonso was pleased with his lot. As the second year of his studies began, he received an increase in his grant. He was protected by the University under which he was living a clandestine life. This kind of financial security, he mused, will hopefully uplift Guiomar's spirit. But Guiomar's reaction defied his logic. She felt even more desperate that their fate will be doomed in Salamanca. The sense of security was her nemesis. For her, complacency meant being lost in a society with which she did not identify herself or her family. Her fears heightened when a few days later Deacon Conejo and a group of locals were found in the basement of his church sitting on the floor and crying over a Hebrew text. Someone betrayed the Crypto-Jews. Who was it, everyone asked.

"We swear to you," said Pablo and his wife the next day to Alfonso and Guiomar, "we assure you we are not the betrayers."

"Who could that be?" whispered Alfonso. "Was it Alcalá? Was it another professor? How can we find out?"

"I am very worried," said María, "I suggest we abstain from talking to Alcalá about private matters."

"What is important is to stay friends and keep calm," Alfonso stated with conviction.

Guiomar's shaky sense of security was shattered. Conejo was the Crypto-Jews' priest and confidante. What will happen to their closed community? Who will be their "own" priest? Conejo gave in to her insistence on home-schooling her children, though they all had to attend Mass on Sundays. By now, her children were 8, 7 and 5 with strong affinity to Judaism. They were tall for their age and had their mother's beauty. What they did inherit from their father was his bright green eyes. Their knowledge of Judaica was growing with each year.

The arrest, torture and burning of Deacon Conejo and his group kept the Crypto-Jews on their toes. They would meet in different homes to discuss their options. Rituals, they agreed, would be conducted in private. People were suspicious since the betrayer remained unknown. No more Conversos were arrested, which meant that the martyrs did not reveal other names. They died with dignity and heroism.

But that was sufficient for Guiomar to leave Salamanca at the end of the school year. She was candid about her plan against Alfonso's pleas. He felt his work would only secure their future, but she would not hear of that. In addition, the new Deacon assigned to their church insisted that Gabriel and Diego should join his school. She could control their Jewish education as long as they stayed at home. She and Alfonso taught them never to speak Hebrew outside their home to avoid the wrath of the Inquisition.

In January of 1508 the University Board announced the vacancy of the Chair of the Department of Hebrew, Aramaic and Arabic. The Board accepted the candidacy of Alfonso de Zamora as recommended by Pablo Coronel. However, soon it became evident that his name would be dismissed. He did not qualify, so the committee argued. But the truth was known that the Inquisition pulled the strings no to allow any New Christian to fill in the prestigious seat. Instead, the University extended Alfonso's contract for two more years with a slight increase in salary.

That was a slap in the face, but Alfonso did not mind. He was indeed unqualified since he had no knowledge of Arabic whatsoever.

Toward the final school year, Alfonso was called to appear before the University Board chaired by Secretary Baracaldo himself. The portentous secretary went straight to the point:

"Alfonso de Arcos, you have done well in your studies of Latin and Greek. This program is complete. From the next academic year, you will carry the status of a junior professor for two years. Your duty as a teacher will be to teach Hebrew and Aramaic to first- and second-year students, using Latin and Greek as auxiliary languages. In addition, you will begin to copy Hebrew manuscripts of the Bible and grammar books for the use of the students. These copied books will remain in the library. I myself have been searching for bookstores and churches and private collectors to purchase these books which will be your source books."

Alfonso was thinking, 'and what about the Jewish homes you raided, and the holy books confiscated and burned?' But his face remained stoic.

Baracaldo continued: "After two years we shall decide whether or not to promote you to join a team for a very important project." He stopped and looked at the papers in front of him on the table. He then looked up at Alfonso who was standing and looking directly at him. "Your salary will be set at 4000 maravedis per year. We are being very generous with a novice teacher like you." His sneering tone of voice was not lost on Alfonso. It will be very difficult to manage with these wages.

Guiomar's mood worsened when she found out the conditions of Alfonso's employment. Nothing would stop her now from carrying out her decision. When July came, Guiomar packed her and the children's personal belongings. Alfonso attended to his own luggage, and the family traveled to their hometown of Zamora.

The families, and especially the grandparents, surrounded them with love and care. It took Guiomar a few days to act.

While Alfonso was helping his father in the store, Guiomar and a maid transferred their belongings to her parents' home. At last, she had made up her mind to stay where she believed she and the children would benefit from a more secure life among her relatives. The unnerving life in a small compound where they lived under constant surveillance by the Inquisition, not knowing who would betray them, was all too much.

When Alfonso came back from work at his father's store, Guiomar and the children were gone. He went over to his in-laws' house where Guiomar was ready to inform him of her plan. He did not imagine she would actualize it.

"Do you understand the repercussions of your action?" Alfonso blurted out.

"Fully." She responded. "It means a divorce. I had two years to think about it. It was not easy to reach this decision, but I have no choice. My duty is first and foremost to our children and to my sanity. I will not teach my children to accept life as Christians."

"Guiomar, my love, I am not master of my own destiny. Cardinal Cisneros controls my life. At least my work gives us respect in the academic society which I never thought possible or ever considered to achieve. It endows me with the power to act as the Rabbi I always wanted to be. This work allows me to develop and reach heights a few Conversos could ever reach. I started with little self-confidence as to my ability to fit in an academic milieu. Those two years have given me confidence of my own worth as a Jewish scholar. I do not walk with bent head anymore. I thank God for my childhood schooling and teachers." His eyes were begging her to understand that on the one hand he was still committed to his heritage, and on the other, he was building his own character and fame among well-known scholars. After a while, seeing that Guiomar was not responding, he resumed:

"If money is the issue, be assured this will also improve with the years as I make a name for myself."

"No, Alfonso. The money is not the issue at all. I have been explaining to you my concerns for the past two years. I cannot take it any longer! I refuse to witness Cisneros's control over your life. It is too painful, too detestable," Guiomar cried in frustration.

"My beloved, you are the love of my life, and I am afraid to lose you."

"I love you, too. Believe me, I have not taken this step lightly," Guiomar said in between wiping her tears.

"Then we have no other choice but to end our marriage. It is very painful. So unnecessary," Alfonso responded in a low voice.

Juan de Zamora and his wife Leonor were called to the Carbajals' home to witness the divorce. They were shocked and upset, but they could do nothing. Juan and Alexandro Carbajal wrote the *Get*, the Jewish legal document of divorce, and two Conversos were brought as signed witnesses. Alfonso left money for Guiomar and the children and promised to continue to support them.

The next morning Alfonso and Guiomar appeared at the local church in front of a priest. Since divorce was not acceptable by the Catholic church, few reasons were. Bigamy, though practiced by Conversos, was strictly forbidden by the Church to the detriment of death. One of the acceptable reasons for divorce was for the husband to find serious fault in his wife. They both agreed to claim the woman's resistance to marital conjugation. The procedure was quick. They were declared divorced, and their case was duly recorded.

Alfonso was grief-stricken. He loved his wife and children. Her presence was his rock. How could he return to Salamanca without his family? But back he went to face his new position as teacher, scribe, and scholar.

Pablo and María Coronel were shocked to find out about the divorce, even though they knew of Guiomar's unhappiness. María lost a close friend, and her children missed their friends. Soon Alfonso was immersed in his new job, preparing curricula for teaching, copying manuscripts that Baracaldo handed him, and analysing and editing books.

The university library was located in a most impressive building. The three floors incorporated the library administration on the first floor, classrooms on the second, and the library on the third. A wide cloister on the first floor was opened for the clergy and the teachers to relax, read and meditate. The library contained rows upon rows of manuscripts on shelves which extended from the ground to half the height of the Gothic ceiling. Some rooms were available for studying and others accommodated special books on science and philosophy, the Classics and Judaica. The smell of parchment and paper was intoxicating. During the day, owls nestled over the top shelves to eat the moths at night.

As he walked along the bookshelves a few days before the beginning of the academic year, Alfonso slowed down at the Hebrew books section. He picked up one: Rabbi Levi ben Gershom's *Maaseh Hoshev*, a famous book on mathematics he had studied in the *Yeshivah*. He opened the last page and read the five lines of notes written by the former owners: "Ishmael son of Moses of Zamora. Born 12 Adar I, 5150. Murdered on the Sabbath, 22 *Tishrei*, 5222, by a mob as he walked home. May *HaShem* avenge his blood"; "Joshua, son of Ishmael of Zamora. Born second day of Succot, 5196. Executed by Bishop Deza for 'offending the Church,' on 29 *Shevat*, 5251. May *HaShem* avenge his blood"; "Eliezer son of Joshua of Zamora. Born 17 Elul, 5234." Alfonso froze. He was holding the ancient book of his childhood friend Eliezer, his *havruta in* the *Yeshivah*. "O, God, I hope he escaped safely," Alfonso prayed softly. "Eliezer's entire library is probably here." He began opening book after book. They all carried names of Jewish owners from around Castile and Leon. He shivered, thinking of his friends and relatives who had fled Spain leaving such treasures behind.

Agitated, he walked to the plaza of the Cielo de Salamanca, with its colorful dome of the zodiac built in the previous century. The plaza was quiet and deserted. He sat down to compose himself from the revelation in the library. He lost himself in time. As the afternoon sun was casting long shadows, he got up and headed back to the library to prepare for his first class.

In the first year he taught basic Hebrew letters and vowels, as he had taught his children. Later he would teach short sentences for simple conversations. Then, toward the end of the school year, he would introduce them to the biblical text. Alongside the Hebrew he would incorporate Latin translation to individual words. In the second-year class, in addition to Hebrew, he would teach Aramaic using the same systematic approach.

As he approached his classroom, the students were still raucous. Apprehensively he stood at the door waiting for them to notice him. Would he be able to exert authority on Catholic students, something he had never experienced before? How would he introduce himself? Professor? Mister? He had no official title. The only title he could call himself was "Rabbi." The thoughts were running around in his mind. Someone said: "The professor is here." They felt awkward. They knew he was a Converso just like most of the teachers at the university. Conversos were despised but disrespect would cause them trouble, even expulsion.

Alfonso entered the classroom and took his seat at the podium. He put his notebook on it, looked at each student in turn and motioned them to sit down. He then began:

"My name is Alfonso de Zamora and I'll be teaching you Hebrew. You will refer to me as Rabbi. Now, each of you will stand up and tell me his name." There were 12 of them. He pointed to the first boy on his right who got up and called out his name. And so on they went. He set before them his rules of behavior and academic expectations. "Whatever I write on the board you will copy and then rewrite in your dorms. I will check your work daily." That done, he wrote the Hebrew alphabet on the board. His handwriting was exemplary in its strokes and evenness. It was a celebration of unmatched skill and artistry.

He sighed a sigh of relief when the hour was up, and the students were dismissed. He then headed for the next classroom. At the sophomore students' classroom, he repeated his introduction. "I am going to write short sentences which I will write on the board. Copy them carefully. Then you shall read them aloud, twice. I shall parse the verbs and analyse each part. Words develop from roots, and each root has one or more meanings. In a week or two you will begin to read Onqelos, the Aramaic translation to the Pentateuch with its Latin translation." He looked at each of the fifteen students and said: "You will copy everything I write on the board and repeat them in your dorms. Those who want to excel will compose short sentences using these roots."

Over a year later, in the winter of 1509, Alfonso was invited to a Sunday lunch at the Coronels' home where he met a young lady and an older one who looked like her mother. The young lady was tall and slim. She wore a blue dress with a high laced collar that matched a pair of blue eyes that exuded wisdom and discernment. Her porcelain skin accentuated the dominant blue while her demure mannerism evidenced noble upbringing. Alfonso was smitten by her grace and beauty.

"Please meet my cousin Izolda Adela Coronel Florez from Segovia and her mother Doña Elma Florez, her chaperone."

The mother was dressed in fancy gowns and jewelry and was seated on Pablo's left. Alfonso was seated next to the dazzling young lady. At first, she was reserved and shy, but Alfonso's gentleness and good looks dissolved her timidity. Soon they found themselves in a conversation that flowed naturally. 'She could not be older than twenty,' he thought. Alfonso admired wisdom and educated girls, his mother being his paradigm.

"Are you here for a visit?" Alfonso inquired.

"No. I am here to study writing at the University of Salamanca."

"Have you done any writing before?"

"Yes. I write poetry and essays on women's issues. I wish to break the barriers of stigma in higher education. Fortunately, Salamanca has just opened its doors to ladies like me."

"I am very impressed. You are probably one of the few Spanish lady writers."

Doña Florez was quick to respond: "Such a waste of time and energy! We are living in a world run by men who will not share their monopoly on printing with ladies, even those from the nobility."

"But surely you support your daughter's courage to break down old conventionalities!"

"I wish I had her courage," María interjected, saving Doña Florez embarrassment.

Alfonso steered the conversation to more concrete subjects. "Are you going to read Greek and Latin? If you do, I would be delighted to teach you."

Izolda welcomed the change of subject when she answered: "Yes, I will gladly accept your help." Pablo looked disappointed. His knowledge of Latin and Greek surpassed that of Alfonso. As her cousin, he had hoped to be Izolda's mentor.

Izolda and her mother rented a modest house in the old Juderia to be close to the University and to her relatives. They hired a male chaperon to accompany her to school, and two maids as housekeepers. Since then, Alfonso would meet the two ladies for Sunday lunches at the Coronels' and teach Izolda the classical languages at her home under the watchful eyes of Doña Elma Florez. The attraction between Alfonso and Izolda grew into love and mutual respect. He proposed to her on Easter and the wedding was set for December. As adults they found no reason to wait. Family came to celebrate from Zamora and Segovia bearing gifts and good wishes. Even his cousin Isabel Melendez came with her husband from Guadalajara. After the wedding, Doña Florez left for home and Izolda and her personal maids, Luciana and Camila, moved to Alfonso's home.

Alfonso continued his Jewish observances in the basement and after some time of hesitation, more from fear than objection, Izolda joined him. In the family palace in Segovia, a secret synagogue in the basement served the entire family.

Not a year went by when Izolda gave birth to Juan, named after Alfonso's father. At the celebration Juan Sr. and Alfonso blessed little Juan with the Priestly Blessing and gave him the Jewish name Hananiah, saying *May God pardon us*. Izolda continued her studies while her maids cared for the baby.

But the peace did not last for long. One night the police came for Pablo Coronel. María's screams woke up the neighbors who rushed to the shared yard. "They took my husband away," she cried loudly, "the bloody Inquisitors dragged him from our warm bed. They will hear from our noble family soon enough, these swine."

"Perhaps Cardinal Cisneros will intervene on his behalf," suggested Alfonso de Alcalá. "I myself will go to Secretary Baracaldo and plead with him to release Pablo. Do not worry. Go home. Right now, nothing can be done."

"We'll be here for you whenever you want," promised Alfonso and Izolda. They gently accompanied María to her home.

At their home, Alfonso expressed surprise at that unusual event. Were they going to be next? Could it be that Pablo was accused of Judaizing by the same person who betrayed Deacon Conejo? Was it Alcalá who pretended to be overly concerned? They went back to bed but were disturbed by nightmares.

Next morning María brought her children to Alfonso's house. "I have already sent urgent messengers to our family in Segovia. I am taking food for Pablo. These pigs do not feed their incarcerated but rather leave them to rot in their dungeons." She shuddered, then continued: "Please take my children to school and care for them until I come back. I will also go to Bishop Bobadilla. He is a family friend. Please pray for my success." She hugged Izolda and left in a hurry.

Conversos knew of Francisco Bobadilla. He was a third-generation descendant of Jewish converts of noble ancestry from whom several reached high positions in the hierarchy of the Church.

Another family member, of the same name, became Alfonso's admirer and patron three decades later. There were rumors the Bobadillas practiced Judaism covertly.

After two morning classes, Alfonso went to the Cathedral to see Baracaldo. He found him in the corridor that led to the large sanctuary. "Have you come to seek help for Professor Coronel?" The Secretary asked with a smirk.

"Yes, Your Eminence," replied Alfonso with pleading eyes. "Professor Coronel is loyal to our holy faith and his work here is extremely essential. Please save him from evil and baseless accusations. His faith is blameless. I can vouch for it."

Undoubtedly Baracaldo enjoyed wielding his power. He enjoyed seeing this talented scholar begging. Weren't they all guilty of pretence? But he was constrained by Cisneros to contain his disdain. "So you can," he retorted mockingly. "If he were detained, there must have been good reasons. The Inquisitors must do their holy work: to inquire and to come to the truth. If he is innocent, he will surely be released."

"Please, Your Eminence, would you speak on his behalf! After all, you are Cardinal Cisneros's trusted Secretary. They will listen to you. Your word is like the word of God Almighty. Surely His Holiness the Cardinal is the head of the Inquisition! They cannot turn you down!"

Baracaldo appeared to be flattered. "I'll talk to His Holiness the Cardinal." He turned and went into the sanctuary.

That was encouraging, Alfonso thought. He went back to the library where he spent a few hours examining Hebrew manuscripts. Occasionally Baracaldo or his assistants would leave new books they had purchased or, as Alfonso suspected, confiscated from Jews who had left Spain or were incarcerated or executed by the Inquisition. Very few books were intact. The majority were abused by fire, water, or even cuts. Those with scribbles were touched by Christians trying to study them. He patted each page, as though they were Torah scrolls. Later he met with Alfonso de Alcalá. There was tension in the room. Alfonso asked:

"Did you talk to Secretary Baracaldo this morning? Somebody did, because when I saw him at noon, he had been already aware of last night's event."

"Yes, I did talk to him, but he did not commit himself to action."

"Well, to me he promised to take the case to the Cardinal himself.

"Have you ever met the Cardinal?"

"No, I have not. He channels his orders to us through his secretary." Alcalá was reticent more than usual. 'Did he harbor guilt?' Alfonso wondered.

The Coronel children were back in their home. María did not know the charges against her husband, but she had some ideas. "The Inquisitors will present them to Pablo in due time," she had answered Alfonso's inquiry. In the meantime, she had to bring food every day, but she was not permitted to see him. All that was left to do was wait for her family solicitors.

A delegation of solicitors and representatives of the Coronel clan arrived a week later with letters from Bishops attesting to the indisputable faithfulness of the Coronels. But the letter they most depended on was signed by King Ferdinand, who remembered Avraham Senior, the devoted counselor of his late wife, Queen Isabella. He questioned the wisdom of the Inquisitors to detain the grandson of the royal counselor Don Fernan Nuñez Coronel (as was his baptized name) and ordered the immediate release of the afore-mentioned prisoner.

The Inquisitors did not rush to free their famous victim. They enjoyed the humiliation and torture of powerful New Christians. Neither the Bishops nor the King had authority over them. Only the General Inquisitor could stop their holy mission. But his whereabouts were illusive. Cisneros was traveling somewhere between Toledo, Valladolid and Granada in his capacity as the royal political advisor on the dispute and threat of war with the French because of their conflict with the Papacy. Cisneros was also busy organizing the movement of Spanish troops from Africa to Italy.

It took ten days for Baracaldo's messenger to reach Cisneros. The arrest of one of his top scholars filled him with rage. Not only did the Salamanca Inquisition interfere with his ambitious plan to create the Polyglot Bible, but they also infringed on his unambiguous order to keep clear of his protégés. "I order the Bishop of Salamanca to immediately remove from their positions the Inquisitors involved in this disgrace!" Cisneros wrote in his letter, "I will deal with their disobedience when I next visit Salamanca."

Pablo Coronel left the dungeon a broken man. His health deteriorated and he needed the constant care of Doctor Carlos Heredia. His body ached from the four weeks of relentless torture. His tormentors wanted names of Judaizers from among the Converso community of Salamanca. Pablo at first persisted he knew no one, but they rejected his denials, so he remained silent. Upon his release, he stayed at home convalescing for a few weeks, during which time his two colleagues taught his classes.

A melancholy spirit took over the Conversos. Each regressed to minimize contact with others and exhibited ultra-devotion to the Church in attendance and donations. It had been understood that the Coronels were immune from Church abuse. Perhaps the wrath of Cisneros would rid the extremists from the local Inquisition and thus allow them a window of relief. Alfonso returned to his work encouraged by Cisneros's strong reaction.

His new assignment was to copy Scriptures facing the Hebrew text against its Aramaic column, listing the roots of all the verbs and nouns on the margins. These would establish his teaching material and would be later copied into the Polyglot itself. Hebrew text was translated into Latin over each word interlinearly, consistently and tirelessly. Rarely did he add Spanish or Greek. He began adding colophons at the end of each copied manuscript using a formula he created as his special marker. Alfonso built a system of scribal signs based on his Jewish tradition to suit his own aims. He used a variety of Hebrew scripts according to the type of text, whether it was for official use or personal, or according to his moods. When he wished to highlight an important issue in restored and copied manuscripts, he would sketch a hand or a finger, or leave vertical lines. To show his delight in the manuscript, he would paint geometric designs, some fancy some less so. Indeed, he had a talent for art. Often his depression would be reflected in his notes on the manuscripts themselves or in his private diary. However, his official works were meticulously and beautifully executed.

His diary was well hidden in the basement. His thoughts and observations of the clergy around him were too sensitive to undesirable eyes.

At the end of the 1510 school year, Alfonso was again summoned before the University Board. "Your work has been reviewed by your peers and students," said Baracaldo with a forced smile, "we are happy to inform you that the reviews are very positive and encouraging. The University Board has decided, therefore, to extend your contract to two more years. Your salary will be 5500 maravedis. In addition, from now on you are officially a team member of the Polyglot Bible project. Your first assignment is to prepare and supervise a Hebrew etymological onomasticon of the Hebrew Bible and the New Testament together with Pablo Coronel and Alfonso de Alcalá. Your personal task, without the help of your colleagues, will be to prepare a Hebrew grammar book for the Polyglot. All the books you need are found in the library. You have already used some for your classes."

Alfonso set the format for the onomasticon: The names in pointed Hebrew letters would begin each line followed by a pilcrow, a paragraph symbol. Then the name as it appeared in the Vulgate would follow by another pilcrow as a divider. Next would come the meanings of the name according to its Hebrew parsing of logic and etymology. No name would be missed even if it had recurred in previous chapters. The three men would be involved in each stage of the work. Sometimes they would work in the library, at other times they would meet in the cloister. At the same time, Alfonso was assigned to find the best Hebrew text of the Bible to designate as the official text for the Polyglot. To do that, he edited and compared several *MiqdashYah* (complete and edited Hebrew Bibles) and other biblical manuscripts.

To prepare the grammar book for the Polyglot, Alfonso gathered all the available books stored in the library written by several grammarians, most of all Radaq (an acronym for Rabbi David Kimhi of the 12th-13th century), his older brother Rabbi Moshe Kimhi, Rabbi Yonah Ibn Janah (10th–11th century), Rabbi Avraham Ibn Ezra (11th–12th century), and Rabbi Yoseph Ibn Caspi (13th–14th century). Alfonso admired these grammarians, philosophers and scientists for their clear and logical format and interpretations. They constituted the basis for his grammar book.

At the end of 1511, Alfonso was again summoned to the Cathedral, but this time it was an audience with Cardinal Cisneros in person. Cisneros donned the fancy garb of his status, a blue robe with a golden high collar and a matching tiara. On his fingers he wore rings adorned with precious stones. His face was stern and harsh with high cheekbones and deep wrinkles. At that point he was the most powerful man in Spain, second to the King. He sat behind a mahogany desk upon which a stack of papers lay, while his secretary stood behind him like a totem pole.

Alfonso bowed and was clearly apprehensive. So, this was the generous yet vicious man who hired him! Cisneros looked at him with a piercing glance for a minute or two then said in a high-pitched voice:

"I have read of the quality of your work here and have found you to be a respectable and competent scholar. The Polyglot Bible is progressing as planned and your students' and colleagues' evaluation is commendable. I have been constructing a new school for Oriental Languages at the University of Alcalá which will be ready for the next academic year. You will chair the committee of the Polyglot that you began here. Your two colleagues Pablo Nuñez Coronel and Alfonso de Alcalá will join you there until the completion of the project. Of course, the University will provide you with a suitable residence and your salary will increase according to your new status, beginning with 7000 maravedis. You will officially be inducted into the University on July 4th."

The Cardinal watched Alfonso's reaction. Alfonso was speechless. He did not expect this dramatic change. He had found a secure livelihood in Salamanca, the oldest and most respectable high institute of learning in the land.

"I thank Your Holiness for his confidence in my worth. I am too humble to speak." He stopped to inhale a deep breath, then added: "The books I need for my work are in the library of this University. Would I get permission to transfer them to the new library in Alcalá?"

"Certainly. Let my secretary know which books you need, and he will organize their shipment. Anything else?"

"No, Your Holiness."

Secretary Baracaldo motioned with his hand for Alfonso to be dismissed. Alfonso walked backward until he reached the door. The guard let him out.

Alfonso stood immobile for a few minutes before the entrance door. His emotions and thoughts were running high and low trying to analyse the advantages and the disadvantages of the news. His major concern was Izolda's reaction. Would she be permitted to continue her studies in Alcalá? Would she welcome the move? On the other hand, Alcalá is so much closer to Segovia than Salamanca.

He buttoned up his light coat and rushed back to school. Many more hours of work awaited him.

When he arrived at home, tired and hungry, his dinner was brought by the maids. Izolda sat opposite him. When he was done, he told her of his meeting with the Cardinal for the first time. Alfonso described the benefits of moving in glowing colors despite his own misgivings. Izolda was deep in thoughts. Alfonso watched her, waiting for some reaction. "Of course, if you could continue your studies, I will support you fully. What do you think?" The painful reaction of Guiomar still resonated in his memory.

At last, Izolda smiled. "Yes, my love, I will be happy to move with you. Conditions will be so much better for us, and you will be forever remembered for your important role in the Polyglot." Alfonso signed with relief and content. He got up and hugged his wife.

They both agreed that the move of the Coronels will ease their own change of location. By then they had forged a deep and strong friendship based on mutual respect and transparency.

CHAPTER 8

Dedicated

Tell of His glory among the nations, His wondrous deeds, among all peoples; for the Lord is great and much acclaimed, He is held in awe by all gods. Psalms 96:3-4

Alfonso and Izolda planned to travel north to Zamora to visit Alfonso's family before they continued to Alcalá de Henares. Juan was a year old, just beginning to walk. He looked more like his mother with light skin, blond hair and blue eyes, unlike the Zamoras who were darker in color. Several coaches carrying their belongings had left ahead of them driven by expert coachmen as the family trailed behind. Old Miguel Hernandez, the reliable coachman, drove Alfonso's private carriage. Luciana, the younger maid, was in charge of little Juan.

'How many times have I been forced to relocate?' Alfonso mused as he sat in his carriage looking at the familiar landscape. 'This is our lot, the wandering Jews! Moving from one place to another in the hope for better circumstances. How many of my people were lost since we left Zamora, first to Portugal, then back?' He covered his face with his hands and prayed: 'O, God, haven't we suffered enough? Show Your might and redeem us before it is too late.' His tears flowed and he began to tremble.

When Alfonso's coach reached the Zamora family, everyone was overjoyed, even Guiomar. The older children were delighted to see their little brother and immediately took over. Izolda felt welcomed and at ease.

As soon as the news of Alfonso's arrival spread in Zamora, the local bishop invited him for an audience. He wanted to meet with the famous professor who has been working in close contact with

His Holiness Cardinal Cisneros. He inquired about the Cardinal and his inner circle and about the most exemplary literary work that was being created.

"I am elated and proud that one of the most important writers of the Polyglot Bible is a native of my town. This is a great honor for me and for our holy Church. I have already ordered a parade in your honor for next Sunday morning, which will culminate in Mass at the cathedral." He shook Alfonso's hand and with this, the meeting ended.

On his way out, Alfonso chuckled triumphantly. How life has changed since those days when Bishop Deza would force the Jews to stand motionless as he paraded in the streets of the *Juderia*! How many Jews were thrown under the feet of the horses and carriage or dragged to the cathedral's dungeons to be flogged and tortured or murdered! This was his small vengeance. He was still standing tall, and the bishop was bowing to him.

His parents and children laughed at the irony and the vicissitudes of fate. They were of course proud of Alfonso's great achievement. His name would be forever remembered, Alfonso de Zamora, son of Juan and Leonor. "No," insisted Alfonso to his family, "Jacob Gabbai, son of Hayim and Sarah."

Sunday arrived and the residents of Zamora came in droves to honor their son, the closest to the most admired Cardinal in the land. Cisneros was remembered as the Cardinal who cleansed Spain from its non-Catholics. The fancy carriage, which once carried the most hated and feared Bishop Deza, now carried the once humiliated denizen. Mordekhai of Shushan's victory parade was re-enacted. Priests and altar boys dressed in fancy Sunday garb carried Christian symbols and icons of the Holy Family, spreading incense and singing hymns. Thus, they rode around town while the Zamoran population lined up to cheer for Alfonso. The parade ended as the procession returned to the Cathedral followed by the cheerful spectators. The joy overflowed as their son brought honor to their city.

The bishop sat the Zamora family in the front seats. He reached his pulpit and began his flowery sermon:

"We bow our heads to our son, the most honorable Alfonso de Zamora, who was selected from among numerous scholars in the land to spearhead the divine vision of our beloved Cardinal Jiménez de Cisneros, the defender of the faith. The Polyglot Bible will allow everyone who can read Latin or Greek to understand better the Holy Scriptures." The Zamora family wondered how many in that audience could read Spanish. "Mother of God, Holy Mary, and her son Jesus Christ, may their faces shine upon him and direct him to life of scholarship and fame."

He stopped to look at the front row: "The families of Juan de Zamora have seen the light of our holy faith and have exhibited exemplary faithfulness to our Holy Father and the Holy Mother of God." On and on, the bishop praised the Zamoran families, their contributions to the community, and their devotion and donations to the Church. No one dared motion to leave for there was a rumor of the dispensation of food and beer after Mass. At last, the bishop sat down and Mass began. The people lined up and each was given a small box with food.

On Monday, Juan Sr.'s store saw an increase of residents bringing their shoes and leather goods for repair or to order new ones. In the evening, Alfonso and his sons went down to the basement to study Torah. He was immune from the Inquisition. Didn't the Bishop state publicly that his family members were exemplary Catholics? Cardinal Cisneros was their personal angel and patron. The irony!

Before moving on to Alcalá after two weeks of rest, Alfonso hugged his sons, Gabriel, Diego and Francisco, and encouraged them to visit him in Alcalá. The carriages were ready to start the long journey. Unlike the voyage from Zamora to Salamanca, the distance to Alcalá necessitated two stops for the night. As Hernandez knew the way well for he had taken that road numerous times before, he selected the inns on the way and cared for the horses.

At the end of the three-day journey, Alfonso arrived at the gates of the city. He handed the guard Cisneros's letter and was at once accompanied to the University offices. As in Salamanca, he was welcomed by the University Church representatives and shown into his new residence in the old *Juderia*. The house was more spacious than his former home in Salamanca and came with an extra room for a maid. It was very similarly situated, with the rear facing a common yard that served several families. He realized he was given a house that had belonged to a Jewish family whose fate he could only imagine. Nearby, a synagogue was boarded-up.

It was not demolished because its location among the homes and its small size lot, had no value for the Church.

Alcalá de Henares was an old town conquered and rebuilt by the Romans. The Visigoths, the Moors, and the Castilians took over the city in turn and left their significant marks on the city, especially on its fortifications. Under the Christians, the city was granted to the Bishopry of Toledo, about 75 miles away. The city is situated by the Henares River. Until the Expulsion of the Jews, Alcalá included a sizeable Jewish community with its own *Juderia*. Commerce was run by the Jews and the Moors. Remains of their famous marketplace rapidly disappeared.

The Complutense University in Alcalá constituted a city within the city proper. Its structure resembled that of Salamanca. Apart from the school, it contained several churches, a police station, hospital, printer, dormitories, library, and gardens. Later, shops opened to serve the teachers and students and the population at large. Among others, they provided writing material, clothing, shoes, and household items. The four sides of the campus of the Oriental Languages faculty comprised three floors of Moorish architecture, with a surrounding balcony. The outside columns were decorated by Cardinal Cisneros's coat of arms, crosses and birds. In the middle of the cloister there was a well. The main entrance faced the new church on the left side of the plaza and the old *Juderia* where all the teachers lived. The three entrance gates were locked at night.

The first floor contained the classrooms, the dorms for the underprivileged students, and a room where students, who broke the school rules, would be arrested for three nights. The library was located on the second floor with additional rooms for poor students, and on the third were the paying students' dormitories. All rooms were furnished minimally: a bed, a desk and a chair.

For Cardinal Cisneros, a fortress-like palace in the shape of the cross was built with towers, gates, gardens, and large yards surrounded by high walls. The focal tower ended with a tiara-shaped octagon centered upon a large cross, adorned by animal statues. A private church was built on the left of the main entrance. Rumor had it that he objected to the opulence showered on the palace. The back of the palace faced the *Calle Mayor* of the *Juderia* with its homes, stores, and former synagogues. Except for the one closed synagogue, no sign was left of the many Jewish public structures. However, the Jewish hospital which was built in 1483 was now run by nuns and Converso doctors.

Alfonso kept studying on his own and his intense work limited his free time. He studied in his basement where his Jewish paraphernalia and family books were kept behind crates and boxes or under rugs. He did his best not to miss his morning, evening, Sabbath, and Festival prayers. The copy of his father's *Mahazor*, a series of prayers and *piyyutim* for the High Holy Days that he had copied diligently during his years in Arcos, were stashed away safely.

Fortunately for Izolda, the University welcomed ladies for a writing class for the first time ever. It was safe to walk alone during the day. She needed one more year to graduate.

By the end of 1513 Alfonso's contribution to the Complutense Polyglot Bible was nearly completed. He had handed over the etymological onomasticon after a complete rearrangement of the format: Instead of repeating the names according to biblical chapters, now the order was set alphabetically. The Hebrew Bible was completed. The Aramaic text of the Pentateuch was nearly ready for publication as well. The grammar book was going through a final editing. However, this and the onomasticon, and the fifth volume of the New Testament, would be the last to be printed. It was an unmatched endeavor of tedious and colossal dimensions. Coronel and Alcalá were still busy with the last phase of the Latin and the Greek translations.

Alfonso's teaching methods developed gradually with each year and with each group of students. He dared to introduce *piyyutim*, the Jewish poetry sung during religious worship and composed by his beloved Ibn Gabirol, in the guise of Spanish poetry. Jewish parables and proverbs learned from his mother and grandmother were introduced as Spanish wisdom literature. He taught commentary of Scriptures through the Hebrew grammar by Radaq and Ibn Ezra, or snippets of Rambam's philosophy from *Moreh Nevukhim* as Spanish thoughts. All this was inculcated in small measures albeit steadily. No one complained or suspected. On the contrary, the students admired the unusual teacher with his innovative methods and the variety of literary texts. In the winter days, when the sun was warm, Alfonso moved his classes to the cloister to the delight of all.

Several books he was given or copied were left in his possession. He argued that he needed them as source texts or to conduct comparisons for teaching purposes. Throughout the years he accumulated a considerable library that included volumes of Rabbinic literature strictly banned by the Church. Many of them he "borrowed" from the library. These books served to further his knowledge. He studied books by Jews on astronomy, medicine and other sciences, or translations by Jews of non-Jewish scientists, like the perceptions of Averroes the Moor on Aristotle's philosophy.

Alfonso knew that his teaching, the preparation for the Polyglot, and his private study widened his range of knowledge immeasurably. His appreciation for his literary heritage deepened and grew by leaps and bounds. It would not have been achieved but for his divine switch from a rural shoemaker to a scholar in the top universities of his time.

Fortunately for many Crypto-Jews, *Yom Kippur* fell that year on a Saturday when Alfonso observed the Holy Day alone in his basement. The old *Juderia* was quiet, shutters closed. Suddenly, out of the stillness in the air, sounds of marching boots began infiltrating the basement. Alfonso hurried to hide his *Mahazor* and *tallit* and ran upstairs covering the floor entrance behind him. He messed up his hair and put on a house coat. In a few minutes the Inquisition police knocked on his door. They knew who he was for he was well known at the University.

"What brings you here, honorable policemen?" he said with a faint voice. "Please excuse my appearance for I am ill."

"We would like to check your home, Professor de Zamora," the highest in rank answered.

"What do you think you might find?" Alfonso asked naively. His face exuded sadness and pain. He held his head with his hand and let them in. "Please do not mess up my books. If they are damaged in any way, I shall report that to our beloved Archbishop Cisneros. And please do not disturb my son's and wife's rest."

They noticed the Madonna statue on a shelf at the entrance and immediately bowed their heads and crossed themselves. They checked every corner of the house but found nothing incriminating.

"Would you like to inspect the basement, too?" He asked with sarcasm. The Conversos among the University faculty were particularly protected by Cisneros and the police knew that well.

"No, we have seen enough. We are sorry to disturb your rest. May our Lord Jesus and his Holy Mother grant you good health." They hurried to leave stopping again at the entrance to bow to María's statue.

Even though no harm was done, the mere fact that these cursed people invaded his space was unnerving. Sitting down to relax his agitated nerves, he removed the rug over the opening of the basement and went back to his prayers. On Sunday morning he sat down to write a letter to his sons whom he missed terribly. He told them of his soon-to-be-completed work. He was proud of his achievement because this Polyglot Bible would encourage thousands of people, in Spain and abroad, to start reading the Bible on their own and be introduced to Hebrew and Aramaic as Jewish texts. His copied books would be studied by Christian students and teachers as well as by church clergy. He was doing God's work and people appreciated his talents.

Gabriel's and Diego's letters arrived a few months later, written in Hebrew. They were restless living in this land. "Dear *padre*," they wrote, "we feel chained and enslaved. We seek freedom to worship as we please. We want revenge for what Spain has done to our people. Mother would not hear of that. She claims we are too young to go away by ourselves, but we are strong and ready. Yes, we must plan every move carefully. For this purpose, we listen to adults talk about the fates of their relatives who survived the turmoil of their travels. We contacted survivors, collected information on secure ways out, and saved money to accomplish all this. In the meantime, we have been accumulating skills to be useful wherever we go. We have been training in medicine in Doctor Calderon's surgery and in the production of leather at our grandfather's shoe store." They ended by assuring their father of their good health in body and mind. Regards from mother.

Alfonso was proud of their clear thinking and escape plan. 'They will accomplish what I had in mind but failed,' he thought. Writing in Hebrew gladdened him to no end. They reminded him of the competitions in his *Yeshivah* who could best speak and write Hebrew. He always won. "You will be a great Rabbi," they used to tell him, and he believed them. His eyes welled up.

He heard of a group of Conversos meeting for Sabbath services at the house of Julio Cardoza. One room in the back was transformed into a small synagogue. At first, he was hesitant, but after talking to Cardoza in private, his fears were alleviated. Cardoza had a loyal cadre of guards he chose himself. Alfonso joined the group on the Sabbath occasionally, then on Holy Days. The group would enter and exit the house through a back door. This went on for a few years until he recognized a plain-clothed policeman walking slowly in front of the Cardoza's house on Saturday morning. He could not afford the exposure. The next morning, he passed by the house and made a vow: 'I will not go into this synagogue.' He paused, then added 'for one year.' Alfonso kept his vow. When no harm was done to Cardoza, Alfonso joined his group again, but less frequently.

In 1514 Alfonso received a lengthy and unusual manuscript to edit and restore which he greatly cherished. It contained the Writings with commentaries by Rashi, Radaq, Ibn Ezra, and Ralbag, accompanied by the Aramaic translation. The richness of the commentaries and Ralbag's unique methodology of "benefits", provided him with a rare opportunity to study them and offer his own comments. Two more works were added which Alfonso would copy several times later: *The sale contract of the evil Haman who was sold into slavery to Mordekhai*, a humorous midrash on the book of Esther, together with *Massoret Seyag LaTorah* by Rabbi Meir HaLevi Abulafia. Any top official, from the King and Cisneros to the Inquisitors and the arrogant judges and lower clergy, served as a reflection of the evil Haman. 'In every generation we have at least one Haman, but here, nowadays, we have so many,' he observed.

Alfonso added his own commentary in every possible free space and in every margin in a variety of inconspicuous ways: wavy lines differing in length and thickness, sketches of fingers or hands, and a script that only he could read. However, he had been warned to skip Radaq's nine rebuttals against the Christianization of certain parts of Psalms. In these rebuttals, Radaq quoted Talmudic support for his arguments. Talmudic references were strictly forbidden. The Church wished to hide these forbidden Talmudic responses to Christian subversion of the Hebrew Scriptures from Christian eyes. To comply, Alfonso would write the marginal note "skip until ..." This would ignite the readers' curiosity to ignore the injunction, especially when he left the text untouched.

The editing of this manuscript took Alfonso many weeks, for he read every column and enjoyed the profundity of these Rabbis' wisdom. 'No one could compare to such deep understanding of Scriptures, and such power of illumination,' he contemplated proudly. In mid-1514, the team members assigned for the creation of the Polyglot Bible completed their tasks. The prepared quires were taken to Eguia the printer. The printing process was laborious and took several months to accomplish. But alas, only 600 copies were printed, because in the meantime Dutch Erasmus sued Cardinal Cisneros before Emperor Maximilian and Pope Leo X in order to halt the printing of the New Testament, which was ready for publication. Since Cisneros wished to publish the complete Polyglot Bible, he was forced to wait for a few more years. But that did not concern Alfonso anymore. He returned in full swing to his teaching, copying, and editing work as well as restoring Hebrew books.

That same year Izolda gave birth to twins, Jeromillo and Sofia. The pressure on Alfonso to support a growing family exacerbated his frustration of mounting work.

CHAPTER 9

Avenged

The one who dug a pit and deepened it, would fall into the trap he made. His evil deed would recoil upon his own head, his violence would come down upon his skull. Psalms 7:16

Alfonso heard of Adalberto Muntaquez, the new counselor to Cardinal Cisneros, in place of Baracaldo who fell ill. When next he was summoned to Cisneros's palace, Alfonso was introduced to Deacon Muntaquez. The man was tall and dark skinned with noble features. He was dressed in the proper garb of his position, but without the excess of Secretary Baracaldo. Alfonso welcomed him to Alcalá and asked him: "You look familiar. Have we met before?"

"I think I remember you from Salamanca where I studied Theology."

"That's right!" Alfonso replied. Indeed, he remembered seeing him on numerous occasions in his first years there. How could he forget this impressive man! Alfonso recalled his years of misery and fatigue in Salamanca. "Did you get your Deaconship there, too?"

"No, right here in the faculty of Theology."

"How did you happen to be hired by the Cardinal?" Alfonso was curious.

"He came to teach a few times in Salamanca and, I suppose, he was impressed by my diligence and argumentation." He did not sound arrogant at all, but rather an assessor of skills, as a matter of fact, without being apologetic. Alfonso liked that. In turn, he recounted how he was hired without mentioning his Converso background, but he assumed that Muntaquez might have guessed.

95

A friendship was formed in a few minutes in mutual admiration and respect for the other's accomplishments. When Alfonso followed Muntaquez into Cisneros's inner chamber, he noticed how Cisneros's face lit up. Alfonso thought Cisneros was glad to see him, the hero of the Complutensis. But he was wrong.

Unbeknownst to anyone in Salamanca or Alcalá, Adalberto Muntaquez was born in a palace in Málaga in 1486 by the name Yusuf al Hassan Ali. His grandfather, Sultan Abu al Hassan Ali, had just transferred Granada to his uncle, Muhammad XII to hold on to his shriveled emirate as the Spanish army was preparing their final assault to regain control of all of Spain. His father, Nasr al Hassan Ali, preferred his horses to politics and lived in a large estate in Málaga. His mother, Princess Suraya, was the daughter of the city's ruler, the Sultan's nephew. Málaga fell when Yusuf was a year old, and the nobility was given the choice to convert or be exiled. At night, Suraya, Nasr and baby Yusuf escaped the city in a carriage drawn by four horses, trying, not always successfully, to avoid the littered bodies strewn on the streets and alleys. As they drove west, they looked back from the top of a hill, and saw their palace and city in flames. Fortunately, they reached the Granada palace safely.

"Málaga has fallen, Your Majesty," said Nasr Ali to his brother the king. "The infidels have slaughtered the soldiers and the civilian population, and set the city on fire. The palace has been ransacked and Prince Salem and his family have been executed. We have survived by the Merciful Allah."

"May Allah avenge our people. I cannot estimate how long we can hold on against the infidel army. We are not certain if we shall survive until the end of the year. In the meantime, the servants will take care of your needs."

He clapped his hands and three servants appeared. "Make the Prince and Princess comfortable as can be." Nasr and Suraya bowed down and left the room.

Life in Granada was tense, for the population knew their turn would come next. In 1492, the king capitulated and signed an agreement with Cisneros to protect Granada from the Inquisition. Only the king, his wives and children were allowed to go into exile in Fes. Yusuf's family was forced out of the palace.

However, the peace did not last, for Cisneros could not in true faith allow a pocket of Moors to live on Christian soil. He decided to use as much force as possible to rid the land of Muslims. Two years later, when he returned to Granada, he proclaimed the agreement null and void and Islam banned. He didn't wait long for the rebellion to materialize. Cisneros's army massacred the rebels. He further demanded of the local elderly Archbishop, Fernando de Talavera, to hasten the process of baptism.

Talavera preached for tolerance: "Agreements must be honored. Won't it be more Christian-like to bring the Moors to Christ by love?" His words sloughed off Cisneros's conscience.

"Love for these barbarians is useless," was his response, "I am here to ensure the immediate baptism of the Granada populace. I have no patience or mercy for these enemies of our Lord Jesus."

During those two years, Yusuf's family experienced poverty and hardship while hiding in an abandoned farm at the outskirts of the city. They kept their royal garments and heirlooms in a small bag for Yusuf to keep. "Guard them with your life, my son," his father said, "This is your legacy if we do not survive." Together they buried the bag by the southern wall that surrounded the house. Yusuf was a bright child, groomed to be a royal prince. At the tender age of 8 he understood the precarious situation of his family.

Where the former main mosque used to stand, a Catholic cathedral now towered over all other buildings. A high platform was erected in front of the cathedral where gallows waited for action. No dungeons would be needed, for it would be either public torture till death or baptism. The citizens were ordered to appear on Sunday morning in front of the platform. In the meantime, troops were sent to the fields to look for hidden Moors.

When the soldiers found them, Yusuf's parents were beaten savagely before his eyes and taken to the city where thousands of people lined up in silence in front of the new Cathedral. Cisneros climbed the platform and sat on a royal chair taken from the palace. His purple cassock with amaranth trim, the golden cross, and the bejeweled heraldic golden mitre shone in the sunlight. Yusuf speculated that this man was the most important among the victorious celebrants. When his father's turn came, the Inquisitor asked him to choose baptism or death. His father held his head high and announced in a proud voice:

"I will not give in to barbarians. I am ready to die in the name of Allah." Suraya held Yusuf's hand and whispered: "Remember this day and these people. You must live to take revenge. Agree to baptize and rise to power. You are a prince from the glorious House of Nasrid. This is our legacy to you." She pushed him behind her and said: "Stay behind. Do not follow us. Always remember our love for you."

His father was already standing on the platform in front of Cisneros when Suraya walked with dignity to join her husband. "I am ready," she said loudly to the executioner, "and may Allah avenge our blood." Her words were forever engraved in Yusuf's memory. His hands were clenched and bleeding, but he kept his eyes focused on his parents. Cisneros gave the sign, and the executioner pulled their clothes off their bodies. He then began to flog them until both collapsed to the ground. Two other Inquisitors lifted them to their feet, and one by one they were hanged. Cisneros gave the sign to remove their dead bodied which was duly done. Now Yusuf focused his eyes on the head executioner, the fancy-clothed man, with the bejeweled crosier and rings. He looked long and hard to remember his face. 'Yes, mother, revenge will come,' he promised himself.

He was taken to the font and baptized. He presented himself as an orphan who was thrown to the streets by his evil uncle. His beautiful face attracted the attention of Bishop Talavera who took him under his wing. When all of Granada's denizens were either killed or baptized, Cisneros came to depart from the local Bishop. There he saw Yusuf, who was renamed Alberto Talavera. Young Alberto froze when he saw his parents' executioner. "Alberto, kiss the ring of the good Archbishop Jimenez de Cisneros," Talavera encouraged him. Obediently Alberto approached the honorable guest and kissed the outstretched hand. He shivered slightly. Cisneros stroked the child's head and said to the elderly Talavera: "Such a well-behaved child, and so handsome! You will take good care of him."

"I promise," replied Talavera.

Cisneros looked at Alberto and said in a fatherly fashion: "Perhaps we shall meet again," he told Alberto. 'Indeed, we shall,' thought Alberto.

The indoctrination of young Alberto began first at the Granada Cathedral school. In his will, the kind Talavera bequeathed Alberto a large sum of money "to further his education." As he neared his last year of schooling, Bishop Talavera's convulsions and heart failure baffled his doctors. These ailments were symptomatic of old age, so the Diocese priests and doctors reasoned. At his tomb, Alberto mourned the untimely passing of his "adoptive father" who raised him with love and taught him to love Lord Jesus and the Church.

He graduated from school with the highest accolades. Immediately before graduation, Alberto asked the principal to change his name to Adalberto Muntaquez, "to begin my new life on my own," as he explained. By then no one recalled the origin of Talavera's protégé. With this new name, he arrived at the Salamanca University Faculty of Theology where Cardinal Cisneros taught and frequented. The new name fit his life mission. 'Adalberto' meant in Spanish 'aristocratic and bright' and 'Muntaqum' meant in Arabic "avenger". His background as he presented to the school, did not mention Talavera. If faced with the facts, he would reason that he wished to be responsible for his own successes.

At the age of 18 in 1504 his impeccable Spanish, his sharp mind, good manners and looks boosted his popularity among students and teachers alike. This was not lost on Cisneros when he began teaching Adalberto's classes. Feeling a strong and indelible attraction to this young man, Cisneros admired beauty and brain, which he found plenty in this student.

Adalberto excelled in all his classes. When he graduated after six years, he realized that Cisneros spent more time in Alcalá. He then decided to follow him by registering for two more years of Canon Law. Cisneros taught there, too, and the young star would approach him for advice. Cisneros was flattered and their communication strengthened. It was 1512 when upon graduation he was bestowed the title of Deacon. Cisneros himself handed Adalberto his diploma. As he shook his hand in congratulation, there was no shadow of recognition of that young boy under Talavera's patronage. Adalberto was at once hired by the Dean to head the Faculty of Theology. He began writing essays on theology and law, lectured in cathedrals and synods, and began teaching. He was considered the rising star of Catholicism. And all this time Adalberto continued to flatter the old Cardinal by seeking his advice. A gift here and a gift there grew Cisneros's heart fonder and fonder.

Two years later, when Baracaldo was too busy with the Complutensis, Cisneros asked the new star for occasional help in a myriad of functions. When Baracaldo lay sick and incapacitated for long periods of time, Adalberto accepted with ostensible humility the full-time employment. It was time to carry out his plot. And so, the process of poisoning began. His experience with his "beloved adoptive father" served him as the steppingstone to the ultimate goal.

It was at that point in his life that Adalberto, wearing a hood over his long cassock, appeared at the library where Alfonso was studying. It was clear he was looking for Alfonso, for he came straight to his seat and sat next to him. He looked at Alfonso's inquiring face and went right to the point in a whispering voice: "You know who I am, I assume."

"Of course, I know, my friend. You are Cardinal Cisneros's faithful assistant."

"No, I mean who I really am, where I came from, who my parents were, my people?"

"I don't want to speculate, so why don't you tell me if you wish."

"I first want to know if I can trust you. I need a loyal friend in Alcalá."

Alfonso raised his eyebrows in surprise. "It depends. You probably know who I am and consequently what my fears and concerns are. I cannot give my hand to any heresy or acts of religious insubordination. People like me are not safe personally or secured in our positions."

"That is why I am here. I understand you more than you can imagine. That is why I seek your friendship and discretion. I am willing to gamble on you, for we are like two peas in a pod."

Alfonso realized Adalberto's need to bear his soul was urgent. He liked this noble-looking man and admired his knowledge and sharp intellect for such a young man. He got up and made motion to follow him to a private room off the main hall. Alfonso locked the small door behind them and lit another candle. "Now we can talk," he said as they took their seats facing one another.

"I cannot divulge every detail of my life but suffice it to say that I came from the royal family of Granada." Alfonso watched him closely as he had never done before. 'Why am I not surprised?' he thought. 'Why is he telling me this?'

100

"You must be wondering why I am telling you this," Adalberto said with a smile. "Because you know how a Converso feels. As long as I have some power over the Cardinal, I shall protect people like you and me."

"The Cardinal protects Conversos. He is benevolent to us," responded Alfonso.

"This is not how we look at him. I mean we, the Moriscos, those who were forcibly baptized."

"Why do you say that? Didn't he build a religious free-zone in Granada for those among the Muslims who refused to convert?"

"At first, yes, but soon after, he dragged everyone to the baptismal fonts or murdered those who refused."

"I didn't know that. Why did he change his mind?"

"Because he was afraid Jews might be flocking there to find religious shelter."

"Oh!" said Alfonso, "I did not know this. Did you lose family members there?"

"Not only my family, but many of my people lost their lives. He tricked us which led to a rebellion. Cisneros depended on it to happen, for that gave him the excuse to kill them and ban Islam from Granada."

"So, what are you planning to do about it? Kill Cisneros? It is preposterous! I hope this is not your plan."

"Don't worry, my friend. But one day I'll need your help."

"Not for any criminal act, I beg of you." The handsome prince got up, hugged Alfonso and left. Alfonso remained quiet thinking about the man's revelation, hoping and praying that he would not do anything stupid.

Alfonso figured that Adalberto came to forge a bond between the two of them, sharing years of suffering, humiliation and forced conversions. He realized how deep was Cisneros's assistant's hatred of the Cardinal and his Church. The difference was that he, Alfonso, was ambivalent about the proper reaction to Cisneros's viciousness whereas Adalberto's could be decidedly controversial.

Adalberto traveled with Cisneros in his many political and religious missions. They said that the handsome and bright counselor became the closest servant of the great Archbishop of Toledo. He not only composed Cisneros's correspondence, but oversaw his attire, meals and wines. Wherever they visited, their rooms were adjacent to each other. Adalberto encouraged this total dependency of the aging Cardinal, and Cisneros trusted him blindly.

"I have good news," beamed the assistant one day. "I met a wine merchant who just brought barrels of red wine from Rioja. He said that this particular wine was blessed by the Bishop of St. James shrine at Santiago de Compostela. He allowed me a taste and I just had to purchase one whole barrel. Here," he held half a glass of red wine and handed it to Cisneros, "enjoy!"

It was sinfully delicious! Cisneros asked to fill up the glass which his assistant was more than happy to oblige. Adalberto knew his story would be received without any questions. His plan has just begun, and it was a good omen. Since then, a small measure of white powder was added to the wine as he had done with Talavera. The Rioja wine became Cisneros's favorite drink in every meal. Every so often Adalberto Muntaquez would meet with the Granada merchant who supplied him with the powder, for the Moors were experts in the production of poisons.

Adalberto introduced new menus of stuffed pork and veal, new vegetables brought from the new world cooked in a variety of spices brought from the Far East, pasta from China and coffee from Africa. In the spicy dishes the loyal assistant added some more powder. "You are spoiling me," 'complained' the Cardinal mischievously. "You have been so good to me. How could I have lived without your devoted service!"

Adalberto smiled sheepishly. "You are the spiritual and political leader of the Spanish empire! You deserve every bit of comfort and happiness. You have dedicated your life to our Holy Faith and to the glory of our Catholic Church. You are the Grand Inquisitor who rid our land from the infidels. Enjoy the fruits of your toils." If only Cisneros listened to the undertone coming from the mouth of his devoted assistant!

Cisneros thought for a while and then said: "Your words are true. It is our Lord Jesus who has brought me to these heights of power. I am the most powerful man in Spain and in the Americas!" He filled his mouth with sweet green grapes and closed his eyes to savor.

'What a swine,' thought Adalberto, 'your day will come.' Time and again the Cardinal would invite his assistant to share his table, but Adalberto would refuse saying: "How could I, of humble beginnings, share a meal with the holiest man in Spain? My deep respect for you forbids me from doing so. Allow me, Your

Holiness, to take my meals in the adjacent room." Cisneros could not know that the young Deacon shunned pork.

Adalberto stayed close to his master, indulging him with every satisfying nourishment, especially the rich wine that soothed the spirit. It was one cool night on one of their stops when he left a window open. Cisneros shivered in bed: "It is so cold tonight," he remarked, "please ask the servant to bring extra blankets." Adalberto at once went out and closed the door behind him. He did not search for extra blankets. He waited awhile, then returned apologizing: "I did not find anyone awake, for all the monks have retired to their quarters."

The 79–year–old cleric did not object when his beloved counselor slipped into his bed to keep him warm. It was pleasing and delightful. It ignited in him uncharted and suppressed feelings he willingly welcomed now. 'Oh, dear Lord Jesus,' he thought, 'forgive me, for my compulsions are weak! I am an old man who has missed so much pleasure in life! Only now do I understand why the 400 Granadan priests escaped with their Moorish mistresses to North Africa and converted to Islam. I foolishly insisted on asceticism! How long am I going to live, anyway?' There was nothing egregious about this, for so many clerics maintained male and female lovers.

Queen Isabella had died in 1504 and her husband, King Ferdinand, maintained his position over Castile. However, the Castilian Cortes declared his daughter Joanna the sovereign of Castile. She was soon found unstable, and her husband Philip was crowned King. But alas, in six months he was dead under the suspicion of being poisoned by Ferdinand who legally became the Regent of Joanna and her son Carlos. Before his death in January 1516, Ferdinand bequeathed Castile to Cisneros as the Regent for his 15-year-old grandson, Carlos. In one of their private meetings, Cisneros described to Adalberto his political dilemmas: "My duties are overwhelming, my dear Adalberto, and I am not so young anymore. But as the closest counselor to the King, I must act without delay. The vacuum and the uncertainties created by the death of the King's son-in-law have given rise to rebellions in several locations. The most urgent ones are taking place in the kingdom of Navarre and among the nobles of Castile."

"What are you planning to do? With your political experience and determination to your royal position, you will no doubt choose the right response to these abominations." Adalberto's subtle advice to use violence against Christians served his purpose. His words impressed Cisneros and he made up his mind. He could not show weakness in the eyes of his "admirer."

"I must deal with them with force and resolve once and for all." 'Did he ever deal with his opponents differently?' thought the young assistant with contempt and hatred. "Brutality is what they deserve," resumed the old Cardinal, "my duty is to keep Spain safe and strong for young Carlos."

And indeed, he viciously conquered Navarre and eliminated many of the leading nobles. Apart from wars and executions during those two years of unrest, he established the courts in Madrid, and organized a popular army. His schedule was exhaustive even for a man half his age. In all these meetings and decision making, Adalberto was present, taking notes.

The heir to the throne of Spain was then living in Ghent, the Netherlands. Carlos V, as he became known later in Spain, was anxious to fill his late father's shoes. But he had to wait, for Cisneros was not too willing to give up his supreme power and Spain was not too welcoming. He was considered a foreigner, Germanic, who barely spoke Spanish.

Archbishop Cisneros called his assistant for an urgent meeting. He seemed agitated and unusually apprehensive. Adalberto realized something very important had happened which upset this powerful man. "Your Holiness," he opened, "what in the name of our Savior has happened? How can I be of assistance?"

Cisneros clasped his jaundiced, wrinkled hands. "Prince Carlos covets the Spanish throne before his time. He has traveled to Valladolid to meet with his mother, Queen Joanna, to force her to change her designation of his brother Ferdinand to succeed his grandfather. This is a clear affront to my years of hard work. He has not consulted with me!" He began pacing the room slowly, with visible discomfort.

Someone knocked. Adalberto went to answer and returned with a scroll embossed with the seal of the Queen. "It is a letter from Her Majesty the Queen."

"More aggravation! More betrayal!" He raised his voice in despair. He stopped pacing and took the letter from Adalberto's hand. He broke the seal and began reading. His face turned white. "They have declared him King together with his mother!"

"Who are 'they'?"

"The Castile Cortez," he shouted with acrimony. "I have held on to the regency for two years. We must rush to swear allegiance to the new King lest I be condemned as a usurper or a traitor. I must reach him before he returns to Asturias on his way back to Ghent. I must resign from my supreme post and bow down to this arrogant youth!"

"But, Your Holiness, you are not well, and a new epidemic is causing havoc throughout Spain. Traveling is inadvisable. Can you send the King your resignation by a courier?"

"No, I must present it in person. Let us hurry."

And hurry they did. The sick perished every day providing Adalberto the perfect cover to fulfill his vengeful plan. Even before they set out in the archbishopric carriage, Cisneros was not feeling well. His jaundiced eyes bulged, and his muscles cramped with agonizing pain. Adalberto massaged his legs and soothed his eyes with warm compresses. He had written Cisneros's reluctant resignation letter and kept it in his personal bag. They stopped for the night at a cathedral where the devoted assistant personally took care of the ailing Cardinal's meal and wine with a good measure of the mysterious powder.

Early morning, they went on their way. On the second night, in Roa, Cisneros's condition deteriorated rapidly. Lying in bed, sweating and vomiting blood, Cisneros felt drowsy. Adalberto sat by his bed smiling. The dying Cardinal looked puzzled.

"Am I dying, my dear Adalberto?" He whispered.

"Yes, Your Holiness, and I have made certain to see to it. Is your pain unbearable?"

Cisneros was confused. He took a deep breath and said: "Yes, it is. What is going on? I need a doctor. Please hurry."

"No doctor is coming. Your day has come. You see, Your Holiness, I am the child whose noble parents you murdered, there in Granada, 25 years ago. You left me an orphan and forced me to live a life of the infidel. I swore then and there to avenge their blood, the royal blood of the Hassan Ali dynasty." He stood up straight, his handsome head high, victorious. He looked royal, noble, in command of the situation. "I am prince Yusuf of the Nasrid dynasty, named after the founder of the dynasty whose life you destroyed. I am the avenging angel, the Muntaqum of the Adalberto, the bright aristocrat." He took the pouch with the powder out of his pocket and dangled it before the infected eyes of the panicked sick man. "This is arsenic. My people are skilled in producing it. This you have been consuming for the past two years, slowly and steadily." With satisfaction, he looked at the dying man's face turn white. "The benevolent and merciful Allah has avenged the blood of his devotees. Now you are going to get the last potion." He poured a large amount of the arsenic into the cup of red wine and forced it into Cisneros's mouth.

The sick man pursed his lips to resist, but he had no energy left to fight. He knew in a few minutes he would die in more agony and convulsions. The Muntaqum sat there calmly as the murderer of his parents and people took his last breath. He shattered the glass of wine on the floor near Cisneros's bed to appear broken accidentally by the dying man. Having finished staging the death scene, the Muntaqum carefully wiped the dead man's foaming lips from the arsenic and went to his room.

Before going to bed he sat down to write an official letter of recommendation to support Deacon Muntaquez wherever he went as the private messenger of the Grand Inquisitor. He signed it with Cisneros's seal. Another document he wrote was the completion of his life story and the mission he had just accomplished.

In the morning Adalberto wailed as he "found" the lifeless body of the Most Honorable Cardinal and rushed to tell the news to the bishop of the cathedral. He cried and looked disheveled and deeply distressed. The bishop had seen the Cardinal's failing condition the night before and was not surprised to see him dead. Adalberto explained that Cisneros probably was infected by the latest epidemic and the bishop kept a distance.

"Get me a coffin to return the body of our beloved Cardinal to Alcalá. Make sure he is wrapped well." He handed the Bishop Cisneros's letter of resignation sealed with red wax. "Take this important letter to Valladolid and make sure it is handed over to the new King. This must be done urgently before he leaves town."

In another letter handed to the bishop to be delivered to the King, Adalberto described in great sorrow the passing of the Archbishop. As the last preparations for the return voyage were made, a letter from the King arrived thanking Cisneros for his services. This letter was intended to reach Cisneros before leaving for his trip.

A small group of mourners from the cathedral joined the Cardinal's carriage on its way back to Alcalá. After taking care of Cisneros's burial arrangements and delegating Alcalá officials to erect a monument inside the local cathedral, he excused himself from the city. But before he left that Sunday, he did two more things: He furnished himself with Cisneros's money and jewelry, and he stopped at Alfonso's home. Alfonso was surprised to see this mourning Deacon at his front door.

"Please, come in, my friend. What can I do for you?"

"Sorry, but I cannot stay. I am on my way to see my family," said Adalberto. "Do you remember our conversation in the library? I kept my promise. Before I leave, I would like to give you something for safekeeping. You will understand this, my friend, for our people suffered from the same enemy." He took out the document of his life story, the poisoning of the highest cleric in the land, his devious plans, Cisneros's vicious acts and their carnal intimacy, and handed it to Alfonso who was still looking at him puzzled. "I trust your discretion," Adalberto said.

"But ..."

Adalberto did not give him a chance to ask the next question. "I know you have questions, but I have no time to explain. I must leave."

He held Alfonso's hand warmly. As he was leaving, he called out: "Make sure it is published." And with this he turned around and walked briskly to his new and splendid carriage. Automatically, Alfonso shoved the rolled-up paper in his pocket. 'Was this prince urging him to leave Spain?'

Alfonso closed the door but remained motionless. What happened just now? He was still standing there when Izolda appeared to ask who was at the door.

"Adalberto Muntaquez," he said slowly as though he saw a ghost.

"Why?" She was curious but not too overtly, as befitting a lady. "To say goodbye. He is leaving Alcalá." He was asked to be discrete which meant that the document contained an important secret. He was trusted with it because Adalberto felt a common bond with him which he must respect. 'But why couldn't he take it with him to wherever he was going?' Late at night, in the basement, Alfonso unrolled the paper and began to read. He was stunned. The detailed descriptions of the most admired Cisneros's blatant sexual encounters would be damning to the Church and its authority. He understood he possessed a bombshell of a document. He had to hide this inculpatory confession lest his own life be in danger. He might be accused by the Inquisition for colluding with the Morisco. He placed it in a leather pouch and hid it among his most precious things.

'Why did he leave his diary with me?' Alfonso kept wondering. 'Could it be that he wanted me to share in his personal vendetta? Did he insinuate that he acted on our behalf? Or did he suggest that we, who shared history, had no courage to fight back? Under what circumstances could he imagine this sensation to be published? Definitely not now and not in Spain!'

After a while his thoughts shifted direction: 'What a great man! How courageous and brilliant! We surely lack such temerity. May God watch over him until he reaches his destination safely.' He could not go back to his study for that mysterious man had left him with mixed feelings of admiration and worry. He should watch his steps with extra care and trepidation. At the same time, he felt guilty for not divulging the secret to his beloved wife. It would be safer if she did not know.

Adalberto headed south. His forged letter of recommendation by Cisneros opened all doors on his way. Every cathedral welcomed him with great fanfare. In Málaga, his birthplace, he drove to the old, abandoned house where he and his parents hid for a while. There, near the southern wall, he dug a hole until he found the bag he and his father had buried. He opened the precious box and found his parents' royal clothes and their heirlooms intact. He hired a boat and crossed the sea to Fes where the last king of Granada had found refuge. Outside the city, in the dunes, he burned his rich garments of the Deacon and wore his father's royal apparel of the nobility.

As Adalberto crossed the Mediterranean Sea, the physician who examined Cisneros's body raised doubts as to the cause of death. He had seen many corpses of people who died of the plague, but the body of the Cardinal lacked any of the disease's manifestations. He reported his suspicions to the Alcalá Inquisitor General. Rumors of the poisoning began to circulate.

CHAPTER 10

Disappointed

Enjoy happiness with a woman you love all the fleeting days of life that have been granted to you under the sun. Qoheleth 9:9

In the two years prior to 1517, Cisneros barely visited his Alcalá palace. Considering his ill health, Baracaldo held the reins as fiercely as he could. Alfonso kept a low profile, doing his work to everyone's satisfaction.

At one of these rare occasions, when Cisneros resided in Alcalá, and a few months into the school year of 1515, he called upon Alfonso with new instructions:

"There are not enough Hebrew grammar books for the library. My secretary Baracaldo has recently collected several such books. You will copy them and prepare notes for your students on how to be a skilled scribe. Another order is that when you copy the Holy Scriptures, you will note all the foreshadowing references to Jesus as the Messiah. You will pass these citations to your students diligently. As you well know, Jews have been hiding these truths from us, and you will reveal them for all to see. And not only in the Hebrew text are they hidden but within the Aramaic translations as well. To achieve this, you will copy all the Aramaic translations for the 24 books of the Bible. Moreover, whenever you date a book, you must note it by the days and years since our Lord Jesus was so brutally murdered." He looked at Alfonso as if to suggest he had something to do with the matter.

"And finally, you will translate all the books from Aramaic into Latin. Yes, it is a heavy load, but you will get an assistant upon request." He pointed to the four books on his desk for Alfonso to pick up. Alfonso did so, stepped backward, then remained standing.

"What is it that you want?" Cisneros asked.

"May His Holiness allow me to copy these books into one manuscript and keep it in my possession so that I could teach from that text?" These books were precious and rare in Spain. He wanted a copy for himself.

"I grant you the permission on the condition that you make such copies for the library." Baracaldo, who stood behind the Archbishop, motioned to Alfonso that the meeting was over.

By January Alfonso completed the copying of the four books which he named *Kiryat Arba'*, 'The City of Four', alluding to Hebron, the city where the Forefathers and Mothers were buried and where David was anointed King. He further added a long list of instructions for scribes on how to retain an accurate copy of the Holy Scriptures. His examples, some humorous, were drawn from his *Yeshivah* days. Since he would keep the book, he added numerous sheets to express his deep personal emotions and assessments of the politics of the day. The memories from his childhood schooling were strong and haunting. His work allowed him to relive those days with pride and longing.

A poem he composed reflected a person physically and emotionally sick and overwhelmed with work: "Do not be surprised if my script is uneven because I am distressed. I wrote this book at night being exhausted from my regular work. Do not reproach me for my strength has weakened and my eyes have become dim to see, for I am closer to old-age than to childhood, as I am 42 years old."

In his first attempts he was not able to find convincing evidence for Jesus in the Hebrew Scriptures, even by using *gematria*. However, for Christians, manipulating Hebrew words looked smart, and even sophisticated. He saw no other way but to manufacture evidence and based his "findings" on two elements: the number three, which he attributed to rationalize the Trinity, and the word 'messiah,' which he attributed to Jesus. The latter was mostly found in the Aramaic translation and thus began a series of claims for years to come that kept his employers satisfied. If Jews read them, they would be amused by such a superficial premise.

Alfonso further reported the story of the 72 elders of Israel in Alexandria who translated the Hebrew Bible into Greek, and the conscientious changes they made for religious and political reasons. In this way, he wished to create a clear separation between the Septuagint's Jewish concerns and the many deliberate changes

Christians made in the Septuagint. He would teach both redactions to his students and plant the seeds of doubt in the Septuagint's holiness vis-à-vis the original Hebrew Bible. This was also a statement of pride that 72 elders, put in individual rooms, came up with the same translation! The power of the true Scriptures! In quiet defiance, he transmitted information directly from the Talmud despite the strict royal order to burn and discredit it.

In this manuscript Alfonso also introduced his own original and sapiential observations on the biblical text which he called "new insights". He used the methodological tools of the Talmudic sages such as *notarikon, gezerah shavah* (syllogism) and *midrash* showing knowledge and pride in his Jewish tradition. He summarized his belief by the statement that God created the world for three things: the Torah, circumcision, and the Sabbath, and that man should "fear God and observe His commandments, for the whole world cannot match to that." Indeed, he stated, he followed his own conclusion. This codex would not fall into unwanted hands, at least not during his lifetime.

Alfonso also accumulated teaching material in this manuscript. As he translated the Hebrew Bible into Latin, he marked the changes in Jerome's Vulgate translation. These changes troubled him for a long time, and he made a point to draw his students' attention to them. In his private annotations and in poems, he noted that Jerome's version could not be reliable any longer, and that his own careful marginal and interlinear translation was superior to Jerome's and should serve the scholars exclusively. As Jerome himself did in his introduction to the Vulgate and as Alfonso argued time and time again: Readers should turn to the original Hebrew for clarifications of difficult passages.

This firm stand came as the University of Salamanca was competing with the University of Alcalá for prestige, students, and donors. The department of Oriental Languages in Salamanca lacked a Chair for years even though there were many suitable luminaries among the Conversos. But the Inquisition would not allow such an appointment. As he said to Pablo Coronel on several occasions: "The inferiority of the University of Salamanca vis-à- vis Alcalá is demonstrated by its emphasis on the sciences and the neglect of the spiritual learning of the Hebrew Bible and the classical languages. Salamanca focuses on the material, the business studies, and the corporeal while abandoning the soul and the theology."

"I agree with you," responded Pablo on one occasion, "there is nothing we can do, unless we jeopardize our livelihood. We have no power against the voices which argue against the need to study the Scriptures in their original language."

Alfonso responded passionately: "It is imperative to retort to those who speak ill of the Hebrew language, claiming that the Latin translation of Scriptures renders Hebrew obsolete. You know as I do that without understanding the Hebrew verbs and adjectives, person and number of masculine and feminine cases, one is incapable of perceiving the text! Latin could not possibly convey the various nuances of the Hebrew!"

"As long as they consider us outsiders and untrustworthy, our influence to change policies is nil."

He was right, for the long-awaited building for the Department was at last erected in 1561. However, it took more than two hundred years later, in 1753, for the position of Chair to be filled, this time by the Converso "Rabbi" Joseph of Cartagena, a descendant of the Zamoran Jews who were forced to baptism and remained there.

Before reporting on the historical events in *Kiryat Arba'*, Alfonso wrote an essay on the two major *differences between the fat Gentiles and the wise Jews*: righteousness and gratefulness. "The Spanish masses live for the present," he wrote, "to satisfy their carnal desires. They have no soul or spiritual existence." Here he noted a mistress for the first time. Without mentioning a name, he complained of the ungrateful mistresses. In another lengthy essay under the motto of *Money answers every need* (quoting Eccl 10:19), Alfonso wrote without fear: "Because of our sins we have the physical and the spiritual weakness, for this is an enormous curse for the entire human race. Come and learn this from the Holy Father who looks forward to silver, and all the more so—to gold; and the King and the officers, and all the more so—the masses; and the wife with her husband; and the son with his father; and the brother with his brother; and the uncle and the kinsman; and the neighbor and the friend; and the slave and the bondmaid, and all the more so—the mistress; and the merchant and the salesman; and the people and the priest; and the slave and his master; and the bondmaid and the lady; and the lender and the borrower; and the creditor and the debtor; and the scholars and the students and the teachers; and up to the infants who, if they cry and are given a silver or a gold coin, they soon shut up and soon laugh. And no one cares."

Such was the society, plagued with greed and unethical conduct, and no one spoke against it. Alfonso held his grim and helpless view of the Spanish society in the late 1510s which did not spare the Pope, the "Holy Father."

When in 1517–1519 widespread uprisings by the farmers in response to heavy taxation imposed by King Carlos, Alfonso sided with the oppressed, the *Communeros* movement. He titled his documentation *The Story of How Spain Was Lost*. He recorded those historical years, emphasizing the foreign origin of the tax-collector; his indulgences in food and wine (he especially expressed disgust of the stuffed pork) while the farmers were starving; his viciousness and apathy toward the peasantry. He described the rise of the young King upon the sudden death of his father, and the escape in shame of both the tax-collector and the King. Even though he resented the way the King mistreated the Spanish poor, he was more disappointed by the nobles for their collusion with the King and abandoning their responsibility for their farmers.

By the time this manuscript was completed, Alfonso fell sick. He remained in bed for a week, cared for by his loving wife. It was not clear whether his sickness was due to the plague, which visited upon Spain throughout the 16th century, or the result of exhaustion or depression.

Upon the completion of his part in the Complutensis, Alfonso's name gained popularity and high officials in the Church sought his employment, but he turned them down because of his excessive work assignments. However, as Alfonso accomplished that large manuscript, Cisneros ordered him to do the same for Diego López de Suñega, the original Director of the Complutensis project, himself a scholar of Hebrew, Greek and Latin. Again, Alfonso was immersed in copying for over a year. He of course welcomed the extra income, but his spirits sunk deeper.

Now with five mouths to feed and his workload growing more burdensome with each year, he began experiencing sporadic periods of melancholy. With aching body and soul, his attention to his family weakened. In his self-absorption, he did not feel appreciated and respected by his wife. Izolda was frustrated by the amount of work she had. Taking care of three small children despite the help of the two maids, took a toll on her time and energy. Her writing suffered as she no longer found time to compose poems and essays. Since the birth of the twins, her health slowly declined.

In this time, Alfonso heard of a beautiful young madam in the *Juderia* whose husband had lost his life in the epidemic and contemplated as to whether to engage her services. He decided to seek her company when Izolda was menstruating early in July of 1519. Refraining from intimacy during menstruation was a Jewish custom that he and Izolda strictly observed. The mere fact that the front entrance of the madam's house was sheltered from the main street bolstered his desire. A maid let him into the inner chamber which smelled pleasantly of incense. The madam sat on a plush sofa dressed in a red flowing gown, her brown hair coiffed above her head with ribbons and golden pins. She was indeed beautiful. His shyness amused her as she reckoned, she was probably half his age.

"Come closer. Don't be afraid." He moved a few steps forward. "Here, sit by me." He sat down keeping a distance. He was not sure he was doing the right thing. He was 45 and needed the touch of a woman without restrictions.

"What is your name, sir? You seem to be an intelligent man."

"Alfonso," he replied meekly.

"Come on, Alfonso, you are safe here. No complaints by the wife, no noise by the children. Just peace and relaxation. I can see this is your first time to visit a lady like me."

He mumbled in agreement.

"Lie down on your back, Alfonso, and I shall massage your neck and shoulders. Come," she coaxed, "You will feel relaxed and serene."

He turned and lay on his back with his head touching her thigh. "Good. Now close your eyes and imagine floating in a boat down the Duero River. The water is clear and cool. Flowers and vegetation on the banks sparkle in dancing colors. You are free of all obligations and demands. You float in the air, happy and at ease."

Alfonso closed his eyes and began to relax. The smooth touch of the madam's hands was magic. Her soothing voice was hypnotic. He fell asleep.

He woke up to see the madam standing over him, smiling. He sat up and smiled. "That was so enjoyable. Forgive me for falling asleep." He stood up embarrassed. He kept quiet for a minute or two, then said: "I did not ask for your name."

"You may call me Madam Aurora," she replied holding her head up. "This will be our first meeting, a kind of an introduction."

"Oh." Alfonso was disappointed. "May I see you tomorrow?"

"Contrary to my name, I sleep late. Come at 8 tomorrow night."

Alfonso's face lit up. "What is your fee, Madam Aurora?" he asked. Would he be able to support a mistress, too? She set a price and he agreed. He paid her for the visit, and she showed him out.

He walked home in high spirits. He made the first step for clandestine happiness. He had never done something like this before. He felt odd. He got home to sleeping children. Izolda was waiting. She noticed the change in his face but said nothing. When he came closer, she smelled a suggestive scent and recoiled. The maid brought his dinner and left. Izolda excused herself and went to bed. They did not share a bed as long as she was not purified.

The next day he looked forward to his nocturnal visit with beautiful Aurora. Entering her familiar salon, he lost his shyness and insecurity. She began with a short session of a therapeutic massage and then invited him to her bedroom. She took off his clothes one piece at a time, slowly and seductively. He stood still, eyes closed, to savor the experience. "Now take off my clothes, slowly, without touching my skin," she whispered. By the time she led him to her bed he was ready for her. But she took her time, prolonging his yearning for a more satisfying experience. As they at last lay coupling, she whispered: "Lie still. Let me guide you." But when she sensed he was going to climax, she allowed him to penetrate her body.

As he was lying exhausted and smiling, she got up and went to a side room to wash herself, dressed, and waited for him. He felt free, as though his soul reached uncharted heights. He wished he could stay there forever. Aurora touched his arm. "It is time to go."

He got up, taking his time, dressed and moved toward her for an embrace. But she stretched out her hand forward saying, "No, we are done. Please leave your payment on the table." He did so and asked: "May I come next week, same time?" He realized this business could bore a serious hole in his finances, but he was too excited to bother now. Yes, he could. He walked home on a cloud of joy.

He did not consider having a mistress an ethical infringement. Spanish Jews were permitted by Jewish law to have a second wife, but as Christians, bigamy was strictly forbidden by the Church and could incur death. A mistress became a safer arrangement.

As the months passed, Alfonso realized he could not afford Madam Aurora any longer. She demanded precious gifts and soon enough changed her attitude toward him. His visits grew infrequent until they ceased altogether. He wrote in his diary: "Woe to mistresses who are ungrateful and require silver and gold." He explained his sexual need in simple terms: "The urge haunts me."

CHAPTER 11

Fulfilled

He clothed himself with garments of retribution; wrapped himself in zeal as in a robe. Isaiah 59:17

The two brothers, impatient in Zamora, looked for the best time to escape from Spain and live freely as Jews. They were taught Judaism by both their paternal grandfather Juan and their mother Guiomar. In the cellar they had many books of Scriptures, prayers, Rabbinic literature, liturgical poetry, and Sefaradi customs. They collected information on survivors who made it to safety in the Mediterranean basin.

The time was ripe in 1517 when the country was in a social and political turmoil with rebellions, suppressions of uprisings, the Cortes embattling the young King for power, and the Inquisition busy with heaps of cases of heresies.

Europe was alien to Jews or Conversos, for it was mostly controlled by King Carlos or the Pope. The Ottoman Empire was encouraging Jews to reach their shores, and North Africa was relatively tolerant. The New World was enticing but unknown and therefore precarious and threatening. "New Christians" were forbidden to reach these shores, so they had heard. Rabbi Sabba, they knew, found a haven in Fes. Others reached Tunis or Egypt safely like Rabbi Moshe Alashkar and Rabbi David ben Zimra. North Africa lay the closest to the Spanish territory. Logically this would be their first destination. They sent a letter to their father in Alcalá to inform him of their decision. "Bless us, *padre*, and do not worry about us. We have planned our escape well." In his response Alfonso blessed his sons and wished them success. "I should have done so years ago," he wrote back, "Be strong and resolute as

God blessed Joshua bin Noon upon leaving exile and entering the Promised Land." The messenger carried money in a pouch.

But Guiomar was worried: "You are too young to travel by yourselves. The dangers are many, especially for people like us."

"Do not worry, dear *madre*. We have planned well. We shall take the highway that leads directly to Seville and from there to Málaga. We heard it is safe to cross to Morocco from there. We shall be dressed as monks."

"As what! Who would sell you monks' habits?"

"You remember Antonio Herrera and Luis Gonzalo from the local monastery, admirers of our father. They sold us two of their robes and large crosses the type they wear over their coats. They also gave us identification papers as Gabriel Herrera and Diego Gonzalo, and a letter suggesting a secret mission on behalf of the Zamora Bishop."

"Why do you reckon the Málaga port is safe for crossing?"

"The Moriscos, who still control the city and the port, ensure the crossing of Jewish Conversos and of any dissident of the Inquisition. They can be trusted for we share a vicious and hated enemy."

"Have you prepared enough food and water?" Guiomar insisted. "Not yet, *madre*. Would you please prepare some food for us? We shall travel light. We'll take a few clothes, two pocket-size Hebrew Bibles and a family *Mahazor*."

Guiomar worried for her teenage sons' venturesome undertaking. But at the same time, she hid her pride in their courageous resolution.

In a week they were ready. Only after Guiomar secured her sons' luggage did she let them go in peace. The sons parted from their families and hugged their mother long and tight. Early morning one day in March of 1517, they began their voyage upon a one-horse coach. Gabriel was barely 18 and Diego 17.

The two brothers did not encounter any difficulties on their way. They stopped for the night in monasteries and filled up their water supply, fruits and vegetables. When they reached Málaga they could not but admire the thousands of Moriscos who in such a short time took back their city. They controlled the economy and kept their city clean and green and attractive for all visitors. No ghettos were to be found. The streets were wide and lined with rows of tall trees and shrubs to the delight of the population. The brothers walked about mesmerized by the contrast to Zamora, its narrow and dirty alleys, where churches dotted every corner and plaza. Here, there was a sense of retained freedom and pride in the history of the population.

Walking among the Moriscos felt uneasy as they were still dressed in their monk's garb. People were staring at them with a subtle contempt. "I think it is time to get rid of our habit and put on the local clothes," suggested Diego.

"That's exactly my thought," agreed Gabriel.

This time they stayed at an inn. In the morning they bought local attire and put them on in their room. "Perfect!" Exclaimed Gabriel. "I already feel free," replied his brother. They threw their travel clothes in the first public garbage bonfire they saw at the port. The brothers befriended an old sailor who was willing to take them and the carriage on his boat across the Mediterranean to Tetouan. When they landed, they wrote a letter to their mother of their safe voyage. The old sailor promised to pass it on for two *reales*. As his boat disappeared over the horizon, they turned to the east and prayed: "Thank you, *HaShem*, for protecting us and bringing us to this land. You are our Shield and Rock, and in You we trust."

In order to travel to Fes on the unsafe roads, they joined a caravan one early dawn. To secure their passage from hostile travelers, they presented themselves as escaping Moriscos. Their lack of knowledge in Islam was understood and forgiven as all Muslim literature, including the Quran, were strictly banned. During the evening rest the brothers were surrounded by admiring Muslims who took it upon themselves to teach them some prayers and statements of faith.

In Fes they headed for the *mellah*, the Jewish quarter, situated close to the governor's palace. They inquired about Rabbi Sabba, but to their disappointment they were told that he had left to Tlemcen eleven years earlier. They decided to continue on to Tlemcen where a larger Jewish community resided. They were invited to stay with the family of Aharon Melamed until after the Sabbath. Gabriel approached Aharon sheepishly when he admitted never to have attended services in a synagogue.

"It was always done secretly, hurriedly and with fear," he explained. "Now we would like to experience real services, unafraid and proud."

119

"You are welcome to join us. You are not the first Conversos who landed in our home from oppressed Spain. We heard the same stories time and again. My community has been helping people like you for the past 25 years."

For the first time in their short lives, Gabriel and Diego entered a synagogue above ground where they could loudly read from their *Siddur* and not feel oppressed by fear. People surrounded them with loving smiles and hugs. They wanted Shabbat to last longer. At the Melamed home lunch became a communal event. People wanted to hear the story of these teenage heroes and they stayed until the evening prayers. The boys were so astounded by the sight of free Jews a few days journey away from the Spanish border.

As they walked to their room, Aharon said: "A caravan of coaches is leaving tomorrow to Tlemcen, among them a respectable number of Jewish merchants. It will be safe to travel with them."

Before leaving, Aaron filled their bags with food and water and said: "May *HaShem* watch over you wherever you go. May you find your destiny of peace."

The caravan drove slowly. Armed guards against robbers secured the merchants. Daily prayers were conducted in concert with the prayers by Muslims. The brothers watched in disbelief this peaceful and tolerant scene that could not ever occur in their place of birth. The Jewish group cast their protection over the two brothers. As they entered the metropolis of Tlemcen, the boys were overwhelmed by the magnitude of the city, its buildings and squares, gardens and diverse population. The architecture was stunning in its beauty and grace. No one appeared to be abused because of his skin color or faith.

The Jewish merchants drove to the Jewish quarter and introduced the brothers to the head of the community, Menahem Abulafia. Gabriel and Diego were invited to the house. They settled down, washed, prayed, and sat down with the family for dinner.

Mira Abulafia's family, descended from a noble family from Cordoba, escaped from the massacres of 1348 and settled in Fes together with the families of Abulafia and Maimon. Scholarship and trade defined their families' greatness. As they were dining, the family inquired about the brothers' escape. The family admired the courage and conviction of such young boys.

After dinner the men moved to the living room and sat on plush pillows. Abulafia said: "Now that you told us your story, what are you planning to do? The Jewish community will do its best to help."

"Our plan is to exact vengeance on the Spanish for what they did and are still doing to our people. We are young and skilled in medicine and leather goods. Can you suggest a way where we can be useful?"

Abulafia sank deep in thought when his son Meshulam, in his early 20s, said: "There is a group of Jewish pirates whose base is here in Tlemcen. They have ships that attack Spanish and Papal vessels to disrupt their trade routes in the Mediterranean Sea. They are fierce and this desire is burning deep in their veins. If only my father gave me the permission, I would join them."

Menahem Abulafia retorted: "This occupation is not for you, my son. You are our only son with obligations to our family. It is time for you to wed your fiancée and start a family. Gabriel and Diego have suffered under the Spanish, and they have a mission to carry on with the permission of their parents."

Gabriel and Diego looked at each other. "We like the idea." Gabriel said. "Where can we find the pirates?"

Menahem told them to be ready the next day for a meeting. The brothers went to bed excited in anticipation. God has led them to the right family.

The office of the Bnai Sefarad was near the docks. When Menahem came in, the occupants rose in reverence. "What an honor, Hakham Abulafia," one said, "please have a seat and we shall bring tea." He rushed to an inner room while Menahem introduced the brothers:

"These are Gabriel and Diego of Zamora who have just escaped from Spain in order to strike at their enemy, the execrable Spaniards, who have murdered and tortured our people. They have prepared themselves to be skilled in medicine and leather production. They are here to help you destroy your common enemy."

"You have come to the right place. We need people like you. Right now, our leader, Sinan Reis, is at sea and we expect him back within the next ten days. In the meantime, we can train you for life aboard ship. Everyone must be trained in all aspects of sailing."

As dessert was served, Gabriel and Diego savored every sip of tea and bite of pastry. So delicious were these treats, they knew their guardian angel was smiling upon them.

"When can we start?" asked Diego, the younger brother.

David, the pirate officer, was pleased with their enthusiasm. "Come back tomorrow. In the meantime, where will you stay?" He looked at Abulafia.

"When they join your organization, they will not be able to live with us. You understand this, of course."

"Of course," answered the brothers. It was time to leave.

The next morning, Gabriel and Diego packed up their belongings and drove their coach to the pirates' office. "We live humbly, and our personal property is minimal," said David. "We share the booty and pay a percentage to the local ruler. Both sides profit from our mission." He led them to a house nearby where they unpacked. They drove their coach to the market where they sold it for cash. They had plenty of savings to see them through for many years to come.

A group of pirates were practicing their maritime skills with ropes, swords and daggers on the beach when David and the brothers approached. After a short welcome and an introduction, the pirates began teaching the new members about life at sea and their philosophy. The boys listened attentively and with excitement. And so, they spent the next ten days practicing and forging friendship with the group. "Trust in God and in each other is the basis of our mission. Each member is part of a family whose wellbeing is our utmost concern. Unity, dedication to the goal, loyalty to the group and leaders make us strong and unbeatable." David's words were inspirational.

It was mid-April when Sinan Reis and his men arrived at Tlemcen for Passover. They came in two ships, "The Sting" and "The Scorpion". These vessels were of a Fusta type with masts and oars. Long and fast, they were superior to the heavier and bigger Spanish ships. The waving pirate flag carried the Jewish symbol *Shield of David* which in Islam was called *Shield of Solomon*. The booty was divided among the pirates, and the ruler got his cut. Captured Christian boys, men, and young women were sold as slaves in the city's market.

David introduced the Zamora brothers to Sinan who welcomed them warmly. After hearing their story, he said: "Many of us have similar stories. We have a mission to damage the Spanish and Catholic economy as devastatingly as possible. With God's help, together with our ships and our men, we shall succeed."

Local Jewish families invited the pirates for Passover, among them the Abulafias who opened their home to the Zamorans.

The fervent two weeks leading to the Festival were busy with cleaning and cooking special meals. When the brothers entered the house, they were enveloped with intoxicating smells of faraway memories. The long table, covered with white cloth laden with vegetables in beautiful dishes, reminded them of a humbler celebration at home. Bottles of wine were placed along the table. On the center plate there were the seven food items that symbolized Passover. The baked *matzot* were stacked before the head of the family. Each person received a copy of the *Haggadah*.

Mira Abulafia assigned seats for the family members and guests. Slowly, the sound of the people abated as they took their seats. A cup filled with wine stood before each attendant, and grape juice for the children. Abulafia began the ceremony with the blessing over the first cup of wine. The reading of the story of the deliverance from Egypt almost twenty-seven hundred years earlier began as each participant read a portion. Abulafia would pause from time to time to explain and discuss the text. Songs were sung and prayers chanted or read. Gabriel and Diego sensed the extraordinary event they were experiencing among these co-religionists.

After telling the story of Exodus and the divine miracles, it was time for the feast. The atmosphere relaxed. Words of praise to the hostess for such a delectable meal were heard from all sides.

Gabriel asked permission from Menahem Abulafia to speak. "Dear hosts, we are deeply moved by your invitation, for this is the first time we celebrate Passover as God commanded, not in hiding and not in fear. Its significance for us is unfathomable. We truly feel the actual sense of liberation from slavery, here, among our Sefaradi brethren, to observe our traditions unmolested. If only our family could dare leave their land of slavery."

Mira Abulafia got up and hugged the two brothers. "You must be missing them very much."

Gabriel's countenance became serene. He continued: "As our body and soul are liberated, this is a good time to liberate our Spanish names and choose Hebrew ones."

Mira Abulafia was the first to react with a smile: "Gabriel, your name need not change for it is Hebrew. It means "God is my strength', but your brother needs a change. Diego, do you have an idea for a name?"

Diego thought but could not come up with a name. Abulafia suggested: "What about Pessah? It means 'Passover'."

"I like the idea," responded Diego, "it is appropriate and well expresses the Exodus from slavery. No more Diego! I have been reborn as a Jew!" The attendees clapped their hands and uttered words of agreement and encouragement. The comradery and joyous occasion were palpable and exhilarating.

"In this happy occasion," Gabriel got up and announced, "We would like to revert to our original family name, Gabbai, and thus severe ourselves completely from cursed Spain."

"I agree wholeheartedly," responded Pessah with great emotion.

A letter was sent to Alfonso to inform him of their change of names.

Passover gone, the pirates prepared their ships for the next mission. Gabriel and Pessah joined in every aspect of the repairs as every other member did. The pirates worked fast and skillfully, motivated by their zeal to make the Spanish suffer. Everyone had a story to tell about the torture and death of their families, their impoverishment and public contempt by the Inquisitors and the Spanish mobs. Emotions ran high by all.

Sinan convened the last gathering before the new mission: "New and refilled supplies, such as food, water, wine, ropes and weapons, have been brought aboard and stored safely. Cooking, serving, and cleaning duties would be shared in shifts. Basic medical care was extended to everyone thanks to the Zamora brothers' skill as medical practitioners. We are blessed to have them join us." He looked at the two young men, beaming with pride. "We greatly appreciate your contribution to our family of avengers. We are looking forward to our new success with God's blessing. Let us all pray for His blessings as we smash the Catholic Satan." Sinan led the prayers. The shared enthusiasm was intense.

Gabriel and Pessah were swept by the religious fervor of trust in God's protection. They were moved by Sinan's words of encouragement and faith, his youth and charisma. He seemed to be a born leader. Only a few raids at sea, and Sinan was attracting men willing to give their lives for the cause.

The ships set sail toward the island of Malta. "Certain Spanish merchant ships would stop there," explained Micah, one of the sailors, to Gabriel, "then continue to Corfu bearing such items as yarn and textile, domestic vessels, cocoa and fancy items for the ladies. Such ships are our best targets."

"Can two of our ships pose a threat to these large vessels?" Pessah asked.

"We are usually fortified by Arab ships joining us in Tunis. The latter would wait in the tiny island of Zembra to force the Spanish toward the island of Pantelleria, between Sicily and Tunis. Here we and the Arabs would engage in artillery battle until the enemy surrendered."

"Very clever," responded the brothers.

The successes were complete, and four ships were pillaged, some people taken captives, and the rest, together with the ships, were sunk. The coordinated attacks and the ensued successes assured a symbiotic relationship of trust and dependency between the Jews and the Muslim crews. They celebrated their victories and friendship in Pantelleria. And so, they would wait for the next Spanish or Papal ships coming from either Rome or Venice. They avoided areas where battles were being engaged often between the Pope's army and the Italian principalities.

The Zamoran brothers made a name for their bravery and loyalty. Their Jewish faith deepened, and their knowledge expanded beyond their early horizons. On Sinan's ships Kosher meals were strictly observed and communal prayers were conducted when possible. However, on major Holy Days the pirates would return to their home bases in Tlemcen or Santorini. In the 1520s, Sinan's name became synonymous with terror on the high seas. The British and the Holy Roman Empire fleets watched out for Sinan's ships and reported on their movements. They accordingly kept their fleets away from battle. Several times Sinan sailed to Egypt to acquire additional ships as more Sefaradi fugitives joined the cause, and the desire to smite the enemy remained a high priority.

Their adventures drew the attention of another buccaneer who worked in the service of the Ottoman Sultan Suleiman the Magnificent. Hayreddin Barbarossa, the admiral of the Ottoman fleet, had been attacking Spanish, Portuguese and Papal ships to undermine their maritime powers in the Mediterranean Sea. The two great corsairs agreed to meet in Tlemcen to combine forces.

It was soon after *Shavuot* when Barbarossa visited Sinan's men for the first time with a large contingent of sailors. He was an imposing figure exuding strength and leadership. Sinan detailed to his men the purpose of the Ottoman's visit: "We have all heard of the great buccaneer Commander Hayreddin Barbarossa. He has proven himself as a bold and brave man. His political goals meet our religious goals and therefore our combined fleets would serve both of us well. Welcome his men as brothers. We shall plan our raids and execute them with honor and fortitude."

Sounds of agreement filled the air as the two groups of men cheered with promises to put the fear of God or Allah in the hearts of the Infidels. With food and drinks, they consecrated their brotherhood.

From that time on, Sinan sailed officially under the Ottoman flag, still retaining the *Shield of David* symbol and keeping kosher foods. Their legendary exploits expanded to the entire coast of North Africa and even to Britain and the Netherlands.

Time passed when in 1538, Barbarossa and his men visited their counterparts in Tlemcen again. They were seated on the lawn in one of the town's gardens. Barbarossa opened the convention. His voice resonated like thunder:

"As you recall, our combined glorious successes aroused the belligerence of the Infidels three years ago when they tried to capture Tlemcen. They suffered inglorious defeat which left them vulnerable and irrelevant. However, our intelligence has reported that a new coalition is being formed among the Spanish, the Pope, and the Holy Roman Empire together with the principality of Venice and the Maltese Knights. They have nominated Andrea Doria, the admiral of the Republic of Genoa, as their commander. Their goal is to redeem their shame for obstructing their secure access to the Mediterranean Sea."

Sinan got up and spoke: "We are planning a daring and a complicated mission to decidedly smash the coalition once and for all. It will demand perseverance and devoutness of objective. Our faith will keep us strong and ensure our complete success." The sounds of cheering men and the clapping of hands were deafening.

And indeed, the Battle of Preveza became a turning point in maritime history when the European Catholics were put to shame and derision by the Ottoman nations. Under the command of Sinan and Barbarossa, the two fleets devastated the coalition and secured the Mediterranean Sea to the Ottomans for many years to come. From now on Catholic ships avoided the Mediterranean Sea altogether and reached India and the Far East by circling the coast of west Africa and the Cape of Good Hope.

During these years of maritime activities, Gabriel and Pessah planted roots in Tlemcen when Gabriel married local Tita (endearing name for Esther), Menahem Abulafia's youngest daughter, and a few years later Pessah married Haniya (endearing name for Hannah), the daughter of Rabbi Daniel Almosnino, a descendant from a distinguished family of scholars from Seville. Their marriages were duly reported to their families in Zamora with whom they occasionally continued to communicate.

In 1544, after 26 years as pirates, the Gabbai brothers decided to retire and focus on their growing families. They exacted their share of revenge. It was time to enjoy a quiet life.

Their children studied at Rabbi Almosnino's school and thrived as scholars, scientists, and traders. Hayim, one of Pessah's children, named after his paternal grandfather, was a prodigy of the Kabbalah. Kabbalah was gaining an honorable place in Jewish studies throughout the Mediterranean and the Middle East thanks mainly to the Kabbalists of Safed in the Galilee and of Egypt. With the blessing of his parents, Hayim traveled to Cairo to study under the Kabbalist Rabbi David ben Solomon Ibn Zimra (the RaDBaZ), a native of Zamora. He later joined the mystics in Isaac Luria's Center in Safed.

CHAPTER 12

Challenged

Examine me, O God, and know my mind; probe me and know my thoughts. See if I have vexatious ways; and guide me in everlasting ways. Psalms 139:23-24

When his mother died in 1521, Alfonso's depression escalated, and he fell sick with abdominal pains and high fever. The doctor was called in and left with some potions he mixed in a jar. The children were kept away and Izolda and the maids took turns to care for him. The maids knew unorthodox remedies which appeared to be helpful more than the doctor's recipes. These Alfonso recorded in a notebook to be published later. However, his obligations to the students and the library forced him to resume his work before he recuperated fully.

What exacerbated his psychological and physical health was the passing of his father in the winter of 1523. This sent him back to bed with a severe case of colitis and heart palpitations that kept him incapacitated for a longer period. The maids fed him a variety of concoctions, vinegar, garlic and olives, chicken broth with saffron, cow fat, egg yolks and milk. He smelled rose water and perfume, and when he developed fever, they fed him pink sugar. He was certain, as the doctor suggested, that he had contracted the plague.

A Converso friend, Fabricio Álvarez, had recently come back from a trip to Rome. As a Crypto-Jew and a teacher, he stayed in the ghetto of Rome searching for new literary material. When he visited the ailing Alfonso, he brought with him a rhymed poem made up of a series of philosophical questions, based mostly on biblical events, that delighted Alfonso: "How did you come to own it?"

"I purchased it from the most popular Hebrew poet Joseph Tzarfati himself. As you can tell by his name, he originally came from France. I met this Jew in Rome and was totally impressed by his Jewish sagacity and scientific mind. As the personal physician to Pope Clement VII, he is also the representative of the Jewish community. As such, his title is *hakham kolel*, "a master sage, a sage of eclectic subjects." The book has been a sensation among Jews and Christians alike, and it was printed by the most respected publisher Daniel Bomberg. I enjoyed reading them tremendously."

"You have chosen one poem to bring to my attention?"

"Yes, because of its amusing biblical content and poetical format. I know that as a Bible scholar you shall appreciate it. You yourself write poetry using biblical references and poetic elements, don't you?"

True to Fabricio's opinion, the poem delighted Alfonso who was so impacted by it that he composed his own questions, ten in number, adding them to Tzarfati's list. He needed the spiritual link to that Jewish genius, and through him, to the Roman Jewish community. Most of his questions centered on his criticism of the immorality of the Spanish society, a subject he repeatedly brought up in his writing. But his lines had no running motif or purpose and therefore they lacked cohesion. His ailment blocked his literary muse. He showed his latest poetic work to his wife who was a literary scholar in her own right. She did not want to address the lack of thematic focus in the poem, so she responded to the conclusion:

"Interesting. I agree with your doxology. You thought the words through with resolution and faith. This is the essence of life."

"Yes. I like the words: 'And it is better for man to always persevere in God's worship, for He is his soul's redeemer. And He shall redeem man from his misfortunes. And he will merit to see God in the pleasantness of His manifestations.'"

"Now, these statements of faith remind me of the proverbs you teach our children. You should put them on paper for all to learn." Izolda was looking for a literary occupation for Alfonso while he was sick.

"This is a great idea," he said enthusiastically. "In this way I shall perpetuate my mother's teaching and pass it on to my students." His spirits were raised, and he asked for writing materials.

It was a work of love in honor of his beloved late mother. He was still stricken in bed when he completed the book which he named *Loor de Virtudes*, "Praise of Virtues." Upon recuperation, he headed straight to the University printer, Miguel de Eguia, who published it in 1524. The book became so popular that it was published several times and sold around Castile.

In late Spring of 1523 Alfonso was asked by Pablo Coronel to meet him in Toledo "for an important event." Missing details meant a secret meeting. When they met at the inn, Coronel shut the door and whispered:

"A Jewish trader arrived in Salamanca and stayed at a local guest house. He knew exactly the name and address of a contact in the *Juderia*. Because of the danger in organizing a meeting there after the raid on Deacon Conejo's group, he sent a word to meet him in Toledo where a large group of Crypto-Jews can gather safely in a certain church. He mentioned you in particular. He also gave us a code word to identify us at the meeting. The meeting is tonight. Let us rest before we leave."

They ate their dinner in the room and rested until sunset. After dark few people challenged the streets. The church was situated in the old *Juderia* atop a dismantled synagogue. From the outside, the building looked unoccupied. Even before they knocked on the back door, someone whispered for the code. Hearing it, the door was opened to let the two slide in. They were guided to a side room lit by several oil lamps and candles. Shadows from the statues and crosses gave an eerie feeling of ghosts lurking from every corner. A few people were already seated around a long table speaking softly. Upon entering the room, the people stood up to welcome them. When they stated their names, the men in the room shook their hands with words of praise and pride, for the Complutensian Bible and its authors were well known among the Conversos.

More people sneaked in individually or in small groups. At last, one of the preeminent leaders of the Toledo Converso community, Doctor Manuel Toledano, entered with the secret guest. They all stood up in reverence. The majority did not know his identity or mission in order to secure the safety of the meeting. The guest wore foreign attire though he looked Sefaradi. Each attendant stood up and identified himself by name. Toledano introduced the man as Moise Abendano, a Jewish merchant from Tlemcen, Algeria. Seated at the head of the table, Abendano began to speak:

"My dear brothers. Thank you for coming to this meeting from all over Castile. I came as the messenger of the Jewish *qahal*, community, from Tlemcen to bid you peace. In order to convince you of my true mission, I have with me a letter from the Rabbi of Tlemcen, Daniel Almosnino. I will pass the letter around so that each and every one will read it. Our *qahal* has been growing in number and in import ever since we were expelled from this cursed land. Many settled first in Fes, but the favorable conditions did not last for long. Higher taxes were levied, and new restrictions were announced. Famine and pestilence did not discriminate between Jew and Muslim. Twenty thousand Jews perished in those years. Many of the Jews moved to Tlemcen where the ruler welcomed them and enabled them to worship in peace. They were allowed to practice any profession or skill which improved the economic and the social life of all residents. Tlemcen now is a prosperous haven for the Jewish pirates who prey on the Catholic ships, pillage and abduct males and females alike for slavery. These young and brave pirates are heroes to us all. Among them is Gabriel and Pessah Gabbai, the sons of the honorable Alfonso de Zamora, who is here with us." He turned his face to Alfonso, followed by the rest of the attendees.

Alfonso stirred in trepidation. 'Has this man brought bad news from my sons?' He thought. The guest continued:

"As you know, the Spanish Inquisition has no jurisdiction over Jews who come from other lands as traders. Even though I was born in Spain, I am free to travel everywhere. However, I am not permitted to speak to Conversos, for the Inquisition knows full well that most of the Conversos continue to live as Jews secretly.

I have come here today not to encourage you to stay faithful to our God and tradition (this goes without saying), but to encourage you to move to Tlemcen. There, you can live as Jews openly and without fear of persecutors. If you wish, from there you are permitted to settle anywhere in the Ottoman Empire, including the Land of Israel where a Jewish *qahal* is growing in large numbers. You have options. You can teach your children Judaism in safety or watch them get lost to us here. You practice Judaism secretly but without rabbis or qualified leaders. You live under the constant fear of the nefarious and the murderous Inquisition. Your children must attend Church schools and you must worship on Sundays and on their festivals. Your children may follow your teaching, but their children will not. Please save yourselves and the next generations. Crossing the sea is simple and short. Our *qahal* is ready to absorb you and support you when you come, as they did for the brothers Zamora."

He stopped and looked around. Many of them were nodding their heads. His words found a favorite ear around the table. A soft sound was heard in the room. One said:

"I agree with you. I have been planning to go north, to Amsterdam and from there to Germany and Italy. But I think your plan makes better sense. Europe is full of hostile Christians."

Another said: "I am glad you came. You give me the incentive to escape while my children are still young."

And so they spoke making decisions and commitments to heed to Abendano's plea. Alfonso and Coronel were emotional as they read Rabbi Almosnino's letter. The vow of each man excited them, but they remained quiet. After a while Pablo stood up and said:

"I am the grandson of the infamous Avraham Senior. My parents are still living in Segovia in our family estate. If I and my family leave, I will break their hearts and hasten their death. I cannot carry this on my conscience. I thought long and hard about fleeing this damn land, but not at this time. We will when my parents are gone." He sat down. It was his first time revealing publicly his secret commitment to Judaism.

Alfonso looked at him in surprise. He never suspected his close friend was plotting to leave Spain. He knew several of his relatives had left in 1492 and found their way to the Ottoman sphere and to the Land of Israel. Abendano looked at Alfonso who so far did not say a word. Alfonso took his time because he did not know how to verbalize his situation.

"My father has just died, two years after my mother," Alfonso began, somewhat embarrassed. "We all planned to leave when we reached Portugal, but conditions were against us, and we were baptized and returned to Zamora. We have been keeping our tradition in secret to this day. However, I came to realize that through my work as a scribe and a teacher I have been disseminating Judaism. This is my way to get back at the Catholic Church. No Gentile realizes this. No Gentile knows the secret I keep inside me. I am glad that two of my children left when they could and are exacting revenge upon the Catholic enemy in their own way. And all my children married Conversos like us." He stopped to contemplate.

"I know I am proposing an excuse, but I truly believe I am doing *HaShem*'s work. One day, I hope, my true identity will be known to our people, and to the Catholic world. This will be my dagger in the heart of the enemy." His eyes filled with tears as he looked at the people seated around the table and sat down.

Doctor Toledano stood up and said: "We have no right to criticize anyone. Each one has done his part to survive." He looked around and continued: "I see that most of us are going to answer our guest's call, and the sooner the better. I, too, will leave within the next year or two. Our children grow fast, and we tend to wallow in the routine and the familiar. I will close my clinic and find justification for moving away." He paused again and addressed the congregants: "If you have questions for our esteemed guest, please ask now. It is getting late."

Questions were asked about the opportunities in Tlemcen and in Thessaloniki and other safe shores. Abendano took his time to answer in detail. At the end, he said: "Please spread the word. Spain is not our land. Do not let the Catholic Church annihilate our faith. We have survived many despots who wished to eliminate us. This is the third attempt in our history to cleanse a land from Judaism, but as the Maccabees saved our people 1680 years ago, the Catholics will not defeat us. Be strong and strengthen each other. Trust in *HaShem*, our God the redeemer."

They answered "Amen" in unison. These were Alfonso's prayers at the end of his copied or restored manuscript. He closed his eyes and repeated them silently.

Abendano looked at Alfonso and said, this time in fluent Hebrew: "Let us talk in private." They moved to a corner. "I have a letter for you from your sons. They are doing well and are well-known among friend and foe. They are brave and committed to avenge our people. I know them well and am proud of them." He took out a sealed letter from his inner pocket and handed it to the very emotional father. Alfonso held the letter to his heart and tears welled up in his eyes. He would read the letter later when he returned to the inn. Alfonso had many questions about his sons which Abendano answered with alacrity.

The entire evening was invigorating and inspiring. Alfonso was so impressed and excited from that clandestine meeting, that he later recounted that "very good, indeed, excellent" meeting in his diary, adding: "The Messenger and I spoke in fluent and rapid Hebrew, both understanding each other." He mentioned that encounter three times in his diary, the last time in 1534 upon his return from Toledo on a failed mission.

Alfonso was surely making a name for himself as a Hebraist, and patrons were seeking his services. After Diego López de Suñega in 1518, it was Fray Juan de Azcona in 1523 following his return from Toledo. But a very dramatic event in late 1525 shook Alfonso to the core. He was called to appear before the new Archbishop of Toledo, the Grand Inquisitor, Alonso III de Fonseca. He had met him briefly before when the Archbishop took his place of residence in Cisneros's palace. Alfonso then was introduced to him together with the rest of the University staff.

Fonseca wore a heavy crimson robe with a hood and a very large ornate cross held by a golden chain. Except for his Cardinal ring, he wore no other jewelry. Alfonso knew this Cardinal descended from a highly noble and prestigious family. His kind and pensive face controverted his zealous nature against Conversos and Moriscos. He, nevertheless, respected Alfonso for his achievements and (albeit ostensible) dedication to the Church. Despite his noble upbringing and his high political and religious stature, Fonseca was known as a down-to-earth man who shunned pretence. He went straight to the point:

"I order you to put aside your current work in order to concentrate on one specific task, which is, to compose an epistle to the Jews of Rome. You shall write it in Hebrew with interlinear Latin. In it, you shall raise all the anti-Jewish polemics found in the Jews' Bible and what they call Rabbinic literature. You have produced before similar evidence for the Christian truth and the references to our Lord Jesus Christ in this sea of literature. You must convince them to abandon their illogical devotion to their faith and admit their errors. Break their stubbornness. Until now you wrote sporadically on this subject for the sake of our students. Now you shall gather all the evidence in one manuscript. This work is urgent so start at once. You are dismissed!"

Alfonso left walking backward, pondering the urgency of this task. He knew he would have to do this against his hidden religious loyalty which was clearly in support of the Jewish faithful. But he was not the master of his own life. Refusal or hesitation signaled heresy and death, not only for him but for his family. But why was he to address the Jews of Rome, of all exiles, so far and disconnected from the Conversos of Spain? And more so, the bidding did not involve the Inquisition! Why do they need a Latin translation? Or is it for the Christian editor to control and censor the content? He sensed that the real reason for this urgent task was a secret to which he was not privy. And indeed, it was a most wild and delusional event.

He had never heard of David HaReuveni. A year before, in 1524, this mysterious and charismatic adventurer arrived at the gates of Rome riding on a white horse. He was welcomed by a sympathetic Cardinal Egidio da Viterbo, a close friend of Pope Clement VII, and a Christian Kabbalist. The Cardinal's support of the self-claimant to Davidic ancestry endeared HaReuveni to some of the local Jews. Cardinals and Princes came to Egidio's house to consult with HaReuveni "from morning to evening." But when he fell ill, he preferred to stay in the house of the physician and rabbi Joseph Tzarfati, the same eminent poet who wrote the Questions Fabricio Álvarez had given Alfonso. HaReuveni remained in Rome for exactly one year. The Cardinal facilitated HaReuveni's audience with the Pope who showed some willingness to respond to the magnetic Jew's political requests. However, at the same time, the Pope used HaReuveni as a ploy in his conflict with King Carlos for the hegemony over Italy.

HaReuveni's claims were contradictory and nebulous. To Rabbi Tzarfati he claimed to have descended from the tribe of Reuben, rather than Judah, and a brother of the Jewish King Joseph who lived in Arabia! His mission was to form an alliance between the "Head of the Christians" in Rome and the Portuguese King on the one hand and the King of Ethiopia on the other to destroy Mecca and the Ottomans in Arabia and in the Land of Israel. Together with a Jewish army he would muster, he promised to rid the Land of Israel of Muslim control. He appeared ascetic with an aura of a mystic that caused many to believe his fantastic stories. In their meeting, the Pope gave him two letters, one to the King of Portugal, the other to the King of Ethiopia with some vague commitment.

The honor shown to HaReuveni aroused messianic aspirations in some quarters of the Roman Jewish community. However, after he met with King John III in late 1525, the reactions among the Portuguese Conversos reached unprecedented heights. Rumors swelled of Conversos burning crosses. Thousands of them paraded in the major streets shouting: "We are Jews! We are Jews! Death to the Inquisitors! Away with evil!" They renounced Catholicism and returned publicly to Judaism. The Inquisition retaliated swiftly by burning these heretics in spectacular public celebrations.

Alfonso was not aware of these happenings, for HaReuveni's efforts did not affect Spain. Yet, HaReuveni's enthusiastic welcome in both Rome and Portugal raised the alarm among the Spanish Inquisitors who found it imperative to squelch any messianic hope that might come from their neighboring country, or from the Papal capital. In December of 1525, Archbishop Fonseca devised a plot to use Alfonso against this religious threat since Alfonso was the most famous authority on Jewish culture and tradition. Fonseca believed that pre-emptive action would curtail any threat. He reasoned that if the Jews of Rome, where the cancer of messianic hopes began, denounced that messianic hopeful, the Conversos in the Iberian Peninsula would follow suit. But Alfonso was oblivious of these events.

Anti-Jewish essays had been written by Jewish converts and disseminated by the Church for the past three centuries. In all these polemics the authors debunked the illogic of Jewish laws and found "evidence" in the Jewish Scriptures for the prophetic announcement of the first coming of Jesus. A special school was founded to raise new generations of Christian "scholars" who would be armed with the right Scriptural references in public disputations with Jewish luminaries. Such writings gave birth to the establishment of the Inquisition in Spain. The most notorious composition, studied and quoted often by later Christians, was *Pugio Fidei* ("Dagger of the Faith") penned by Raymond Martíni in the 13th century.

Alfonso went to the University library and began to read Martín's book. He was devastated by the lies and misinterpretations before his eyes. He went home and showed it to Izolda. She read the first few pages and her face turned ashen:

"These are malicious words of nefarious people. They twist the wisdom of our sages and trample on holiness."

"Yes," agreed Alfonso, "and yet I have no choice but to join this farce."

"This time they have pushed you to a corner from which you cannot escape."

"I will do my best to tone down the poisonous condemnations. I will interpret any mention of 'three' as referring to the Trinity and make up new ones that will be doubtlessly received in complete ridicule. I doubt the Jews of Rome will read this vacuity, let alone be persuaded to convert."

Alfonso divided his letter into seven parts doing his best to draw illogical ideas from Rabbinic and Kabbalistic sources, the same sources he praised in his personal notes. He repeated these erroneous ideas in every chapter while adding more he himself found pathetic in his clandestine writings. He especially liked his new insight on the attribution of the triple "holy" in the *Amidah* prayer to the Trinity. It was so ridiculous that any Jew reading his *Epistle* would certainly understand it as pitiful and pernicious Christian propaganda.

The bulk of the essay contained biblical quotes to establish the Jewish erudition of the author. Alfonso opened with a gloomy depiction of people forsaken by their God because of their own aberration of path, and refusal to see the light of Christianity: "God bestowed power to the Christians," he wrote, "evidenced by their number and wealth. Listen to my words of wisdom, for I have heard a decree of utter destruction upon you."

He then went on to detail "the evidence": "The mysteries of the Trinity are numerous, in every oracle of the Prophets. As Zechariah said: *And they shall look up to Me, the one they pierced.* That is, all the remaining families will convert and look up to Jesus our Messiah whom they pierced. The verse in the Book of Daniel refers to the son, where it says: *And the appearance of the fourth looks like the son of God.*" Who, among the Jews, would miss the contradiction between three and four?

And on and on he quoted and misquoted verses out of context and intent. However, he ran out of references and out of steam in mid-composition, so he turned his criticism to the Hebrew language, and the sagacity of the Rabbis: "I have studied all the Hebrew grammar books and found them inept in methodology, as pedagogical works, and in focusing on the essential rules. The result is that their students can never study and master grammar.

Authors and students are the object of ridicule by non-Jewish scholars. They all lack the spiritual aspect of the sciences." He did not bother to explain the link between the Hebrew grammar and the sciences.

In confounding thoughts, Alfonso hoped to appear ridiculous and unscholarly. In his last chapter he returned to the Trinity through the Kabbalah in a fuddled demonstration. On the one hand, he called the words of the Kabbalah "words of divination and women's fables," and on the other, he withdrew from it "proofs" for the Trinity.

"Your sages composed the science of the imaginary Kabbalah, which is your wisdom and intellect, but not in the eyes of the nations who ridicule you for the debilitating use of *notarikon* and the *gematria* and the transmutation which is a *nut orchard*. The three letters of *gnt* (=orchard) denote the Trinity. Pico della Mirandola considered the Kabbalah as a major source which affirms the divinity of Jesus. Yet we know the futility of its esoteric teaching. Many secrets are embedded in the Kabbalah, in its numerology of the letters or by analogy, and in the *notarikon*, or in superfluous words in scriptures. I shall herewith bring to you proofs which you would not be able to counter, for they are strong and valid to magnify our holy faith. And let me say now that the name Jesus whom you call Yeshu in three letters only, denotes indeed that Jesus was born from YHWH and from his mother Miriam, for in *gematria* Jesus and Miriam and YHWH are similarly strong. For the sum of 'Yeshu' is like the sum of 'Miriam YHWH.' And if you call him 'Yeshu,' its significance indicates essence, because he created essence from nothing, and all essence emanates from him and under his hand. And if you call him 'Yeshua' it indicates then in its significance that he is a savior and a redeemer. Furthermore, Moses said: *See now, for I, I am He,* to denote the mystery of the Trinity in the double words which are the words of the Father who says that He and His son are one."

As he began, he ended his "masterpiece" with a warning: "I assure you, the rebellious Jews of Rome, a total annihilation if you do not convert to the Holy Faith."

When he showed the finished *Epistle* to Izolda, she burst out laughing: "Excellent composition. I cannot find any logic nor consistency of thought. The Hebrew lacks mastery and the style is immature and diffused. It is completely garbled, dear husband."

"This means I have created a superb oeuvre." Alfonso was pleased. "No Jew will take this letter seriously, and my masters will be content."

However, by the time this *Epistola* was printed as an addendum to the second edition of his Grammar Book in 1526, its necessity was lost. The Portuguese Inquisition quenched the religious fervor in blood, and the book with its "letter" never reached Rome. Alfonso could sigh deeply in relief.

It was 1525 when a scholastic relationship began in earnest between Pedro Ciruelo and Alfonso. They knew each other before, for Ciruelo taught Alfonso Latin in Salamanca, and in Alcalá Alfonso taught him Hebrew and the Bible, subjects to which Ciruelo devoted himself in the 1530s in Segovia. In Alcalá, Ciruelo was teaching theology and mathematics, astrology and philosophy since 1509, and was well known and respected in academia. When Alfonso was preparing his re-edited Grammar Book, he sought Ciruelo's help in the Latin translation. Alfonso, therefore, dedicated the 1526 edition to his *best supporter, the teacher and great sage, the master theologian.*

Archbishop Fonseca called Alfonso for an audience in his palace on the outskirts of the *Juderia*. The rain had not stopped since the night before. The air was cold, and the wind sent chills to the bone. Alfonso hurried to reach the front door. When the door opened, the warmth was a welcome change. Fonseca, sitting high in his chair, was dressed in his bishopry attire. This time he was smiling.

"I am very impressed by your successes, especially that of the Epistle to the Jews of Rome. I, therefore, order you to launch the Latin translation of all the books of the Old Testament. That was, as you know, Archbishop Cisneros's wish. To establish a unified format for the series, you will begin with the book of Genesis as a paradigm. Professor Ciruelo will guide your Latin and approve the format of two columns of text with an interlinear translation. There are 24 books to copy and translate, so do not waste time. You are dismissed."

Hiding his hands in his long sleeves, Alfonso dashed out to return to the library. At least the library was heated and protected him from the troubles in the outside world.

The first book in the series was dedicated to Pedro Ciruelo with similar flattery which, Alfonso knew, was sweet to his ego: *To the great theologian, for his name is throughout the land.* It was completed on January 14, 1527, with an honorable mention of the current Rector Antonio de Cascante.

As people returned to their work and routine after Christmas and the New Year, Ruiz Fernández Guzmán, the former Kosher butcher of Zamora and now a sheep breeder outside the walls of Alcalá, was ready for the visits of the Conversos. This was the right time to bring their growing children to learn the procedure of Kosher slaughtering. Alfonso's family ate little meat, mainly on Holy Days and special occasions. It was early Sunday afternoon when Alfonso and his children prepared to drive to the farm.

"Here are extra blankets. It is snowing outside so put on your boots," called Izolda.

The twins were almost 13 and ambivalent about what to expect. Juan had seen it three years earlier, but he loved the ride. It was a cold and cloudy day. The white carpet of snow carpeting the hills and the valley with green dotting the horizon was a delightful sight to see. The children felt pity for the horse treading on the snow and exposed to the chill of the day. All bundled up and huddled together inside the coach while the breath-taking scenery compensated for the cold.

"Do not be alarmed at the farm. Mr. Guzmán will show you how he inspects the sheep for blemishes and what type of knife he uses. He will sharpen the knife to a degree of perfection. He will place the head of the sheep in between his legs to allow him to cut the throat in one strong swoop to prevent unnecessary pain. Then he will let the blood drain over the soil. His sons will first shear the animal, then cut up the meat into specific parts. Because of the cold weather, we will be able to wrap the meat in snow."

"Please allow us to play in the snow, *padre*. The snow in town is really dirty."

"After we accomplish the purpose of our visit." Alfonso promised with a smile.

Soon they entered the gates of the farm and drove directly to the barn. They descended and walked toward Guzmán and his sons. A corpulent sheep was eating peacefully unaware of her immediate fate. Alfonso and Ruiz greeted and hugged each other. Alfonso said:

"I have prepared my children for your demonstration. Now, you take over."

Guzmán was a big man with rough hands and a hardened face. He had demonstrated his work to children umpteen times, with patience and sensitivity.

"Are you ready?" He asked watching them closely. "If you cannot bear blood, step back." He kept on watching them. They did not move or respond. "Well, are you ready?" He asked again. "If you are, then draw near." Like sheep, they followed the farmer's hand which pointed to a patch of dirt. Guzmán's sons seized the unaware sheep and led her forward. Guzmán examined the sheep and found her without blemishes. He then held the knife in his hand and sharpened it on a whetstone. He cut a piece of linen to show the children how sharp the knife was.

"Come closer and see the knife. Sharp, right?" The children nodded. He placed the sheep's head in between his legs and said in Hebrew: "Blessed are You, *HaShem* our God, King of the Universe, who hallowed us with His commandments and commanded us on the slaughtering." And before they noticed it, the head was severed, and blood began pouring onto the dirt. Sofia jumped and closed her eyes. She opened them slowly to see Guzmán's sons shearing expertly. This done, they cut the sheep open for their father to examine her lungs for any infection. The sheep was declared kosher for butchering.

"Wow!" Jeromillo blurted out in fascination. Juan watched with no particular interest.

"The usual cuts?" Guzmán asked.

"Yes." He turned to his children and said: "Now you may go out and play in the snow." Alfonso conversed with Ruiz while the latter washed his knife and hands. He put the knife away and with his sons, covered the blood with soil. They cleaned the area for the next customer.

"It is getting dark," Alfonso called out, "it is time to go!"

"Can we stay some more? We are having fun," Sofia begged.

Her father always capitulated to her whims. It was a rare occasion for them to play in the snow outside of town. "Of course, but not for much longer," he gave in with a smile.

At home, Luciana and Camila immediately cooked some of the meat and the rest they salted. It would last them throughout the winter months.

The series for the University of Alcalá did not follow the paradigm, nor was it complete. Out of the 24 books only four were accomplished, Aramaic written in one column with interlinear Latin translation. It took two years to complete them, for more urgent assignments were demanded of him.

However, Ciruelo desired a similar series, and only nine years later in June 1536 did Alfonso return to it, beginning with the entire Pentateuch. This time the accolade reflected Ciruelo's whereabouts: *The master theologian, no one is like him in Spain and France, and the whole world.* Instead of an epilogue, Alfonso composed a poem addressed to the New Christians, in which he warned them against trusting in Jerome's Latin translation. "Jerome," Alfonso contended, "was a true Christian and a fine translator, but many ignorant copyists had for centuries changed the text. Therefore, turn to the Holy Language for the truth!" His intention was to arm the Conversos, who might read it one day, with pride in the Hebrew language and the eternal truth of their Bible. In his introduction to the poem, he wrote: *This poem is for you to sing, for I wrote it in the same meter as Solomon Ibn Gabirol's piyyut 'My heart, Keep an Answer.'* This was Alfonso's signal to the Conversos as to its real meaning and purpose. Gabirol's poems were very popular among the Sefaradi Jews and the Conversos, and they continued to be sung on the Sabbath and on festivals.

Alfonso's calculated writings, geared for Conversos in the guise of Christian compositions, were getting bolder and bolder, especially in his private messages.

Five months later he completed seven more books for Ciruelo which years later found their way to Salamanca. The sporadic work of two sets of the same series for Ciruelo and for his university had to be halted for years as a result of a more ambitious schedule. Alfonso had already translated Radaq's grammar books. The new set for the University of Salamanca was brokered by his friend and colleague Pablo Coronel who came in person to Alcalá.

"I was recalled by the University Board and ordered to hire you on a new venture," he told Alfonso as they dined at Alfonso's home. "I had to sign off my property as collateral to ensure their investment. You are to copy for them most of the biblical books in their Aramaic translations. You shall prepare the Latin in a parallel column. I shall oversee the payments."

The new task exhausted his day and night relentlessly. By 1530 Alfonso succeeded in accomplishing the copying and the translation of a large portion of the Hebrew Bible twice, once for his school, and another for the Salamanca Library. Alfonso recorded the progress of work and the incremental payments in his diary.

Amid this hectic life, he received a letter from the English Ambassador to Spain, Edward Lee, with a personal request that Alfonso copy Radaq's Grammar Books with a Latin translation. "You have been recommended as a highly skilled scribe and scholar of Hebrew writings. Since my residence, at His Majesty King Carlos's royal palace in Valladolid, is temporary, I would appreciate timeliness. I assure you, you will be rewarded tidily." The emissary handed him a heavy pouch with coins as a down payment.

Mr. Lee was a Catholic theologian who had graduated from the top universities of Europe. He served King Henry VIII in a variety of ambassadorial positions, including petitioning the Pope's consent to the King's divorce from Katharine of Aragon, King Carlos's aunt. In his pursuits of further knowledge of Hebrew, Lee traveled to Salamanca where he met Coronel. To his inquiry, Coronel recommended Alfonso's services as he himself was too busy and in ill health.

In his letter to Alfonso, Coronel explained the urgency of the upcoming request: "Ambassador Lee is a busy diplomat. Right now, he is in the process of brokering an alliance with France. That is why his continued residence in Valladolid is uncertain. Good luck." Alfonso immediately set out to work, but he used a semi cursive script while the Latin was quite hasty.

The ambassador gave Alfonso six weeks to complete the task, after which he arrived in Alcalá on his way to Paris. The meeting took place at the Dean's office, where a welcome party was prepared for the honorable English diplomat, with the entire staff dressed up in their regalia standing behind him.

The Dean opened the ceremony with a long speech that bored everyone: "We are exceedingly honored to welcome the most learned diplomat Mr. Edward Lee, whose place in our royal court is of great significance for our two countries." He went on to enumerate Lee's political and parochial achievements in England and Europe.

Lee's humility was genuine: "You are too kind, distinguished Dean. I am delighted to visit your esteemed university whose fame is well known in my country. I thank you all for coming to honor me with your presence. But I must mention the person who is the reason for my visit, and this is Professor Alfonso de Zamora."

"Of course," hastened the Dean to respond as he pushed Alfonso forward. "We are all very proud of our accomplished scholar, teacher, author and poet. He has brought great honor to our institute."

Lee turned to Alfonso and shook his hand, finally handing over a heavy pouch as the last payment. Alfonso bowed his head in reverence: "It was a work of love, Your Eminence. It was a privilege to be chosen by you." He gently handed the ambassador the manuscript.

That night, the ambassador stayed at Fonseca's palace and left early the next morning to Paris where he had a few weeks to study the manuscript. However, as he was called to report to King Henry on his negotiations with the French King and Council, he decided to gift the precious book to the Royal Library.

Throughout the years of overwork and sickness, Izolda stood by Alfonso attending to his every need. But she could not forget the years he spent at his mistress's. Her fury was masked by her noble upbringing and would not permit her resentment and anger to surface. However strong she appeared to the outside world, the emotional turmoil deep within, which was gnawing at her soul, took its toll. Suffering from fainting spells after a short walk or physical activity, she found joy and solace in her writing and in raising her children. In 1528 Juan was 17 and a diligent student at the University, reading arts and the classics. He wanted to go into business, to import commodities from the New World like their neighbor Alfonso Gomez did.

The twins, on the other hand, now 14, were spoiled and lazy. Jeromillo skipped school and associated with the wrong lot. He resented his parents' Jewish teachings and wanted to be like the rest of his friends. He hated going to Mass or observing anything that smelled of religion. He liked to read of far-away adventures and royal intrigue. He was a dreamer without an anchor.

Sofia was aware of her beauty and poise. With her charm she could get anything she wished for from her doting father. Izolda scolded Alfonso for his indulgence and often reprimanded him for his weakness. Sofia was smart and a quick learner which bored her to apathy. School was too easy, and the Church setting was not to her liking. The priest-teacher was besotted by her beauty and sharp mind, and therefore she was the first to leave the classroom. Unlike the rest of the students who came from afar, she and her brother dashed home for lunch. But there were days that instead of going back to study in the library, they would stay at home and nap. Izolda was too sick to control the twins.

On one such day, in early 1530, the twins came home to find their mother collapsed on the floor and the maids tearing at their hair.

"Stop wailing!" Sofia ordered, "Carry your mistress to her bed. Fast! You, Camila, fetch the doctor. Hurry up!" Luciana, the older maid, kept tapping and massaging Izolda's heart and wrists but by the time the doctor arrived, there was nothing else to do but declare her dead.

The funeral was heart-breaking: "It is my fault, my sweetheart Izolda," Alfonso wept at the grave site. He was murmuring: 'How could I betray you, a woman I have loved and adored! You have been a devoted wife and mother! How can I face life without you! You were the rock of the family upon which each of us leaned and found stability. I admired your wisdom, your talents and strength. I was so engrossed in my own work and pleasure, that I neglected the treasure I had at home.' He remained kneeling in grief and remorse. Slowly, the children walked him from the cemetery up the road to the empty home.

The maids, who nursed Izolda since birth, refused to stay on: "We have lost our baby," they cried. "We shall return to the Coronels' palace in Segovia."

"You have been like mothers to us. You raised us since we were born," pleaded Sofia. "Please stay, at least until we find a replacement."

The maids agreed. After all, Izolda's three children were their babies, too.

Alfonso returned to overworking himself as a means of self-punishment. Again, this resulted in complete exhaustion which compelled him to ask Cardinal Fonseca for an assistant. The *bachiller* (high-school graduate) Langa, a former student, arrived in April just before Passover. Alfonso kept him in the library, away from the clandestine activities in his home during the Passover week. After two months, Alfonso felt strong enough to fire the devoted assistant: 'The man's progress is too slow and his Hebrew handwriting is immature,' he reasoned. He tore up the last two pages of the manuscript and finished it in his own handwriting, signing off with his formulaic colophon.

Warm winds in the air and the rebirth of flowers and trees in their wealth of colors soothed his aching soul. One day in May as he was walking home, he noticed a young girl dressed in rags begging for food. She donned neither shoes nor coat. He was moved by her appalling condition, for she was probably Sofia's age or a little younger. "What is your name, child," he asked.

"Maria, sir," she answered in a whisper. She was clearly fearful of this kind stranger. She suspected his true intentions. Her eyes pleaded 'do not hurt me like the others have done.'

"Where are your parents, child?"

Hesitantly she said: "They died in the plague, sir." She was quiet, then asked: "Do you have a piece of bread, sir? I am hungry." She began to cry.

"Come with me to my home. I will take care of you. Come on, give me your hand."

She did not move. She looked at him with consternation.

"Do not worry, child! My children are your age. We will take care of you." He smiled and raised her from the dirty ground. She obeyed and together they walked home.

He called the maids and said: "This is María. As you can see, she needs a wash, clothes and food."

The children came to watch the frightened girl being taken to the washroom. Sofia went to her room and found fitting clothes, socks and shoes. Since her mother's passing her manners improved and compassion replaced her vanity.

Clean and properly dressed in Sofia's clothes, María was taken to the kitchen. Luciana brought out bread, cheese and olives.

She warmed some milk and placed it in front of the poor girl. María ate voraciously. The hapless orphan was pretty with brown eyes and black hair, a typical girl from the nearby villages.

"Do you have a family?" asked Sofia. "An aunt or an uncle?"

"Yes." She held the cup of milk to her lips and drank. "They took over my parents' farm and chased me out. I have no one and nowhere to go."

Camila, the younger maid, said: "Would you be able to take care of a household? We would like to return to our hometown."

"I doubt if she could," interjected Sofia. "She is too young and inexperienced."

"What if I stayed for another year until she could be a responsible maid?" offered Camila. Luciana looked at her with astonishment. Were they not returning to Segovia together?

"That would be a very good idea," opined Alfonso, who could not afford a disruption of his family's daily life. He looked at María and asked: "Are we settled, then, child?"

Maria's eyes sparkled. "Yes, sir. I will be much obliged." And with this, everyone went to bed for the night.

In a few days, Luciana was ready to leave. The children wiped their tears as they escorted her to the carriage, for they felt they were losing their mother again. "It is time for me to retire. The Coronel family will take care of me in my final years," Luciana had reasoned.

Camila was in tears. Luciana was like an older sister, loving and caring: "I shall join you in no time," she promised.

Since *Loor de Virtudes* was published in 1524 in several cities around Castile, the publisher, Miguel de Eguia, withheld Alfonso's royalties. He avoided Alfonso's visits and ignored his requests for payment. Moreover, Alfonso was treated in the same fashion after Eguia published the second edition of his Grammar Book titled *Introductiones Artes Gramaticae Hebraicae*, or *Artes* in short. *Artes* was a simpler version of the one he prepared for the Complutesian Polyglot Bible. Even though Alfonso dedicated the book to Archbishop Fonseca, he owned its rights. After five years of withholding payment, Alfonso sued for royalties.

From the beginning, the case went nowhere. The judges constantly postponed the hearing and demanded new conditions and more evidence. Alfonso turned to Fonseca for help in his capacity as the head of the University and the supreme judge in Spain. Fonseca was non-committal:

"As long as you work at the University, my duty is to protect you from any Inquisitorial harm. But in the current case, the lawsuit is a private matter. Let the courts hear your case and justice will prevail. I trust our justice system."

"How can I get justice if the judges avoid setting a date for a hearing?"

"I can do that for you. I promise to force the local courts to set a date for the hearing."

The date was set for May 30, 1530. Still, it was well known that in such cases when the plaintiff happened to be a Converso, the verdict would result against him. But Alfonso had to try. Perhaps there would be one righteous judge?

On the day of the hearing, the judges sat at the podium with a stern sense of self-importance. Juan, Sofia and Jeromillo stood at the back of the room. As he later recorded in his diary, Alfonso described the event in vivid words of acerbity and disappointment. Eguia, the publisher, brought with him a cadre of witnesses who swore, one by one, that they had been privy to the payment in full of Alfonso's royalties. Among the witnesses Eguia paraded was his "personal servant Navasquez; the arrogant judge Baquedano, the one with soft words; the preacher-priest wearing some kind of black clothes; the fat preacher; leaders of the community; and the trustees of both Archbishops, Cisneros and Fonseca." The civil justices and the Inquisitors, together with the audience Eguia invited to fill the room to capacity, were his "prosecutors and foes." The audience kept expressing words of sympathy for Eguia, and whenever Alfonso spoke, he could hear them yell "Liar! Liar!" The set was staged and manipulated.

At the conclusion of the charade, the head judge declared: "We have listened carefully to the witnesses' testimony. We, the judges, have concluded that the plaintiff, Prof. Alfonso de Zamora, did not prove his claim that he was extorted of his labor." He turned to Alfonso with a grave face: "Therefore, we sentence you to pay a fine of 1000 maravedis to the court, and 2000 in remunerations to the innocent Eguia for suffering and shame."

Another judge continued: "You are here reprimanded for smearing the good name of an upstanding Christian who has been an honor to the University and to Alcalá."

The mob in the room yelled "Hang this apostate! Burn this enemy of Christ!" The police were called to restore order and accompanied Alfonso and his frightened children home.

Alfonso's hopes were crushed for good. From then on, in his repeated criticism of the Spanish society in his diary, he always sent poisonous arrows toward the *fat, ignorant, hypocritical, and vicious priests.* To his children he said: "No Jew should ever seek justice in non-Jewish courts, for not only would justice not be served, but it would demean our tradition and culture." He made a note of this in his diary.

During the year 1530, Alfonso worked incessantly, copying books in Hebrew and Aramaic with Latin translation either as a paralleled column or interlinearly. Some of his work was on assignment for the University of Salamanca, but he mainly worked for his university. He was paid as he completed a certain number of quires. Sometimes Professor Coronel would be the messenger, at other times it would be a special envoy. Alfonso recorded these installment payments in Hebrew in his diary.

The high expenses of the trial dwindled Alfonso's coffers and he decided to add a new venture to his already very demanding schedule. He announced to his children: "I am joining my good friend Andre Martinez in the business of olive oil distribution. He would pick up the oil from the presses outside of Alcalá and bring it to his home. We would look for clients and sign the contracts. We need an accountant and a delivery man." He looked at Juan: "Would you like to join the business? This might open the door for you to branch out in the future to other commodities. What do you think?"

Juan thought for a while and then responded: "I think that would be a splendid opportunity to be independent and take responsibility."

"I am pleased of your answer, my son. I will discuss the matter with Martinez."

Martinez was another Converso who resided in the *Juderia* with a variety of successful enterprises. He had a good name of an honest and trustworthy businessman. It was agreed to assign Juan to deliver the olive oil to the clients' homes, receive payment, and oversee the accounting.

Juan was a diligent worker whose looks and manners captivated his clients. The business was doing well from the start to the satisfaction of the two other partners. The number of clients grew by the month. One of their eminent clients was Fray Bernaldino, a charismatic and a brilliant preacher of Jewish descent, and an agitator of the *comuneros*, an anti-royal movement. Alfonso warned Juan of the man's credibility: "The man is clever and cunning. Do not be misled by his promises and smooth talk. Insist on payment at the time of delivery, for he keeps changing residences, probably to discomfit the authorities. He is infamous for being a fornicator, gambler, cheater, drunkard, and a profligate. He shows no restraints from poking jokes at high officials in the Church, including Archbishop Fonseca. He has been living in Alcalá for a short time, but I won't be surprised if soon he will be apprehended."

"Has he been hiding or avoiding the police?" inquired Juan.

"It does not seem so. Complaints against him are mounting and he is becoming *non-grata* in Alcalá."

"So how come he is still free?"

"Because his supporters are high in the Church hierarchy, and concrete evidence is hard to gather, especially when his victims are threatened. His place in the active *comuneros* ensures his immunity. But as King Solomon said: *Power does not last forever.*"

True to his word, after many years of attempts to find him guilty, it at last happened. On Friday evening, October 13, 1531, as Juan was approaching the Fray's home, the Police came and arrested Bernaldino.

In the evening Juan reported to his father the stormy event he witnessed: "Even before he opened the door for me, the police assaulted Bernaldino's house by breaking the door. I was so scared they might arrest me as an accomplice. I showed them the olive oil bottles and they asked me to leave. You should have seen the crowd that assembled in no time to cheer on the police. What a day!"

His father laughed at his son's excitement: "*How the mighty have fallen,*" he quoted King David's words.

Another business Alfonso established with Martinez and Juan was trading in grains. These businesses, too, turned to be profitable for the partnership. Apart from this venture, Alfonso gained three more patrons for his scribal work, the most noble of them was Bishop Diego Ramirez, the private counselor of Queen Joanna. The other two were Diego de Toro and Professor de la Parra, high University administrators and teachers. Alfonso could now loan money to private residents and give charity to an orphanage and to the poor.

Two people were the subject of Alfonso's charity. Whenever Alfonso needed a messenger to take the completed quires to his patrons, he used either Fabricio or Etiense. Fabricio was a quiet man who did not complain about his misery. One day in winter, Alfonso noticed Fabricio's worn-out shoes. "Come with me, my good man, you cannot walk around with these shoes." They stopped at Alfonso's house. "Wait here, I'll be right out." In a few minutes he returned with thick socks. "Now, put them on and let us go to the cobbler."

At the cobbler's, Alfonso bought Fabricio a pair of warm boots. The other poor man was Etiense who survived by doing odd jobs, but he could not afford to rent a decent room. Alfonso approached him and said: "Etiense, I have heard that Ozido, the book seller, has an extra room to rent out. I know him well and he is a good man. Let us talk to him."

At Ozido's store Alfonso began to haggle: "Ozido, my friend, this poor man needs a room to rent. How much do you want for your room?" But Ozido looked at Etiense's tattered clothes and refused to let him rent his "clean and respectable residency."

"Do not look at his miserable sight. He is a fine and decent man. He deserves a roof over his head, just like you and me. Please, in the name of our friendship, give him a chance and you will do a good deed."

"All right," at last he answered, "thirty maravedis per week."

"Etiense, can you afford this rent?" Alfonso looked at the poor man.

"I can afford half," Etiense replied sheepishly.

"I have been generous," responded Ozido, "I cannot agree to his offer."

Alfonso took Ozido aside and said: "I shall pay the balance. Tell him you accept his offer."

Two months later Ozido doubled the rent when a new tenant offered to pay more. Etiense could not pay the new rate and a vocal row ensued. Ozido entered the room and threw the few possessions the poor man had, out the door. The shouts attracted many spectators who took either side. The police were called and Etiense was imprisoned. From his jail room he sent a message to Alfonso who became extremely upset. At Ozido's store he exploded with rage:

"What you have done is reckless, heartless, and greedy. You gave me your word to give him shelter as long as his rent was paid on time. You have broken your word to me."

"It is business, not charity. I have a better offer. That's life."

"Money is not the only thing in life. Character matters." Alfonso turned and left agitated.

He looked around for a cheaper rental which the pitiable Etiense could afford. He then went to the police and paid for Etiense's release.

It was early August when Camila went out to the market, and Jeromillo was alone at home with María. When he raped her, she screamed in pain and shame, but no one could hear her. When Sofia came home, she found María locked in her room. One look said it all for Jeromillo had been harassing María ever since she moved in with them.

"Was it Jeromillo?" Sofia asked even though she knew it was a rhetorical question. She was furious. This was unacceptable behavior from the son of Jacob Gabbai. He had to be punished.

Maria nodded. She was huddled on the bed, dress torn, and hair disheveled, crying in shame and pain.

Alfonso came home and was very disturbed by the rape. Sofia insisted that he banish Jeromillo from their home. "He has shamed our family. He has shamed the memory of our mother and our tradition. He has forfeited his right to reside here."

Alfonso agreed. Ethical behavior and respect for women were taught and practiced in Alfonso's household. He himself wrote in many of his essays and annotations that the highest degree of righteousness is to observe God's laws as commanded in the Torah. Yet, Jeromillo came home later expressing no remorse.

"You have shamed God and your family. I will not tolerate such an abomination in my house. Apologize to María and take responsibility."

"She is only a maid," Jeromillo said with contempt, "she wanted it. I have not done any wrong and I am not going to apologize."

"If you refuse to take responsibility, then you are not welcome in my house." Jeromillo was stunned, for since the passing of his mother, his incorrigible ways were tolerated or overlooked by his overworked father.

Sofia had already packed a bag and shoved it to her twin brother. "You may return when you understand your wicked act and show remorse," said Alfonso.

Jeromillo left without a word.

Despite Camila's efforts to help María overcome her trauma, María's work suffered. Tenderly, Sofia comforted her, but she was busy with school and with preparation for her upcoming engagement. Two months later Alfonso conferred with Camila who suggested that a change in residence might help María heal. María was sent to work at the home of Don Manuel, a wealthy man with a large family. Camila said she could manage by herself, but everyone knew she could not, considering her advanced age. She could not fetch water from the public well any longer or carry the groceries from the market. Alfonso had no choice but to hire his neighbor's maid as a part-time aid.

Alfonso's worries and the feverish pace of life during 1530 took their toll in August when he collapsed from physical and mental exhaustion. He again complained of weak eyes and aching body and soul. However, soon enough another event shook his busy life.

It was September 15, 1530, and Alfonso was summoned by the Inquisition as an expert witness in the case of Isabel Melendez of Guadalajara. Her case of Judaizing was going on for the past two years without a conviction. Isabel was Alfonso's cousin who had moved with her husband from Bejar to Guadalajara many years earlier. They kept in touch by letters and meetings on occasional family events. They never forgot their vow to love God and each other. Alfonso still kept her brooch in his pocket at all times. He knew she observed Jewish customs at home and passed them on to her children.

When he entered the Inquisitor's office, the secretary was seated behind the table ready to record the process of testimony. Isabel was seated at the back of the small room. No one knew the relationship between the accused and the expert witness. The Inquisitor, dressed in black, necklaces and rings, and wearing a tall biretta, addressed Professor Alfonso de Zamora with suspicion, for testimony by "New Christians" was always tainted, for they could not tell whether they were lying or mocking them. Alfonso planned to resort to these two strategies. He was offered a chair facing the inquisitor. "State your name, profession and residence," barked the Inquisitor. Alfonso obeyed. "Now put your hand on the Holy Scriptures and swear to speak the truth." Since he was given the New Testament, Alfonso did so without hesitation. The secretary recorded every word and every body movement.

The inquisitor began: "We have a witness who saw the woman Isabel Melendez lighting four candles before sunset on a Friday. Is this a Jewish custom?"

"No," declared Alfonso, "they must be five as the number of the books in the Torah. Where did she light the candles?" Alfonso feigned an interest to help the Inquisitor.

"This was done behind the kitchen door."

"Well, that is definitely not a Jewish custom. It can be done anywhere in the house, except behind the kitchen door. At what time of the day was she caught lighting the candles?"

"At sunset on Friday."

"I have heard some do this then, but the correct Jewish custom is to light them anytime between sunset and sunrise on Saturday," Alfonso responded with authority. "This is the Jewish Law as commanded in the Torah." Alfonso knew the Inquisitors were not Bible scholars. If educated, they were mostly Canonists.

"Our witness also said that there is no pork in the Melendez house, or hare, or shrimp. Are these forbidden foods among Jews?"

"No, absolutely not, but they are found to be injurious to the delicate bodies of Jews who from time immemorial avoided these foods. It is simply a question of health, not religion."

The Inquisitor looked at him confusedly, but Alfonso's face remained stoic and anxious to be helpful. After all he was the authority on Jewish rituals and customs. The inquiry continued:

"The maid observed that clean bed sheets were changed every Friday and that the family wore clean clothes on Saturday."

"As I said before, Jews are highly health conscious, and changing linen and clothes is part of that obsession. You might say they are mentally sick, but it has no religious significance whatsoever." Although Alfonso's heart twisted with disgust, he managed to keep an impassive face. "Thank our Lord Jesus that we are not health conscious like these poor souls." The Inquisitor and the secretary nodded in agreement, looking pitifully at the prisoner.

"Furthermore, the maid said that Isabel Melendez covered the kitchen table with a clean white tablecloth every Friday evening. Is this a Jewish ritual?"

"No, it is part of their obsession with health. They are afraid that they did not clean the table well enough, and therefore they designated Friday as the day in the week to cover the table. They simply do not wish to see any dirt left from the past week. It is pathetic, wouldn't you say? It is a perverted obsession but not religious."

"But the maid testified that the woman Melendez slept in a separate bed during her menstruation period." Now the Inquisitor was begging for an indictment. That was the last accusation on his list.

"Yes, I have heard of this silly superstition," smiled Alfonso, "these fools believe that at that time of the month the devil enters the woman's body and grows two horns on her head. Would you like to sleep with a woman like this? Oh, but of course not you, most learned Inquisitor!" said Alfonso with reverence. "And anyway, the Lady Melendez is too old to menstruate. I suggest you punish the maid for perjury," he added with resolution. "Furthermore, I kindly suggest you free this miserable, foolish, superstitious woman without delay. She deserves our sympathy and scorn, not jail." He then added: "I will mention your name to our Most High Archbishop Fonseca, my mentor, supporter and master at the University of Complutensis. I will tell him of your sense of justice in releasing a demented woman from your jail."

The Inquisitor was pleased to hear Alfonso's promise and he ordered his assistant to free "the Melendez wretched woman" forthwith. Alfonso volunteered to take her home before she frightened the good citizens of Guadalajara. Outside, Alfonso barely controlled his laughter as he left the pompous Inquisitor utterly bewildered yet full of self-adulation.

At her home, the reunion of his concerned cousin's children with their defiant mother was celebrated with hugs and hushed voices.

Armed with his experience, Alfonso composed lengthy advice in his diary on how his fellow Conversos could circumvent the interrogators. He further wrote under the title *A Great and Secret*

Message: "If they seize us, the scholars, because they suspect that we do not believe in the faith of Jesus, then we shall reply that they debase their intelligence more than their fabricated accusations. The Inquisitors are ignorant, and they will always wonder about us. And we, the accused Conversos, do not believe in their faith of Jesus."

Another essay he titled *Against the Inquisitors and their Fabricated Charges and their Hatred*: "The Inquisitors are not theologians, and they know nothing of apostasy or enlightenment. Yes, they possess great power, but we shall not fear and dread them because we possess wisdom. We shall tell them that if they continue to harass us, we shall move to another country where people are not burned."

Alfonso later lamented the state of the Conversos in Spain. They, who were once compared to the cedars of Lebanon, chose the fires over Christianity. He called his effusive poem *Verses*: "The mighty have cut down the cedars and despised the remnant. Lowly and broken down, they chose to burn by fire, by the viciousness and deceit of the powerful toward us. Yes, they hold the power now, they pretend to be righteous, but they are devious. The Ultimate Judge will punish them," Alfonso wrote. "The Gentiles are evil. They tell us: 'Why do you think we want your destruction? We want you to lead the life of the righteous, for we are merciful with love in our heart!' But God created the world to judge the evildoers, and He shall surely judge them."

He chose to express his boundless feelings of contempt and hatred for the Inquisition and its evil doers in his diary. Thus, he was able to remain outwardly silent to ensure his and his family's safety.

The preparations for Sofia's engagement went into high gear at the end of December. The groom was one of Andre Martinez' sons, a *bachiller*, in partnership with his father in the distribution business of quality fabrics for the nobility, from central to the northern kingdom. He was in his mid-20s and well-spoken of in the Conversos' community. Sofia was a young lady of 16, doing well in school, and looking forward to life with Danilo. He was getting their new home ready for the next Spring.

It was Alfonso's responsibility to prepare the banquet and for this he spared no expense. He ordered the best pomegranate syrup, almond and date pastes, chickens, roosters and beef tongue from Converso farmers as far away as Valladolid district, purified water from the private well of the Villalbilla noble family east of Alcalá, and beer from the local brewery. Alfonso also ordered the traditional trousseau, new shoes and quality linen from the mills of Santa Yusta in Segovia, a factory belonging to the Coronel family. Camila baked the bread and the cakes, the pies and the quiches.

The festivities were joyous as the couple's friends played music, sang, danced and joked. From Zamora came Francisco, Alfonso's third son. Luciana promised to come to the wedding which was scheduled for the week following *Shavuot*.

Alfonso hoped for a less hectic year than 1530. The pace of teaching, copying and restoring Hebrew books was indeed slower. However, for the first time in the history of Alcalá, his classes were opened to young ladies. He found it awkward to teach them and shared his resignation with Sofia:

"These ladies come as they please and expect short talks and no homework. They urge me to skip this or that subject and to focus on subjects they like. I have no authority to excuse them from my classes for they come from noble families and pay full tuition."

"So how do you keep them in line?"

"I teach them of the brave and exceptional women in the Bible as a paradigm of proper character and behavior. They were exemplary wives and mothers and community leaders. For example, I point to Ruth as the most proper lady, not because of her beauty, for she was not praised for her looks, but for her loyalty to her mother-in-law and the traditional obligation to marry the next of kin to ensure the memory of her deceased husband. Of course, I cannot praise her for converting to Judaism. Tomorrow I will complete the list of the praiseworthy ladies of the Hebrew Bible."

The next day, after discussing the list of women, one student asked: "But, sir, what about the Mother of God, Mary? Didn't she surpass all the Hebrew women?"

Alfonso's face flushed. He was not thinking of the New Testament at all. For him it was not considered "Bible". For him,

Mary's character was summed up by being the mother of Jesus, the Jew, who was killed by the Romans.

"Of course," he blurted out, "she surpassed them all." What else could he say? He made a mental note to add her to his list in his teaching notebook.

Alfonso did not like to teach the ladies. They were reluctant to study logic and philosophy. He vented his resentment for having to teach them in his diary: "Learning at a university is not a capricious or a frivolous affair. There is logic and purpose in teaching and learning, otherwise one cannot reap joy from the experience. Students have no right to dictate to teachers the trajectory of learning in order to suit their whim." But he could not find the fortitude within him to express this to them directly. He felt his place was not to entertain the ladies but to teach them character and biblical values in order to be fit for marriage and to be dutiful wives to noblemen.

To his students, mainly the boys, he excused learning the biblical history as necessary in order to understand the times of the Prophets who were a high priority in Christian theology. He taught the subject from a variety of angles, sometimes through the teaching of the good and the bad acts of the kings, or through the miracles that God performed for the righteous kings. Another way was through the "Serving Angels" or the messages of the Prophets. In whatever way, he taught that one should speak what God had put in his mouth, like Balaam who blessed Israel against the direct order of his master King Balaq.

Alfonso was preparing his teaching material in his study when Sofia entered. "What are you writing, *padre*?"

"I have noticed that in order to keep the students' attention and excitement, I have to find methods and subjects that will astound them, for I find these privileged students dull and bored. Their wealth and arrogance are obstacles to building a character based on biblical values. I have decided to tell them stories about rich and vain princes who learned their lessons of humility and empathy from the wise and the poor while traveling the world. Wisdom, my daughter, is essential for the everlasting soul, surpassing wealth and Canonist dogma. One reaches Wisdom through theology which is summed up by observing God's Laws which are the foundations of the Torah."

"Don't they complain that your teaching does not draw from the New Testament?" asked Sofia.

"Not anymore since I explained to them that in order to understand the teaching of the New Testament, we first have to study its foundations in the Hebrew Bible from which it developed. And anyway, teaching the New Testament is not my responsibility, for there are other teachers for that subject."

"On what do you focus your high school and adult classes?"

"I focus on the beauty, logic and meaning of the Hebrew language. I teach them that logic is integral in each root, which was developed through their verbal forms. Like a tree of knowledge, meanings are alive, breathing and expanding. Hebrew is *sweeter than honey, than drippings of the comb*," he quoted Psalms 19. "Letters, the building blocks of the words, could twist and turn positions to create mysticism and links to the divine. As the first ever language spoken by man and God, Hebrew will return to be the only spoken language in the Messianic era as prophesied by the Prophet Zephaniah." He then added: "Studying the Hebrew Bible in Latin is futile and misleading, because of the numerous errors and changes made throughout the centuries. I have been saying this often."

"Yes, *padre*, I have heard that before," smiled Sofia and left the room.

Sofia's wedding was approaching fast. Alfonso's orders were even more extravagant and the wedding dress, adorned with precious stones and lacework, was in the last phase of sewing. The preparations were almost complete, yet when Danilo heard of the details, he teased Alfonso that not enough was being spent. Alfonso was deeply dismayed as he worked in several capacities to give his only daughter an exceptional wedding. He could not match Danilo's father, whose businesses reached neighboring countries, even the New World.

"You are being insolent. I am doing my best to give you a memorable wedding. Be content with what we have. Remember, 'Who is wealthy? The one who is content with his lot,'" quoted Alfonso from *Pirkei Avot*.

Danilo blushed. "I am sorry, sir, I was just kidding. I appreciate your generosity."

The wedding vows were taken at the church, after which the family and guests arrived at the large home of Don Martinez for the reception. The elite of Alcalá attended with their fancy clothes and jewelry driven in their spangled coaches. Martinez hired the servers and provided the chairs, tables and dishes in concert with Alfonso who provided the food and drinks. This time the sumptuous dessert was prepared by the host's bakers. The wedding was the talk of the town for months to come.

The young couple moved into their new quarters with maids and wealth beyond Sofia's imagination. 'If only her mother could attend,' ruminated Alfonso sadly.

Almost a year after María the maid was sent off to Don Manuel, Camila was coming back from an errand when she recognized her former assistant walking aimlessly in the *Juderia* streets. She was aghast to see this poor teenager back in rags. It was August and the street cobbles were burning the soles of her shoe-less feet. Camila stopped María and said:

"Why are you on the streets? Were you fired by Don Manuel? Tell me, child!" She realized the street was not the place for María's story. She must be hungry. She put her hand on María's shoulder and said, "Come home with me. You will tell me your story since we last saw you."

Maria's eyes showed consternation and Camila understood. "Don't worry, Jeromillo has not returned home. You are safe." She gave her a sympathetic smile.

Before settling down, Camila gave the girl a bath, clean clothes and nourishment. Then they sat on the couch:

"Now you can tell me your story. What has happened to you since last October?"

Maria sighed and answered: "At first I was happy in their house. I did my job to the satisfaction of Mrs. Manuel, but then her husband began coming to my room. I was afraid to shout because he said he would throw me to the streets. I tried my best to avoid him and locked my door at night, but the maids' quarter was away from the main building, and he dismantled the lock. Pilar, the head maid, would not intervene on my behalf because this happened to her and to the rest of the maids, and she wanted to keep her employment. I begged her to protect me, but she abandoned me. It was up to me to stay or leave."

She stopped. Camila handed her a glass of warm milk.

Maria resumed: "He impregnated me. Pilar took me to an old woman in an alley and aborted the baby. I lost much blood and could not work. Pilar let me rest for a week but then I had to get back to work. I was still bleeding when Mrs. Manuel noticed the blood. I had to tell her the truth. The next thing I knew I was out the door. A man took pity on me and promised to take care of me. I did not know Estefan was a pimp. At first, he was kind and generous, but it did not take long when he brought men in. He said I had to pay for his hospitality. I was locked in at all times. One day when Estefan was busy with the client and the door was unlocked, I snuck out and have been on the streets ever since."

By then Camila's eyes welled with tears, thoroughly disgusted with the Alcalán society. "What animals," she exclaimed, "what kind of people live here? To take advantage of a poor and helpless orphan!" She hugged María and promised: "As long as I work in this house, no harm will befall on you."

When Alfonso came home, Camila told him María's story. She said: "I am getting old, and I need María's help. She is a good and loyal maid. You are a man of God, sir. Please allow her to stay."

Alfonso gave in. He had been supporting Alcalá's orphanage with money and clothes. It was the right thing to do as he remembered Isaiah's words: *Share your bread with the hungry and take the wretched poor into your home. When you see the naked, clothe him ... and you shall be like a watered garden, like a spring whose waters do not fail.*

That was the time when Alfonso decided to look for a new mistress. He never considered going back to Madam Aurora after Izolda passed on. When Aurora died of syphilis, her clients scattered to all directions like roaches. It was a miracle he had left when he did.

Juan Álvarez de Toledo, the son of the Duke of Alba, had an idea for which he was willing to pay handsomely. He studied theology in Salamanca where he later taught. Before he was appointed the Bishop of Cordoba in August of 1523, he was a member of the Order of Friar Preachers and was known to be fervent and pious. An important composition in the curriculum at the University, as in every other theological school, was the infamous anti-Jewish polemics of Raymond Martín's *Pugio Fidei,* "Dagger of Faith." This poisonous and garbled "references of truths" from Rabbinic literature ate away at his conscience when he realized the wide scope of Conversos who clung to their faith and pretended to observe Christianity. He had to act, and he had an antidot: *Pugio Fidei* had to be translated back into Hebrew and taught in all churches on Sundays. But he did not know the right person to accomplish this. It was also an excellent opportunity to celebrate 260 years since its publication.

In the summer of 1531, he visited Salamanca where he mentioned his desire to the local Bishop Luís Cabeza de Vaca. Luís Cabeza immediately suggested Alfonso de Zamora, "who himself has penned a similar masterpiece in his *Epistola to the Jews of Rome* five years earlier. He is a devout New Christian, and no one else is more capable to translate the truth of Martín's book into Hebrew than him."

Upon his return to Cordoba, Juan Álvarez sent a letter to Archbishop Fonseca in which he wrote, among others: "Your Holiness knows, as much as I, the fraudulent New Christians' adherence to our Holy Faith. We must force them to see their errors with direct proof from their own Scriptures. We must put a stop to their charade by forcing them to listen to a voice of reason and logic. I have heard of the perfect scholar who can translate into their language the set of evidence to shatter their belief. I would like to ask your permission to hire this scholar to do the translation. He will also be charged in placing a Spanish translation parallel to the Hebrew. My Bishopry will finance this entire work." He then detailed his plan on the logistics of the dissemination of his "scintillating idea".

Fonseca loved the idea. The bishop sent an urgent letter to Alfonso with the order to translate the Latin text into Hebrew with a paralleled column in Spanish. A copy of *Pugio Fidei* was in the Alcalá library. At the time, Alfonso was editing and punctuating Don Isaac Abravanel's lengthy commentary on the Prophets. He enjoyed his work especially those passages against Christian and former Jewish scholars' distorted interpretations, even though it was tedious and time-consuming. It would take him three more years to return to the unfinished job, but then he would have no more time to properly complete that work.

Yes, Alfonso remembered Martin's manuscript, for he perused it for his *Epistle*. He had even left his marks on it. However, now he had to translate each page punctually. The irony was that the Latin text was a translation from the Hebrew or Aramaic of the Talmud and the *Midrashim*. His job was, then, to translate it back to its original texts. He knew he would have no time to execute the Spanish translation because he had a major assignment waiting in line for the University of Salamanca. That suited him fine. Alfonso sent several quires every few weeks and was paid in return. He completed the Hebrew column on February 19, 1532, and was eventually paid in full. He hoped that with this, his responsibility ended as he wrote to the bishop: "Your Eminence, these are the last quires of the Hebrew translation. Due to a prior obligation, I will not be able to accomplish the Spanish column. If the Bishop pleases, I might be able to do that in a year or two." However, a note came back with all the quires: "Please append the Spanish as soon as you finish your obligation." Luckily for Alfonso, this manuscript, as was the fate of his *Epistle*, never saw the light of day. Five years later, the good bishop was moved to Burgos and the assignment was neglected.

Nine days after completing *Pugio Fidei*'s translation, the "Work of Salamanca," the Aramaic translation of the Prophets into Latin, began in earnest. Pablo Coronel had come with the papers and the down payment: "I am assigned to write the Latin translation. To do this, I'll wait until you finish your part of the Aramaic. I am also required to purchase five copies of your *Artes* and *Loor de Vitudes* in a fancy cover for my university." However, Pablo fell ill, and Alfonso ended up executing both translations. He hired the courier Fabricio to deliver the completed sections to the Salamanca University and get his payment.

By March of 1532 the "Work of Salamanca" was done, and with a deep sigh of relief Alfonso handed over the last quires to the courier. He then resumed his assignments for his university.

Apart from teaching teenagers in the closed and restricted Alcalá campus, Alfonso taught priests as part of their canon law studies. Many of these students went on to become Bishops around

Spain or served as counselors and diplomats in the royal court. Almost all came from the nobility: sons of Dukes, governors and yes, Bishops. Among the most distinguished students were Pedro Ciruelo and Francisco Mendoza de Bobadilla. Ciruelo was already a renowned mathematician and theologian when Cisneros invited him in 1510 to teach at the College of San Ildefonso at the University of Alcalá. A few years later, as Alfonso established himself in his new cathedra, Ciruelo joined his Hebrew classes. His long-time wish was to read the Hebrew Bible in its original language. From that time on Alfonso and Ciruelo collaborated on several scholarly endeavors.

In the 1520s, it was a young and brilliant Francisco Mendoza de Bobadilla who joined Alfonso's Hebrew and Aramaic classes. Bobadilla was born to the first marquis and Viceroy of Navarre, a descendant of Jewish converts during the pogroms of 1391. Several of Bobadilla's relatives reached high positions in the Church as a shield from the Inquisition. Even though some of the Bobadillas lived as Jews secretly, young Bobadilla had already made a name for himself in Salamanca before moving to Alcalá. After he was granted a doctorate in civil and canonical law, in an act of defiance against the "pure blood" law, he authored a revelatory essay *Tizon de la Nobleza de España* which traced the genealogies of all the nobility of Castile and Aragon to Jewish roots. Indeed, he was not the typical Converso high cleric, but one proudly grounded in his heritage.

He exhibited a keen interest in Hebrew and with Alfonso's help, mastered the language with ease. He was a natural scholar who delved into the works of the Medieval Jewish commentators and grammarians with enthusiasm and deep insight. He enjoyed his conversations with Professor Alfonso, showing him great respect.

Bobadilla's admiration was not confined to his teacher's knowledge, but to his latent pride as a Converso as well. He noticed Alfonso's unique methods of teaching, the contents and the emphasis he used in class. In his genius mind and resplendent observation, he perceived Alfonso's goals. In his last class of the semester, Bobadilla stayed on to speak with his teacher.

"I thank you for your teaching. I have learned much and will always cherish this opportunity to study from the master."

"It was my pleasure to teach such a noble and bright man. If all my students were to possess such a mind as yours, my life would be so much less aggravating. Well, I should not say that. I do enjoy my work, even though it keeps me busy until late hours."

"Do you keep busy on the weekends, too?" asked Bobadilla.

"It depends. Sunday mornings are spent, of course, at Church. Then I meet with my children for lunch. If there are still some hours to spare, I go back to my work."

"And on Friday nights and Saturdays, do you work?" pressed on the bright and inquisitive student.

Alfonso turned pale. 'To what was this son of a Duke, and himself a Deacon, aiming?' he thought. 'I better watch my words.' His hesitation confirmed Bobadilla's suspicions. He did not wish to trap his teacher or embarrass him, but he wanted to make sure his observations and deductions were correct.

"Nothing happens on Friday nights, and on Saturdays I work, depending on the urgency of the assignment. In good weather, I like to walk in the countryside and enjoy nature. We must take time out to relax. Don't you think so?" Alfonso seemed to beg Bobadilla to change the subject.

"I agree with you. I, too, like to walk on Saturdays. Walking relaxes me." He looked at Alfonso with his penetrating eyes as though to say: 'Your secret is safe with me.' They parted as friends. Soon after, Bobadilla moved back to Salamanca where he taught civil and canonical law. He never forgot his teacher, and a few years later he became his patron.

He met Aldo, as Alfonso called Aldonza, one Sunday afternoon at one of Andre Martinez's parties. The ladies he invited would choose their clients only by his recommendation and patronage. Alfonso was introduced to a lovely lady seated casually on a couch and dressed in the latest fashion. Aldo knew what this introduction meant.

"So, Alfonso, I have not seen you before at Don Martinez's soiree," she began their intimate conversation. "Are you a friend or a business client?" Her red lips moved seductively, her voice rich and pleasant. 'She no doubt comes from an educated family, far from Alcalá. Her good taste in clothes, shoes and jewelry suggest a rather high-end kind of a woman,' he mused.

"Friend, partner and family member," he answered her curtly. "But it is my loss for not attending Martinez's parties before," he finally revealed a coy smile. "I am very busy and since my wife passed on, I have increased my workload. No time to frolic."

"Well, isn't it time to relax, Alfonso dear? Life will pass you by without really living. Would you sit next to me so we can start enjoying the party?" She did not move. He was going to sit down when he noticed she was holding an empty glass.

"May I fill your glass with wine?" He stretched out his hand and she obliged. At the bar, Martinez approached and whispered in low tones: "I see you are progressing well. She is one of the best in town. Well educated and a smart businesswoman. Just be careful. She likes gifts. Expensive gifts. Be aware of the responsibility of having a mistress."

"I am not interested in a mistress. I am too busy with my life."

"Oh, yes you are. I have known you for a long time. You need a woman in your life. Go back to her. It is rude to keep a lady waiting." He laughed and nudged Alfonso in her direction.

"Here you are, Aldonza." She received the glass gracefully as he sat to her left. She brought the glass to her lips and took a sip, sighing with pleasure. "You have not told me what keeps you so busy, Alfonso." She let her shawl fall to her lap revealing flawless and enticing skin. Her made-up eyes were riveted on his face. She wanted to know. She needed to know.

He told her and she listened without disrupting. Behind his job description she recognized the frustrated Converso. "Can we talk about it more in the comfort of my house?" she suggested when he was done explaining. She was a businesswoman, after all.

Alfonso was taken aback by her directness. When he pulled himself together, he said: "Perhaps you will tell me your story, Aldonza. You seem to be schooled in academia and in business. I wonder where you have achieved these skills." Then he hurried to add: "The truth is, I am busy during the week and the only time I have to socialize is Sunday afternoons."

"That suits me perfectly. Let us meet, then, next Sunday. I will tell you my story then." She held out her hand to him and he took it as he stood, both bowing to each other as he stepped away. Alfonso went home looking forward to his next adventure. The anticipation kept him up at night.

Sunday came and as everyone in the *Juderia* gathered at church for Mass, Alfonso was anxious for the services to be over. Conversos like him would murmur a curse before stepping inside the church.

This custom was imbued with Conversos for generations, though the meaning was lost to them, but the Hebrew formulation remained on their lips. Alfonso went home with Juan, Camila and María for lunch. Sofía and Danilo would meet them there. After a nap he headed to Aldonza's place with a bouquet of flowers.

As she opened the door, Alfonso handed her the flowers. She seemed to be a little disappointed, but she smiled and thanked him "for such a colorful and fragrant bouquet." She was provocatively attired: her long dress accentuated her bosom, and a high slit revealed a naked leg in a high-heeled show. She was carefully made-up, and her long black hair was tied in braids around her statuesque head. 'Absolutely stunning,' thought Alfonso following her to a spacious living room. The room was tastefully and richly decorated with an attention to detail. After filling an Italian vase with water and putting the flowers inside, she sat down on a blue and gold couch. On a side table there was an open book. She took the book in her hands and asked Alfonso to sit next to her. He did. He did not expect the next question:

"When will the Messiah come, Alfonso?"

He looked at her confused. 'What Messiah is she talking about? Is she laying a snare for me? Is she testing me? Is she an agent of the Inquisition?' Alfonso was thinking rapidly. He would better keep quiet.

"Well, you are a Bible and Talmudic scholar. You must have asked yourself this question, have you not?" She was serious. She placed the book on her lap and began reading, in Hebrew: "Rabbi Joshua asked the prophet Elijah: 'When will the Messiah come?' Elijah answered: 'Go and ask the Messiah himself!' Rabbi Joshua asked: 'And where is he sitting?' Elijah responded: 'At the southern gate.' Rabbi Joshua asked: 'And what is his distinguishing feature?' Elijah responded: 'He is sitting among paupers afflicted with disease.'

He went and met the Messiah. He asked him: 'When is master coming?' 'Today,' the Messiah answered. Rabbi Joshua went back to Elijah. Elijah asked him: 'What did he say to you?' 'He lied to me, for he said to me: 'I am coming today' and he has not come!' Elijah said: 'This is what he was saying to you: *Today, if you heed His voice.*"

She stopped and looked at him. "This passage does not offer a clear answer. Can you elucidate on this *qushiah*?"

Alfonso was speechless. This high-end lady of pleasure not only was reading Hebrew, but could engage in a Talmudic teaching, straight from *Tractate Sanhedrin*. She wanted him to know that she was a Conversa and that she knew who he was.

"I'll answer your question later, but first tell me how do you know Hebrew and Talmud? I am stunned!"

"I have not revealed this to anyone before. I feel that I am safe with you. You see, my grandfather was the rabbi and the *shohet* in Trijueque, a short distance from Guadalajara, with estates in town and in the countryside. His farm supplied the kosher meat. All his children studied at his school, including the girls. In 1492, as he was about to cross the border to Portugal, he was detained and returned to Trijueque. There, he was forcibly baptized in front of the remaining Jews of his community in the Inquisition's effort to convince the Jews to come willingly to the baptismal font. His hair still wet, he publicly denounced Christianity and called his congregants to either escape or die. For this he was burned alive together with his righteous wife. His house in the countryside was destroyed and gutted to its foundations. How I wish I met him and my grandmother! His children escaped to Amsterdam and from there to Constantinople. His youngest son, my father, who was to take over the rabbinate, remained. He vowed to continue his father's mission.

He taught Judaism clandestinely in different locations. He married my mother who was one of his students. We took part in the studies and vowed to remain Jews. Like his parents, he and my mother were caught and tortured until they died. I have retained most of my father's books and I keep on studying."

She paused to reminisce. "Because my father was the youngest, he did not know much about his grandparents. I wish I knew something about them. How I miss my family!"

Alfonso listened attentively, hanging on every word. She could put him to shame for her defiance of Jewish learning. He remained quiet, pensive. At last, he said: "How can you live this kind of life after what your family suffered?" He looked at her seductive clothes and connotative room.

"My patrons come mostly from top Church clerics. I torture them physically and emotionally and they pay heftily. I seduce them but they cannot go beyond my rules of engagement. They spend a fortune on me, and I give these hypocritical priests drinks laced with slow-acting poisons. I make them sick, I make them die. With this money I support Crypto-Jews around Alcalá and beyond. Do you know that many of the orphans are of Jewish families? I help them survive." Her face reddened with anger. She took a deep breath.

"Are you not afraid I will deliver you to the hands of the Inquisition?" challenged Alfonso.

"No," she responded, "I have done my homework and I know where your heart is. You hide the same type of books I have from my father. We two are like brother and sister. No, you will not deliver me to the Inquisition."

"You are right, Aldonza. I studied to become a rabbi but could not. However, my work here is sacred because I teach Judaism through our books and traditions. Except for one, no one realizes that. They tell me to find evidence for Jesus in our Scriptures and Rabbinic literature and I make up statements and they mindlessly accept them as gospel. This is my revenge, spreading Judaism at the time of the Renaissance. Many of us do our share of defiance." He paused to see her reaction.

She smiled, then said. "Let us go back to my question and do some learning."

Alfonso began: "Rabbi Joshua learned that the Messiah's coming depends on everyone doing his share of goodness in this world. We live to obey *HaShem*'s Law and support each other. *HaShem* is our Rock and Redeemer as King David said: *O God, my rock and my fortress, my deliverer, my shield and the horn of my salvation, my high tower.*"

"Yes, I like this explanation."

"However," Alfonso continued, "Abravanel has suggested a different interpretation by reading the *daled* in the meaning of 'of'. So instead of 'southern' he reads 'Rome,' that is, the Messiah was found sitting at the gate of Rome where the most afflicted people reside. Rome, as you know, is euphemistic for Christians."

"I know," said Aldonza, "and I like Abravanel's reading which depicts Christians as cursed by God, cast away by their people and God."

And so, they continued their studies until she stood. At the door she hugged him and expressed her wish to see him again, same time next Sunday.

Alfonso walked home with an elevated spirit as though he was back at his beloved *Yeshivah*. He was happy he found a kindred soul. He understood Aldonza's interest in the coming of the Messiah. All Conversos yearned for their redemption and the collapse of the Spanish tyranny. Life under the roving eyes of the Inquisition engendered constant fear.

He could not visit Aldo every Sunday due to the pressures of his work, but he brought a gift every time he did. One Sunday in May, she looked pale. "Sorry, my friend, I cannot see you today. I am menstruating." For both, menstruation meant no physical contact or the touching of holy books.

Teamed with Andre Martinez and his father, Juan's business thrived in its expansion throughout the district of Alcalá and its venture into a wide variety of commodities: grains, fruits, vegetables, leather, wool and coal. Alfonso prodded Juan to start a family, but he always made the excuse that he was too busy.

And so it happened that in one of his wool deliveries to Emilio Verdugo, a young woman welcomed him inside. The 21-year-old Juan had never seen her before and was mesmerized by her gentle features and poise. She went to call Don Emilio, the maker of woollen sweaters and coats. Verdugo invited Juan to his office where he paid for the wool.

"If you please, Don Emilio," asked Juan bashfully, "Is the young woman I saw your daughter?"

"No, she is my niece. Her mother died last year, and her father passed away recently. She just moved in with us." He looked at him inquiringly, "Would you like to meet her."

"If you don't object, sir."

Verdugo left the room and came back with the young woman. "My dear Anabel, meet Juan de Zamora." They bowed their heads, but Anabel's head remained low. Lovingly, her uncle raised her head and said: "Would you like to spend a few minutes with Juan? He is a dependable trader from a good family. His father is a renowned professor at the University. He himself is a graduate of that University."

Anabel watched Juan with her blue eyes and nodded. Verdugo invited them to the front room and left. She was probably 18 or 19, dressed modestly with no jewelry. Her blond hair was gathered at the back of her head, held by a few decorative hairpins.

"Your uncle tells me that you live here. From where do you come?"

"Guadalajara," she replied. They were still standing. "Please sit down, I am so ashamed of my manners." They sat down keeping a respectable distance from each other.

"Do you know, by any chance, my great cousin Isabel Melendez and her family? We don't see them often enough. A pity. I find family very important."

"Yes, we do know them. We lived in the same neighborhood, and I grew up with her children."

"Did you spend time in their home?" Juan needed to know if Anabel was a Conversa.

"Yes, we often shared their Friday night dinners. Sometimes they would be our guests." Relieved, Juan knew he chose the right girl. His father would be pleased.

"Have you studied at the University?"

"Yes, in Guadalajara. I took writing. I have joined my uncle only a month ago, after my father ..." she stopped talking and her eyes welled up.

"I am so sorry." He wanted to hold her hand, but it was against the proper rules of engagement. She wiped her eyes with a handkerchief and sat straight again.

"I lost my mother last year, and I miss her every day. You would have loved her. She was an educated woman who was involved in helping women in her community." Like her, he was proud of his late mother.

Don Verdugo reappeared. It was time for Juan to leave. "May I see your niece again, Don Verdugo?"

"Perhaps in two weeks, when you bring the next batch of wool." Juan thanked him and was escorted out.

He told his father of the encounter with lovely Anabel, and Alfonso was delighted. He was encouraged to hear of the relationship between Anabel's family and his cousin Isabel's. "That is a good omen, my son," he responded, then went back to his work.

Juan was smitten, recalling their first meeting again and again, further fueling his attraction until the next meeting. He bought a necklace with precious stones and presented her with the gift two weeks later. Anabel appeared to have been waiting for this encounter as excitedly as he was. Their engagement was short since their families gave their blessings. A new house was readied with the latest comforts and in early 1533 the young couple was wed. Within the next three years, their two children, Raúl was born.

CHAPTER 13

Threatened

And your life shall hang in doubt before you; and you shall fear night and day, and shall have no assurance of your life.
Deuteronomy 28:66

Another bout of exhaustion in August 1532 sent Alfonso to bed for a week. Juan and Sofia, concerned for his frequent decrepitude, visited him every day. Camila cared for him with home remedies.

In the winter of 1533, a new sponsor requested copies of the Former Prophets. It was Antonio Ramirez de Haro, Abbot of Hervas, the nephew of Diego Ramirez, Bishop of Cuenca, for whom Alfonso made copies of several biblical books three years earlier. Abbot Ramirez served King Carlos and his children in numerous political capacities and like his uncle, amassed great wealth. Later, as a high Inquisitor, he proved to be the most zealous cleric in the land.

In most of 1533 Alfonso focused on his daily work as a teacher and scribe. At the age of 55 he seemed to have slowed down. The following year made a great impression on his life and career. It began with the February death of Archbishop Alonso III de Fonseca who protected Alfonso and the rest of the Converso professors from the long and sharp claws of the Inquisition. He also determined which books Alfonso would copy, translate or restore. So far, this relationship with the two Archbishops Cisneros and Fonseca secured an honorable and fruitful life. Rumors were spreading that the very nefarious and low-class Juan Pardo de Tavera was a serious candidate.

Tavera was already a rising star in the Church hierarchy. As the nephew of the infamous Bishop Diego Deza, hater of Jews and Conversos, young Tavera graduated from the Salamanca University in Canon Law and was immediately appointed the rector of that same University. From then on, his rise to power was fast as he moved from one county to the next until he became the president of the Royal Council in 1524. Seven years later Pope Clement VII made him the Cardinal priest at the consistory. The next natural step was the Primate of Spain and the Archbishop of Toledo in April of 1534.

Tavera detested the vibrant department of Oriental Languages at the Alcala University because of its many "untrustworthy" Converso professors. His appointment guaranteed closer scrutiny by the Inquisition, and the elimination of protégés. The fear among these professors concerned the closing of their department and the termination of Converso academicians from other faculties.

Right after Tavera's nomination was confirmed on April 27, 1534, Alfonso penned a five-line poem in Hebrew, full of riddles and mysteries. It was written inside Abravanel's Commentary *on the Prophets* which he kept at home. The poem addressed Alfonso's angst, his fear for the Conversos and their secret life, and a deep contempt for the new Cardinal:

> *Always be very low and please do not walk in the*
> *congregation of the arrogant and the powerful;*
> *Look at the hyssop in the wall, it rests in the stormy wind,*
> *but He breaks cedars.*
>
>> *His wife immersed. It is good for him, good for her,*
>> *not good for us, for immersion has been forbidden.*
>
> *After the man, who, by the merit of his grandeur,*
> *was called cardinal and a son of a cardinal*
> *and a repairer of fallen walls;*
> *My mule in the name of Cardinal I [must] call,*
> *for his father was an ass, Cardinal of the land.*

In the first paragraph Alfonso advised the Conversos to keep a low profile and disassociate from the arrogant and the powerful, that is, the Clergy. 'Take the example of the hyssop,' he wrote, 'which bends its branches to withstand the storm, and pray to God to break the mighty. Perhaps this catastrophe will be only temporary.' Inactivity was a sure way to avoid suffering.

He then expressed his fears that whereas Conversa women would find ways to immerse after the period of menstruation was over, which was considered a beneficial custom for couples, now they needed to be extra careful.

In a very clever wordplay, the last paragraph revealed the menace to them all. While the late Cardinal came from a noble family and was the son of an Archbishop himself (though born out of wedlock like others who were fathered by hypocritical top clergy), Fonseca knew how to build political alliances and calm down rebellions. In contrast, the new Archbishop had no pedigree. He rose to heights not because of his merits but because of nepotism: his uncle, who raised him like his own son, was Deza, the Archbishop of Toledo and the Cardinal of the Land. But Alfonso reckoned, the Archbishop was an ass, while the nephew was a 'mule,' *pered in* Hebrew, alluding cleverly to his name *Pardo.*

However strong his misgivings, Alfonso had no choice but to show allegiance to the uncouth new Cardinal Pardo for he was, after all, the de facto head of all the universities in Spain. Alfonso and his fellow Converso professors understood they had better go to the pigsty and genuflect in order to ensure their livelihood.

He left early Monday, May 4, and in the afternoon reached the inn in Toledo. The first thing on his timetable was to prepare a draft of his "insurance card" in honor of "the Divine" as he referred to Tavera. In his anti-Jewish composition comprised of six full folios addressed to the "rebellious and blind" Crypto-Jews, the chapters were arranged as questions whose supposed answers pointed to biblical "evidence" glorifying Jesus and Christianity.

Alfonso opened with an apology: "I apologize for keeping the message short because my trip to Toledo was not planned, but rather done hastily." He continued with the same repeated claims against the Jews and Judaism he had presented in previous polemics, which would certainly delight Tavera:

"The Hebrew Bible and the Talmud are incomprehensible, confusing and contradictory, which have prevented the Jews from knowing the truth ... For the converted scholars everything is clear and clarified. The Jews are deficient in the spiritual meaning of the fine points of the Holy Scriptures, but not so the converted who perceive Jewish theology better than the Jews. These great scholars are joyous in their choice because they are erudite in theology and all other disciplines. The righteous Queen Isabella and King Ferdinand were urged by these enlightened converts to burn the Talmud for it contained useless things."

In contrast to the enlightened converts, Alfonso depicted the Jews as "evil, ignorant, stupid, immoral, sinful, and corrupt." Tavera would love it.

As in his two previous polemics against Jews and Judaism, Alfonso knowingly misquoted Daniel, the prophets, Targum, and the major commentators as purportedly offering Christian interpretations. Among his examples, he outlandishly claimed that in his commentary on Jeremiah's *the queen of heaven*, Radaq agreed with the Christian interpretation "that the people hoped the queen would give birth to Jesus." In several places, as he did in previous essays, he briefly forgot that he presented himself as a true Christian and included himself with *my people*. His people were still hoping to be redeemed by God and were still counting the *Omer* (the 50 days between Passover and *Shavuot*). He suggested that "His Holiness enjoined the reading of this letter in every congregation during Mass throughout Spain." Knowledgeable Crypto-Jews, he figured, would undoubtedly understand the true message behind the "evidence" presented to them. Alfonso concluded with a prayer "May God, in His mercy, get you (the Crypto-Jews/Conversos) out of darkness into the light according to the wish of your servant, the author, Alfonso de Zamora." Alfonso knew his ambiguous arguments and references were confusing and illogical, but he hoped that Tavera would ascribe them to the character of the Jews.

He then edited his essay and translated it into Latin on fancy paper in his beautiful handwriting. The next day he went to the seat of the Archbishop of Toledo and handed it to the guard at the gate. His Holiness would not grant him an audience.

Three weeks later Coronel sent Alfonso a letter: "Please accompany me to Toledo. I have been summoned by the Inquisition to answer a few questions. I am very worried for they are on my case relentlessly." The location of the interrogation was in the center of town, that is, at the seat of the new Archbishop. They both remembered well the first time Coronel was arrested by the Salamanca Inquisitors. Had he been under surveillance all these years? A summons from Toledo meant trouble. Yet, Alfonso thought that Coronel would have been apprehended in Salamanca if the charges had been serious or substantiated. Coronel shivered as he entered the interrogation room. The torture he endured a few years earlier was still fresh in his mind. The scars would attest to those weeks of torture. Alfonso waited in the lobby, pacing the floor.

When Coronel came out sweating and shaken, Alfonso rushed to him: "What the hell did they want from you this time?" asked Alfonso as he hugged his friend.

"They had been informed that Alfonso de Alcalá was secretly Judaizing. They could not arrest him because of his prestige and protection by the Dean. Since we work together, I was ordered to report to the local office of any suspicious activity. My own life and the life of my family would be jeopardized if I refused to oblige. What could I say?"

"God damn them!" Alfonso exclaimed fuming. "Why Alfonso de Alcalá? Do you think he is a Judaizer? I thought he was the rat who delivered you to the Inquisition." He was truly surprised.

"Since then, I have kept our relationship strictly professional, so I have no inkling to his activities outside the University."

"Trust in HaShem for ever and ever. For He has brought low those who dwelt high up, has humbled the secure city, humbled it to the ground, leveled it with the dust," Alfonso quoted Isaiah.

"Amen and Amen," responded Coronel, still shivering of the horrid experience.

"We need nourishment and then we shall get out of this wicked city. You have a long way to get home."

Coronel's interrogation in Toledo intensely affected his health, and four months later he suffered a massive heart attack. He died on September 30 of that year. His wife María sent Alfonso a note of Coronel's passing, and he rushed to Salamanca to express his condolences. María and her children, together with Alfonso and his children, went to the grave site to say Kaddish.

At that time, Alfonso was working on the restoration of four biblical books: The only Targum Onkelos with *Tosseftot* he had ever restored; the only Ramban's *Commentary on Job*; Radaq's *Commentary on Isaiah* which served as his source for another copy a year later; and Radaq's *Grammar Book*. His teaching was praised unanimously by his students and colleagues at the end of that school year. His relationship with Aldo was going strong and their shared study generated much joy.

However, 1534 was a year of frustration, sadness, and overwork. Despite his contempt for the level or commitment of Hebrew studies in Salamanca, Alfonso was invited to teach there as a guest professor in 1525-26 and again in 1533-34. He described the value of his existence as "the greatest act of kindness God has done in order to make the Hebrew language in Salamanca known in its truth. The second divine act of kindness was exposing the folly of Sanchez who had magnified himself in deceit." Alfonso suspected that Sanchez cheated in his final exams and in his application for a teaching job at the university. Sanchez was among his students who, according to Alfonso's evaluation, flunked his class, failing all twelve basic course qualifications.

In 1534, when he discovered that Salamanca University was considering hiring Sanchez as professor of Hebrew, Alfonso was appalled and infuriated. This was proof of the unequivocally low standard of education being pursued in the Hebrew Department despite his efforts to raise it. He sent an urgent letter to the Dean decrying their decision: "It is an abomination to confer the title of Professor on my failed student. The twelve requirements to pass the Hebrew proficiency have not been met, and therefore he certainly cannot qualify as a Hebrew teacher." Alfonso's letter was ignored, and Sanchez joined the faculty as a junior teacher.

Alfonso's teaching curricula did not change, and a new cadre of scribes was trained for future assignments. Having had extra time at the end of 1534, he resumed his work on Abravanel's *Commentary* in September, but his eyesight did not allow him to punctuate the tiny, printed letters in the books of the Minor Prophets. Between 1535 and 1537 he copied only three manuscripts with Latin and restored one. His finances were solid, and he was enjoying his grandchildren. As for Jeromillo, he had not seen him since he raped María. In the meantime, Camila, their devoted maid, passed on and faithful María took over the care of the house and of her master.

In the cold night of February 9, 1535, the sound of pistol shots was heard in the streets of the *Juderia*, an event never transpired before. No one dared to come out. The next day the residents found out that murder had been committed in their midst. The respectable Alfonso Gomez, the wealthy businessman and a graduate of the Alcalá University, was the target of the murder attempt. But more shocking was the murder of his slave he had brought from the new colonies. According to his own report, "a gang of three former soldiers were roaming the streets when they came upon my carriage driven by my Indian servant. They appeared drunk. The gangsters stopped the horses and threw slurs at my slave and challenged him to a fight. I begged them to leave us alone, but they dragged my poor slave to the ground and began beating and kicking him. I offered them money, which they took, but their bullying did not abate. They started shooting when I began to yell for help. The slave was shot several times and a bullet grazed my arm. I took the reins and directed the horses toward the police station. The gang dispersed to all directions."

Policemen were immediately dispatched to the homes of the gangsters, and one by one they were arrested. The next morning the Chief of Police convened the public in the Plaza Major and reported on the events of the night before. His eyes were red from insomnia: "We will not put up with such disgraceful behavior by disorderly soldiers or anyone else. We will not tolerate shooting in our quiet and respectable city. We will charge the three criminals for murder and attempted murder within a few days. Rest assured that such abominations will not happen Here's more."

The mob that gathered in front of the police station shouted: "No apologies! Hang them!" "Hang their parents too! Shameful upbringing!" "Uproot evil from us!"

Don Gomes took to the podium and silenced the agitated civilians: "Let the police do their job! We thank our Chief of Police who acted quickly and courageously so that no such crime would be repeated. Let us all thank him!" Citizens cheered loudly for several minutes.

"Please return to your home. You are all safe. Thank you for your trust and patience," the Chief concluded.

Alfonso, like the rest of the crowd, returned home. He was still troubled by the violence in his town where most of the residents were university-affiliated or were wealthy merchants. He documented in his diary the incident in a confused and unclear manner. He was so upset!

At that time Alfonso copied the book of Genesis with interlinear Latin in his diary. He prepared his own commentary based on his views of his society and of his own life. The Hebrew text availed him with a great opportunity to criticize the Spanish elite in general and the Inquisition in particular. He viewed the Spanish elite as "fat and boorish, who follow the filth and maliciously despise the poor, who are wise in their eyes and believe they shall inherit heaven, but their destiny is hell. The educated among them are the naturalists who perceive the world like Aristotle, rather than the spiritualists who have a better grasp of the purpose of life. They, the spiritualists, perform acts of kindness, and therefore they shall attain the World-to-Come. The multitudes of Spaniards are fools and stupid and ignorant and evil, like the Flood generation who deserved annihilation. They are known to be vulgar in matters of science. And as for the priests, they take advantage of their flocks. They are malicious who spend excessively on their own comfort."

Contrary to the Gentiles of his day, Alfonso depicted the Jews in this Genesis commentary, as "brilliant scholars like the Rambam, and the Talmudic and Midrashic Rabbis. To stay spiritual and ethical and reach the World-to-Come, one must observe the 613 commandments. Jews must be ready to fight their enemies, for God would always protect His beloved and holy people Israel. Through His *Shekhinah,* Israel will be forever divinely protected."

But to be worthy of God's grace, Alfonso turned to the Conversos and advised them to pray: "YHWH, God of our ancestors, pray, redeem us! My people, be strong and fear not the Inquisitors! When caught, hide your true faith deep in your heart and do not give up your secret life. Tell them what they want to hear. Distance yourselves from the *Minim,* those sinners who had abandoned their Judaism, for they are carnal and know not spirituality."

Alfonso personally felt that God was testing him as He tested Abraham, but he kept his faith and did not waver: "I am like Joseph and Daniel who served their masters in exile but never gave up their faith. And more so, through Judaism they contributed to the betterment of their society." "The Expulsion," he wrote on another occasion, "is another divine test for all the Spanish Jews. I am doing my part in perpetuating Judaism through the teaching of Hebrew and Jewish literature, while pointing out the errors of Latin and Greek translations on which Catholicism depends. In my interlinear or parallel Latin translations I offer a more traditional and accurate text." He felt safe enough in his diary to reveal that "no one knows my secret life."

When Spring came and flowers bloomed in bursts of color and fragrance, a man appeared at Alfonso's university office holding a folder in a bag. Appearing anxious to meet the famous scholar, he could not sit still, pacing up and down holding his bag tightly to his chest. He waited for over an hour until Alfonso showed up carrying his books and a shoulder bag. A student was following him carrying some of Alfonso's manuscripts. Alfonso placed his load of books on his desk and asked the student to do the same and leave.

The guest stopped pacing and faced Alfonso who looked at him perplexed: "How can I help you?" He sat on his chair and waited for the reply that did not tarry to come.

"I am so honored to meet you, Professor Zamora," began the man who looked tired, as though coming from a long voyage. "Your name is known throughout Spain. In Guadalajara we are very proud of you."

Alfonso could not understand at first what was the purpose of this information. Was he sent by his cousin Isabel? Was she ill? Did she pass away? "I guess that you have come here from a distance not to tell me how proud you are with my work."

"You are right, sir. I have come to consult with you on a delicate matter."

"What delicate matter you are talking about? I am not a physician nor a reader of astrological signs. In what way can I be of help to you?" He paused, then continued: "Perhaps you start by telling me your name as you know mine."

"Doctor Francisco de Medina of Guadalajara is happy to make your acquaintance," he answered bashfully. "I have here in my hands a parchment of Hebrew nature, which I would like you to translate. Of course, set your price and I will pay whatever you charge. I know your translation will be executed perfectly."

Alfonso now understood the pride of this man and his community. Medina was a Jewish name, meaning 'town' or 'walled area' in Hebrew. Many Conversos lived in Guadalajara, as did his cousin's family. "And how do you know I have the time, dear Doctor Medina? I am a busy teacher with many obligations to my university and my students."

"Here, look at this paper and tell me if it will be too time-consuming, sir," the Doctor pleaded. He approached the desk and laid down his precious document in front of the professor. Despite the stains from humidity, the old parchment could still be read easily.

Alfonso read the first few lines and held his breath. It took him a few minutes to relax as Medina watched. This time Doctor Medina was perplexed. Alfonso asked him to sit down. "I have been so rude. Please rest from your travel." He got up and went to the corner by the window and poured water into two glasses. He placed one in front of the guest and one for himself. The two men drank.

"Before I decide whether to accept your request, please tell me how this paper came into your possession? Does it belong to someone you know? Do tell me."

"No, I don't know its owner. I received it from a farmer who resides in Trijueque, a short distance away from Guadalajara. He was rebuilding his farmhouse on top of existing foundations when he noticed a brick was missing. He felt his hand in the space and came out with a cloth bag that contained this parchment."

"Has this farmer been living on that farm for generations?"
"No. As far as I know he was granted this farm by the Archdiocese 43 years ago." Medina looked at Alfonso to detect an acknowledgment of information. Alfonso remained focused on Medina's face. He did not know if it was wise to reciprocate in this game of insinuations. The Inquisition had its way of planting mines under the feet of Conversos. Medina's answer confirmed his suspicion that the farm had belonged to a Jew. And he knew who that Jew was.

"The subject matter appears to be interesting. As I said, I am a busy teacher. However, if you please, leave this parchment with me. I promise to translate it within the next two weeks. Come back then and we'll set the fee."

Medina was pleased. His excitement was tempered in his reply: "Very well, Professor Zamora. I will be back in two weeks."

The two men got up and shook hands. Medina left in high spirits while Alfonso sank into his chair and began re-reading the old *ketubah*, the marriage contract of Aldo's grandparents from 1473, a year before he himself was born. He could not wait for Sunday to meet his friend and mistress. He dashed to her home right after his workday was done, not even stopping at home for dinner. When she opened the door, he went straight inside without greeting her.

"You look upset, or are you agitated? Something profound has seized your emotions. What is the matter, my friend?" She poured him a glass of water mixed with wine and asked: "Have you had dinner yet?"

He shook a parchment he was holding in his hand and sat down on the sofa. "No, I am not hungry. I am excited and moved for you, my love. Come, sit next to me. I want to show you something that concerns your family."

She looked puzzled but she obeyed and handed him the glass which he emptied in a few gulps as if there was no time to waste. He told her about his encounter with Doctor Medina at his office. She began to understand as the unusual story was unfolding: "Trijueque. A farm in Trijueque. The farmhouse that was demolished to its foundations. The Archdiocese that owned it. It makes sense." She remained pensive.

"Exactly," said Alfonso. "Now let us read this *ketubah*. No, you should read it aloud, for it belongs to you."

She began reading the Hebrew text: *On Thursday, eighth day of the month of Tishrei, year five thousand and two hundred and thirty four to the Creation of the World, (the ninth of October, one thousand, four hundred seventy three to their counting), here in Trijueque, the honorable Rabbi Joseph, son of Rabbi Avraham, may he be well, who is a Doctor, said to Simha, daughter of Rabbi Shem Tov, may he rest in Gan Eden: I take you for my wife according to the law of Moses and Israel. I shall provide you with a home, clothing, jewelry and protection. I shall govern you according to the law of the Jewish men who provide and adorn their wives fairly. And I shall give you as a gift for your virginity 200 maravedis that are yours to keep, and for your maintenance, and for your coverings and clothes. And I shall come to you according to the way of the world. And this Simha the bride consents to be his wife, and he consents to these stipulations. And he shall secure for her an additional 300 maravedis.*

Moreover, I, Rabbi Joseph the groom, consent to secure for her a four cubits grave near her family plot. All these are here notarized, plus 400 secured maravedis for the decoration of the bed and the house.

And I, Rabbi Joseph the groom, take upon myself, may I be well, not to take another woman over her and not to take her out of this county to another county against her will. However, if I do take another wife over her, or take her out of this county without her will, she will pay me all that she spent on herself, and I shall release her without libel. And this condition is fortified according to the condition of the children of Ruben and Gad.

And so, Rabbi Joseph the groom takes upon himself and upon his heirs, and upon his furnished estates in Trijueque and in the country, all these conditions according to the law of the Sages, may their memory be a blessing.

And we received the obligations of Rabbi Joseph the groom, about all that is written above according to the use and order that were set by the sages of the Holy Congregation in Toledo. May their Creator keep and shelter them and be their help and have mercy on the remnant who serves Him, who keeps the truth forever. Amen.

Signed: Joseph, son of Rabbi Avraham. Notarized by Rabbi Avraham, Witness. Rabbi Samuel, Witness. Rabbi David, Witness.

By the time she finished reading the marriage contract of her grandparents 62 years ago, her eyes were filled with tears. The two remained quiet, absorbing the words uttered at the wedding ceremony.

"I never had them hug me or bless me or even see me. These righteous people were slaughtered by the murderous Inquisitors. I can see my grandparents removing one brick in their farmhouse foundation where they hid their precious *ketubah* before escaping this cursed land. Like so many others, they believed that the Expulsion was temporary, that they would return soon after. By the time they were dragged back to Trijueque, their estates were in ruins, thanks to the quick action of the Church."

Alfonso felt her pain and longing. "When the Inquisitors arrested them at the border, they forcibly baptized your grandparents. Now as Christians, when they denounced Christianity, they could be charged as Judaizers and sentenced to death. The Inquisitors fell asleep needed them only to aid them in the conversion of the rest of the congregants."

"Yes." Aldonza wiped her eyes and nose with a handkerchief Alfonso handed her. "I can now imagine my grandparents' wedding day. How respectable they were, both coming from leading and learned families. Now I know that Rabbi Joseph was also a doctor.

As I told you on the first day we met, he was also a *shohet* who provided the kosher meat for his congregation. These two righteous people come alive for me. They are real. I can touch them through this sacred paper." Deeply touched, she held the *ketubah* to her heart. "Now I know the names of their fathers. My father told me of his parents' love and respect for each other during their short nineteen years of marriage." She remembered her righteous parents, defiant of the Catholic Church and its ferocious inhumanity.

"I don't believe in coincidences. God meant for us to meet, and He meant me to be where I am now." Alfonso thought of the fate of the Jews and the Conversos. 'How many such stories have taken place around Spain? Didn't his father hide sacred books in his basement? Didn't Jews hide precious documents in graves?'

"You understand that this document must stay with me. It belongs to me. It is my heritage that links me to my murdered family," she implored.

"I think this can be done. Doctor Medina requested a translation. He did not mention the return of the original. I doubt the farmer needs this old paper that is devoid of any significance for him. When Medina returns in two weeks, I will ask him to leave the *ketubah* with me. It is yours, and no one has the right to it."

At last Aldonza smiled. She handed the *ketubah* to Alfonso, who got up, hugged her and left.

In two weeks, Doctor Medina was back in Alfonso's office. Alfonso welcomed his guest with wine and refreshments. Now he was hospitable and respectful.

"Here is the translation as you requested. I have made a copy of the Hebrew text in case you wish to have one. The parchment is old and damp. As you can see, if not secured, saved and restored by expert librarians, it will soon disintegrate and be lost."

"Well, I agree with your opinion. The farmer asked only for a translation. I doubt he cares for the Hebrew text which has no meaning for him. I will give him your copy of the original to compensate him in case he demands the parchment. He is simply curious of the paper he found."

"Then this matter is settled. And since you leave the parchment with me, I will charge you half my fee. I hope this is agreeable to you." Alfonso smiled benevolently.

Doctor Medina agreed. He paid as he was charged and left satisfied.

One day in early 1536, Alfonso came home to a weeping María. The house looked like a hurricane had just passed through. Every cushion and mattress, every cabinet and rug were overturned, strewn everywhere. Clothes were on the floor and some dishes were broken. Ashes from the oven were scattered around the living room. "Who was here, María?" Alfonso asked. He did not really need to ask. The Inquisition was looking for something incriminating. He knew what they were after.

"Several priests came with policemen. They asked me to stay outside in this cold and it took them three hours to finish their search. They had the audacity to help themselves to food and wine." She went on weeping.

"Did they go down to the basement?"

"I am not sure. They might have, because the rug over the floor door seems to have been disturbed."

"Calm down. I shall help you take care of the chaos."

They went from room to room and returned order. María was cursing the priests as she was cleaning. When they finished reorganizing the house, Alfonso took an oil lamp and went downstairs to the basement. The Inquisition agents moved the furniture to the center of the long room, and a variety of items were strewn on the floor. They did not touch the books, nor his desk. They apparently had orders to respect the famous Professor's teaching tools. Adalberto Muntaquez's written incrimination of Cisneros and confession, as well as Alfonso's diary, were intact. The cache of his Jewish rituals was still deep in the secret drawer in one of his trunks. Thank God they were so ignorant. That was the second time the Inquisitors raided his house for Adalberto's document. Somehow, they found out of its existence and of Adalberto's visit at Alfonso's home before leaving Alcalá. It was no more than suspicion, Alfonso hoped.

The next day Alfonso appeared at the local Inquisition office and asked to see the head priest. Fabela was seated at his mahogany desk looking very important. Alfonso was ready for a fight. Fabela pretended to be unaware of Alfonso's reason for the visit. Usually, he encountered Conversos in dungeons.

"Your Honorable Priest Fabela," Alfonso asserted. "Your people invaded my privacy and harassed my maid. They turned my home upside down and caused damage to my property. Will you explain this unacceptable conduct?"

Fabela looked at Alfonso with apathy. Although Alfonso was well known and respected at the University, he had no supporters in the Inquisition. Since Archbishop Fonseca died two years earlier, the University was patronized by the anti-Conversos' Archbishop Tavera who gave the Inquisitors a free hand to harass and abuse the Converso professors. Fabela was a master at doing as he pleased, especially with the Conversos.

"Professor Alfonso de Zamora," Fabela spoke slowly, as though each word was an insult, "I do not need to divulge to you the reason for our search. But since you have come all this way, I will grant you the honor. You see, it came to our attention that a certain Morisco man in the service of our most beloved Grand Inquisitor, Archbishop Jimenez de Cisneros, caused his untimely death. He had documented the execution of his plan on paper, and we believe that this said document is held in your possession. We would like to retrieve it."

"What is this documentation, as you claim, doing in my possession? Why should an assassin trust such an important and incriminating paper with me? His Holiness Cisneros was my patron and benevolent master, and I was his faithful servant. Can you explain this?" 'Interesting,' thought Alfonso, 'the matter of the sexual liaisons with the so called "servant" was not mentioned! This must be the underlying fear the Church needed to suppress.'

"No, I cannot explain this, but we heard from a reliable source, that you were the recipient of that document."

"Who is that, as it were, your 'reliable source'? If it is a Morisco man, perhaps it is a hoax to denigrate the Catholic Church? He dug a trap and you fell into it."

"We keep spies in Fes who would have no compunction in killing their parents for large sums of money. I have no doubt he was telling the truth."

"Your informant is lying. I do not know anything of a document written about that murder. Have you considered that he left it, if there is such a paper, with someone who was close to him? We were never friends or colleagues. I and my family have been faithful to our Holy Faith without a blemish! Your invasion of my privacy was an evil act, and I do not expect to see your men ever again in my home."

This time Fabela was quick to respond: "Not an evil act. Unfortunate, perhaps." He motioned with his hand to dismiss Alfonso.

Alfonso turned his back to Fabela and exited his room holding his head up. 'I might have not convinced him of my innocence, but at least I planted suspicion of a possible error,' thought Alfonso as he headed to the University, quite pleased with himself.

For thirteen years Alfonso kept Gabriel and Pessah's letter and whereabouts from Sofia and Juan. He needed to be certain of their adherence to the Jewish faith. As long as they lived with him, they observed the tradition, but now that they were married and had their own children, there was no room for error. He began visiting them on Friday nights, Saturdays and Holy Days. He was pleased. They kept kosher, the women lit the candles, and the meals were conducted as he had taught them. They were careful to hide all signs that might incriminate them for they knew the consequences.

One Saturday night Alfonso called his children for a private talk. María cleaned up after dinner and retired to her room.

"My dear children," he opened, "I have never told you about your half-brothers, Gabriel and Diego. They left Spain in 1517, when Spain was going through tumultuous times of rebellions and violence. They ended up in Tlemcen and joined a group of Jewish pirates fighting the Catholic fleets in the Mediterranean Sea. They have had great success in avenging our Expulsion and our people's suffering and murder. I have kept a letter they sent me thirteen years ago through a messenger. I would like you to read this letter. It describes their new and fulfilling life, their religiosity, and their thoughts and hopes." He handed them the letter and they read it together by the lamps. He watched their beautiful faces as they became serious then excited. They smiled and Alfonso was relieved. His worries proved groundless.

Sofia was first to respond. Her green eyes, like her father's, were glittering and one might say, mischievous. "I am so proud of them! What courage! What dedication! I have heard of these brave pirates, but I had never imagined that two of my brothers would be actually part of them. This is amazing! I can't wait to tell Danilo. He will be flabbergasted!" She was laughing and hugging her brother.

Juan was dumbfounded. "My own brothers are pirates! I am stunned! They are there fighting our war, and we are here living in opulence! What a waste of life we are leading! Instead of taking revenge, we accept the fate forced upon us by the same people who murdered and expelled our brothers and sisters. I am ashamed!" He was not laughing like Sofia. His face was serious and red.

"Forgive me, my children, for holding this information from you all these years. Our families will be in danger if the word leaked out that my sons, your brothers, are actively killing Catholics and destroying the Spanish economy. By now there have been thousands of Catholics who have been killed or abducted into slavery and forced to convert to Islam. Eye for an eye, said *HaShem*." He paused, looking at Juan who was still in a daze. "I suggest that you approach the subject with your spouses delicately. Do not express your views yet. Wait until they responded honestly. Your lives might be in danger. One more thing," Alfonso added, "to give meaning to his new life, Diego changed his name to Pessah."

They hugged each other and Sofia and Juan drove home in their carriages. Juan was still serene when he arrived home. His wife Anabel noticed his strange and contemplative mood at once.

"What happened? Did you hear bad news? Come to the kitchen and have some tea." She held his arm and gently led him to the chair.

"No, no bad news. Just astonishing news."

She prepared the tea for the two of them and sat down opposite him.

"What do you know about the pirates in the Mediterranean Sea?" he asked watching her reaction.

"Not much, only that there are Jews and Muslims who attack Spanish ships in retaliation for the Expulsions and the Inquisition." She was surprised at the question. The Spanish did not report their losses to the masses. They did not wish the Conversos to rejoice or join their brethren. Foreign traders passed on the news in private communication or in the markets. "Why are you asking about them? You have never mentioned them before."

Juan took his time to respond. "How do you feel about them?"

"They are Jews, like us, right?"

"You did not answer my question." He was not going to answer her question, so she continued: "Fine. I shall answer your question first. How do I feel about them? I suppose they chose one way of vengeance. Men are different than women. We are anchored at home with our families."

"But are you proud of them, or do you find them evil? Or maybe criminal?"

"Look, I do not believe I will be happy if you joined them," she chuckled. "Don't tell me you are planning to leave us to become an adventurer?" She looked at him and then stopped chuckling.

"What would you say if your brother became a pirate? How would you feel then?"

"Well, that's different. If I had a brother, I would be very proud of him. Look at us, accepting the fate that others imposed on us. We do our share in keeping the faith, but will our children and the next generations continue the tradition? I doubt it."

"So, what you are saying is that taking action to assert our independence and tradition is honorable?"

"Yes. Such people are heroes, and we are cowards." Juan felt uncomfortable hearing her strong words about being a coward, but in a way, he concurred with her assessment. His brothers were heroes. He was unaware of his wife's strong feelings about the situation of the Conversos in Spain. He was in a way proud of her.

"If this is how you feel, then I have something to tell you." He began the story of his half-brothers. At the same time, on her way home, Sofia imagined several scenarios and looked for the right way to open the conversation with Danilo. She was an assertive person, someone who always found the right way to express her views and desires. But now she was not unsure.

"This meeting took a long time. Why did you meet your father tonight, darling?" Danilo asked, coming closer and embracing her. He looked at her with anticipation.

"He had something important and secretive to tell my brother and me." 'Good,' she thought, 'he opened the conversation.'

Danilo was even more bewildered. He thought he knew everything about his wife and her family. "Secretive?" he asked, "about himself or his family? I can't imagine anything secretive about his life. I thought we knew it all."

"Well, not really." She wondered how to get to the point, so she remained silent.

He wondered whether or not to press on, so he remained silent watching her struggle with herself. Sofia realized this standstill could not continue, so she blurted out: "Are you comfortable with our life? I mean, life here in Spain. Yes, I know business is good, but is your soul at ease?"

He did not expect these questions at all. Life was good, in fact, very good. They could afford anything they desired. They were healthy and happy.

"My dearest, are you sick or unhappy? I will do anything for you, you know that. What is it about the soul? You are my soul and my reason to live. What is bothering you, my love?" Now he was worried that something was indeed the matter.

"I meant a different denotation of 'soul,' I meant the spiritual side of existence, the real, raw consciousness that links you to the divine, to our heritage. Does our history as a people touch you? Do you wonder about our fate here in Spain?"

"I suppose these were my parents' dilemmas and considerations.

I was born into this reality. I accept it."

"But it is important to you to observe, at least some, of our traditions and pass them on to our children. Isn't it?"

"Definitely. My grandparents are still alive, and they would be devastated if we did not. My parents are less strict but nonetheless they observe basic tenets of our faith and expect us to do the same."

He focused his gaze to the beautiful face of his wife and asked: "Sofia, my dear, what is the real question behind this conversation?"

"If I understand you correctly, we simply accept the Spanish treatment of Conversos without some type of reaction."

"Do you mean to take up action like a rebellion or sabotage?"

"Or attacking ships on the high seas?"

Was Sofia serious? Did she really mean literal action against Spain for the Expulsion and the suffering of the Conversos?

"Are you serious? What do you have in mind? Would you like to take up arms and leave your comfortable life behind? I am really confused."

Sofia smiled for the first time. "Do not worry, my dearest husband, I am not going anywhere. But what would be your reaction to, let's say, retaliating by attacking Spanish ships?"

"It sounds dramatic and daring. That would not be my choice, but those who risk their lives to avenge their families, are courageous and praiseworthy."

"I agree. What would you say if I know two such people who are courageous and praiseworthy?"

"You do? Do I know them?" Danilo's curiosity level was piquing up and up.

"No, you do not know them. They are my half-brothers from Zamora, Gabriel and Pessah. In fact, they are doing extremely well as pirates. They refused to live among murderous and evil people and chose liberty and revenge. I am very proud of them. So now you know."

Danilo's mouth opened in surprise. When he recovered, he said: "I salute them. They are much better than I am. But this should not go beyond these walls."

"I concur. I was not sure about your reaction. Forgive me, my love." They stood up, embraced each other and kissed passionately. Then they went to their bedroom, Sofia's head on Danilo's shoulder.

Soon after Alfonso completed his final commitment for Professor Pedro Ciruelo, he met his former student, now Bishop, Francisco Mendoza de Bobadilla who was visiting Alcalá. "I am planning to write a medical book. What do you think of this new venture?"

"This is exciting. Allow me to sponsor this essay. It will be an honor," Bobadilla responded.

After an initial objection, Alfonso accepted the offer. He titled the work *A Treatise in the Time of the Plague*. Its subtitle served as the opening of this unusual composition: *A most necessary and most beneficial treatise, which contains a brief regimen to be able to control the health at the time of the plague. Also, to know how to cure and remedy those who are affected.*

This handbook in twelve pages focused mostly on prevention and on treatment in short sayings. The front page identified the patron as *the most illustrious and most reverent Lord Don Francisco de Bobadilla, Bishop of Coria, Archdeacon of Toledo*, to whom Alfonso dedicated this work. Four years later their collaboration would repeat itself.

Scholar and humanist, Bobadilla was a friend and supporter of the controversial Erasmus who faced much condemnation. As such, and especially as an elite ecclesiastic, he commissioned books and original works, and supported literary works such as this treatise. Now, in 1537, at the young age of 29, he was already a Bishop and an Archdeacon, an unheard achievement.

The second dignitary to whom Alfonso dedicated his work was *the most famous and virtuous, Doctor Antonio de Cartagena, professor of medicine in the most prestigious university of the most noble town of Alcalá de Henares.* The Doctor edited the medical aspect of the treatise. Following the two dedications, Alfonso introduced himself as *the author, who is an authority on the Sacred Scriptures, and who is a professor at the University of Alcalá de Henares, with other spiritual disciplines for the superior clerics and the ecclesiastics.*

Compositions on how to deal with diseases had been written before. Plagues recurred in Spain in disturbing frequency and thousands lost their lives. Avicenna (Ibn-Sina) had already written *Canon de Medicina* in the 11th century, which was translated into Latin by Gerardo de Cremona between 1150 and 1187. Maimonides, in the second half of the 12th century, in the fourth chapter of his *Mishneh Torah*, offered advice on preventive medicine for the body and soul.

After the outbreak of the plague in Spain in 1348, several other medical treatises were composed. One was written in Toledo following the outbreak of pestilence there in 1489 or 1506–1507. The identity of the author of this treatise had not been established and he was known as "the Licenciado Vazquez" of Toledo. His *Tratado Contra la Pestilencia* did not save him from the Inquisition which prosecuted him as a Judaizer. This work and perhaps previous such essays came to Alfonso de Zamora's attention and inspired him to add his voice. He, after all, suffered ailments throughout his life.

"On what do you base your knowledge of symptoms and treatments?" Bobadilla had asked.

"From my own experience of sickness, and from my maids' therapy," Alfonso had answered.

Whether affected by the plague or not, his two older maids, Luciana and Camila, used natural home remedies to treat him, which were mostly useful and beneficial. He began writing notes on their concoctions and advice at those times which gave him the idea in the first place. The text was written in a short series of poems or proverbs and at times appeared to be either confusing or contradictory. He began with an ode "to the most high and eternal God, the Creator of the world, the powerful, who lights my ingenuity, and who grants health to mankind and helps me through times of sickness." The purpose is stated next: "Since the plague is very painful, one needs to have faith in the Sacred Scriptures and their arguments and reasoning, otherwise insanity prevails. The plague in Spain is constant and certain. It has spread to the homes where 28,500 people have been suffering in great torment." His holistic approach viewed the symbiosis between body and spirit to be essential to complete recovery.

"Preventive measures begin with the trust in God," Alfonso advised. "The right attitude is paramount, for to be sick brings anger and sadness. To combat sinking into melancholy, the wise patient must look for pleasant environments. A sense of humor can disperse the ghosts of death and can enable the sick to reach the other side, where complete light reigns."

He continued: "The proper diet for a healthy body is to avoid excessive intake of sweet delicacies. Scents of fine perfume and rose-water, as well as vinegar in sauces, are always beneficial, especially in the summer. Water and wine are always good beverages. The afflicted should limit the intake of dry fruits and avoid fish in winter, but garlic and olives are always beneficial.

When sick, in order to increase perspiration to overcome the infection, and to add relief for the overall sense of sickness, pink sugar is the right medicine. While the infection is ravaging, chicken broth and saffron, cow fat, egg yolk or milk are perfect remedies. Intimacy has no place during the battle for healing. It must be strongly resisted. Extreme work and walking in the summer are to be avoided at all costs, for warm winds engender the outbreak. If possible, the afflicted should refrain from talking and rather resort to listening, especially to the wisdom of the holy prophets. And of course, the sick person should trust in the merciful God to help doctors find remedies.

The infirm must keep calm and surrender to the prescribed medicine by the Doctor, whose goal is to alleviate the pain. The involvement of friends and brothers in the care of the afflicted is crucial, even though it takes sweat and blood and bravery. At a time of emergency, all measures ought to be taken to prevent further damage, like a house on fire which needs dousing. Some people remain apathetic and deny the man's suffering, whereas others believe something must be done. At that time of affliction, people come up with odd remedies like taking poison. But poison goes straight to the heart without losing a moment, and then the journey of life comes to an end." He reminded the readers that "the affliction is blind, for it affects any age." Baby Princesa was still on his mind.

Alfonso concluded with the advice "to be of a clean soul, and to pray to the Redeemer, the King of Heavens, who saves us and grants comfort to the supplicants." Considering his two Catholic patrons, Alfonso then penned a few lines in honor of "the holy Virgin, who gave birth to the son of God because of many sins." This is followed by a poem dedicated to his educated readers, in which he quoted the great poet Juan de Mena. Alfonso ended with the dedication of the treatise to "Jesus and his mother in applying the corporal regimen to the spiritual."

For many years, Alfonso was obsessed with the great poet Juan de Mena, quoting from time to time his short proverbs of observations on life. Alfonso felt that he could imitate those proverbs at the end of this treatise. When he looked back, he was pleased with his creation. His proverbs, some analogies, were as good as Mena's. Here they were, pearls of wisdom, to uplift the spirit of the afflicted: "The careless shepherd finds deceit; at night darkness is very certain; to use prudence, in time it is haunting; it is much madness to put oneself in danger; all the property of larceny or the tailor's disaster, are relative."

It was by no means a scientific article but rather an attempt to combine several sources with his own observation and experience. He felt proud by his venture into a brand-new territory and by the patronage of two extraordinary scholars. That was a tremendous achievement for Alfonso the professor of the Holy Scriptures to associate with those luminaries. The two patrons helped him publish his new venture, but this time, not by Eguia.

Partly retired, Alfonso took his time to copy books, either for the universities or for himself. By now he had accumulated a large library at home. At the age of 67 his old patron, Francisco Mendoza de Bobadilla, still the Bishop of Coria, commissioned him to copy Radaq's *Commentary on Psalms* for private study. Coria was a long way from Alcalá, and the communication and payment were bartered through messengers while the Bishop stayed in Toledo. It was a lengthy assignment but fortunately Alfonso had two books from which to consult. However, both contained Radaq's nine rebuttals of Christian interpretations, which were banned by the Catholic Church. On the other hand, did the bishop choose this particular book to study the Jewish rebuttals against the intentional Christian misinterpretations? It would be safe to leave them out.

Alfonso invested much time and effort to satisfy the quest for knowledge of this famous Bishop of Jewish ancestry. Alfonso's square and uniform Sefaradi script was strong, and beautifully executed, his artwork remarkably artistic. With black and red ink, he decorated and embellished each page tirelessly, sometimes intricately, with rich ornaments in a variety of motifs and in large characters. The margins were also flanked by two vertical lines ending in crosses. The few opening words of each chapter, and of some verses, as well as the acrosticon of alphabetized Psalms, stood out in larger red letters. Biblical references were largely noted on the inside margins.

Several marginal annotations and remarks carried both Jewish and Christian perspectives, conveyed covertly and overtly. Alfonso felt he could trust his patron with his views, recalling their last conversation as professor and student. When Radaq meant the First or Second Temple exile, Alfonso ascribed it to the "Spanish expulsion of the righteous under the hand of the evil ones." He referred to the Jewish leaders of the past as "my Rabbis." He could not extol the Jewish mysticism of the Kabbalah as Radaq did, so he offered a different angle by saying that in that case "Kabbalah meant the Hebrew Bible, which we must believe in and never deny." Alfonso could not resist this directive, which had been his habitual tendency throughout his life's work. All the annotations were penned in Hebrew, a communication that pointed to the common heritage with the Bishop whose knowledge of Hebrew was commendable.

When the copying of the fourth book of Psalms was done, Alfonso wrote, "we shall begin the fifth book, with the help of the God who completed His work on the sixth day." This was his coded reminder to his patron that the day of rest was the seventh day, not Sunday.

In his dedicatory finale, Alfonso depicted Toledo as "the laudatory city," a borrowed expression from Ezekiel, who thus named Tyre-on-the-sea, then confident in her maritime power. In that passage Ezekiel prophesied total destruction for the Phoenician city. Alfonso left double coded messages in which he hoped for the destruction of Toledo, the center of the hateful Inquisition, and a condemnation of Spain as a maritime hegemony in the 16th century as Phoenicia was in days of yore. His allegiance was preserved for his sons fighting the Spanish fleet.

Even though the anti-Jewish texts had been removed, Alfonso still mentioned Radaq's arguments whenever Radaq claimed that those specific Psalms had nothing to do with Jesus or Christianity. As in other manuscripts, Alfonso presented Christian interpretation devoid of substance, and often repeated flat claims that its Christian attribution was right. At least Bobadilla could see Alfonso was trying to show some adherence to his new faith. Alfonso's attitude to the commentary was clearly ambivalent by design in order to remain protected.

Bishop Bobadilla cherished the book and took it with him when he moved to Italy in 1546. Before returning to Spain in 1552, he sold it to one of the book traders. A century later the book was sold to Henri Dormal, a Belgian-educated librarian of Cardinal Francesco Barberini, and a speculator in manuscripts. It is unknown under what circumstances did the book reach the Napoli Brancacciana library, its latest repose.

Juan Pardo Tavera became the Primate of Spain, the Archbishop of Toledo in 1534, and the Grand Inquisitor in 1539. His absolute power had the official cachet of the King. From this elevated and powerful seat, he began scheming against the New Christians who held professorial positions in universities across Castile. The Dean of the Alcalá University announced to the teaching staff: "Cardinal Tavera is targeting our academics and books written by Jews. However, fortunately, he is busily involved in the politics of King Carlos, whose wars and intrigues keep him often away from Spain. As a result, he has appointed Archdeacon Gaspar de Quiroga to represent him at our establishment."

"Why has he targeted our university?" one faculty member asked.

"For Tavera, the study of Hebrew and Aramaic at the Salamanca University has been more than sufficient for these subjects," answered the Dean.

Quiroga had a lean and pale face with a pointed beard. He loved to dress in fancy clothes, a full-length embroidered cassock, and a bejeweled mitre. He ardently believed that appearance engendered respect and fear. Settling comfortably in Cisneros's palace, he began earnestly to intervene in the administration of the Alcalá University and its faculty. He put constant pressure on the Dean and the Council to close the department of Oriental Languages. When they refused, he pressured them to fire or at least to decrease the number of the Converso professors. These professors taught in every department, especially in the sciences. When again the Board refused, he asked to see the curricula of the University. He immediately ordered the removal of all the books written by Jews, such as Avraham Zacuto's *The Great Composition* and Geronides's *The Wars of the Lord,* both on astronomy which were translated into Latin during their lifetime. Again, his order was ignored. It was unheard of for the Church to force Universities such as Salamanca and Alcalá to determine the type of books to teach or the teachers to hire. The Inquisition, though, could obstruct the promotion of the department heads.

A committee was formed to handle the situation. The Dean announced at the meeting: "The pressure from Cardinal Tavera through Quiroga is mounting. We must bypass them by approaching the King directly. For many years the King has been our protector and chief supporter. We shall send a special and reliable courier to His Majesty the King."

"But I understand that King Carlos and King Henry VIII are right now invading northern France in an attempt to break the French- Ottoman alliance that had conquered Nice," reminded one professor. "It will be very difficult and dangerous to find him on the battlefield."

"Yes, I am aware of the awkward circumstance that is working against us, but we must act now. It will take weeks until we hear from the King, and in the meantime Tavera and Quiroga can devise new strict measures."

The debate continued with a consensus to take the Dean's advice. The courier was selected carefully and secretly. Not a word should reach Quiroga. Two days later the courier left with a letter signed by the committee members urging the King to remember his commitment to the free academic policy at Alcalá. It took the courier ten days to reach the battleground and safely present the letter to the King. In his reply King Carlos wrote, among others: "I order you, Archdeacon Quiroga, to stop at once all hostile actions and respect the University laws. I shall deal with the problem in more detail as soon as I return to Spain," he admonished.

The Committee was very pleased and encouraged. They sent a representative with the King's letter and presented it to Quiroga together with Pope Paulus III's protection documents signed a few years earlier, and with those from former Popes, in which they restricted any Church official from meddling with the university policies and autonomy. But not only did Quiroga tear the documents, he slapped the face of the representative.

As Alfonso was getting on with age, Tavera's lack of respect for the University's academic freedom greatly accelerated his failing health. In his 32 years at this prestigious institution, he worked to exhaustion in order to pass on his love of Jewish traditions and literature, and he raised a new generation of disciples who became famous in their own right. He also ensured the livelihood of other Conversos. He would not give up on his achievements. As he previously wrote in his diary, "A Jew has to be ready for war when faced with evil Gentiles."

Around his seventieth birthday, in the early spring of 1544, the faculty met again to discuss the next step. Many of them, including Alfonso, remembered how they rushed to Toledo ten years earlier to swear allegiance to the new Archbishop of Spain. What fools were they! Such disappointment and humiliation!

The meeting was boisterous, and feelings of rage filled the air. Professor Sebastian de la Cross stood up to speak: "A group of us Board members are willing to respond favorably to His Holiness Tavera in order to ease the pressure and to continue the good grace and support of the highest cleric in the land."

"How can you allow the bullying of the New Christian professors?"

"The well-being of the majority must prevail."

"But the majority of the staff are New Christians!" called Alfonso. "Everyone here has the same rights under the law!"

"If some New Christians are thrown to the lions, so be it!" de la Cross argued. "Weren't our early Fathers thrown to the arenas to be devoured by lions? Some sacrifices have to be made so that our future is secured."

De la Cross's bold position was rejected, and a consensus was reached to write to the only person left superior to Tavera, the Pope himself. They agreed on the content and let Alfonso, as the senior professor in the department, write the letter in Latin.

The letter he composed on Monday, March 31, 1544, was written in Hebrew in the name of Sornoza, Judge and Director of the University, and the entire staff. He was more comfortable and familiar writing in Hebrew, especially when he quoted heavily from the Hebrew Bible. This would serve as the draft for the Latin translation. He addressed the Epistle to *His Holiness, Paulo III, who sits in Rome, and whose wisdom is as vast as that of King Solomon.* In flattering words, replete with biblical references, he rationalized the learning of the biblical wisdom as the foundation for the love of God and the elevation and magnification of the Christian faith, "for if we truly follow this truth, then we shall attain the Heavenly Kingdom. The Hebrew language," he argued, "is essential for the understanding of the holy text, for even St. Jerome taught so. And we, all the scholars at the University of Alcalá, your servants, kiss your holy feet and hands in utter obeisance, and are asking and pleading Your Holiness to save us from the hand of our enemy, the Archbishop of Toledo, who has been persecuting us for no fault of our own."

The letter went on to describe "the utter disrespect Tavera has for the protection edicts by the King, by the Popes, including the current one, and by Cisneros the founder of the University. Tavera is the master of this town, who brings upon us every day, always, many atrocious troubles. And not only did he not uphold the past edicts, but he appointed a judge over us, Quiroga, in great malice, who tore up your holy documents. We are in great trouble with him. He views us as a flock going to the slaughter. We do not know why he commits this perversion, whether out of jealousy or hatred of wisdom, or mammonism, or to lessen the memory of the preceding Archbishops of Toledo." The letter ended with a personal plea from Sornoza and a prayer that God glorified His Holiness.

Alfonso edited his letter and when he was satisfied with the result, he sat down to translate it into proper Latin. He reread his letter, found it satisfactory and put it aside. The Hebrew draft was penned in a most flowery language that revolted himself, but that was the only way to elicit the Pope's sympathy for the scholars. This flattery caused him to reflect on his own life. Here, a Crypto-Jew, trying to save the department of Oriental Languages from another Haman, and he, Mordekhai, was doing his best to hang this despicable man. Will he succeed? Was he influential enough to stem the tide unleashed by the second most powerful man in Spain? Who was he, at 70, but an old man among a gentile society he disrespected and despised? He began writing an addendum, for his eyes only. No, for the next generations of Conversos or Jews who would one day read his diary and realize the truth behind his facade:

"This epistle was written and completed by me, Alfonso de Zamora, teacher of the Hebrew language at the University of Alcalá, for whoever wishes to learn it. And here I am, nearly seventy years old, and I have not enjoyed even one good day in my life. And I wrote this epistle with its vowels so that any mediocre man will understand it, even if he is not a scholar, for scholars do not need vowels. For I am left alone from all the scholars of Spain, from the Expulsion by the Kingdom of Castile, which transpired in the year five thousand and two hundred and fifty-two to the Creation of the world, according to the counting nowadays by all the Jews who dwell throughout the world in exile. Praise to God."

How odd! This was the first time, since working for the Catholic Universities, that he deviated from the formulaic dating in his colophons. He dated it by the Jewish calendar! He looked at the words and smiled. At last, his consciousness came through freely, truly, honestly. He was alone and he was writing in his diary. This felt good.

Alfonso showed the translated letter to Director Sornoza and the committee that night. "Very good, Alfonso, your letter tells it like it is. Still, there is no guarantee the envoy would be granted an audience with the Pope. What is our next step, anyone?"

One professor suggested: "Let us request Pietro Paolo Parisio, Cardinal of Santa Balbina, to be our liaison, for he is the Pope's representative on the University of Alcalá Board of Trustees," he reminded them.

"Good idea," responded the Director, "through him the University has benefited by numerous protective measures to safeguard its academic and administrative freedom. Cardinal Parisio has free access to Pope Paulus who has elevated him to the current high position at the Grand Basilica Church in Rome. He will surely agree to speak on our behalf." Before joining the Church, Cardinal Parisio was married. A celebrated jurist, he taught at the Universities of Padua and Bologna. After he was widowed, he entered the Church and served as a teacher for many years. His sympathy for the University of Alcalá's professors gave the grieved academics great hope.

Sornoza turned to Alfonso and said: "Prepare a letter to Cardinal Parisio along the lines of your letter to the Pope. To secure its safe arrival you will be our honored emissary. I shall provide you with all the necessary documents signed by all the professors."

Alfonso was alarmed. "I am not in good health to travel long distances, Director Sornoza. A young and healthy envoy will better suit this mission. However, the letter will be ready tomorrow for your inspection."

"We'll see. Right now, it is time to go home."

The next morning, April 1, 1544, Alfonso composed the letter to the benevolent Cardinal using almost the same content and style. It was shorter and with fewer biblical references but with similar words of flattery. Alfonso depicted the Cardinal as a "supreme judge whose obligation is to listen to the grievances of the people and repair everything evil and crooked." He compared the professors to the "oppressed people of Jerusalem whom their leaders ignored... The source of our oppression is Don Juan Tavera, who has brought upon us troubles and misery, as our advocate will report to you with the evidence he will carry ... Tavera refuses to honor the laws and privileges that were granted to us by the Holy Father and the former Holy Fathers. He dishonored his name. His representative, by the name of Quiroga (a very evil man), tore the documents of the Holy Father."

On and on, Alfonso described the audacity of Tavera and added: "That is why we, your servants, are reporting all these to you so that you will report them to the Holy Father, who is the earthly representative of God. He is a holy man of God. We have borne all these troubles hoping to get your help. We have all been teaching theology in order to magnify our holy faith. And if you carry out our request, then YHWH will watch over you and keep your foot from stumbling. We bow down to Your Eminence and every day we pray to God to prolong your life, for we have not forgotten the great kind acts Your Eminence has done for us until now. May God save Your Eminence from evil. Amen."

The committee's hope for a sympathetic ear did not last long. Before Alfonso was ready to leave on the long voyage, the news of Parisio's declining health reached the faculty. Alfonso's trip was canceled until they heard better news. The majority of the University Board of Trustees resisted Quiroga and ignored his demands. Fortunately, Cardinal Tavera's political activities kept him away from Alcalá and the pressure was lifted. Quiroga centered his malicious activities on surveying Conversos' movements, especially those of the professors he detested.

Alfonso was slowing down due to declining health. Juan arrived to visit his father alone, for he wanted to let Alfonso know of a very important and secretive decision. They hugged and sat down at the kitchen table. María brought tea and pastries and left the room. Juan went straight to the point:

"*Padre*, Anabel and I have decided to leave Spain. Our children are growing up fast and have adjusted to the Church teachings too close for our comfort. We do not wish to raise them in this Catholic environment. Several of Anabel's family have successfully reached Thessaloniki and we hope to join their trade network. There is constant movement to other safe havens such as Amsterdam, the Caribbean islands or North Africa."

Alfonso listened quietly. He admired his son's resolution and strength of character. He was reminded so much of Izolda, Juan's mother. "Go in peace, my son. I will miss you greatly, but you are doing the right and the courageous thing which I should have done at your age."

"Thank you, *padre*. We were certain of your approval, and we would not leave without your blessing. You have been a role model for all of us and we are proud to be your children. We know that our children will miss your teachings and kindness, love, and personal attention."

"What are you going to do with your business?"

"We have already sold our share to Andre Martinez. Our house was sold last week to Anabel's uncle, so that no suspicion will be raised by the authorities. We shall take the bare minimum to enable us to cross the Mediterranean to Africa. We would rather avoid Christian lands. We plan to visit our brothers in Tlemcen. It is time for a family reunion." He smiled thinking about that moment of engagement.

Alfonso was excited about the idea. "Good planning, my son. When are you leaving?"

"Early morning next Monday, the eighteenth of *Iyyar*. We shall, God willing, celebrate *Shavuot* with Gabriel and Pessah. The children think we are going on a trip, and they are looking forward to this adventure."

"Have you saved enough money to carry out this plan? You know you will have to bribe your way to cross the sea, and even later as you travel further east."

"Yes, we know, and we are ready. We can't wait to get off this disgraceful land."

They continued to talk about the strategy of traveling through Spain, the goals of the emigration and what to expect at the last station. "In Constantinople I hope to engage in import-export business as I have done here. There are ships owned by Jews who trade with China and India. The Portuguese colony in Goa offers entry into India for Spanish traders. There are many opportunities in the Far East for businessmen like me." He chuckled. "Perhaps I will get special privileges from the Sultan for being the nephew of the famous Zamora brothers?"

Alfonso laughed. "Did you know that the Portuguese conquered Goa from the Jewish Kingdom of Cranganore? After the area was flooded, the community moved to Cochin. There have been new migrants from the Iberian Peninsula to that area ever since the Troubles who might be of great help to you."

"Good to know. Did you say, "a Jewish Kingdom"? I must see this place. This is so exciting!"

"As I said, the kingdom does not exist any longer, but there are several Jewish communities in southern India. They were well-known for centuries, even from the time of our holy First Temple. Rambam's brother was a trader who sailed from Egypt to India many times."

Before Juan left, he promised to bring the family for a parting blessing.

The next Sunday, the entire family gathered at Alfonso's house for dinner. Sofia was emotional to see her beloved brother go away. She declared: "I do not know exactly when we shall follow you, but rest assured it may be sooner than later." She had tears in her eyes. Juan's and Sofia's families were close. They made sure the little cousins grew up as siblings. Sofia had revealed to Juan her plan to escape from Spain "only after father will no longer be with us." Theirs was to settle in Constantinople, like Juan, where a growing number of former Conversos from Spain and Portugal had settled. Danilo, Sofia's husband, kept business ties with several of them and hoped to join the Jewish traders on the Silk Road to Afghanistan and China. Who knows?

After dinner, Sofia and her family left, leaving her brother's family to say farewell in privacy.

Alfonso called his grandchildren to come closer. He put his hands on the heads of Raúl and Izolda and quoted Jacob's words to Joseph's sons: "*May the Angel who has redeemed me from all harm, bless these children. In them may my name be recalled.*" At that turning point in the life of his son's family, Alfonso became Jacob Gabbai again. Now it was his time to shed tears. "May God make you like Ephraim and Rachel." He hugged them and said: "Wherever you go, always remember you are Jewish. Observe our tradition with pride, for *it is a tree of life to those who grasp it, and whoever holds on to it is happy.*" So often he had quoted these words in his lifetime!

Anabel and Juan knelt at Alfonso's feet and bent their heads. Alfonso placed his hands on their heads holding back tears, and quoting Moses, he said: "*May HaShem bless you and keep you! May HaShem bless you with His light and be gracious to you! May HaShem lift up His face to you and grant you peace!*" How many times did his own father used to bless him with these words when he was growing up!

Knowing this was the last time their family would be together, everyone let their tears flow and hugged each other for a long time. As Juan and Anabel prepared to leave, Alfonso asked Juan a favor. "I have something to give you for safekeeping." He took a silk-wrapped pouch from under his pillow and handed it to Juan: "This is incriminating testimony against the Church written many years ago by a very special man who escaped from Spain. He entrusted it to me for safekeeping. The Church would do anything to get its hands on it. It must be smuggled out of Spain. He was a Moorish prince whose uncle was the last king of Granada. I do not know if he is still among the living. When you are safe in the land of the Ottomans, publish it. But until then, guard it like a hawk. This will be one way to take revenge upon the Catholic Church which has destroyed our people and is still persecuting us."

"A real prince! But why did he entrust you with this secret?"

"All that he insinuated was that I, as a Jew, represented a nation that suffered like his people by the hand of the same enemy. He might have wanted me to know who killed the man responsible for the death of so many Moriscos. At the same time, he might have hoped to plant in me a desire to be bold and somehow kill another oppressor, perhaps even Archbishop Fonseca, Cisneros's successor. He wanted me to share this bond between the Jews and the Moors and be proud of him. Or perhaps he hoped my children would follow his footsteps and leave this oppressive land. I am not certain of his motivation because he may have several. I can only speculate."

"Did you know him well?"

"Not really. Our paths crossed on several occasions as we both served Archbishop Cisneros. We certainly respected each other."

Juan took the pouch and put it in his inside coat pocket. They embraced again and then they were gone. Alfonso watched them from the front door until their coach disappeared in a distance. He went back inside filled with mixed emotions about his children: He was so very proud of Juan who graduated from the University at the top of his class and with whom he shared a successful business. He buried the memory of his son Jeromillo deep in his subconscious. He felt the rays of joy from his daughter Sofia and her two children for their goodness filled up his sad heart. This was a diametrical contrast to the awareness that he did not experience one true happy day in his life as an employee of the Catholic Church. The Hebrew dating he used in that personal note was the proof.

In July, the University of Salamanca sent him an invitation to teach in the Fall semester. Alfonso declined without a second thought for he could not go back to Salamanca where his best friend Pablo Coronel no longer lived. He would not leave his daughter's family in his old age. His health was deteriorating and the medicine he prescribed in his *Tratado* was ineffective and Doctor Fernando Citron's medicine resulted in little improvement. Yet, despite his ailments, Alfonso would not rest. He enjoyed reading his Bible and producing more copies, some for himself, others for the university library.

Maria never forgot Alfonso's kindness in rescuing her from the streets. She was devoted and kept his secrets unswervingly. She prepared his favorite foods and fed him patiently when he was incapacitated. She took care of his needs and never complained.

Sometime in June of 1545, Alfonso took a respite from listing the 505 wonders God had brought upon the Jews as documented in the Bible. He called Sofia to come over. She placed a chair in front of him and sat down as he reclined on the sofa. She noticed his yellowed face, sunken cheeks, and weight loss. He was breathing slowly and painfully. He asked María to bring tea and cake.

"My dear daughter. I named you Sofia because I value the wisdom of our people more than anything else. No other nation, past or present, has ever surpassed our written or oral heritage. Millions of Gentiles have adopted our literature but have never been able to reproduce anything that is remotely close to its ethical and infinite teaching. The Inquisition is here to stay, gaining increasing influence as the years pass by. As I see it now, the Inquisition will continue to yield much power and will continue to persecute and annihilate us. Be careful. Follow your brothers and do not look back."

He drank some more. Sofia handed him a slice of cake. "Sofia, my daughter, I shall leave you with my will as Jacob our Forefather had done to his children. My greatest regret was not taking the chance to join Rabbi Sabba when he left Portugal. As you can see, I do not know how many more days I have left. And this is the point for calling you here today. Soon your eldest son, Luís, will turn 13. Danilo and you shall take him outside of the city and teach him his obligations as a young adult Jew. Make him aware of why you do certain things differently than others. Instil in him the love for our heritage. Yes, I know you two have lived Jewishly as much as you could, but he needs to know the reasons behind our rituals. Take him to the Guzmán farm where I took you at his age, to learn how the slaughter is done properly. Teach him the laws of *kashrut* and their reasoning. Make him a proud Jew."

Sofia interjected: "Yes, father, we have already been planning to do just that, as you did to us when we were children. And as we revealed the day Juan left, we shall leave Spain soon. We do not know exactly when."

"Good." Alfonso closed his eyes and rested for a few minutes. He opened his eyes and looked at his beautiful daughter: "I, too, do not know when I am leaving, this world, I mean. It seems sooner than later. When you do leave Spain, take my diary with you. Here it is under my pillow. I still fill up pages in which I record personal activities as well as criticism of the Spanish society. I have composed many essays against the Inquisition and many counsels for Crypto-Jews. I have recorded names of Priests, their furtive and illegal activities, dates and names of their mistresses and offspring. All this must be smuggled out of Spain, and when you reach safety, publish this documentation. I must offer my own contribution to the destruction of the Inquisition and its Church."

Sofia helped him sip more tea. He continued: "If you leave before me, I will hand it over to you. However, if I leave this world first, you will find the diary hidden under the basement floor by the desk." He groped under his pillows and brought out a thick notebook. "This is my diary. I have also written my will for you to cherish. These are precepts and customs by which I have lived."

"I promise, *padre*, to uphold your teaching and will make sure they are observed by my children. I will keep your diary and faithfully carry out your will. Next Sunday we shall all come to visit you as we have done in the past."

She got up and bent over her sick father to kiss him. After she left, her sweet smell lingered on which brought a smile of pleasure to Alfonso's dry lips. He sat up straight and went on recalling on paper the rest of God's miracles. He had already listed the 613 divine commandments once before for his students and now in his diary for his children. Tomorrow, or perhaps the day after, he would copy Isaiah for he was certain that this would be the last time he would have the chance. The book of Isaiah was his favorite, words and prophecies he loved, by the prophet who said, "Here I am, send me" when God asked the angels, "Whom shall I send?" Was his soul the reincarnation of Isaiah? Wasn't he sent to spread Jewish literature and ethics among the nations? It was not extrinsic nor coincidental that Baracaldo had chosen him to teach in Salamanca and eventually in Alcalá.

He copied Isaiah slower than he estimated. Too weak to keep writing for more than an hour at a time, he completed Isaiah almost two months later, on August 28, 1545. At its conclusion, he composed a colophon in Hebrew as was his custom, in which he noted being infirmed. He also mentioned the current Dean, Andre Abahat, and ended with "Praise to God." He turned the page and rewrote "Praise to God" in large red letters. These would be his last words, he decided, for they encapsulated his reason for working and living: to thank his ancestral God for protecting him from evil Spain.

He lay down and ruminated about his life. He thanked God for his parents and wives and children. Well, his youngest son was a great disappointment. Yet, his code of ethics was the foundation of his existence that guided the discipline of his children. Three sons succeeded in escaping from Spain and his daughter would soon follow suit. He took out the letter from his son Francisco in Zamora written two years earlier, and reread it:

"Dear *padre*, I hope you are well, for I worry about your health. I have sad news to tell you about *madre*. She was well until last year when she slipped on the wet cobbles and broke her hip. She suffered indescribable pain and was completely helpless. I hired a live-in maid to answer to all her needs. Her immobility was probably the cause that hastened her death, and she passed on last week with intense pain. She is greatly missed.

It is time for you to retire and spend the rest of your days among us. Please consider our invitation."

The completion of the copy of Isaiah signaled to Alfonso his retirement from academia. The salvific prophecies that ended the book of Isaiah projected their hope on Alfonso: *"For as the new heaven and the new earth, which I will make, shall endure by My will, declares YHWH, so shall your seed and your name endure. And new moon after new moon, and Sabbath after Sabbath, all flesh shall come to worship Me, said YHWH."*

'Yes,' thought Alfonso, 'the Gentiles will come to Jerusalem to worship the God of Israel and witness the death of those Gentiles who had persecuted God's people. God will create a new world where His people will lead the world in unity and faith. Then the Gentiles would be blessed by God for they would come with new hearts of purity and goodness.' What a wondrous scene! He fell asleep with a peaceful smile.

As the newest wave of arrests by the Inquisition created panic among the Conversos who hurriedly partook more often in Church rituals, Sofia and Danilo decided to hasten their escape. *If not now, then when?* they quoted Rabbi Hillel. But first they had to safeguard Alfonso's well-being. No family member was left in Alcalá who would be obligated to care for him. They visited Alfonso on Sunday afternoon. He was lying in bed comfortably and happy to see Sofia's family. After the usual inquiry about his health, Sofia began: "*Padre*, the Inquisition has launched a new wave of persecution and we are worried. We therefore have decided to leave as soon as possible. However, we will not leave you here alone. We think that you should move back to Zamora where Francisco and Leonor would care for you. What do you think?"

Alfonso was ready for this scenario since Sofia and Danilo revealed their desire to escape from Spain. "I was expecting this moment for quite some time. I do not wish to detain you because of my health. Since I have completed all my obligations to the University and officially retired, I have come to a decision to move back to Zamora when you are ready to leave. I shall reside in my parents' home which has been rented out since they passed away. I am financially comfortable and would not be a burden on Francisco and his family. In fact, I received a request from Francisco to retire in Zamora. I sent him a letter of intent and here is his reply which was received two days ago."

He handed an envelope on the nightstand to Sofia. She read the short letter and smiled in relief. "Good," she said, "when do you think you will be ready?"

"A week from tomorrow will be a good day," declared the ailing father. He looked at Sofia whose face displayed worry. "Of course, María will be coming with me. Do not worry. She has already begun packing. We will take only what we need and sell the house furniture. The house itself will go back to the University. I will take all my books with me, of course. Francisco will sell them after I die to the Universities of Salamanca and Alcalá, or to any private patron. They will generate a good amount of revenue."

"And the diary? When can I get your diary?" Sofia asked.

"Right now. Here, I have already wrapped it carefully in this tube. Even if you are stopped and searched, no average person or any local priest will be able to read Hebrew. And especially the personal notes I wrote in illegible handwriting so that only learned Jews could read and understand." He pointed to the narrow cylindrical object on the side table. She held it in both hands with veneration and placed it into her coat's inner pocket.

Alfonso asked: "When are you leaving?"

"A day after you move out, that is Tuesday. We will come to say goodbye early next Monday." She then turned to the children and asked them to hug and kiss their grandfather. Alfonso held them tight as his eyes filled with tears.

"Listen to your parents, my precious grandchildren. You will grow to be educated and professional like me. Now, be on your way." He let them go of his embrace.

During his last week in Alcalá, the neighbors came to bid Alfonso and María good luck in their new home and showered them with small gifts. Their expressions of love reminded him that leaving a home and a community where he had lived for thirty-three years was not as simple as he first imagined.

The week passed and Alfonso's personal belongings and books were packed in crates and mounted on the carriage. Having taken extra care securing the secret treasures once hidden in the basement, María walked from room to room knowing she would miss the only home she ever had for the last 14 years. Here was Camila's and Luciana's room which became her own. Alfonso's deference and kindness slowly dampened the memory of the suffering she endured from his son's cruelty, for he treated her like a daughter. Who knew what was waiting for her in Zamora on the Duero River? She broke from her reverie to the sounds of Sofia's children, Luís and Edmondo. She felt guilty, for she could not extend the usual hospitality. All the food was packed for the voyage.

Alfonso called them to the living room where he sat on the sofa. Knowing this would be the last time they would ever see each other again, he clung to the children even longer. Sofia and Danilo bent down before him, and he blessed them. He then put his hands on the heads of their two sons and blessed them with the Priestly Blessing. "You are going on a long and exciting journey. May the God of Israel be your guide."

'Here you raise children and then they go on their way, and you are left alone with your memories,' Alfonso and María were thinking alike. María and Sofia helped Alfonso climb the carriage and sit comfortably. The coachman was seated high in his front seat, the reins firmly in his hands.

Sofia embraced María. "How do you feel about your move? You were born in this district, and this has been your only home."

"But this is the place where I suffered abuse and degradation. If not for you, I would be long dead. I owe you my life and I am grateful for whatever joy came my way." She stopped to think, then she continued: "I am not expecting much from the new location, but as my master taught me: *A change in place, a change in one's luck.* I hope my master's son Francisco will be as noble as Juan and you."

"Yes, he is, from my father's depiction and from the few times we met at family events."

"I wish you success in wherever you settle. I shall miss you greatly."

"I shall miss you, too. You have been good to my father, and I thank you for it."

The two women fell upon each other in a warm embrace. Both were crying.

The coachman called for the horses to move forward, echoed by the mimicking sounds of the children. Amidst their mischievous mood, Sofia began sobbing as the carriage turned a corner. Danilo embraced her and stroked her hair, murmuring words of comfort. The children stopped running around and looked at their parents feeling ashamed of their own misbehavior.

Much had happened since he moved to Alcalá in 1512, a stranger in a strange city, invading a home of former Jews. Here he married his beloved Izolda, and here he raised his three children. Here he spent years of teaching and working for the same Church which enslaved him, and thousands like him.

Zamora invoked many ambivalent feelings of happiness and of suffering. He was going "back home," to his childhood, to memories of his parents and grandparents, and to his son and his family. 'Alas,' he thought, 'Guiomar passed on two years ago.' He would have loved to see her again, perhaps even to rekindle that love and closeness they had shared.

As he thought about the past, he was oblivious of his surroundings: green fields with isolated farms. Calls to stop disturbed his reveries. A horseman was approaching fast. María looked through the rear and side windows and wondered aloud: "What does he want? I hope we are not being robbed or worse! But he is waiving a paper! He looks official!"

Alfonso's coachman stopped and waited for the horseman to reach him. The rider remained seated on the horse and addressed Alfonso: "Are you Alfonso de Zamora?" Alfonso was not addressed by his title which raised his suspicion as to the reason for this stoppage. María propped him to a seating position. He examined the man and answered: "Yes." He was not going to waste words on this insolent man.

"I have here in my hand an order to search your belongings. Descend the coach at once."

"Who empowered you to search my belongings?" Alfonso retorted.

"This order is signed by His Honorable Quiroga, the representative of His Holiness Cardinal Tavera." He showed the document to Alfonso, who gave it a good look. Yes, it was an authentic signature.

"What is the purpose of your search?"

"It came to our attention that you possess a diary that might cause great damage to our Holy Church. My order is to burn it."

'Just as you burn people' Alfonso thought. He kept the man waiting until the coachman intervened: "Don't you see Professor Zamora is sick? Have compassion, young man! Shame on you! How dare you order him to descend the coach?" He would have continued with his chastisement of the impudent rider if he hadn't been slashed in the face with the man's whip. Despite his wound and dizziness, the coachman held on to his reins. "I will not tolerate this type of bullying and disrespect for the great Professor," he said as he tried to control his pain. He stretched his hand to seize the document, but the rider was quick to move his hand.

The coachman was caught off guard by a second attack, this time the whip caused his ears to ring, and his head felt like it would explode. Still, he held the reins firmly. In self-defence and with the anger of humiliation, he pulled out a knife from his coat and lunged at Quiroga's agent who was taken by surprise by what he thought was a mere low-life peasant. When the knife entered deep into his chest, the man fell off the horse that then galloped away. María was first to overcome the momentary shock. She descended the coach and picked up Quiroga's document from the dust. The official's blood was gushing profusely. He was as good as dead. In a commanding voice she ordered the coachman: "We cannot leave his body lying on the road. Give me a hand and let us bury him under some bushes. Quick!"

They dragged the body to the next large assemblage of bushes. He went back to the coach and brought out a spade and began to dig a hole. The coachman removed the agent's clothes and shoes, and any valuables he found in the dead man's pockets. He then went on to bury him, making sure the grave was well hidden. He covered the blood with dirt. María treated the coachman's cuts, and they were again on their way.

Alfonso was still shaken from the violence he had just witnessed. On the one hand he was revolted by the killing, but on the other, he was calculating: 'What if the agent went through my personal belongings and found my Jewish ritual items stuffed at the bottom of the crates? Heresy and Judaizing charges would be lodged against me immediately. I would not be able to withstand the torture, and my place in history would be obliterated. My good work would evaporate from memory. And yet, a man's life was taken away before my very eyes!'

María understood Alfonso's silence. "Master," she reasoned, "this was not murder. Our man was viciously attacked, and it would not be far-fetched to assume that the attacker would have killed him. Church agents, like this horseman, abuse their power and regard us, the hapless, as non-human with no rights or worthy of considerations."

"But a human's blood has been spilt! I agree with your evaluation, but couldn't we just put fear in him and avoid escalation?"

"No, wicked Quiroga would have sent a large contingent of soldiers to punish us. What we have done is preferable."

While he kept quiet contemplating over her reasoning, the coachman was fuming with anger, outraged of the horseman's gall. He had no problem with the outcome of the confrontation. In his mind, such a man had no right to life.

CHAPTER 14

Prevailed

Let the Lord guide your way, trust in Him and He will deliver.
Psalms 37:5

Tuesday was a good day to start a long and hazardous journey, for on the third day of Creation God declared twice "and it was good." The plan was to reach Seville, the industrial city of silk and wool industry, where the local wealthy trader was business partner of Andre Martinez and his son Danilo. "Garcia de Higuera is a Morisco who, like us Conversos, was forced into baptism," Martinez had told Danilo and Sofia. "His commercial success is due to his genius in enterprise and the innovative color schemes of his textiles. His business owes its might from his close-knit network of family contacts in the Spanish and Portuguese colonies around the world. His family, mostly refugees from the Expulsion, controls much of the textile industry. In addition, Higuera's empire owns a fleet of medium-sized ships which dock in the port of Seville, and which enjoys the protection of the Ottoman pirates in the Mediterranean Sea."

"What has brought prosperity to Seville?" Sofia had asked.

"When the population in Spain was decreasing at an alarming rate mainly from recurrent plagues and the economy in Castile was in decline, Seville in the south prospered. The high taxes by the Church and the Crown were mostly waived thanks to gifts and bribes. Moreover, the plagues have barely reached Seville which adds to the stability of the population."

"In 19 days, the Jewish New Year will begin, and we hope to celebrate it with Sofia's brothers," Danilo revealed to his father.

"If, for any reason, we shall be delayed in Spain, we hope to reach them within ten days' time for Yom Kippur."

"Do they know of your plans?"

"Yes, we have already sent them a letter through an Algerian merchant."

Danilo and family headed directly to Seville via Cordoba to get Garcia's help in crossing to Tlemcen. The parents wore the large crucifixes over their pilgrim's attire. Before leaving, they were endowed with a letter from their parish priest which described the young parents as fulfilling a vow they had made to Holy Mary when their children were born: to visit the Cathedral of Our Lady's Resurrection in Cordoba, and then The Cathedral of Seville, the largest Gothic church in the world. They would thank the Mother of God and her Holy Son for the gift of the birth to their two healthy boys.

They began their "pilgrimage" to Cordoba on the 10th of Elul, 5305 (1545) on a trek of approximately 250 miles, with their personal coachman, Raphael Santiago, at the helm. Driving with frequent breaks and resting only at sunset, they hoped to reach Cordoba in twelve days. Upon arrival, they dined and rested at the respectable inn Posada del Potro. In response to the children's complaints of the boring vacation, Sofia and Danilo promised to visit the historic city the next morning.

Once breakfasted, the family set on foot to see the resplendent buildings and gardens of this former Moorish capital. Finding the old Jewish quarter was their goal. Their first destination was the major mosque turned into a cathedral. The cathedral, built atop part of the grand mosque, ruined the overall sacredness and glory of its former unequaled architecture. Danilo reminded Sofia of that which King Carlos had said when he first saw the new cathedral: "You have destroyed what was unique in the world." The children marveled at the vast Hall of Prayer and the beautiful calligraphy on the walls. The marble columns and floors, and the awe-inspiring decorative arches, were magnificent to behold.

They walked on to the Alcazar castle and marveled at the exquisite gardens, ponds, fountains, trees and aromatic plants. They climbed downstairs to the old Moorish bathhouse and came out deeply impressed by the splendor of the place. On they went to visit the Royal Stables of the Andalusian horses. Here the children became excited and wished to stroke a horse but were denied access for fear of an accident. "They are too young to approach a horse," said the guard to their parents.

Outside they noticed a circular tower. "What is the function of this tower?" Danilo asked a passer-by.

"This is the State seat of the hated Inquisition," answered the stranger. Before he moved away, he spat with obvious disgust. They turned around toward the old *Juderia*.

The alleys were narrow and the houses, now occupied by Christians, still carried Jewish emblems over the doors, panels and walls. They walked with sad faces. "Imagine the Jews walking in these streets, studying and working, trying to maintain their peaceful Jewish life," said Sofia to the children.

"Can we find signs of Jewish life here?" asked Luís.

"No, my child," replied his mother, "for the Jews were first massacred by the Moors, then by the victorious Christians."

Danilo said: "But there are still some remains of an old synagogue. We are now heading to visit it. Be quiet. Do not ask questions, for it might be too dangerous."

The old synagogue was easy to identify by the Hebrew letters over the front door. It had been converted into a hospital which declared its name on the gate and wall. Above the name a large cross was now engraved.

They stood and stared at the building imagining Jews wrapped in *tallitot* coming and going at a time of relative religious tolerance that seemed now eons ago. A nun, dressed in a brown habit, coming out of the hospital, watched them and then asked if someone needed to go in for treatment. Danilo and Sofia were caught without an answer. Sofia was first to regain confidence: "My old father is sick with Hydrophobia, and we suggested to bring him here for treatment. But he won't listen to reason."

"Would you like us to send two men to bring him in?"

"My mother needs to be convinced of this move first. She would rather take care of him herself. We would like to find out about the treatment and the charges, though. Hopefully she will change her mind."

"Please come in and our Mother Superior will give you the information."

Sofia realized she went too far with her story, for now she could not turn down the invitation. As she hesitated, Danilo said with a smile: "Certainly, good nun, we shall follow you."

They followed the nun to a large room. "Mother Superior is in a conference and will be back shortly. Please wait here." They were left alone.

Restlessly, the children looked around the room. Sofia told them to sit next to her on the bench. Reluctantly, they obeyed. "I am tired of waiting here. Such a dreary place," said Luís. His brother, Edmondo, added, "We have just begun to enjoy the vacation. Now we are stuck in this prison."

"Patience, my dears, this should not take long." But it did. An hour passed and they began to suspect that something went awry. Danilo left the room looking for the nun in brown. Several nuns were walking about, each glancing at him with a stern face. With an aura of danger in the air, he rushed back to the room and said: "Hurry, we must leave this place at once." Just as Sofia opened her mouth to ask a question, Danilo responded: "No time for questions. I'll explain outside."

They had just rushed down the stairs when the front door opened. They knew they were trapped. At the door the nun in brown was pointed at them as she talked to a heavy-set man dressed in the garb of the Inquisitors. "These are the people, Father, pretending to show interest in our holy work." She turned to Sofia and Danilo and scoffed with a wicked sneer: "You are not the only Jews who come here pretending to have a sick parent. You always come with your children, damn you!"

The priest motioned for them to go back inside. A small dagger was dangling on a rope around his waist. The nun entered sneering wickedly. Instructing them to sit down, he turned to Sofia and barked: "Take off your clothes! You, too!" he demanded, looking at Danilo.

"This is outrageous!" called Danilo and stood up. "I protest this treatment of faithful Christians. We are not Jews, never have been. Here," he took out the letter from his priest and shoved it to the Inquisitor's hand, "We are pilgrims on the way to the holy places of Cordoba and Seville."

The Inquisitor pushed Danilo back to the bench. He read the letter and threw it on the floor. "You all do the same thing: come here with a phony letter of faith but actually wish to visit your old synagogue. We are not stupid, you know!"

"We are coming all the way from Alcalá de Henares on a holy pilgrimage. We do not know the town. If we had known it was a synagogue, why would we have brought our sons? We are not stupid, you know!"

"Do not be smart with me, you filthy Jew. Your denials do not work on me. Now, shut up and undress."

The children clung to their parents, but the priest pushed them to a corner and ordered them to undress as well. Crying and calling out to their parents, Danilo responded, "Do not worry, my children, do as he says." The nun hurried Sofia to disrobe but Sofia took her time, thus asserting her defiance, stopping only when she reached her underwear. Once the Inquisitor searched the children's and Danilo's clothes and found nothing incriminating, he allowed them to redress. He then approached Sofia and lustfully ogled her naked body. He would do whatever he pleased with her for he was not concerned at all with the nun's reaction. They had been collaborators for many years, after all.

When the priest got too close for Sofia's comfort, she stepped back and looked straight into his eyes. Face-to-face, he moved forward to touch her, but she stepped back again. "Take your filthy hands off my wife!" Danilo shouted just as the nun rushed to him and pushed him back. He almost hit her. The children, now dressed, held on to his arms, looking at the people in the room with terror.

The priest began searching Sofia's clothes. She became apprehensive. What if he found her father's diary? She said: "I am cold. May I have my coat, please."

"Not too fast, Jewess. I have all the time in the world. Let me see what is in this coat of yours." He brought out the contents from the outer pockets and examined every item, discarding them on the floor. He checked the hem. Nothing there. The inner pockets were searched next. He brought out a variety of small items but then his fingers touched a solid and long bag. "Aha! What do we have here?" he exclaimed triumphantly.

Sofia caught her breath for a second for she had to find an excuse, and fast. Danilo blurted out: "These are business notes for my partner in Seville. You can check. He is a very respectable Christian with many friends in the high echelons of the Church. You have probably heard of Garcia de Higuera."

"Yes, I have heard of him, but he is in Seville, and we are in Cordoba." He opened the cylinder case and drew out Alfonso's diary. "What do we have here! Hebrew, right? This is the language of commerce these days? I doubt the honorable Higuera speaks

Hebrew. Arabic? Perhaps, but definitely not Hebrew." He started to peruse, then stopped as though he was hit by lightning. "This is blasphemy! How dare you defile the name of our Holy Sea and his majesty the King! Surely this will land you in the fires of hell! The Inquisitor General of the state of Cordoba must see this!"

The nun moved toward the priest, gazed at the diary and laughed. "They all fall into this pit of deception." She yelled menacingly at Sofia and Danilo: "You fools! Don't you know our priests can read Hebrew? This honorable Inquisitor, in his sinful days, had once studied to become a Rabbi but he saw the light of our Holy Mary!" she cackled as if possessed by demons.

Danilo looked at his wife. She nodded. Understanding that they had to act fast lest they leave that room in chains, she lunged at the nun and strangled her until her lifeless body fell to the floor. Simultaneously, Danilo tackled the priest who fell forward, too heavy to resist the sudden attack. The priest screamed when his face hit the ground, his nose shattered. Danilo grabbed the priest's small dagger while straddling the priest's back and pulled the priest's hair back toward his chest. In one quick movement of the hand, he cut the fat man's throat as he had seen the *shohet,* Mr. Guzmán butcher the sheep. He got up and put on his coat to hide the blood on his clothes. The children were aghast, holding their breath at the sight of the slaughtered man and the lifeless nun. They moved backward and began to mumble incoherently. Danilo hushed them to be quiet. In the meantime, Sofia dressed and returned the case containing her father's diary back to the inner pocket of her coat along with the other once-scattered contents: "Let's get out of this damned place," she whispered as she held the hands of her boys.

Danilo opened the large window facing the back garden, checking to make sure the coast was clear. They moved fast, locking the door behind them. He pushed the key under the door. When the bodies are found, Danilo reasoned, a thief would be blamed for the double murder. They rushed outside. No one saw them going out. The nuns who had seen them earlier, gave them only a cursory look; only the nun in brown and the Inquisitor saw them or knew of their plans. On the street they walked fast, pulling their sons behind only slowing down when they saw their inn from a distance. Knowing not to look dismayed or anxious in any way, they met coachman Santiago and informed him that they were to leave first thing in the morning. They ate in their room, washed and went to bed.

The children were still in a daze. "Try to forget what you saw today and don't mention it to anyone," cautioned Sofia, holding them tight. "Anyone! Understood? You must be brave!" They understood the gravity of their situation and remained quiet but scared. "Don't worry, my brave sons, everything will be fine." One by one they climbed into their parents' bed and fell asleep in their parents' embrace.

"Early morning, they breakfasted in their room. Slowly walking to their coach which was waiting at the inn court, the coachman asked: "Did you enjoy your tour of the city yesterday?"

"I liked the paved streets, and the glazed tiles in the cathedral floors. The gardens were such an inspiration! Such serenity and brilliance! So different from Alcalá. Right, Danilo?"

"Definitely. We must stop here again on the way home." He looked at his children and put his finger over his lips, noticing their dispiritedness.

The scenery was enchanting with its mountains and valleys and brooks. The topography differed markedly from that of Castile. It was hotter and dryer at some areas and greener in others. "Look at these olive trees. They must be at least a hundred years old," noted Sofia who attempted to distract her children's thoughts with the surrounding landscape. "Look at these large estates scattered in the distance." There was no response. "Do you know that there were barely any people living here before the *Reconquista*? You did learn about the *Reconquista*, right?"

They nodded. It was encouraging so Sofia continued: "These large and prosperous estates proliferated in this region 300 years ago, but still, the number of the population has barely grown." She looked at the children and asked: "Why do you think the number of people has not increased, even though there is so much land?"

Edmondo made an effort: "Perhaps because there was no work available?"

"Excellent deduction, Edmondo. What do you think, Luís?" asked Danilo.

"Perhaps because all the lands are owned by the Church or the King?" He was not certain his answer was as logical as that of his brother.

"Excellent, Luís!" said Danilo encouragingly, "I am very proud of the two of you!"

"I can think of two more reasons," suggested Sofia. The children turned their attention to her. "One, that the former Muslims and Jews who lived here left to escape the Christians, and two, that people moved north to find better jobs."

"Good answer, *madre*," said Danilo.

"I have another answer." Edmondo was happy to be part of the conversation. "Farming is really hard work and not many people want to work hard."

"Together we came to some logical observations," summed up Danilo.

The children smiled. The power of deduction made their parents proud.

The traffic was sparse but the closer they reached Seville, the more populous the area became. The golden color of the church towers on the horizon dazzled in the sun. Now the Guadalquivir River could be seen, its water shimmering in the distance. Ships and boats of all sizes and shapes looked like toy miniatures. Even the children, who complained of their boredom most of the time, were excited by the change in scenery. Perhaps this place will be more suitable as a vacation spot.

They stopped at the first inn on their way and sent coachman Santiago to ask for directions to Garcia de Higuera's house. "I can see you are a stranger in the city," the innkeeper said. "Everyone knows where the Higuera's palace is situated. Here, let me give you advice. Be wise to avoid the beggars and the pickpockets and the many criminals who roam the streets. This city is renowned for its ruffians. I better send one of my boys to show you the way." He returned to his office and came back with a young man. "This is Jesus," he told the coachman, "He will lead you safely to your destination. And don't forget to mention my name, Don Manuel Lora de Carmona, to the honorable Don Higuera."

"I certainly will. Thank you for your kindness." The coachman and Jesus climbed the carriage and on they drove through the multitude of shoppers and hagglers, prostitutes and gamblers. Horse-drawn carriages passed as ladies in fancy clothes and jewelry looked unabashedly through the windows. 'God!' Sofia was astonished, 'this kind of public exhibition would never be tolerated in Alcalá!'

The homes of the rich and the powerful were painted white, the windows were draped in lavish fabrics. The balconies were laden with colorful potted flowers, as though competing for commendation. Women coiffed and dressed in satin or silk were seated there provocatively to be admired or desired. The separation between the elite and the rest of society was surreal with so many people coming and going or congregating in every street and alley. As far as Sofia knew there was no Christian festival to be celebrated at that time. She turned to Jesus:

"Jesus, why are there so many people on the streets? The next holy day is November 1, All Saints Day, over a month from now."

"At this time of year, the ships return from their long voyages to the Americas or the Far East. People flock here from around the district to find work and to take advantage of the many charitable organizations. The crowds provide fertile ground for criminal activities from pickpockets to assassins. There is quite a well-organized criminal underground here in Seville. Ladies and even gentlemen do not walk on foot but are driven by private carriages and bodyguards."

He signaled the coachman to stop for they reached their destination. It was a massive building behind a high wall that hid the first floor. Jesus knocked on the side heavy gate. A guard opened a small window and asked for his business. Jesus pointed to Danilo who responded: "We are Don Garcia de Higuera's guests from Alcalá de Henares."

The guard said: "Yes, sir, we have been expecting you." He opened the gate widely for the coach to enter. Danilo paid Jesus for his kindness and coachman Santiago followed the guard's directions, driving to a side area where other carriages rested. The gate guard probably rushed to fetch some employees for as soon as Danilo descended the coach, two burly men ran to help with the luggage. Danilo helped Sofia and the boys dismount and they followed the two porters.

A butler welcomed the guests holding a silver plate with four glasses of water with slices of lemon. "Please refresh yourselves before I take you to your suite." He waited until they finished, then said: "Please follow me."

The suite was roomy, with open windows and bright drapes pooling on the floor. The ambiance was that of a princely Moorish villa: low sofas decorated with brilliantly colored cushions, laced netting draped over a large four-poster bed, a wash station, towels and slippers nearby.

"I feel we have entered a fairy-tale," Sofia observed having admired every part of the room. The children lounged on every sofa, then jumped on the bed. "Let us see the children's room," Sofia called walking through a connecting door. They all stood at the entrance to admire the sight. "Such a happy space!" rejoiced Sofia.

The children ran to one corner of the room where a wooden horse, decorated in the typical colors of the Andalusian equestrians, invited them for a ride. Luís, being the elder, went first. Edmondo raced toward another corner, where never-before-seen games were stacked on shelves. "Hey, Luís, let us try these games!" But Luís was in a different world of horse racing.

Someone knocked on the door. Danilo called to come in. It was a maid who was assigned to the Martinez family. "My name is Mariana. You probably need to freshen up. I will prepare your bath in that room over there. Dinner will be served at the dining room at eight. I will come to escort you."

"Will the children be dining with us?"

"No, I will take care of their meal after which I will put them to bed."

"Thank you," they all responded unanimously.

By eight Danilo and Sofia were ready to meet their hosts. They were accompanied downstairs to the main dining hall. In the middle, a beautifully decorated table was surrounded by several guests chatting amicably or standing with glasses of wine. As the Martinezes entered the room, the host, Don Higuera, hastened to welcome them.

"Danilo, my friend," Higuera said gaily, "welcome to my home. How is Don Martinez? I hope your family is enjoying life in Alcalá. It is such an honor to host the son of my trusted friend and partner."

The two partners gained much wealth by their association. Martinez was in charge of central Spain and Higuera's sphere was the south. Higuera's way to defy the Spanish conquest was to smuggle Jews and Moriscos out of Spain in close alliance with the pirates. His parents were forcibly baptized and, like Jews, lived double lives.

Danilo introduced his wife and Higuera took them over to meet his wife, Narina. Warmly greeted, they were escorted to their seats. Among the guests were the town mayor, the Bishop of Seville, merchants, admirals, and an architect. It was a display of the district's most influential citizens in the realms of politics, religion, and the economy. Higuera introduced the Martinez as business partners who were moving their enterprise to Granada "with the blessing of the Holy Mother." The Bishop hastened to write down the name of Granada's Bishop as a potential patron while one merchant suggested that Danilo contact his brother and partner, an importer of Berber carpets from Morocco.

Danilo turned to the architect who was seated to his left. "How busy are you in this city of contradictions?" he asked.

"Busy, indeed!" He answered excitedly. "The number of churches, nunneries, convents and private homes has exploded since the turn of the century. This city is wealthy beyond imagination. Bankers, traders, and stone, metal and wood craftsmen from every European land have settled here. This city holds the trade monopoly in Spain."

"Are all artisans foreign?"

"No. Churches constitute the unmatched source of wealth and therefore they hire the best craftsmen available. Their power is unrivaled: No ship leaves without their blessings. No festivities are celebrated without their sanction and leadership." He lowered his voice and said: "Who would guess that just fifty years ago this land was ruled by the Moors!" He shook his head in astonishment.

"Yes, who?" echoed Danilo who pondered the whereabouts of the Jews who used to live here among Moors and Christians.

People discussed various subjects, resulting in an enjoyable and informative evening. Danilo and Sofia listened to the descriptions of managing big enterprises, of progress of new construction, anecdotes of smuggling imports without taxation, or the amount of gold and silver brought in this season from the New World. Everyone boasted of their contribution to alleviate the poverty in the city.

As the guests left, Higuera whispered to Danilo: "Sleep well. We shall meet at breakfast to discuss our business."

That night, the boys slept on two luxurious beds in their fancy room. The adventures they experienced since the traumatic episode in the Cordoba hospital, took their toll and they fell asleep while talking to each other.

After breakfast, the maid took the children for a ride around town while Danilo and Sofia remained with Higuera in his office. As a businessman he went straight to the point: "Where do you plan to go? Across the Mediterranean or across the ocean?"

"Across the Mediterranean to Tlemcen."

"Fine. For this purpose, I need to smuggle you aboard one of my ships that sails to Egypt early morning tomorrow. I will instruct the captain to make a short stop in Tlemcen. I am aware that Tlemcen is the pirates' home port, but that will not be a problem since we have a pact with them. Some of our sailors are either Moriscos or North Africans whose ancestors fled from the Christian forces. Like you, they vowed to exact justice and revenge. You two will be dressed like sailors and the boys will be smuggled in crates under my direct charge. Church representatives like to snoop around but they will be directed to the galley for a few glasses of wine. I myself will lead them ashore." He watched their faces. They were not worried.

"You will be given your disguises after sunset. Make sure you are ready tonight because tomorrow morning a throng of onlookers and criminals will gather to see the ship set sail. We also must avoid the bishop's public blessings. You will leave your carriage here and I will compensate you for it." He opened a drawer and handed him money. It was more than fair and would be insulting to refuse. Danilo pocketed the money and thanked their host for his care and kindness.

"One more thing. Will you please send off my coachman back to my parents' house in Alcalá? Here is some money to cover that expense." Higuera would not hear of that and any of the customary insistence was futile. They parted until dinner.

Narina prepared a large basket of provisions for the Martinez family. During the day Danilo and Sofia discussed the escape plans with the boys, who listening intently looked forward to new adventures. "Until we are aboard ship, you must keep quiet in the crates. This is imperative because spies will be everywhere. You will be carried to our room and only then let out. Remember, complete silence until we let you out."

"Is our vacation over?"

"For now, yes. When we reach our destination, your vacation will resume with many more surprises."

Early morning, dressed as sailors, Danilo and Sofia waited in the living room for Higuera's signal that everything was ready. "Good. If I did not know you, Sofia, I would not recognize you. You really look the part. Would you like a job as a sailor?" They all laughed, breaking the tension. Two burly men came in with two padded crates and directed the boys to lie inside. The lid and side walls were outfitted with holes for ventilation.

"Are you comfortable?" asked Sofia.

"I am fine," replied Luís. His younger brother said: "No problem. I only wish I had a book and a lamp." Sofia laughed. "Soon enough," she replied.

Sofia and Danilo hugged Narina and Garcia. "We are indebted to you. We don't know how we can ever repay you," they said.

"By getting safely to your final destination. Be well and may God watch over you. Remember, I will be with you until the ship sails," Garcia de Higuera allayed their masked apprehension.

The three walked out and ascended the imposing carriage. They arrived at the dock where the Doña Narina anchored. A few sailors were taking care of last-minute preparations, setting lights, going up and down the stairs without giving Garcia's party a second look. The two porters, carrying the crates containing the boys, were heading to a lower level when suddenly, a Church agent appeared from nowhere. He greeted Garcia with "good morning, Don Higuera. What is in these unusual boxes?"

Garcia replied without missing a beat: "Two dead Moriscos on the way for burial in the high seas as befitting sailors. Here are the two replacements. Oh, what a disaster! What an awful death!" His voice quivered in grief.

"What did they die of?" Inquired the priest.

"Cholera." Higuera continued to mourn their death, wailing. The priest inched back: "Perhaps they need a blessing?"

"Oh, no, no, no! For this you will need to open the box. You don't wish to see their bloated, demon-possessed bodies. Stand back! The devil seeks new hosts! This is contagious. Please, no one needs to know, otherwise the sailors will mutiny. Here is a donation for your church to pray for these lost souls."

The priest's face turned white. After he grabbed the money and hurried off, they all sighed with relief. The two "sailors" followed the two porters and Higuera as they descended the stairs. In their quarters, the porters delicately placed the crates on cushions and left. They came back shortly with the parents' personal trunks. Danilo paid them and they left again. He and Sofia opened the crates and found the boys fast asleep from the constant motion. Gently, Danilo carried them to their crude beds. The empty crates were stationed outside their door. Someone would come shortly to remove them.

Higuera knocked on the door softly. Danilo opened the door a few inches wide. When he saw his benefactor, he let him in, whispering, "Thank you so very much for your help. Everything is going according to plan. We owe you our freedom." Higuera murmured some apologetic words, "If I could only send you off with more comfort!"

As they hugged, Captain Alejandro came by to greet them. He first saluted his employer, then looked around the room: "If I could only afford you better accommodations." Higuera and Danilo looked at each other and laughed. "We thank you for your hospitality. The room is more than adequate," Danilo replied with a smile.

"Tomorrow you will be dressed like traders and your meals will be brought to your room." The captain noticed Sofia's apprehension: "Don't worry, it is not the first time that we'll be stopping in Tlemcen with human cargo." He gave them a wink, saluted Higuera, and left.

After checking the water supply in the room and all necessities, Higuera hugged the two "sailors" again and left, too.

Because the ship was sailing to the Mediterranean Sea, there were no missionaries on board. No one would inquire about the unscheduled stop. And anyway, the voyage would not take more than three days, so they were told.

Early Saturday morning, the 28th of *Elul*, 5305, the ship set sail southward through the Guadalquivir River.

Hundreds of spectators shouted farewell until the sails disappeared in the horizon. Only then did the Martinez family, now dressed in civilian clothes, dare to go up to enjoy the green banks and the serenity of the countryside. Toward sunset, the ship reached the Atlantic Ocean and turned southwest to a calm sea and cold wind. The next morning, they sailed through the Strait of Gibraltar. On the third day, as they neared the port of Beni Saf, a pirate ship approached. Captain Alejandro brandished a red and white flag, their mutual signal of identification. The pirate captain, Moise Diez, climbed the ladder thrown over the deck and with hugs and kisses the two greeted each other.

"I have a cargo of four people to disembark in Beni Saf," said Alejandro. The Martinez Four came closer. Danilo greeted Moise: "*Barukh haba*! My wife's brothers, Gabriel and Pessah Gabbai, are expecting us. We are sorry we could not make it to the first day of the New Year."

"You are not too late." He looked at the boys with a smile: "I guess these are your sons."

Curiously, the boys looked at the scene unfolding before their eyes. They had never seen a pirate before, only in books. The man did not look devilish, nor particularly ugly.

Moise shook their hands and said: "Welcome to Africa, the land of wild animals and brave hunters!"

They looked puzzled. Moise laughed: "Don't worry, they are far from the shore."

"Any relative of the Zamora brothers is a relative of mine," Moise said as he turned his attention to Danilo and Sofia. "We will escort this ship to the port to see you safely on land." After a short conversation with Alejandro, Moise Diez climbed down the ladder to return to his ship. Both ships sailed slowly until they reached the port. Danilo and family thanked the captain who ordered their luggage securely reached the shore. Luís and Edmondo insisted they could disembark by themselves. As their feet touched the sand, Sofia and Danilo, and their sons echoing them, prayed: "Thank you, *HaShem*, our God, King of the Universe, who has granted us life, sustained us, and enabled us to reach this moment. Amen."

Captain Moise and several pirates hired two coaches to drive the Martinezes and their luggage to Tlemcen where they were greeted by the sounds of the New Year celebration and the greetings of their extended family. Gabriel, Pessah, Juan and their families' loving arms melted away any weariness the newcomers may have felt. Shouts of welcome came from all directions as everyone clung to Sofia and her family: "Perfect timing! It's the second day of *Rosh HaShanah*!" and "Thank God you are here, safe and sound!" greeted them in every turn.

Luís and Edmondo were at the center of attention. Raúl, Juan's son, tugged at their sleeves to navigate them toward their new cousins, the children of Gabriel and Pessah. So these new relatives were the surprises their parents had promised them in Seville! They believed the three days aboard ship was surprise enough, but now, this was overwhelming! So many names to remember! It seemed that the entire Jewish community congregated to welcome them. The highlight of the day was meeting their mother's two brothers, the pirates who filled their imagination with brave adventures.

Gabriel and Pessah embraced their nephews: "Thank God you have all arrived safely." And to his and to Pessah's children, he asked that they take good care of their new cousins and show them to their room. "Make them feel at home."

Maids offered trays of pastries and beverages to the newcomers. No one could go to bed, for the atmosphere was charged with joyful electricity.

Sofia and Danilo told their harrowing story of escape through the early hours of the morning. Getting up late later that day, they joined in the festivities, knowing full well that in order to face God on *Yom Kippur*, they would need to cleanse their soul. To this end, both Juan and Danilo prepared to go through the rite of circumcision along with their sons. Rabbi Almosnino advised and officiated. Since Juan was circumcised at birth, he needed a symbolic bloodletting. Juan took the name his father had given him at birth—Hananiah; Danilo was named Daniel; Luís became Nahum; Edmondo—Micah, and Raúl— Jonathan. Little Izolda jumped up and down: "I want a new name, too! I want a new name, too, *padre!*" They all laughed at Izolda's determination.

"All right! All right! What do you have in mind, little girl?" asked Juan.

"I don't know, *padre*. You and *madre* choose for me."

"Well, what about Sarah? Ruth? Devorah? Abigail?" asked Anabel.

"I like the last one best! Abi-gail!" shouted Izolda with glee.

"So, Abi-gail Izolda it is," laughed Hananiah. "From now on we shall call you Abi-zol." Hananiah could not part from his mother's name altogether.

Little Izolda ran around with the gleeful enthusiasm only a child could muster: "Abi-zol! I am Abi-zol!"

"Since our brothers have reverted back to the Gabbai family name," announced Hananiah, "it is the right thing to do the same."

"So be it," responded Anabel, hugging her husband.

On the night of *Yom Kippur,* they all dressed up in white and went to the synagogue for services. It was the first time ever that the Martinez family attended services in a synagogue surrounded openly and freely with fellow Jews. Their emotional state brought them to tears. The Holy Day was indeed the right time to come out publicly as Jews, to pray for forgiveness, to reflect and realize the profound damage the Catholic Church had done to their people in Spain. They prayed in deep fervor and devotion to cleanse their soul from the defilement in which they lived all their lives.

The day after *Yom Kippur,* the Zamora and the Martinez families constructed a large tabernacle for the festival of *Succot* set to begin on Sunday night, the fourteenth of *Tishrei.* Gabriel taught the newcomers the *Succot* traditions involving the building of the *Succah* and the significance of the Four Species of palm, citron, two willows and three myrtle branches. There was so much to learn and absorb! This festival was completely unknown to the families of Hananiah and Danilo, since such a public observance could never have been realized in Spain. The children enjoyed decorating the Succah with vegetables and fruits, paper ornaments and amulets symbolizing safety, good health and prosperity.

Gabriel taught his guests: "It is customary to have all meals in the Succah. Some family members sleep there, too." Wishing to completely absorb the traditions of the Festival, Hananiah and Daniel took on the challenge.

Gabriel gave them the special book for the Festivals (a *Mahazor*) as a gift which he had copied from their father Alfonso' book, which he had copied from his father's. At the synagogue on the first day of Succot, Gabriel and Pessah demonstrated to Hananiah and Daniel and their sons how to shake the Four Species to the six directions of earth: "Hold them in both hands. Say the *SheHeheyahu* blessing. Now shake them forward, backward, left, right, down and up to acknowledge God's omnipresence."

Nahum, Micah and Jonathan took their turns. They found the ritual amusing. Little Abi-zol insisted on being included to the delight of her parents. While it was fun for the children, the adults understood the significance of the moment while they each held the bouquet with gentle reverence. Later, Daniel and Sofia privately reflected on the uplifting day:

"To this day we have been yearning," said Sofia, her eyes welling up.

"The travels and tribulations we endured have been amply rewarded by the joy of seeing our sons happy with our extended families."

"I agree. Look how they feel so much at ease, as if they had been going to synagogue every Shabbat." They smiled and embraced.

The eighth day of *Succot* was the high point in Hananiah's and Daniel's spiritual transformation: Hundredsat of Jews from around Tlemcen gathered in the synagogues and spilled over to the streets, dancing with Torah Scrolls, singing and thanking God for reaching the new cycle of Scriptural readings. They were swept by the passion of the occasion and the power of the tradition. How lucky they were to reach that moment!

Hananiah and Daniel decided to stay in Tlemcen until after Passover in order to fully experience the true Festival of Freedom and the Unleavened Bread. In Spain its celebration had been minimal and furtive. And anyway, it was too perilous to sail the rough seas during the winter months. They rented homes to pass the winter with their local relatives. During those months of fall and winter Rabbi Almosnino instructed the two former Converso families with the laws of Judaism and prepared the sons for their *Bar-Mitzvah*. Nahum was the eldest of the children, a 13–year old. Hananiah's son Jonathan and Sofia's Micah were 11.

The month of Adar ushered in the festival of Purim celebrating the courage of Queen Esther. Dressed in costumes and munching on sweet pastries, the children read the story of Esther for the first time and joyously made raucous noises whenever the wicked Haman's name was uttered. Haman's all-consuming hatred was now embodied by King Carlos and the Inquisitor General, Juan Tavera.

Sofia, seated among the family ladies, Anabel, Haniya, and Tita, could not stop crying with joy. Later she told her husband: "Micah and Nahum had such fun! It seems like they have no more nightmares from the event at the Cordoba hospital. Thank God."

"Yes, I noticed that, too. How lucky we are to have reached this day to see our sons becoming Jews without fear of persecution. We have done the right thing by leaving Spain."

"I agree, my love. Learning about our faith has deepened my love for our tradition and heritage. It fills me with tremendous pride and spiritual contentment."

"I know exactly how you feel, my darling." He took his wife in his arms and kissed her.

A month later, Passover was celebrated according to the strict laws of the faith. Because this was a true family festival which necessitated a large room with several long tables to accommodate all the family members, it was decided to celebrate the festival in the inner court. Much preparation for Passover was made since Purim: a thorough cleaning of the house and the shopping for and preparation of the traditional foods. Sofia and Anabel not only watched attentively but insisted on taking part in every aspect of the time-intensive activities. Gabriel's and Pessah's children, now adults, centered their attention on their young cousins, going through the *Haggadah* so they would be able to participate in the reading around the festive table. The children were excited to transfer the special wares of Passover from their crates to the polished kitchen. There was much to learn and much to assimilate.

Nahum's extensive study for his *Bar-Mitzvah* bore fruit when on the Sabbath of the 17th of *Nissan*, he went up to the *Bimah* and read from the Torah in the Sefaradi custom as his large family watched with pride and wept. Trembling with overwhelming emotion, Daniel went up to the Torah for the first time in his life to make *Aliyah* in his son's honor. Nahum then read the *Haftarah* from Ezekiel's prophecy of the Dry Bones. Sofia's stream of tears turned to open sobs when she remembered her mother: How proud she would have been to attend this spiritual event.

When she later met with Daniel, Sofia said: "How appropriate for Nahum to read about the dry bones today. It is our story! I could imagine our dry bones rising up from the field of death and putridity which is Spain, and revitalized with flesh and skin, blood and sinew here among our people!"

"That is exactly what went through my mind." They fell into a long embrace.

The four siblings of the Zamora family spent their time together as frequently as they could. They knew this comradery and closeness would soon come to an end. After eight months it was time to part. A pirate ship was at the port ready to leave

233

for Constantinople. It was a sad event for the whole family. Tita and Haniya were crying. "Thank you so much for your friendship and support," said Sofia and Anabel. "You have taught us how to build a real Jewish home, and for this we are forever grateful." The children became accustomed to spending time with their older cousins and friends from their school.

It was a difficult parting from the community. They made friends especially with Rabbi Almosnino's family. On the day of departure, the schoolchildren and their parents came to bid their goodbyes bearing small gifts. "Remember us," the children said to Nahum, Micah and Jonathan. "Perhaps we shall meet again." "We hope so. It was fun to be with you." Hugs and handshakes were exchanged by all among many words of thanks and prayers for success in their new home.

From the ship's deck, they continued to wave to their family and friends on the dock until they were just specks in the distance.

The ship docked in Constantinople on *Lag BaOmer*. Sofia and Hananiah knew about the counting of the Omer from their father who observed its laws: from the sixteenth of *Nissan* until the Festival of *Shavuot*, fifty days in all, no happy events, such as engagements or weddings, were to be celebrated, except on *Lag BaOmer*, the thirty-third day.

Hananiah and Daniel purchased two large homes adjacent to each other in the Jewish quarter where many former Portuguese and Spanish Conversos now lived openly as Jews. A large number of refugees struggled to make a living, but they were supported by successful merchants who funded soup kitchens and vocational training workshops. The local authorities encouraged Jews fleeing their homelands to settle within the Ottoman borders in exchange for paying a special tax.

It was 1546 and the two brothers-in-law purchased a ship from Egypt, but first all administrative fees had to be paid and sailors, cooks, handymen, and a captain were to be hired. Most of them were Jews with different degrees of experience. Two agents of the company and a former Portuguese navigator were sent to bring in the ship.

The maiden voyage under the ship's name "The Abizol" set out through the Port Said waterway after being blessed by the local Rabbi.

In her numerous voyages, *The Abizol* carried a cargo of European and Ottoman popular and luxury items for Indian kingdoms on the western and eastern shores of the peninsula. From Ceylon they brought tea and spices such as cinnamon, ginger, vanilla, cardamon, and cloves. Salt and pepper were prime commodities. Later, the two entrepreneurs joined Jewish traders in central and eastern Asia who imported silk, jade, fur, and gems among others. By the 1540s, Indian kingdoms engaged in constant wars with the Portuguese rulers who tried to subjugate them by acts of belligerence such as burning villages. Therefore, the enemies of Portugal were welcomed, which enabled the Jewish traders to establish relationships based on respect and trust with the local rulers.

While the ship was away, the brothers-in-law planned to expand their import-export business to Asia Minor and the Greek Islands. For this they needed the help of Anabel's family, the HaLevi's in Thessaloniki, who arrived there after the Expulsion. In a long letter to the HaLevi's, Hananiah detailed their escape from Spain and their mercantile enterprises in the Far East for the past two years. "We thank God for watching over us and for reaching a safe place to live freely. Our children are growing in a Jewish community with prospects for greatness and success. We bid you peace and good health." Anabel and Hananiah signed.

They received an enthusiastic response from Anabel's relatives. "We thank the Keeper of Israel for leading you to safety in these perilous days. Anabel's father could not escape when he wanted and would have been pleased with her choice and bravery." They then wrote about the Jewish Sefaradi community and its impact on the economy of Thessaloniki. "Our community is united in its commitment to the teaching of Moses, to charity and education. We have founded a vibrant organization to resettle new waves of escapees from the Iberian Peninsula. Many of them need help in shedding their forced Christian upbringing and in assimilating back into Judaism and its customs. This phenomenon, as you know, is extant in every major city in the Ottoman sphere. We have created charitable enterprises for the benefit of all the citizens of our town. Tolerance and mutual respect are cherished by all." He ended with an invitation: "My partners and I have been importing coffee from Ethiopia, and carpets and fabrics from Morocco. Would you consider forging an alliance by sharing our resources?"

One weekday Hananiah visited his sister: "It has been three years since we left Spain and we have heard no news from our father. I think it is the right time to fulfill his wish to publish the two secret documents in our possession. What do you think, Sofia?"

"Our father's document is too damaging in case he is still alive. However, you may publish Prince Yusuf's personal diary because *padre* is not mentioned there nor referred to in any way."

"You are right. Tomorrow I shall go to the Soncino office. Hopefully they will find it worthy of publication."

Hananiah met Eliezer Soncino in the publisher's office and showed him Yusuf al Hassan Ali's flagrant documentation. "This manuscript is too long to read now. Leave it here and come back in three days, Mr. Gabbai."

When next time they met, Soncino stood behind his desk holding the manuscript in his hands and looking suspicious: "How did this document come to your possession? You understand that the publication of this scandalous material may cause a political and religious conflagration between Christians and Muslims."

Hananiah was ready to respond. "Yusuf al Hassan Ali was a friend of my father when Yusuf served Cardinal Cisneros as his personal secretary. Of course, he was not known by this name then. My father was a very famous professor at Cisneros's Complutensian University in Alcalá. The document was entrusted to my father's care with the clear request to smuggle it out of Spain and publish it. I don't know if my father is still alive, but I know that he returned to his hometown of Zamora."

"What was your father's name?"

"Alfonso de Zamora. He was the leading ..." Soncino interjected: "Yes, I know the immense importance of your father in the preparation of the Complutensian Polyglot Bible. There are not enough words of praise to describe this genius scholar. But wasn't he a devout Christian? After all, he worked for the Catholic Church for many years!"

Hananiah hastened to reply: "As you can see, I have returned to our faith thanks to my father's adherence to Judaism. My family lived covertly as Jews despite the close scrutiny of the Inquisition, but we prevailed. My parents instilled in us the love for and perseverance to our culture and customs."

Soncino was impressed and touched at the same time. "No one would guess this from his known books and manuscripts."

"Yes, he wrote several anti-Jewish polemics which never went beyond their patrons, but he was ordered to do so. My sister is carrying his diary and she is going to publish it only after our father leaves this world."

"That I would like to see. The diary I mean, not his passing, of course. Please ask her to see me when the time comes." He paused, thinking. Hananiah was rethinking, too. He took advantage of the silence in the room and said in excitement: "What do you say if my sister brought the diary in a few days for your review? If you find it worthy of publication, then you will begin the process."

"We can do that." Soncino could not control his enthusiasm. "Please ask her to visit me with the diary. I will be honored." He paused again to compose himself, then continued. "Let us go back to the document at hand. Did Yusuf intend to publish it? Is he still alive?"

"Yes, to both questions. Before he fled to Fes, Yusuf handed his diary personally to my father for safekeeping. By doing that he endangered my father's life. In fact, word got out that Yusuf had left a damning record with my father, and twice his house was searched and ransacked by the Inquisition. Yusuf may have talked about it in Fes to the wrong people. Is he still alive? There is no reason to suggest otherwise. He was still young in 1517, 30 years ago."

"All right. Publishing this diary may attract much interest among the Sultans' family and the Muslim public at large, now, more so, when the Ottomans have drastically eliminated Christian domination in the Mediterranean Basin. Yes, it may be good and beneficial for our patrons, the Ottomans."

"There is only one condition, that my father's name is not mentioned anywhere in the publication. This I insist. We still have family in Zamora."

"This goes without saying," promised Soncino. They conferred a little longer to discuss details.

With her head covered, Sofia and Daniel arrived at Eliezer Soncino's office the next Sunday. Even though it was a hot day, she wore a light coat with the hidden pouch. As she entered, she removed her scarf with her delicate hand. Sofia's noble stature and beauty were dazzling. Soncino called his secretary to bring cold drinks, tea and cake. When the refreshments were served and the secretary returned to his room, Soncino began:

"Thank you for coming. I am very honored to meet you two and examine that which you have brought with you. I will need, of course, to read the diary first to find out its content and value."

"Of course," replied Sofia. "I would remind you that my father wrote his notes and essays, poems and biblical commentary in complete secrecy. Like my brother whom you met last week, I cherish this document and have kept it safely at all times. In Cordoba we were almost killed for it. It is very precious to me for it is my father's legacy as a Crypto-Jew and as a father who lived on a very tight leash under the watchful eye of the Inquisition. If not for his bravery and resolve, we, his children, would not be here today to reclaim our freedom and faith."

Soncino was moved by her devotion to her father and her pride in him. "I promise you, this diary will be protected in my office like Don Isaac Abravanel's commentary to the Prophets."

"I saw that book in my father's home! He edited it for four years and punctuated it so very patiently and respectfully. My father left there many annotations for himself and for his students. He especially loved Abravanel's rebuttals to Christian polemics and distortion of the biblical text."

Soncino stirred in his seat. "Is that so? I am deeply honored! That book was published by my father 28 years ago! He will be thrilled to realize that the great Alfonso de Zamora studied and punctuated it." His face brightened as he sipped his tea with pleasure.

Sofia handed over the diary still in the cylinder. Holding Daniel's arm, they left the office.

In three days, Sofia returned alone. She was led to Soncino's office with much fanfare. The young publisher was excited to see her back. "My father could not sleep knowing that the great Complutensian scholar actually held the book he published in Italy in his hands to study and edit. He was so relieved and pleased to know that Alfonso de Zamora was a Crypto-Jew and that his children have made it safely to Constantinople. He would have loved to meet your families."

After a few moments of silence, Soncino said: "As in the case of Yusuf al Hassan Ali's diary, this one may cause a serious flagrance in the Catholic world. But this is good for publication and does not concern the country we live in. On the contrary, there will be much mocking and derision of the Catholic Church, of Spanish society, and of the Inquisition's religious intolerance. With all its power and viciousness, the Inquisition's failure to turn an entire people into devout followers is clearly exposed."

"I would appreciate if my father's name was not mentioned."

"In this case it would be difficult not to mention him because he wrote his name in several places. Without stating his name, this diary will carry no weight or import. Remember, the irony here is that a famous man, trusted and respected by the top Church hierarchy, deceived them all and survived. That will encourage other Conversos to either go underground in defiance, or devise ways to leave Spain. Your father kept this diary in order to become a force to lead his people out of what he called "the Trouble." He saw himself as Joseph in Egypt and Daniel in Persia who stayed in exile to do God's work. He led you out of bondage. Help others do the same."

Sofia ruminated for a while. "You are right. My half-brother in Zamora seems to be a devout Catholic. If not him, perhaps his children will dare to revolt against the existence in which they live."

"So this is settled," Soncino responded. "Now, let me tell you how I am going to organize the mixed material. It will be presented as a testament against the corrupt and evil Catholic Church and the Inquisition, the political leaders, Spanish society in general, and their education system. In separate chapters we shall submit the author's criticism of the Conversos, his personal notes, longing for his homeland Zion and the rebuilding of the Temple, jokes, teaching material, his biblical commentary and new insights. The subjects he dealt with are many and varied. However, the most pressed subject he wanted to expose was the lists of corrupt priests, Bishops, and Popes, their criminal and immoral actions, their mistresses and progeny. This will be the crux of the publication. What are your thoughts?"

"Putting them in order is a good idea. If you need my help with my father's various handwritings, it will be a privilege to lend a hand. Also, I can shed light on his personal notes. However, we still need to verify if my father is alive or not before publication."

"Agreed to both." Respect and protection of the Zamora family was non-negotiable. And decorating his office with Sofia's nobility and beauty would be a desirable asset.

The two discussed their work arrangement to mutual satisfaction: They would meet five mornings a week while her children studied with their tutors. Her son Micah and Hananiah's son Jonathan were preparing for their *Bar-Mitzvah* the next month.

It took two months for the publication of Yusuf al Hassan Ali's diary. Soncino presented the first copy by hand to His Majesty Suleiman the Magnificent in a short ceremony. A week later, the *Kanuni*, as the Sultan was known in his realm, ordered 50 copies to distribute among his palace counselors and officers. He said he would like to award the daring Secretary the highest medal of honor. He kept his word and sent a special royal galleon to bring Prince Yusuf to his palace as befitting a Moorish prince. Yusuf was in his mid-60s, still vigorous and noble in stature.

For the occasion, Sofia, Daniel, Hananiah and Anabel were invited as the Sultan's guests. When they were introduced to Prince Yusuf, he was ecstatic: "I never imagined I would live to see the children of my good and trusted confidant carry out my wish. My thanks to you are profound and sincere. In my last words to your eminent father, I hoped to plant the seeds of liberation: liberation from Catholic Spain and from the bonds of loyalty to the University. And here is the result!" He bowed to Sofia and kissed her hand. He then turned to Hananiah and with two hands he shook Hananiah's hand.

"Throughout his adult life my father regretted not attempting to leave Spain. But at the same time, he believed he was doing God's work by teaching Judaism in an indirect way. He sensed your trust in him was the highest honor he could receive from a true sympathizer." Hananiah smiled at the handsome prince.

"You must have stories to tell about your escape," encouraged the Prince.

Sofia and Daniel smiled. "Indeed!" said Sofia reminiscing of their adventures in Cordoba. "We were almost seized by the Inquisition! Instead, we had to kill their agents to survive."

"You must tell me your stories, I insist." They sat down and recounted their horrid adventures. At the end, Prince Yusuf got up and requested the Sultan's permission to speak in public.

"I have just heard of the dangerous tribulations the two children of my famous friend in Spain, with whom I entrusted my diary, suffered. I would like to thank them in public for risking their lives for my dangerous request. I knew the Inquisition had sent spies to assassinate me. I was a coward and involved an innocent person and his entire family in my personal vendetta. Thanks be to Allah that no harm befell on them. I beg your forgiveness." He looked at Sofia and Hananiah who stood a few feet away. "If I can do anything for you, it will be my utter pleasure and honor."

Sofia and Hananiah came closer. "The honor is ours," Sofia replied. "What you can do for us is accept our invitation to be our guest. Let our children meet the great Prince of Spain." He accepted without hesitation.

The Sultan announced: "I have ordered a royal parade to introduce Prince Yusuf and the Zamoran families to the Ottoman population. Muslims and Jews have cooperated in defiance of the evil Catholics for centuries. Jewish refugees are welcome in our empire. Their value is incalculable to our growth and might. Now," he looked at the orchestra, "Let us enjoy music and dancing!" Beautiful young women appeared in bright silk costumes revealing more that the mind's eye could imaging, rushing forward as they danced.

Among the throngs at the parade were book collectors and agents of the European ambassadors and of the East India Dutch company who wanted to see the family behind the infamous exposé.

The book sold out in a few months and a second edition was duly published, then a third. There was a large market throughout the Ottoman empire that enjoyed the clever revenge of the young Moorish prince. In Renaissance and Protestant Europe, readers joined in the mockery of the hypocrite Catholic Church, remembering the scandalous *Decameron* by Giovanni Boccaccio, which was still a best-seller two hundred years later.

Due to its complicated format, the publication of Alfonso de Zamora's diary took a little longer. It was finally ready for distribution in the autumn of 1549 after Sofia's cousin, Avraham Gabbai, had returned with news from Zamora of their father's passing.

The book was first introduced in the Italian dukedoms and states of Florence, the Republic of Venice and Ferrara, which were still wedded to the Renaissance movement of free thinking and expression. It reinforced the teachings and criticisms expressed by Martin Luther as practiced by his growing number of disciples. Protestant German and Dutch cities, despite the Habsburg domination, embraced the somber, at times humorous, yet always honest depiction of the same political and religious entities they themselves found faulty and repulsive. In England, the new converts to Henry VIII's modality of religion, found the book most amusing and titillating. It soon became the center of discussion in the salons of intellectuals.

However, when the book first appeared in the papal-dominated states and in King Charles's Holy Roman Empire, it was at once banned. The Pope, first Paul III (who was personally named as one of the most corrupt Popes), then his successor Julius III, as well as the Inquisitor General, Garcia de Loaysa and local bishops, read the book in secret out of curiosity, then burned it.

Sofia and Hananiah carried out their father's wishes. They kept Alfonso's original document in a secret location as a legacy for their children. The success of both books in Europe and in the Muslim centers of learning from Damascus to Alexandria and Fes, was tremendous. For many foreign agents, especially the book traders, these documents generated a fertile source of income.

The second half of the 16th-century saw the import-export businesses of the Zamora clan embracing the world of commerce and finance. The future of Jacob Gabbai's descendants was thereby secured for generations.

CHAPTER 15

Redeemed

The Lord's steadfast love is for all eternity, toward those who fear Him; His beneficence is for the children's children of those who keep His covenant. Psalms 103:17

A lfonso de Zamora moved into his parents' home in September 1545 two decades after his father had passed away, but not before the house went through two months of repair and updating. When Alfonso arrived in town, his son and his extended family welcomed him. Alfonso's son, Francisco, was married to Leonor Rodriguez and together they had six children: three sons and three daughters. Four siblings married Conversos who settled in Zamora and by then had little children of their own. Ana and Gabriel, the youngest of Francisco's children, were reading in Salamanca with two years to graduation.

His parents' house was ready for the returning patriarch. Food had been cooked, water brought in, beds made, bathrooms ready for use. Alfonso walked with a cane and was dependent on his faithful and ever-present maid. María was still young and strong. When the family first gathered in Alfonso's house, Francisco and his wife Leonor went to the kitchen where María was busy organizing the refreshments.

"Maria," said Francisco, "we are deeply grateful for your dedication to our father, but we should not allow you to bear the sole care. We have decided to share your duties among the women. Each in her turn will prepare the meals and clean the house."

Maria's face reddened. "I will not stand for it as long as I am strong and capable. I have been doing this for years to the unwavering satisfaction of my master. I only need a young maid to help with the house chores and would appreciate if you hired one to fetch water and do the laundry. Your wives have their hands full with their own households."

Leonor responded in a soothing tone: "We shall do that. You are a member of the family, and we thank you for your years of service. There is no doubt that you are capable of taking care of our father. Today we have already brought soup and bread, cooked fish, vegetable patties, water, wine and hand towels. Next time you will tell us what to bring. Now, let me help you with the party."

"If you need medical attention, our Doctor Xavier Paltero will be your caregiver. He will visit our father twice a week as we have arranged with him," Francisco added.

The grandchildren had never met Alfonso, for they had only heard of this famous personality. The family sat around two tables, Alfonso at the head of one. Thanking them all for coming, he announced: "In this house I was born and raised by two devoted Jewish parents. Here I shared my *Yeshivah* days with them. Here I was taught our customs and culture. Therefore, I will resume in this house the life of my childhood. I do hope you shall learn and emulate."

Francisco rushed to the kitchen and brought a jar of water, a basin with a hand towel, and soap. He helped his father wash his hands, then he washed his own hands. Alfonso blessed the bread and began eating. When he stopped, his eyes welled up. He could see himself running home at night with his childhood friends Eliezer and Samuel as the heavy steps of Deza's hooligans echoed in the *juderia*. He saw his mother opening the door and he, seated at this very same place, on this same chair, eating his mother's soup and the warm bread from the oven. He choked back tears.

Francisco came to his side. "*Padre*, what is the matter? I hope the soup is to your liking. This is grandma's recipe."

"Yes, I know. It has conjured up long-ago memories of my childhood, sitting right here, talking with my *madre*, may peace be upon her."

Francisco hugged his father. At the end of the meal Alfonso asked the rest of the family to move to the living room. Father and son remained in the dining room to discuss life post "the Troubles" and the daily struggle of keeping the faith.

"Do not give up, even if you hold on to some customs. Pass on our traditions to your children. They may choose to leave Spain and live as free Jews. Nowadays, there are several lands which are tolerant and afford freedom of faith and occupation. Already four of your siblings have taken that courageous step."

"Yes, *padre*, we do our best to keep the faith." Francisco remained pensive for a while. He then bent his head and said softly: "*Padre*, Jeromillo has been living here since he was banned from your home in Alcalá. He has changed. He has taken on Grandfather Juan's business and is doing well. He has since married a Zamoran girl, and they have been living a few doors away. I am pleading with you to bury the hatchet and see him."

Alfonso was surprised. He had no idea of Jeromillo's whereabout since he raped María. "He must first ask María for forgiveness." He looked up at Francisco's face for a few seconds. He then added: "Let him come tomorrow evening."

"Thank you, *padre*. He will do as you request."

The family left to let Alfonso rest, but he could not relax. He called María and told her of Jeromillo's visit the next evening. He was concerned of her reaction. She shivered. That rape had been etched in her memory like blood on parchment. Her face reddened as her instinct wanted to scream: 'No! He will never set foot in this house!' But after years of learning from Alfonso, she knew to take a deep breath before any crucial decision. Looking into her ailing benefactor's eyes, she saw a hope of reconciliation with his son. 'He is going to die soon. I cannot take this, perhaps last opportunity, away from him,' she reckoned. 'He is married with family, and anyway, I am not afraid of him any longer for gone is that helpless teenager I once was.'

She nodded to her master and left the room. Alfonso's tension abated and he sighed in relief for her courageous decision.

The next day María got herself acquainted with the house and its chores. Alfonso dedicated the day to reading and resting. One of the books he cherished most was Rambam's *Moreh Nevukhim*. He could now leisurely read and reread old books, prohibited by the Catholic church, without fear. He could proudly display his extensive library openly in his living room cabinets. There was no fear of retaliation if an Inquisitor entered his house, for the books were associated with his academic work. His father's books were still kept in the basement. His heart jumped a beat when he heard a knock on the door.

María opened the door and faced Jeromillo. In her mind, she had imagined this moment her entire adult life and she knew what her response would be. She looked stoically at Jeromillo's face and led him into the living room. She did not announce his name, but quietly returned to the kitchen holding her head high.

It was an awkward moment for both father and son. Jeromillo approached Alfonso's bed and knelt before him: "*Padre*, please forgive me. I was a rotten child, irresponsible, disrespectful, and shameless. I have changed. I prayed to *HaShem* with all my heart to redirect my drifting soul, and He answered my supplications."

Alfonso spoke sternly: "I cannot forgive you before you have asked for María's forgiveness."

"I am here to do that."

Alfonso called María to the room. She stood still before her master.

Jeromillo stood up and faced María. "I humbly ask for your forgiveness, María. I did a despicable and awful thing, and no excuse can soften my crime. Please forgive me. Not a day goes by when I don't feel shame and sick to my stomach. I have exiled myself away from my beloved family to suffer self-humiliation. I beg of you! My wife and daughter are outside. She knows of my shame."

María stood erect as she looked at Jeromillo's eyes. They were sincere. She thought for a while, then said:

"I forgive you, for I see you are truly remorseful. I hope your demons will be lifted and your soul healed."

Jeromillo fell to his knees and cried, thanking her again and again. She went to her room gather herself. 'It was not too painful,' she thought, 'thank God it's over.'

Jeromillo turned to his father in anticipation, still on his knees. Alfonso put his hands on Jeromillo's head and said: "I forgive you. Let *HaShem* forgive you now. Get up and bring in your wife and child."

Jeromillo went out and came back with a young woman, perhaps 19 years-old, attired modestly. Her black hair was tied in the back and her black eyes were bright and inquisitive. She was holding a baby in her arms. "This is Reina, my wife." He took the baby in his arms and handed her over to his father. "This is Izolda."

Alfonso embraced and kissed the baby. She was about one year-old with blue eyes like his deceased wife. "Izolda, may *HaShem* keep you and watch over you. May He shine His face over you and grant you peace."

Jeromillo and Reina echoed "Amen." Alfonso inquired about Reina's family. She turned out to be the granddaughter of Martin Padilla, the Zamoran businessman. Padilla and his family left for the mountains of Bejar with the family of Alfonso's aunt. But the Inquisition reached there, too, and they were forced to convert. They returned to Zamora where Padilla rebuilt his business after all Christian debts had been paid. Reina's grandparents had died but her parents were still alive. Reina and Jeromillo took their leave relieved and encouraged.

Francisco returned later with his wife to visit his father. Leonor was above average height with braided long brown hair, green eyes and olive skin. After six pregnancies she remained full figured. In her kind face she reminded Alfonso of his mother of the same name.

Francisco and Leonor had served as the patriarchs of the Zamora clan while Alfonso was away. Meetings, decisions, Holy Days, and celebrations were executed in their roomy house in the old *Juderia*. He now acknowledged his father as the head of the family.

"Francisco," Alfonso said, "I would like to take the opportunity, while I am still able and clear of mind, to reinstate teaching of my grandchildren, as my father had done before me."

"What do you have in mind?"

"Children above the age of three will gather here for lessons in tradition twice a week and every Shabbat afternoon. After the Shabbat lesson, we shall have a family dinner. I suggest that Leonor and Rosa Muñiz, the wife of your son Diego, will orchestrate the event including the food."

"But María would not allow us to bring food. She insists on taking care of your needs all by herself."

"Listen to her and respect María's wishes," Alfonso retorted. "However, I will nonetheless convince her to take Shabbat off. She will consent to accept your help whenever I ask her to do so."

Alfonso's life was busy. He read for hours, wrote notes and looked forward to meeting his children and grandchildren. According to their ages, he taught them the Hebrew alphabet, basic prayers, about Zion and the Prophets, customs and traditions. The mothers would sit in the back and listen so that they could repeat the material at home. And so it went for about two years.

April 1547 came and the family celebrated Alfonso's 72nd birthday lavishly. His health was failing. His eyesight dimmed and a pair of eyeglasses, a relatively new German invention, never left his side. As the party wound down, Alfonso complained of pain in his shoulder and feeling faint. Francisco rushed to call Doctor Paltero who immediately removed Alfonso's upper clothes and examined him. Hearing the heart's fibrillation which signaled a serious problem, the doctor gave Alfonso several herbal potions and ordered complete rest.

His family visited every day for he insisted on continuing the teaching of his grandchildren. Sensing his mortality, Alfonso did not waste time. Most of his life he taught strangers and lying-in bed was against his character. He had to do one more thing before he died. He called his family for an important occasion on Saturday evening. Sunday was inappropriate in his view.

Gathering around his bed, they could guess the essence of this convention. Alfonso was propped up in his bed, looking pale but not yet defeated. When they were all seated, he began:

"My dear family. Like our Father Jacob, I have called you to hear my last Words of Testament. My life began in a happy home. My blessed parents and grandparents were the center of our life. Judaism guided and shaped our souls. I loved my schooling at the Yeshivah and hoped to become a rabbi. But as you all know, the Catholic Kings and the Inquisitors decided otherwise. We tried to escape but were caught up in the deception and intrigue of Kings John and Manuel and their vicious Church. We were dragged to the baptismal fonts kicking and screaming. We vowed right there to never relinquish our faith. All the escape routes in Portugal were closed to us and we returned to Zamora in broken spirit. We survived and did our best to cling to our traditions as much as we could. We got married and sired children. Our external life patterns did not ostensibly differ from the rest of the population."

He motioned to Francisco to hand him the cup of water on his side table. He took a sip, then a deep breath and continued:

"My Jewish upbringing and my years in the *Yeshivah* shaped my life. Because of this I was hired to study and teach at two of the top universities in the nation, if not the world. My skills were needed and appreciated, and for my work I was protected from harm."

After sipping some more water he went on: "It was not easy to live a double life. Several Converso scholars were tortured and left to rot in jail. Others were burned to death in public spectacles. We were extra careful. I was lucky to marry two courageous and devoted women who never wavered from our vow. Often, I wondered if I was doing the right thing instead of trying to escape this hideous land. But I stayed behind to do my job for two reasons. The first was, that even though I was not a bona-fide rabbi in a *Yeshivah*, I was acting like one. I manipulated my academic freedom and taught thousands of Christian students to love our Bible, our language, our Forefathers, Prophets and Kings, our laws of justice, our God—the miracle maker who loves His people Israel—our history, *piyyutim* and poetry, meter and melodies, our Bible commentators and philosophers, and even our traditional Sefaradi proverbs. I taught all these."

He paused to take a deep breath. "I also had the opportunity to study for myself and compose new insights into biblical commentary. I wrote three books which became very popular and gained influential patrons especially within the Church. No one realized what I was doing. On the contrary, the accolades kept coming. I was so indispensable that until two years ago the University of Salamanca offered me a teaching position. That was also the time when I was chosen by my colleagues to compose two similar letters, one to the Pope and the other to a bishop in Rome, to save my department from abolishment. They planned to send me to Rome as their representatives! I fooled them all."

He drank some more, then continued: "I was cheated out of royalties and found no justice in court. The plain perversion of justice was so conspicuous for all to see. Sometimes teachers lay traps in my path hoping that I be demoted or even fired by my patron Cardinal, but the two Cardinals always protected my reputation. I survived well, but I never had a truly happy day in my life because of my constant fears and trepidations. I was often sick, mostly from mental exhaustion and depression which affected my physical health. In those days I turned to Job and to King Solomon's wisdom in Proverbs and Ecclesiastes. For praying and hope I turned to King David's Psalms to be close to *HaShem*."

Again, he drank from his cup which Francisco kept filling. They all waited silently, mesmerized by his testament. They sensed the solemnity of the occasion which would not be replicated. Ever.

Alfonso breathed deeply and carried on. He was encouraged by the respectful silence of his family. "The second reason for staying behind was my age and family circumstances. When we returned to Zamora, I was already twenty-two, and my parents were still alive. As the eldest son, their well-being was my responsibility. My two brothers soon escaped from Spain which chained me further to Zamora."

He began crying, softly, remembering his beloved parents. Francisco hurried to hand him a handkerchief. They waited patiently.

Alfonso sighed and drank some more. He looked around him with satisfaction and remarked: "You have made me proud for choosing the right spouses. I am also proud of Juan and Sofia and their families who dared leave this land even though they were financially comfortable. But they are still young and fearless. I gave them risky assignments to carry on and I wonder if they were successful."

They realized they were witnessing a confession of a proud, but tortured and frustrated man. He was opening his soul for forgiveness without criticism. That was life. On the other hand, he was encouraging them to cling to his faith and make it theirs, forever, with full commitment. He was giving them permission, more than permission—courage, to leave Spain. His days were numbered, yet he was not worried. His loyal María would remain at his side to his last breath.

"My dear children, I have spoken enough. Go home. I will be fine in María's nursing hands." They kissed him and departed silently. Doctor Paltero came several times to examine him and adjust his medications. Alfonso's condition remained stable, but his movements were limited to a few steps a day. He nevertheless continued his reading and teaching. He would never give these up.

In November of that year, as autumn turned cold and windy, Francisco arrived with a foreign visitor. "I found this man wandering in the streets asking people for your address. I asked him for his business, but he would divulge only to you in person."

The young man was dressed in a North African garb even though he came from Constantinople. Spain was in a state of war with the Ottomans, and he would be arrested forthwith as a spy. He bowed his head to Alfonso and introduced himself:

"My name is Avraham ben Isaac Gabbai. My father was born here in Zamora and left Spain still in his teens. He first arrived in Fes, then moved to Alexandria where he fulfilled his childhood ambition to study the sciences, astrology and mathematics. For a while he spent time in Cairo and in Tzefat in the land of Israel to delve into the Kabbalah. Some years later he sailed to Constantinople where he could not find a job in teaching as such positions were reserved for Muslim scholars. Instead, he opened a successful trading business of books and manuscripts. There is much interest in Hebrew books by mainly foreign embassies, Church officials, Christian guilds, private collectors, and Muslim scholars."

Alfonso interrupted. "How do I know you are who you claim to be? You may be an agent of the Inquisition to accuse us of heresy."

"A year or two later, his brother Barukh joined him. Their mother's name was Sarah Melendez and his father's name was Hayim Gabbai, skilled in leather goods and a leader in the Jewish community. We have reverted to our ancestral family name."

"You could have obtained all this information from the Church files." Alfonso was cautious and for good reasons. But the guest continued.

"Right after my father was abducted by the Portuguese priests, his mother miscarried."

It was this fact undisclosed to the Portuguese priests that prompted Alfonso to stretch out his hands to embrace his nephew: "Welcome to my family, Avraham. You must be tired and hungry. First you eat then we talk." He smiled in relief and turning to Francisco he said: "Francisco, my son, meet your cousin Avraham." The two hugged with a soaring exhilaration.

After María was ready with the meal, Avraham washed his hands, said the blessing and sat down to eat. María poured him a glass of water and retired to her room. When he was done, he chanted the after-meal grace. Francisco invited him to sit next to his father. Alfonso opened: "Please resume your story, Avraham."

"In 1546, my father and I traveled to Cairo to study for six months in the Yeshivah of Rabbi David ben Zimra, a native of Zamora. As you know, our families had known each other before the Expulsion. By then, Rabbi David served as the Chief Rabbi of Egypt, teaching the mysticism of the Kabbalah to the many prodigies who flocked from near and far. When we returned to Constantinople in the spring of 1547, we heard of a new Jewish international enterprise run by two brothers-in-law. The name of one of them was Hananiah Gabbai of Zamora. We did not pay attention because there are numerous former Jews from Zamora. However, just before *Shavuot* a sensational book was published by Soncino. It involved the personal account of a Morisco Prince who portrayed a very condemning picture of the Catholic Archbishop Cisneros. Rumor has it that it was kept in Alcalá by a famous Converso whose name was not disclosed. My father wondered if it had anything to do with you. We visited the Soncino office and introduced ourselves. He refused to divulge any detail. We asked if that Zamoran had relatives in the city, and he said yes. We asked him to pass our names and address to these relatives. Sofia and Hananiah did not delay in contacting us, and the meeting was a very happy one."

"I did not know it was published. I guess the authorities have not permitted its sale in Spain. How was the book received?"

"It sent a wave of shock in both the Christian and Muslim worlds. Except for where the Catholic Church is in control, everyone has shown much interest and scorn toward the Church and the Inquisition. Added to that which had been already exposed by Martin Luther, the book revealed major problems with corruption and hypocrisy within the Catholic Church hierarchy. The Muslim world is still saluting and cheering for their Moorish prince who exacted revenge on that pompous and hypocritical Cardinal. Of course, the Vatican has denied any truth to it, and has issued several claims that the old and ailing Cardinal died of a heart attack. They proclaimed the diary to be a fraud and a figment of one Muslim's imagination. Prince Yusuf Ali visited the Sultan and before the judges he swore the document to be true. By the way, Hananiah has returned the original diary to the prince who rewarded him with honors and gifts. The great Suleiman gave a lavish party in honor of the prince and your children for their courage in risking their lives. There was even a parade in their honor in the streets of the capital headed by the Sultan himself!"

"Have you heard of another publication against the Church? I entrusted a very important document with my daughter Sofia. Are you aware of such a document?"

"Sofia told me of a document you wrote which is kept unpublished."

"Do you know why?"

"No, she did not disclose."

"Now I know that the two documents reached their destination safely. I guess that Sofia will release my diary after my passing to avoid retaliation. My soul can now rest that I have done my share in our quiet defiance."

Alfonso closed his eyes. Despite his shallow and rapid breathing, he smiled. He could see his two children and his grandchildren there, far away, in the land of the Ottomans, carry on his heritage.

Avraham spoke: "I have with me two letters from your daughter and son. After you read them, please burn them for they may cause you unnecessary repercussions if found." He took out two envelopes from his coat's inner pocket and handed them to his uncle. Alfonso held them to his racing heart. His hands shook and his eyes welled with tears.

"Let me read them to you, *padre*." Francisco got up. He began with Hananiah's letter describing their stay with their brothers in Tlemcen, experiencing the Jewish Holy Days, and their arrival in Constantinople. He mentioned their joyous meeting with their uncle and cousin, and the publication of Prince Yusuf's diary.

"Prince Yusuf Hassan Ali expressed his indebtedness to you. He knew he could count on you," wrote Hananiah. "We were welcomed by the Sultan and the Prince in a great display of gratitude. They wished you left Spain to spend the rest of your days here as the Sultan's guest of honor. We and the children miss you very much and wish you God's blessings. Your loving son, Hananiah."

Sofia wrote about the family's escape from Cordoba and their smuggle out of Spain by the Morisco Higuera, and about the business success of the partnership between her husband and her brother. She described her agreement with Eliezer Soncino to postpone the publication of Alfonso's diary until it was safe for obvious reasons. "We miss you terribly. The children were sad to celebrate their *Bar-Mitzvah* without their grandfather. They send you their love and hope you will come to live with us."

She ended with an anecdote: "Eliezer Soncino, the publisher, was very moved by your having read and punctuated Don Isaac Abravanel's *Commentary on the Prophets*. He wished you worked for him. He offered me the position of an editor. Imagine this! Me, an editor of Hebrew books! If he cannot get you, he might as well get your daughter! I agreed to work for him. This is a great opportunity to read works by great Jewish minds." Sofia, Daniel, Nahum, and Micah signed their names.

"Too late for me," murmured Alfonso, still very moved. He looked at his nephew and said: "My family is immensely grateful to you for coming all the way to give us the good news. I am too weak these days, so please let them know that we are all fine. Do not report of my poor health. In the meantime, go and meet your other cousin and his family. You will stay here as long as you remain in Zamora. Tomorrow the family will gather here for dinner."

Francisco asked: "Did you come to Zamora specially to bring the letters?"

"Yes and no. My father and I forged a business deal with the Bishop of Granada. He is a learned man who has books to sell and who has ordered books from us. I took this opportunity under the patronage of the bishop to accomplish this personal mission. As you know, the Inquisition has no power over Jews, only over Conversos." Alfonso closed his eyes. María came in and said: "Please leave now. He has had enough excitement for one day." Francisco and Avraham left.

"María, please get the extra room ready for my nephew. He will remain with us as long as he wishes." Alfonso still held the letters to his heart and was crying softly.

"Please, sir, you must rest and not get too emotional. Here is your medication." She spoon-fed him the herbal concoction. "I'll bring your dinner soon." She fluffed up his pillows and covered him with an extra blanket.

In half an hour María returned with a steaming bowl of soup and some bread and sat down to feed him. He was smiling and looked peaceful. She called out to Alfonso, touching his hands which were still grasping the letters to his heart. He remained unresponsive. Crying, she rushed outside to fetch Doctor Paltero and then on to Francisco's house. His wife Leonor was alarmed at María's panic. "Come right now," she called out to Francisco. When he saw María, he said nothing but ran to Jeromillo's house and together they hurried to their father's house. Leonor trailed behind.

When the doctor saw them, he shook his head with sadness.

Francisco fell upon his father's bed and began sobbing. Avraham Gabbai stood crying softly as he watched his lifeless uncle. They all noticed the letters grasped in Alfonso's still-warm hands.

"He died with joy in his heart," Francisco spoke. "He waited to hear from Sofia and Hananiah to know they reached a haven. He could now close his eyes and meet his Maker once his revenge was complete. May his soul be bound up in the bond of everlasting life." A quiet chorus of "Amen" filled the room.

"We must burn the letters as Avraham instructed. They might be precariously damning. But let us read them first." Francisco gently removed the letters from Alfonso's grasp and read them aloud to his family. They listened to the account of their relatives' courageous escape and good fortune. He went to the fireplace and dropped the letters there. The rest of the family came closer and watched the fire sparks die down.

As nightfall approached, Doctor Paltero organized the burial for the next day. One by one, the grandchildren kissed their grandfather, then the daughters-in-law, the nephew, and last came Francisco and Jeromillo.

"*Padre*, I am so sorry to have given you a hard time. I promise to continue your teachings. You have been an inspiration to us all." Jeromillo's sobs echoed throughout the house.

Francisco hugged his wife and children. Speechless, he was not the emotional type, but recognized his profound love for his father. They stood there with their heads bent in reverence and grief. The doctor said: "There is nothing else to be done until early tomorrow morning."

"The church officials need not know of father's death. We do not want any church involvement, no eulogies or ceremonies," advised Francisco. "We shall leave in early dawn in several coaches down to the valley, and with the help of Doctor Paltero, we shall give him a proper Jewish burial without any undesired attention. For now, we shall go home."

They left slowly, heavy with loss.

As the sun was slowly rose, Alfonso's body was wrapped in his prayer shawl María produced from under his pillows. A shroud above it was wrapped around his cold body. Francisco and his son Juan, Jeromillo and Doctor Paltero carried the body to the coach and the procession drove through the city gate.

At the cemetery, the four men dug a hole next to the graves of Alfonso's parents and each shoveled soil atop the body until the grave was filled. Even María, dressed in black and choking back tears, assisted in the burial. Some-time later, the family would place a burial stone with Alfonso's name and a "Jewish cross," a Crypto-Jewish symbol showing a cross on top of an inverted menorah. All returned home with aching hearts.

As was bequeathed in Alfonso's will, María would live in the house for life. With María's consent, Gabriel and Ana, Francisco's unmarried children, would move into Alfonso's home to take care of her and keep her company. The children would divide among themselves his books and his personal Jewish paraphernalia. Alfonso's prayer books and the *Mahazor*, which he had copied from his father's book, would go to Francisco and his descendants.

Avraham, Alfonso's nephew, left with ambivalent emotions. He, on the one hand, fulfilled his personal mission and contacted his remaining family in Zamora. On the other, it would be his duty to tell Sofia and Hananiah of their father's passing. The thought was pressing on his mournful heart.

The Zamora Cardinal found out about Alfonso's death too late to get involved. As long as the Zamora family kept on appearing at Church every Sunday, and donating into its coffers, he had no cause to doubt their faithfulness, or to harm them.

It was in Gabriel's and Ana's lifetime that agents from the European library collectors, such as the Universities of Salamanca, Alcalá, and the newly-built El Escorial Library under the leadership of the biblical scholar Benito Arias Montano, visited the Zamora clan to purchase Alfonso's library. Book traders came to bargain for private collectors. Most of the books, which Alfonso had copied for the purpose of teaching, were sold in no time. These books have been studied by thousands of students and scholars for generations and have been cherished by their librarians.

Some patrons took Alfonso's books with them when they changed addresses, and later bequeathed them to local university libraries, such as in Paris and Naples. During the Spanish Civil War of 1936–1939 some universities and libraries were set on fire, and unfortunately several of Alfonso's books were either burned or damaged. In addition, in the process of studying and transferring the manuscripts, incompetent handlers lost or damaged some pages. In recent times, Alfonso de Zamora's contribution to the proliferation of biblical scholarship during the Renaissance and beyond is finally being recognized and appreciated. Because of his attention to detail, his methodological approach to biblical study, his own biblical commentary, his respect for Jewish biblical commentators, calligraphy, script varieties, and historical documentaries, interest in his work has been expanded. Yet most of all, his persistent criticism of erroneous translations has been acknowledged. His life's work encouraged the creation of other Polyglots in Europe which enabled laypeople, other than scholars, clergymen and royals, privileged to read Latin and Greek, to gain access to the Holy Scriptures in their own languages. This opened the door to a series of critical editions of the Bible which dared to criticize not only the Hebrew Scriptures, but also the New Testament and thus Christianity itself.

Alfonso's work thusly contributed to the Renaissance movement and the free thinking that drove away the last dark clouds of the Middle Ages. Through his teachings, Hebrew and the Hebrew Bible have become a worldwide focus for modern-day scholars.

EPILOGUE

Several generations later, in 1660, Sofia's progeny Jacob, named after his great-great-grandfather Alfonso's Hebrew name, sold the diary to a speculator in manuscripts who worked in the Dutch embassy in Constantinople. Levinus Warner obtained a published copy of the diary from a bookstore in the Ottoman capital. However, Warner wished to acquire the original document, and after investigation, he arrived at Jacob's house.

At first, Jacob denied owning the diary and sent Warner away. But Warner was persistent, and he returned with a lucrative and irresistible offer. He would donate it to a Protestant University Library whose students and teachers would study it with deference, and the manuscript would be carefully preserved. Jacob consulted with his siblings who agreed to the offer.

"The condition of the diary," argued sister Izolda, "has already begun to deteriorate. At least it will be appreciated by scholars as our ancestor intended. It will be preserved for eternity. Selling it to a respectable Protestant University library is a logical and sound proposition."

Her siblings agreed and the sale of the diary was complete.

When the Vatican heard that the original diary was kept at the Leiden University library, Pope Clement IX ordered his nephew, Cardinal Giacomo Rospigliosi, to remove all the offensive pages concerning the priests and their mistresses and lovers, and the lists of their illegitimate offspring. "You are unknown in the Netherlands. I suggest that you present yourself as a reader from Liege. Do not exhibit any emotional involvement. Appear calm, respectful and academically oriented."

Rospigliosi was a Jesuit cleric who studied canon and civil law in Salamanca. At the time of his summons, he was stationed in Avignon. To prepare himself for the mission, he replaced his Catholic attire with that of a simple Protestant minister and dressed in this disguise he entered the Leiden library. He approached the librarian and asked to see the notorious diary. The librarian went to a side, locked cabinet, opened it with a key he kept around his waist, and brought it to the priest.

"Please be advised that you are strictly forbidden to remove the diary from this room or damage it in any way," the librarian sternly instructed.

"Of course," replied Rospigliosi. "I will be sitting at that desk by the window."

After perusing through the diary and marking the targeted pages, he was ready for the right opportunity. When he noticed the librarian left the room, he cut out the marked pages and shoved them deep into his pockets. He left the diary in disarray and in his hasty exit expressed his thanks to the junior librarian who had just entered from the inner rooms. Back in his legate convent, he read the unsavory lists, the unethical behavior of the clergy, the essays against his Church, the Inquisition and the courts, and wondered what was new. He witnessed the same behavior in his own lifetime. But he had an order and so he burned the pages as instructed.

Today, the diary is kept under strict supervision at the Leiden University Library, Holland, its pages are still in disorder. It can be read digitally at https://digitalcollections.universiteitleiden.nl/view/item/1563008/pages

Many of Alfonso de Zamora's manuscripts have been digitized or are available in microfiche at the Israel National Library, Jerusalem, in libraries in Spain, Italy, France, England and the United States of America.

A FINAL NOTE

Many of the descendants of Alfonso de Zamora came to Eretz Israel and live there to this day, bearing names such as Gabbai, Zamira, Zamora, Zmora, Zimri and the like. Beside them live the descendants of his good friend Pablo Coronel (Senor), the grandson of Abraham Senor, the chief adviser to Queen Isabella, who sold his soul to the evil forces of his day. But despite the great publicity made by the Catholic kings to the conversion of Abraham Senor, there is conclusive evidence of the continued secret life of the Senor family.

It is unknown when the Senior Palace of Segovia was taken over by the Catholic Church and turned into a monastery. In the early 2000s, a seventeenth-generation descendant of Avraham Senior visited the Senior Palace following rumors that the Senior family continued to follow the Jewish faith in secret. She was denied entry. With the persistent intervention by the City Mayor, she was allowed in. She found an old synagogue in the basement that confirmed the rumors. However, pursuant to her visit, the resident monks sealed and boarded up the synagogue to prevent future visits.

GLOSSARY OF FOREIGN WORDS

Aliyah:	Going up to the *Bimah* to read the blessing before and after the Torah portion is read.
Bar-Mitzvah:	The Jewish boy's celebration upon reaching the age of 13. He becomes an adult member of the community with all the pertaining obligations.
Barukh Haba:	Welcome!
Beraita:	A Rabbinic discussion not codified in the *Mishnah* that is brought up for support in the Talmud. Aramaic. *Beraitot* in plural.
Bimah:	The pulpit area before the Holy Ark.
Converso:	A Jewish convert to Christianity in Spain whether by force or voluntarily. Spanish.
Drash:	An exegetical methodology of the Torah.
Epistle/Epistola:	Letter. Latin.
Gematria:	A Jewish alphanumeric code of assigning a numerical value to a word based on its letters. Greek.
Haftarah:	A portion from the Prophets read every Shabbat in the synagogue at the conclusion of the Torah service.
Hanukkah:	The celebration of the victory over the Greeks and the rebirth of the Jewish autonomous state in circa 165 BCE.
HaShem:	The name religious Jews refer to God.
Havruta:	Two or more students who study together. Aramaic.
Hebrew Calendar:	Tishrei, Heshvan, Kislev, Tevet, Shevat, Addar, Nissan, Iyyar, Sivan, Tamuz, Av, Elul.
Juderia:	The Jewish quarter in Spanish towns. Spanish.
Kaddish:	The prayer for the deceased.
Kashrut:	Keeping Jewish diet according to certain rules.
Kiddush:	Blessings on the bread and wine before a meal.
Ketubah:	A Jewish marriage contract. Aramaic.
Loor de Virtudes:	*Praise of Virtues* a book authored by Alfonso de Zamora. Spanish.

Massorah:	The codified customs that guide the proper reading of the Hebrew Bible.
Matones:	Bullies. Spanish.
Midrash:	A type of biblical exegesis. *Midrashim* in the plural.
Mishnah:	A collection of Rabbinic laws or rules which formed the basis of the Talmud.
Morisco:	Literally, "a small Moor." A Muslim convert to Christianity. Spanish.
Notaricon:	A play on words in order to derive new words and new meanings. Greek.
Parashah:	One of the 52 Torah portions read every Shabbat in the synagogue. *Parashiot* in the plural.
Pessah:	The Jewish Passover commemorating the Exodus from Egypt.
Pirkei Avot:	A chapter in the Mishnah focusing on wisdom teaching.
Piyyut:	A poem in honor of God and Jewish Holy Days. *Piyyutim* in the plural.
Plaza major:	The Main Square of a Spanish town. *Plaça*, in Portuguese.
Pugio Fidei:	*Dagger of Faith*. Raymond Martini's anti-Jewish polemic. Latin.
Qahal	A Jewish congregation.
Qushiah:	A difficult question.
Rapido:	Hurry! Spanish.
Rosh HaShanah:	The Jewish New Year celebrated for two days.
Sefaradi:	A descendant from the Jews of Spain
Shabbat:	The Jewish day of rest.
Shavuot:	A festival in commemoration of giving the Torah at Sinai.
SheHeheyahu:	A prayer said before eating foods for the first time or experiencing something joyous for the first time.
Shekhinah:	God's feminine emanation that protects the Jewish people.
Shema:	The statement of faith.
Shohet:	A certified Jew to slaughter an animal for consumption according to humane rules.

Sinagoga:	Synagogue. Latin.
Succot:	Literally, "tabernacles." A festival in commemoration of the 40 years of living in the Wilderness of Sinai.
Tallit:	A prayer shawl wrapped around the shoulders. *Talitot* in plural.
Talmud:	Six-volume teachings and discussions by rabbis collected for several centuries.
Tossefta:	Discussions by rabbis not included in the Mishnah. *Tosseftot* in plural. Aramaic.
Yeshivah:	A Jewish school.
Yom Kippur:	The holiest day in the Jewish Calendar.

Cisneros's palace in Alcala

The main street of the Juderia in Alcala

The University where Alfonso de Zamora taught

Cisneros's tomb in the Alcala cathedral

New apartments built on the walls of the old Juderia

The "Jewish cross", a cross over an inverted Menorah

The new Juderia (after 1391) where the Campanton Yeshiva used to be

The Main Plaza in Salamanca

A typical street in the Salamanca Juderia

The entrance to the Salamanca Library

A main room in the Salamanca Library

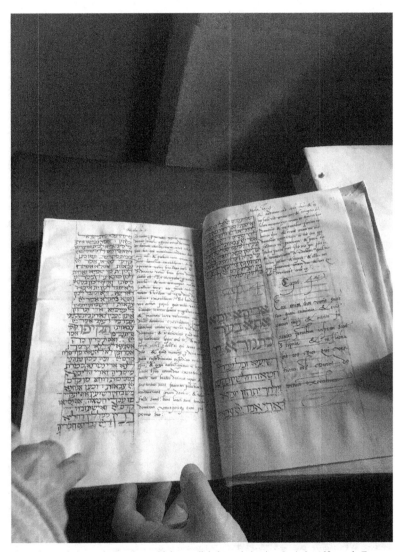

Aramaic translation to the Prophets with its paralleled translation into Latin by Alfonso de Zamora

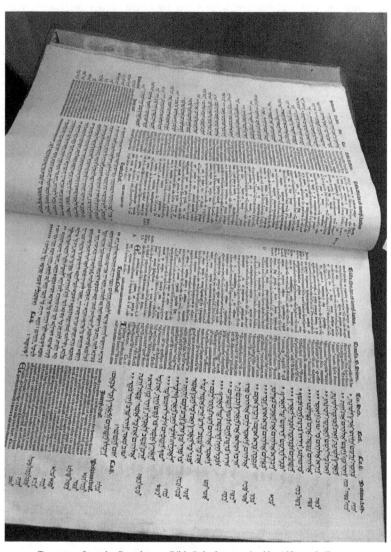

Two pages from the Complutense Bible Polyglot organized by Alfonso de Zamora

272

The Sunega fortress in Bejar where escaping Jews found a temporary haven

Made in the USA
Middletown, DE
04 August 2022

70533302R00156